Praise for Alice Zorn

Arrhythmia

"An utterly compelling story written with a clear, cold eye. Zorn's women navigate betrayal by holding filaments of family and friendships so tenuous you never know which lifeline will snap."

— KATHLEEN WINTER, AUTHOR OF *ANNABEL*, NOMINATED FOR THE GILLER PRIZE, GOVERNOR GENERAL'S LITERARY AWARD FOR FICTION, AND THE ORANGE FICTION PRIZE

"Alice Zorn's debut novel *Arrhythmia* is an ambitious, deftly handled exploration of human beings in love … it seldom misses a beat."

— *MONTREAL REVIEW OF BOOKS*

"*Arrhythmia* is a vivid and elegantly written novel with characters so fully realized, so round and warm and fraught with their own hidden desires and wounds, so sincere in both their misapprehensions and their hard-won resolutions, that the reader inhabits them, smells the rich aromas of their cooking, endures the pain of their longing for what is forbidden, rejoices in their moments of triumph and redemption. *Arrhythmia* holds the reader fast from its opening pages to its wise and satisfying end."

— JULIE KEITH, AUTHOR OF *THE DEVIL OUT THERE*

Ruins & Relics, shortlisted for the Quebec
Writers' Federation McAuslan First Book Prize

"It's a treat to encounter a writer so keenly aware that writing
and reading are a creative continuum.... The titular 'Ruins
and Relics' closes the book. A story of fractious love spun in
new directions by the challenges of a holiday in Tunisia, it
blends shimmering visuals with a nuanced probing of yawning
cultural divides. Even better, it never reads like a travelogue
tweaked into fiction."
— *GLOBE AND MAIL*

"In *Ruins and Relics*, Zorn delivers a strong showing and
promises to be a Canadian writer to watch."
— *VUE WEEKLY*

"I love the range of these stories, the sense of complete worlds,
the way the author quietly and remorselessly closes in on her characters. There is a crack in everything, and Alice Zorn finds it."
— JOAN THOMAS, AUTHOR OF *READING BY LIGHTNING*, WINNER OF
THE COMMONWEALTH PRIZE FOR BEST FIRST BOOK

"Zorn leaves you wanting just one more story, and the end
of the book comes all too quickly."
— *THE STAR PHOENIX*

"A collection of eleven well-crafted and deliberate stories …
recommended for all those who admire the beauty of the
short-story form. These are vivid and authentic characters
brought to life with Zorn's deft talent."
— *ALBERTA VIEWS*

Alice Zorn

DUNDURN
TORONTO

Editor: Shannon Whibbs
Copy Editor: Tara Tovell
Design: Courtney Horner
Cover Design: Laura Boyle
Cover Image: © Robert Aubé
Printer: Webcom

Quotation from "Secrets" in *placeholder* (Brick Books, 2013) by Charmaine Cadeau used with permission.

Library and Archives Canada Cataloguing in Publication

Zorn, Alice, author
    Five roses / Alice Zorn.

Issued in print and electronic formats.
ISBN 978-1-4597-3424-1 (paperback).--ISBN 978-1-4597-3425-8 (pdf).--ISBN 978-1-4597-3426-5 (epub)

    I. Title.

PS8649.O67F58 2016   C813'.6   C2015-906676-X
                                    C2015-906677-8

1 2 3 4 5   20 19 18 17 16

Conseil des Arts du Canada   Canada Council for the Arts   ONTARIO ARTS COUNCIL / CONSEIL DES ARTS DE L'ONTARIO / an Ontario government agency / un organisme du gouvernement de l'Ontario

We acknowledge the support of the **Canada Council for the Arts** and the **Ontario Arts Council** for our publishing program. We also acknowledge the financial support of the **Government of Canada** through the **Canada Book Fund** and **Livres Canada Books**, and the **Government of Ontario** through the **Ontario Book Publishing Tax Credit** and the **Ontario Media Development Corporation**.

Care has been taken to trace the ownership of copyright material used in this book. The author and the publisher welcome any information enabling them to rectify any references or credits in subsequent editions.

—*J. Kirk Howard, President*

The publisher is not responsible for websites or their content unless they are owned by the publisher.

Printed and bound in Canada.

VISIT US AT
Dundurn.com | @dundurnpress | Facebook.com/dundurnpress | Pinterest.com/dundurnpress

Dundurn
3 Church Street, Suite 500
Toronto, Ontario, Canada
M5E 1M2

For Robert, who brought me to the Pointe.

Well, there's one kind favour I'll ask of you
Well, there's one kind favour I'll ask of you
There's just one last favour I'll ask of you
See that my grave is kept clean.
— *Blind Lemon Jefferson,*
"See That My Grave Is Kept Clean"

Holding a letter up to the light
as if there should be more to the story.
— *Charmaine Cadeau, "Secrets"*

1978

THÉRÈSE

The bus hurtled along the highway. Cigarette smoke wafted down the aisle. The crackle of a bag of chips. The innocent movements and sounds of a handful of people heading north out of Montreal on a Wednesday evening.

As the lights of the city receded, Thérèse let herself relax. She and the baby were safe now, weren't they? Who could follow them? No one knew where they were going. She hoped the embrace of her arms made the baby feel safe. That the jiggling of the old bus wouldn't wake her. She slept now that Thérèse wasn't shifting her from side to side to grope in her pocket for money, clutch a ticket, set down and pick up her suitcase. In the subway, if that pretty Indian woman hadn't helped her at the turnstile, Thérèse wouldn't have been able to lift her suitcase across. She'd never before left the house with the baby and hadn't known how hard it would be to shove against doors, count correct change, carry a suitcase, and keep track of a ticket while holding a baby.

"You'll see, we'll be fine," she murmured, as if the baby had heard her thoughts. Nothing was too hard. She would manage, even if she had to hide the suitcase in the trees by the ditch.

When she'd climbed onto the bus at the station, she'd asked the driver if he would let her off at the gravel road before they got to Rivière-des-Pins. He glanced at the baby and the canvas suitcase she'd packed tight with diapers and formula, a bottle and nipples. *Quelqu'un vient te chercher?* Someone picking you up? Nothing but trees out there. She hurried down the aisle without answering.

A few seats away someone listened to a ballgame on a transistor radio. Bursts of tinny hollering. The escalating roll of the announcer's voice.

Thérèse held the baby tighter. The bus window was so streaked and blotched with dirt she couldn't tell if the moon was shining. She trusted that her feet would remember the trail through the woods. The humps of tree roots she had to step across. The dips in the forest floor. So often she'd walked along that path. But never before with a baby in her arms.

She lowered her head to breathe in the tender intimacy of soft baby hair. Her lips brushed the wisps. So sweet, so delicate. She'd bathed her that afternoon. Her own darling Rose.

For the summer, they would be fine in the cabin, but in the winter she would have to keep it warm. She didn't know how Papa had paid Armand for wood, but she would find out. She would ask. Now that she had Rose to care for, she no longer felt timid about talking to Armand.

The cabin had a table, chairs, sofa, a bed. Maples and birches circled the clearing. Around them brooded the hush of a centuries-old pine forest. Armand and the people from Rivière-des-Pins would soon know she was there, but no one from the city would ever find them.

Six months ago she'd scrubbed the wood floors, wiped the tongue-and-groove walls and two windows, stripped Maman and Papa's bed. The furniture stood in place as they'd lived with it. The cast iron stove. The rocker with the rope seat. The plank table where she and Maman had kneaded dough and peeled potatoes — and where they'd eaten, Papa, Maman, and Thérèse. Meals had been silent except for the tap of their forks on their plates and the wet sound of Papa chewing as well as he could with the last stumps of his teeth.

The balding velvet sofa against the wall was for reading the Bible. The difference between kneeling to say the rosary and sitting on the sofa, while Papa read the Bible, was that listening to the Bible was like a formal visit with God. His stories were written word for word on the pages. The rosary had words, too, but requests were still possible. A plea could be mumbled between Hail Marys. Blessed be the fruit of thy womb and please may the traps not be empty tomorrow. Hope was more heartfelt when the hard boards of the floor dug into your knees. Papa and Maman prayed with their heads bent, pinching the beads of the rosary like a lifeline. Thérèse, watching them sidelong, felt less sure. Even as a young girl, she'd wondered if God listened. He'd never answered her prayers for a baby sister or brother. For the girls at school to let her turn the rope when they played skipping. For a dress bought new from the store.

At night the sofa was covered with a sheet, sewn from old bags, on which Thérèse slept. The sheet had been washed so often that the cloth was soft, the lines of print faded. She could just make out the faint pink letters on the cloth tucked across the sofa's back. FIVE she didn't know because it was English, but ROSES were flowers in any language, she was sure. Every morning the ghostly message whispered to her when she woke.

Roses grew in the bushes by the creek. In the forest there were tiny purple violets, bloodroot that bled real blood when you picked it, elegant white *trilles*, trout lilies with sleek, speckled leaves. Maman had taught her the names.

Papa brought Maman home when the doctors in Montreal could do no more for her. She lay in bed, her lungs torn by the coughing that kept all three of them awake. Thérèse fed her bread softened in milky tea, lifted her in bed, and cleaned her. Maman could no longer move herself. Only the ravage of disease moved through her.

Papa still slept beside her, because that was his place. At night, when Thérèse sat with Maman, she saw how small they both were, their bodies flattened by the heavy blankets woven from strips of rags. She was their only child, born to them late in life, a gift God sent to care for them in illness and old age.

When Maman finally died, the cabin was silent. Thérèse missed Maman, but how could she wish for Maman to keep suffering? She didn't know what Papa felt. She cooked for him, and washed their clothes, the floors, and the windows, but they hardly talked. On Sundays they sat on the sofa, with the empty space between them for Maman, and he read the Bible.

One day Papa didn't come home. Thérèse hadn't noticed if he'd gone out with an axe, a wheelbarrow, a shovel, or his gun. The sun had set behind the trees, and still she waited with the *marmotte* stew warming on the side of the stove. From the window she watched the last light blur the outline of the trees. Her stomach watery with foreboding, she strode through the woods and across the field to Armand's farm.

As children, she and Armand used to wait for the school bus that stopped at the end of the gravel road. Thérèse took the path through the woods to the road, Armand the long driveway from his white clapboard house. If Armand got to the road ahead of her, Thérèse paced her steps not to overtake him. He did the same when he was behind her. Both at the end of the road, they stared at the fat pods of milkweed in the ditch. Candelabra goldenrod and feathery purple vetch. In the winter they made footsteps in the snow and watched the crows in the trees squawk and flap their wings. When it rained, they huddled away from each other under separate trees. Armand didn't talk to her. No one at school did. She was dressed in old clothes donated by the church. The other kids jeered when they recognized a sweater or a skirt. They knew she had no electricity or bathroom in her cabin, and they scrunched their noses in disgust, because how could she take a bath? Thérèse could have explained, but no one ever asked. Once a week Maman heated water on the stove to pour into the tin tub. Papa bathed first, then Maman, then Thérèse. She often sniffed her clothes and skin. She couldn't smell anything, but maybe the other kids could because they washed with water that gushed fresh from a tap.

Armand had grown into a tall, rangy man with a moustache. Only from his weak chin could she recognize the boy he'd been. She told him Papa hadn't come home. Armand lifted his rifle from a cupboard and called for his dog. He ignored his two boys, who clamoured to come along. Thérèse waited with a cup of tea his wife made, listening to the ricochet noise of the television the boys watched. When Armand finally stomped through the door, he carried Papa slung over his shoulder, dead.

By herself in the cabin, Thérèse heard each sound echo. The scrape of her spoon in a bowl touched the stove, the window, the stairs to the attic. All week she ate from the same pot of food. The air between the walls waited for what she would do next. She sat on the doorstep until her legs grew numb. She knew no other life and had no one to ask for advice.

Chickadees flitted across the clearing with dry threads of weeds in their beaks. The snow had melted, except for the thin shoulders of ice shrunken beneath the trees. The sky was overcast, but Thérèse could sense the sun behind the clouds — the imperative to stir and awaken. The air smelled of wet pine needles, mulch, and decay. The shadowed hollows of the forest floor. Soon, the fiddleheads would poke through the felt of last year's leaves. The tongues of burdock and trilliums.

Thérèse fiddled loose the wall plank beside Maman and Papa's bed and groped in the dark for the glass jar. Ninety-two dollars. She packed the hairbrush, her nightgown, socks, and a sweater in the canvas suitcase Maman had taken with her to the hospital. She locked the door and hooked the key on the nail where Papa used to keep it.

If she walked to the end of the gravel road to the highway, eventually a bus would pass that would bring her to Montreal. She wore her knit scarf and hat and Papa's old parka. Her braid hung to the small of her back. It was 1978 and she was twenty-four years old, about to start a new life.

Bridges, concrete, buildings, and cars. The pudding faces of people in the subway. Thérèse narrowed her focus to see only what she needed. She remembered how to get to the nuns with whom she had stayed while Maman was in the hospital.

Three years had passed, though. The nun who'd been so kind to her and brushed her hair at night and again in the morning was gone. From behind a large, polished desk, the nun in charge told Thérèse she could only stay for a short while. Charity was not an inexhaustible resource. Thérèse had to find work and a place of her own. In the light from the window, a sore on the nun's lip glistened. Thérèse was willing to work. She had never meant simply to live there, though as far as she could tell, that was all the nuns did.

At the employment office a man in a pink shirt and a spotted tie determined that Thérèse's only employable skill was cleaning.

Every evening, Monday to Friday, Thérèse wound her braid in a bun, donned a blue button-up dress, and rode the bus to a glass tower, where she steered a vacuum cleaner and a cart stocked with dusters and bottles from office to office. She'd never used a vacuum cleaner, and at first marvelled at how it sucked up paper clips. But she had to stoop to scratch at bits of paper that stuck to the carpet, and couldn't manoeuvre the head of the machine into corners.

The other cleaners chattered in an agitated, voluble language, flung their hands at the furniture, their carts, and each other, shouted as if on the verge of tears, only to break out laughing. For a week they pretended Thérèse didn't exist — the same as the kids had years ago at school. Then one of the women asked

Thérèse about her family. When the others heard that her parents had passed away, they crossed themselves and invited her to eat with them. "Come," they said in accented French. "Sit here. Eat this. Mozzarella and tomato."

The women now sometimes spoke broken French so Thérèse could understand. They complained that life was expensive in this cold country. They had to work here and at home, where they cooked and cleaned. Sometimes their husbands were angry, but that was how men were. Their children, whom they adored, were *perfette*. When they called on the Blessed Virgin for mercy on their sore backs, Thérèse remembered Papa and Maman.

She still hadn't found a place to live. The rooms on the list of addresses the nun had given her were dank and airless, and often in the basement. Thérèse had always lived simply. She understood poverty. But the desperation of these rooms — a sagging cot beside a laundry sink — repelled her. They weren't homes but steps toward homelessness.

She wandered down streets with her coat unzipped, the air so warm that she no longer needed her scarf and hat. Back home, in the woods, the violets would have spread a dainty carpet of tiny purple faces. Here, among the rumble of traffic and constant bustle, the earth stayed dead. The city was a world of engines, concrete, glass, and stone, the few lone trees imprisoned by the sidewalk. Thérèse didn't regret having come to the city where she now had a job, a paycheque, and friends. She regretted that the city was so ugly.

Thérèse rarely looked out the windows of the office tower where she worked at night. There were only the lights of other buildings and the unblinking rodent eyes of traffic. She moved from office to office, dusting the radiators and raking the vacuum cleaner across the carpet. She was squirting a spray bottle along a window ledge when she saw the towering, red neon letters — FARINE FIVE ROSES — against the skyline.

Another cleaner, Gemma, called from the doorway that it was break time. When Thérèse didn't move, Gemma demanded, "What's wrong?"

"What does that mean?" Thérèse pointed. "Flour and roses." She tried the strange middle word: "Fif."

"Fayf," Gemma said. "It means *cinq*."

"Why five roses?"

"*Basta!* It's a sign. Look at them — everywhere."

"It's flour?"

"Sure, why not? Come! Ines made *zeppole*."

Thérèse had never tasted sweets as delicious as the snacks these women baked.

The nuns knew Thérèse worked nights and usually let her sleep late. That morning she woke to a tap on the door. She thought she'd dreamt the noise and didn't move. There was another knock, harder and louder. The nun said Mother Dominique wanted to see Thérèse now. Thérèse dressed and quickly braided her hair.

Mother Dominique sat behind her polished desk as if hardened into a likeness of herself while waiting for Thérèse. Her forehead was a rampart of beige skin beneath the starched white band of her veil. The sore on her lip had left a mottled mark. She said she was surprised that Thérèse had not yet found a place to live. "You were given a list of rooms, but it seems you expect —" Her tone bristled with exasperation, reminding Thérèse of teachers who'd patrolled the aisles with soft steps, only suddenly to whack a ruler across a boy's back. "Now you have no choice. By Saturday you must leave."

Thérèse had understood the first time she'd been told that charity was not an inexhaustible resource. Since she began working, she'd paid for her bed and board.

She left the office and the building. She'd only slept for a couple of hours, but Mother Dominique's words had jolted her awake. When the bus she normally took to work drew up to the curb, she stepped on. She didn't get off downtown but stayed in her seat, watching the sky that appeared now and again between the high-rises. Not many people were left on the bus when she finally saw the scaffolding atop a tall brick building with the gigantic letters, FARINE FIVE ROSES.

She yanked the bell and got off. The sidewalk was lined with low buildings with grey plywood covering their windows. Once upon a time people must have lived and worked here. She'd never before seen abandoned property in the city. Except for the odd car, the street was empty. She began walking toward the Five Roses sign, down one street, then another, only to be stopped by a waterway built of great blocks of concrete and stone. The water glimmered, depthless and murky. She peered farther along and saw where a bridge crossed it. The bridge belonged to a main street where cars and trucks passed. The Five Roses sign still loomed in the sky, but she couldn't tell how to approach it. Directions twisted strangely — not like the city roads downtown. More like paths in a forest following a creek or skirting a marsh.

She turned onto a street of aged brick buildings, all joined in a row, close to the sidewalk. Doors canted slightly. Steps were trodden. Scrap lumber had been used to fashion a handrail. A woman walking toward her wore a second-hand coat. Thérèse recognized the hang of shoulders and hips stretched to fit someone else's body. The cars parked along the street were dented and rusty like cars in the country. A boy, still in his pajamas and with a plastic bag of sliced bread dangling from his hand, jogged past and loped up the stairs to a house, shouting *"Maman!"* as the door slammed behind him.

Thérèse heard the strum of a guitar and plaintive singing coming from a house with a door painted bright orange. A hand-lettered piece of cardboard was propped in a window. CHAMBRE À LOUER / ROOM FOR RENT. She didn't hesitate. She climbed the three steps from the sidewalk and knocked. When no one came, she rapped on the glass. The singing stopped. From an upstairs window, someone called, *"Quoi?"* A young man with bedraggled blond hair leaned out on his arms, peering down.

"I came about the room."

"So come," he said and ducked inside.

She waited at the door. When she heard him start singing again, she tried the knob. It wasn't locked. The door faced a large hallway and, beyond that, a broad room opening onto another. Against the walls eddied cushions, blankets, and sleeping bags. There were no tables, no chairs.

Thérèse followed the soft wailing up a broad stairway with a handsome carved banister. Along the hallway were doors, some closed, some ajar. She saw a mattress heaped with rumpled clothes, candles on the floor burnt low in dishes, a girl sitting cross-legged, braiding another girl's hair. Both wore long patterned skirts.

The young man stopped singing long enough to say, "The room's at the end — on the left. Forget about the balcony. It's for the pigeons."

She walked down the hallway. In her body she felt she belonged here. The Five Roses sign had led her to this house — to this room. The plaster walls were nicked with scars, the floorboards bald with age and use. There was a balcony outside the window with pigeons perched along the railing. They didn't fly away until she knocked on the glass.

Thérèse told the young man she was taking the room. "Doesn't work like that," he said. "You have to come back when Stilt's here. Talk to him."

She retraced her walk to the main street where the bus passed. At the convent dormitory, she packed her suitcase. There was no one to whom she even wanted to say goodbye. She waited on the sidewalk for the bus and stayed on until she saw the Five Roses sign and the bus crossed the bridge. She carried her suitcase along the streets of weathered brick row houses.

She didn't knock on the orange door before she walked in because she lived here now. She rooted through the cupboards in the kitchen for a bucket and rag. The windowsill was so thick with grime that she had to change the water before she could start on the floor. She leaned on her knees, fists balled inside the rag as she scrubbed. She paid no attention when one of the kids, then another, stood in the doorway to watch.

She had washed halfway across the floor when a man squatted next to her. "Hey, whoa! What do you think you're doing?"

Thérèse kept rocking forward on her haunches, shoving the rag with her fists.

He laid a hand on her forearm, which made her sit back as if he'd pressed a button.

"Who are you?"

"Thérèse."

He wore strands of beaded necklaces, a leather vest without a shirt, silver rings with great stones on his fingers. She'd seen people like him in the city, but never close-up. His hair, pulled back in a ponytail, frizzed grey at the temples.

She sloshed her rag in the bucket, wrung it, and dropped the twist on the floor. She had to finish in time to get to work.

"Hey, are you deaf? I don't want to play the heavy here, but I'm the one who decides if you can have this room."

She understood now. Like Mother Dominique. She sat back with her head lowered.

"Are you a runaway?"

Run away from the cabin? How did he know?

"Nah," he drawled. "You're too old. You must be like twenty, eh?" He fingered the end of her braid then looped it around his hand.

She clenched her jaw and stiffened, wishing he wouldn't touch her hair.

"Your braid's cool. But you're pretty straight, aren't you?"

She had no idea what he meant.

"Do you have any bread on you?"

She glanced at him. Why would she have bread?

"Money," he said.

She remembered about charity. "I have a job."

"A job's good." He paused. "But I don't think you'll like it here."

"I will."

"Oh yeah? I bet you'll be gone in a week. But I guess I won't kick you out after you already washed the floor. Don't want bad karma."

The next morning, when Thérèse returned from work, she saw that someone had dragged a mattress and a blanket into her room. She was so exhausted she slept despite the gamy stink of the wool and the sunlight from the window. When she woke, she didn't recognize where she was. Then she heard the pigeons. Their roosting murmur had worked so far into her dreams that the sound was already familiar.

Thérèse never set out to explore the house, though day by day she began to clean it. She scooped towels off the floor and hung them to dry. Bagged the empty pizza boxes and takeout containers. Scrubbed the sinks. Swept the hallway and wiped the carved wood moulding.

The house was quiet during the day. The kids only woke or began to arrive toward evening. When Thérèse got ready to leave for work, putting on her uniform and pinning up her braid, she could hear the rhythmic slap of hand drums starting up and smell the strangely scented reek — like smouldering weeds — that wafted through the house. People had always acted in ways she didn't understand. She ignored them.

As the weather got warmer, she tacked a piece of flowered cloth across her window so she could open it without the pigeons trying to fly into the room. Sometimes she woke to a grey tabby curled in the nook behind her legs. The cat liked to pad careful steps across the guano terrain of the balcony and slink in her window. She showed it the route by the hallway but it still chose the balcony, making the pigeons grunt and flutter off.

When Thérèse rode the bus to work and home again in the morning, she watched for the Five Roses sign. She knew it watched her, too, from its height and in spirit. She remembered waking in the cabin and how the words on the sheet whispered to her.

Not far from the house, in a junk shop, she found a large bowl like the one Maman had used for making bread. She bought flour, sugar, lard, and yeast. Like the Italian cleaning women who cooked for their families, she wanted to bake bread for the kids. It didn't matter that she didn't know their names, or even how many lived there. Early in the morning she sprinkled yeast over warm water and waited for it to soften. With a wooden spoon she stirred and beat the dough until it was rubbery. She kneaded in the final cups of flour and covered the dough with a damp cloth. The thick ceramic walls of the bowl kept the dough warm. When it had risen, she formed two balls she set side by side in a single pan. Maman had called bread shaped like this *pain fesse* — buttock bread. She didn't normally mention that part of the body, but that was the name. Two smoothly rounded loaves joined by a seam.

In the house, the kids woke in the late afternoon to the yeasty odour of bread baking. They lumbered down the stairs, yawning and hungry. Thérèse gave them thick slices. She was happy with her new life, her job, the savings she tucked in an envelope taped to the wall of her closet, the old house she kept tidy, the easy company of the kids who said her bread was the greatest. She thought about buying a chair for her room. She stroked the cat, who lay on her blanket and purred. She scratched around its ears and under its chin.

One morning she came home through rain pelting down. Her shoes squished as she ran. She leaped onto the front steps and opened the door to the staccato howl of crying. A girl in a long, wet skirt sat against the wall in the front room. A baby had slid from the slack crook of her arm to her lap. Its face was crimson with rage and bawling, its legs and torso bundled in a filthy blanket.

A boy scuffed into the room, holding a mug of tea. "God, I'm glad you're here," he told Thérèse. "I found her in the park. She's got nowhere to go."

The girl clutched the mug with both hands, letting the baby slide farther between her legs to the floor. Its cry grew thinner, more choked.

Thérèse couldn't bear to see the baby so neglected. She hurried across the room to lift it from the girl who made no move to stop her. Through the blanket Thérèse felt the sodden diaper and tiny limbs. The smell of concentrated urine made her blink. She strode to the stairs and behind her heard the boy urging the girl to come, too. Why? The girl was useless.

In her room Thérèse lay the baby on her mattress. She peeled away the dirty blanket, her fingers careful with the safety pins wedged in the saturated diaper. The baby heaved for breath to cry. A girl, Thérèse saw. She tugged free a corner of her bedsheet to cover the child's scrawny nakedness. How could she bathe her? There were no stoppers for the sinks in the bathrooms.

The girl who was the mother stood by the wall with the boy. Two other kids leaned in the doorway. "Here," Thérèse said. "Someone watch the baby." When no one moved, she said more sharply, "Here!"

The boy took a step closer. Thérèse said, "Don't touch her, just make sure she stays there." She bounded down the stairs to the kitchen and grabbed her large bread bowl and soap. She gushed the water hard, testing it for warmth.

As she walked down the hallway with the bowl filled with water, she could hear the baby still crying, but more weakly, exhausted. The girl sat sprawled against the wall.

"Get her out," Thérèse told the boy. "Give her a bath. And dry clothes."

The girl raised her head with its tangled, bushy hair. "She's hungry."

"Then why didn't you feed her?" Thérèse snatched a towel from her closet, gently wrapped the baby, and carried her to the girl, who fumbled with her T-shirt. She wasn't wearing a bra. Her breasts, plumped against her stomach, leaked milk. She let Thérèse place the baby in her arms. She didn't move to help and Thérèse — disgusted by the girl's lack of shame — had to nudge the baby's chin toward the nipple. The baby batted her fists in protest until a dribble of milk touched her tongue. She latched on now and began sucking greedily. Thérèse had no choice but to wait. The kids stood watching the girl with the baby. Then the boy began telling them how he'd found the girl. Thérèse saw the cat at the window, its tail lifted like a disapproving finger at the crowd in the room.

Excitement bubbled among the kids at this discovery of a girl like themselves *with a baby*. The girl watched them with vacant eyes, head leaned against the wall, breasts exposed, tears dried and sticky on her pale cheeks. Thérèse bent to take the baby, who'd fallen asleep. An instinct or a memory made her hold the baby upright and pat her back.

"Go," she said. "Into the bath." She'd several times dipped her fingers in the water in the bread bowl to make sure it was still warm. She supported the baby's back — so small she was! — on the flat of her hand and slowly eased her into the water. The baby moved her arms but didn't wake. Thérèse squeezed water from a washcloth over her body and smoothed soap over her slippery limbs. She ran her wet hand several times across the baby's scalp.

She wrapped her in the towel and, holding her close, walked down the hallway. The kids had clustered around the bathroom doorway, holding up skirts and jeans they'd scrounged. The girl lay in the tub with her knees and breasts poking from the suds. The bottle of dish detergent Thérèse had brought was on the floor. "I can't wear jeans," the girl was complaining. "My hips are too big."

"Because you just had a baby!"

"No, my hips —"

Thérèse interrupted. "Someone has to buy diapers. I've got money."

A girl with small gold-framed glasses said she would go. She followed Thérèse to her room, cooing at the baby. "*Ooooh, qu'elle est chouette.* The perfect little sweetheart."

Thérèse spread her fingers wider across the baby's back. The baby needed more than pretty words and noises. She wasn't a toy.

At noon Thérèse called in sick to work. How could she leave the baby with the kids? The girl only remembered her when her breasts ached. All afternoon she lounged with the others in the next room. They giggled, shared a large pizza, traded stories about which bands they'd seen.

At sundown they trooped downstairs as more kids arrived. Soon, Thérèse smelled the rank sweetness in the air. The thump and wail of music grew louder. She paced in her room with the baby, who began to cry and wouldn't stop. Thérèse had no choice but to find the girl.

The kids sprawled on the sleeping bags and cushions in the front room, passing around a pipe. Candles lit the gloom. The laziest movement cast long, distorted shadows. Music clashed and groaned. The scene was evil — an image of hell, which had never before seemed real to Thérèse, but which she recognized now that she saw it. She wanted to flee, but the baby had to be fed. Huddled over to protect her as well as she could, Thérèse crept into the room and kneeled before the girl, who could hardly rouse herself to lift her shirt. Jaw hard, Thérèse forced herself to watch. There had to be another way. A better way. There had to.

That night Thérèse tucked the baby into bed next to her. She stroked her delicate cheek and whispered, "I'll take care of you, I promise."

Later, when the baby woke and began to fidget, Thérèse carried her downstairs again. The house was quiet. The girl, still clothed, lay against a boy who was naked, both snoring softly. The girl didn't wake. Thérèse rolled her aside with her foot, freed a breast, tucked the child against it, and gave her the nipple.

For two days and two nights Thérèse cared for the baby. She hardly slept, but she had never felt more determined and awake. The baby was docile now that she was held, regularly fed, clean and dry. While she slept, Thérèse ran from the house to the store to buy more diapers and clothing. There she saw bottles and formula. Slowly, her finger on the package, she read the instructions.

The baby sputtered when Thérèse rubbed the wet nipple across her lips, but Thérèse cajoled and rocked her, waiting for her to taste the few grains of sugar she'd added. "What's your name?" she wondered. She'd never heard the girl say it. "I'm going to call you Rose."

That day, when Thérèse called in sick again, the supervisor told her she would need a doctor's certificate if she called in sick the following night. Thérèse didn't answer. A baby's claims were surely greater than a length of grey carpet.

Rose had taken the bottle several times, but tonight she kicked and gagged on the nipple. Thérèse finally bundled her close to carry downstairs. The front room throbbed with music, flickering shadows, drumbeats, and smoke. The kids slumped in a circle around a tableau of mother and child, not unlike the other times the girl had nursed the baby.

But Thérèse held Rose. A man lay in the girl's arms, his mouth on her nipple. In the wavering candlelight, Thérèse saw Stilt's unshaven cheeks pulling draughts of milk. The girl's dreamy smile. Farther down his body, a head bobbed at his crotch. The other kids lay in poses miming Stilt's. Some only watched or rubbed at themselves.

Thérèse charged up the stairs and slammed the door behind her. She stood with her back against it, her heart pounding hard in her throat. When Rose began to wriggle and cry again, Thérèse grabbed the bottle she'd left on the floor by her mattress. This time Rose took it.

Thérèse paced the room and thought hard about what to do. She flung open her suitcase, crammed in diapers, baby clothes, formula, nipples. Her things didn't matter. She tiptoed down the stairs with Rose hidden against her, suitcase in hand, and slipped out the door.

A groundhog sat upright, its snout twitching at the air. The boys playing in the fields near the woods saw the banner of smoke twisting above the trees. They sneaked as close to the cabin as they dared and spied movement at the window. What if robbers were staying in the cabin and they had guns? The boys scrambled home to tell their father.

Armand paid no mind to their story about robbers — robbing *what* from an abandoned cabin in the backwoods of Rivière-des-Pins? But he didn't like intruders so close to his land.

He didn't take his gun but snapped his fingers for the dog. More annoyed than curious, he trudged through the swish of high grass, across the fields, into the woods. At a distance, the boys trailed him.

As he crossed the clearing before the cabin, he wondered if he should holler and tell the person to come out. He decided to knock.

He stepped back when Thérèse opened the door holding a baby. She hadn't been gone that long. Was she pregnant when she left? Then who ...? He blushed.

"Yes?" Thérèse tapped the baby's back.

"My boys said someone was here."

"I'm here. With Rose."

He looked away, not sure what to say next. He remembered the land. "I ploughed your field when I did mine. I planted corn."

"Good," she said evenly.

"It's your land. I'll give you a percentage."

She dipped her head to smell the baby's hair. It was a protective, yet intimate gesture that reminded him of his wife when their boys had been babies.

Behind Thérèse the house was scrubbed and swept. She had no electricity or running water. She had already left once. Why had she come back? Especially with a baby. No sane person would choose to live like this.

But she looked so content, cradling the baby. As if her life brimmed with riches.

2005

FARA

The roads didn't meet at right angles. One shot off on a tangent that curved tight to dip under a railroad bridge. The car slowed, almost stopped, rolled into a crater in the pavement, then — bump! — jolted onto the asphalt again.

In the back seat Fara felt like she and Frédéric were on a funhouse ride. Which they were, sort of. *House shopping.*

The real estate agent had driven them along industrial streets where transport trucks idled, past abandoned factories with corroded metal grids on the windows. Signs with the letters eaten by rust. Sagging heaps of thawed winter garbage.

The car rumbled across a truss bridge over what looked like a moat.

"Is this even still Montreal?" Fara asked. Frédéric nudged her. *Be polite.*

"The original, working-class heart," Yolette said. "Pointe St-Charles."

Yolette of the plucked eyebrows, signature fragrance, and stretched smiles. Yolette, their guide to a cut-rate mortgage. So far, she'd shown them a house with a stagnant pond in the cellar, another with a tongue-and-groove ceiling so buckled Fara refused to step into the room. Each house would need more than the cost of the house yet again to repair all that was tilted, decayed, broken, leaking.

Fara hadn't expected to see houses again so far south below downtown. Wasn't this where the rail yards and the port abutted the St. Lawrence? But look, here were row houses in faded, crumbling brick. They must have been a hundred years old, maybe older, built by immigrants nostalgic for brick and flat roofs. Didn't they know flat was crazy in a climate that dumped snow from Halloween until Easter? Old Québécois houses had high, sloped roofs.

Fara wasn't convinced yet that they should buy a house. She still wanted to feel footloose, to travel, to — she wasn't even sure what. Hike in the Pyrenees. Learn to paint watercolours in Corsica. *Habla español.* They had no children. Why tie themselves down with a house? Working Monday to Friday to funnel her paycheque into a mortgage would feel like slavery.

Frédéric said owning a house didn't rule out adventure. Real estate was an investment. They could afford to buy if they headed into a scruffier neighbourhood, away from the upscale bistros and grey stone façades.

Fara smirked out the window. Nothing upscale about doorways sunk in their frames, cornices blistered from age and neglect. Outside a *dépanneur* two men slouched on mismatched kitchen chairs, king cans in hand. Was it even noon yet?

Yolette stopped the car before a house covered in beige vinyl siding. "Wait until you see this one. It's really cute!" *Cute* was her gloss on *tiny.* A place where elves might feel cozy, but where Fara and Frédéric hulked like hormone-crazed giants.

When Fara didn't move, Frédéric said, "Fara." He had a tone he used to remind her she wasn't *trying.* She got out and followed the swish of Yolette's skirt up the worn wooden steps.

They had to sidle through the entrance past winter jackets and coats heaped on wall pegs. The two bedrooms were at the front of the house, facing the street. Neither was large enough for their king-size bed. Nor were there closets, which might account for the slurry of clothes and toys underfoot, the winter coats still hanging in the entrance in mid-April.

"The bathroom." Yolette waved gaily but didn't stop. Frédéric did and turned on the light. A minuscule tub with stained tiles. Maybe mould? Fara held her breath.

In the kitchen four adults sat crammed around a table, silent and gloomy, smoking and staring at their cans of Pepsi. The air stank of cigarettes and old grease.

"Outlets for a washer and dryer." Yolette pointed near the floor since there were no appliances to demonstrate. "And there!" Out the window, last year's dried weeds straggled along a bucktoothed fence. "Western exposure — absolutely the *best* for a garden."

As they edged past the coats and out the door again, Yolette chattered about green space, the proximity of the river and the Lachine Canal. "I'll bet you two cycle!"

Once they were in the car again, Fara asked, "What was wrong with those people? They didn't look like they wanted to sell."

"They're not selling. They're tenants."

"Are they moving out?"

"That's your decision. If you buy it as a rental property, they stay — but you can't raise their rent unless you do repairs. If you want to live there, you give them notice."

"Evict them, you mean."

Fara watched the pencilled line of Yolette's eyebrows in the rear-view mirror. How did she do it? Wax? Electrolysis? When they talked face to face, Fara had to remind herself not to stare at Yolette's hairless brow. "I don't want to evict tenants."

"Me neither," said Frédéric.

"Well, what did you think?" Yolette's voice rose. "If you want to buy a house, then the people who live there have to go."

"We thought they would want to sell."

"Eighty percent of the houses in the Pointe are rental properties, so you're seeing mostly tenants, not owners. And look —" She jabbed a red fingernail at a house with windows patched with hockey tape. "No one's taking care of these places, not the landlords, not the tenants. This is inner-city real estate only minutes from downtown, and it's sitting here, a wasteland. It's high time people start moving to the Pointe."

Fara considered mentioning that *people* already lived here. "Aren't there any empty houses?"

Yolette's snort didn't match her chic perfume and clothes. "I think that's it for visits today. I'll drop you at the subway."

Fara leaned against Frédéric, who squeezed her hand. Who cared if a woman with android eyebrows thought their scruples were ridiculous?

Fara woke with her heart thumping, but kept her eyes closed so as not to lose Claire yet.

The dream itself hardly mattered. It never did. The plot dissolved the instant Claire appeared. Across heads in a crowded bus. Framed in the window of a passing car. Heading up an escalator while Fara descended. Sometimes Claire looked at her and smiled. Complicit. Taunting. *You're there, I'm here. Don't try to get closer or you'll wake up.*

In this dream Fara was walking down a street of dilapidated brick row houses. She lifted her eyes to the carved line of weathered cornices against the sky. And there — she almost missed her — in a second-floor window stood Claire. She was looking at the sky, too. Her hair was darker, not as blond as it used to be. Her body thicker. She looked older, as she would have were she still alive. Dream logic was relentless.

Dream logic or conscience? Fara hadn't accompanied the police to the morgue. She'd choked and wept. She *couldn't.* Not after the horror of finding Claire. She'd begged her boyfriend to go identify the body. Now, all these years later, a sly whisper persisted that, since she hadn't seen actually seen Claire's face, maybe it wasn't true. How often had her boyfriend lied to her about money and where he'd been? Why had she trusted him with this? Her sister with the snub nose and thick blond hair, dead at twenty.

She wondered if her parents ever dreamed that Claire was still alive. They hadn't wanted to see her in death. Her body had been shipped from the morgue to the funeral home. Claire was cremated with no ceremony, no witnesses. The reproach of suicide compacted into the smallest possible package.

The dream was already fading. Fara could no longer recall the shape of Claire's body. Only the brick around the window. A lingering aftertaste of sadness. And as always, regret — a useless emotion once it was too late. Seventeen years too late.

Beside her in bed, Frédéric shifted. She slid a hand across his chest to hold him. Or hold herself against him. His solidity was her anchor. His generous heart her warmth.

An early morning breeze made the edge of the curtain tap the wall. A block away, traffic on Parc was starting up. The wheeze of city buses. The alarm would go off any minute.

"Frédéric!" Fara leaned away from the pantry doorway, a box of cereal clutched to her robe, feet cringed in her slippers, grimacing at the shiny black turds around the garbage can. She checked the corners of the cereal box for teeth marks. Glanced along the shelves around the jars of couscous and rice. Mice couldn't climb walls, could they?

"Fred!" No time for the tra-la-la of *Frédéric*. "Would you come?"

He ambled into the kitchen, wiping a towel across his face, wearing only his grey trousers. A tall man with a padding of flesh on his frame. The odd white hair in the sparse curls on his chest. A comma of shaving foam hung from one earlobe.

She waved at the floor, still standing well back. The mice might think the pantry was theirs now that they'd marked it. What if they attacked with sharp teeth and claws?

Frédéric bunched the towel in his hand and turned away.

"Where are you going? We have to do something!" Fara slammed the cereal box onto the counter and followed him to the bedroom.

He reached into the antique armoire for a shirt.

"Well?" she demanded.

"I didn't do it."

"I never said you did. I want to know what we're going to do about it."

"I'm leaving for work."

"So am I!"

"So clean it up when you get home." He nosed his belt through the loops.

"Why should *I* clean it up? Don't we need to get traps? This is exactly the kind of thing I mean about not being ready to buy a house. All these things we don't know anything about. Mice and toilets blocking —"

He watched her as he buckled his belt. His wide cheekbones and eye sockets gave him a candid expression that made people trust him, though it was simply how his skull was shaped. She knew him well enough to see past the bones to the amusement he was hiding.

"What's so funny?"

"How about you aim for the garbage next time you clean a papaya?"

Papaya seeds? Fara spun around and strode back to the kitchen.

A disgruntled queue traipsed off the bus in front of the hospital. Fara waited on the sidewalk for the light to change. Across the street she saw Zeery walking up the wheelchair ramp to the ER entrance. Fara loped past employees dawdling over cigarettes, sidestepped an elderly man who seemed startled by the workings of the sliding door, and tapped Zeery's arm.

Zeery plucked out an earbud. She barely reached Fara's shoulder and had to tip her head to look at her. Light shimmered off her gold hoop earrings. "Hi! How are you? How was your weekend?"

Fara grimaced. "Looked at houses again."

"That's good."

"Only if you want to buy a house."

They got off the elevator on the twelfth floor. Zeery was talking about her cousin who was visiting from Calgary. Fara only half-listened as she assessed the Monday morning havoc. Linen trolleys blocked the doorways to patients' rooms where the orderlies were busy with a.m. care. Inside the oval nursing station bodies milled. The night nurses were busy charting. The nurses coming onto day shift grumbled about their assignment or gossiped about the weekend. The surgeons yelled last-minute instructions as they headed to the stairwell to the OR. "For 27B, d/c every second stitch and Steri-Strip. And that ultrasound drainage, make sure it gets done." The charge nurse scribbled notes and nodded. She knew the spiel. *We hold down the fort while you go play diva with your scalpels and probes.*

Fara had to squeeze between chairs to get to her desk at the head of the counter. "Let me through," she droned. "Let me through or I'm going home." Chairs wheeled aside. No one else wanted to do battle with the phone and the intercom.

Her blotter was heaped with requisitions and consults tossed every which way — the doctor version of a projectile sport. She shoved her knapsack in a drawer and grabbed the phone that was ringing. "Twelve Surgery, yes?" The OR had received a patient wearing dentures.

Fara called out, "Who sent 23A to the OR?" No one answered. She peered at the assignment sheet tacked on the billboard. José had 23A. But José dropped his daughter off at a daycare that only opened when he was already supposed to be at work. When he worked day shift, he always showed up late. Whoever had sent his patient to the OR hadn't checked for dentures.

Fara waved at the orderly walking past with an armload of towels. "Royal, will you go to the OR to get dentures?"

Royal touched a gloved finger to his breastbone. "*Me?* A nurse did that. Send the nurse."

He was right. Of course he was right. But that didn't help her if she didn't have a nurse to send. The phone kept ringing. The intercom, too. She had to giddy-up to the supply room to do her order, which had to be faxed before eight. She grabbed her clipboard and shimmied past the chairs again. The OR didn't have to be so king-of-the-castle. Put the dentures in a cup. Someone would get them later.

In the supply room she scribbled a list of stock that was low. Iodine gauze, #8 cannulated trachs, urine measuring bags, 21G butterflies. And surgical tape. Not a single roll left. She'd emptied five boxes, twelve rolls per box, into the bin on Friday. What did the staff do with tape on the weekend? Take it home and truss up their partners? Not a sex game, just tying them up.

Back at her desk, she filled out the order sheets, faxed them, and began sorting through the heap of requisitions and consults. Without looking, she answered the phone.

"Are you sending someone or aren't you?"

No hello, no goodbye. Probably the OR. Read the fine print on the job description. Unit coordinators had to be telepathic. Able to guess which test a doctor meant when the loop-de-loop scrawl across a requisition bore no visible relation to either of the two official languages. What a demented patient wanted when he toddled to the desk clenching the baggy armhole of his gown. Who *my mother* was when family members asked for information without saying who *my mother* was.

And here was José, trotting down the hallway to the change room. "José! Your patient in 23A went to the OR with dentures."

"Wasn't me, I just got here."

"Right, but she's your patient." And has been for the last half-hour, buddy boy.

José whirled around and saw Royal, who shrugged and walked to the stairway. Nice, Fara thought. He wouldn't go when she asked, but he did it for another bro.

"Farahilde?" Claudette had what Fara thought of as a pencil-sharpener voice. She held the pay envelopes.

Fara opened her hand. "Thank you."

"I thought you were called Farrah for *Charlie's Angels.*"

"It's not spelled the same way and no one remembers that show. You're dating yourself."

Claudette leaned on Fara's shoulder to look at the envelope again. Fara flipped it over and answered the phone.

Fara had been named Farahilde after her father's mother. A good German name. When she was a baby, her parents called her Hilde, like her grandmother. Then Fara's mother heard how the French-speaking neighbours pronounced it *Ilde.* She didn't want a child called Ilde. Fara became Fara. Three years later, when her sister was born, their parents were more familiar with the idiosyncrasies of language in Quebec. The new baby was named after her maternal grandmother, Klara, but they spelled it Claire.

ROSE

People had surgeries where they could never eat again. Throat cancer or stomach cancer, Rose wasn't sure. They had to get liquid nutrients through a tube plugged into their stomach. No more tart autumn apples, oatmeal cookies warm and crumbly from the oven, barbecued chicken, corn on the cob.

But surely being fed through a tube was better than dying? People should be grateful they were still alive. Perhaps at the beginning they were, but as the months wore on, not being able to eat made them feel diminished. Less human. They resented pizza commercials on TV. People walking down the hallway eating a chocolate muffin. One patient scowled when he saw Rose pushing her cart of tube feeding. You ever tried that shit? It doesn't even go in my mouth and I can taste it. He smacked his lips with disgust. Whatever they put in it is gross. I *hate* it.

When Rose had first applied for a job in the hospital, she expected to work with patients. Changing dirty sheets for fresh ones she pulled taut. Bracing a frail waist. She had a broad back and strong legs. She liked helping people.

But not sick people, she realized. Patients who banged their bedside tables, flaunting the right to be miserable — the only power left to them. They loathed their disease, and by extension, anyone associated with it. Even helpless and in bed, they were bullies, rude and demanding. Not *all* the patients, no, but enough of them to make work as a nurse or an orderly demeaning. Rose saw how the nurses fled certain rooms, their mouths pinched with exasperation.

Rose worked in Dietary, delivering tube feeding. She started her shift by counting out cans she packaged in paper bags labelled with the patients' names and room numbers. She measured formula into Styrofoam milkshake cups. The different tube feedings had different ratios of protein, electrolytes, vitamins, and minerals. Rose checked the dietician's list once. She checked it twice. An earnest Santa Claus.

Her trolley loaded, she wheeled it to the elevator, which she took to the fourteenth floor. At the first nursing station the coordinator verified the number of bags and cups Rose carried to the med room. At the second nursing station the nurse in charge signed without even glancing at the cart.

When Rose felt a tap on her right shoulder, she already knew to look to the left.

"Can't fool you anymore." Kenny grinned. He had freckled teddy-bear cheeks and a teddy-bear belly. He worked as an orderly on Six South.

"What are you doing here?" She was glad to see him — a friendly face in a not-always-friendly hospital — but shook her head in reproof.

"Have to borrow an IV pump."

"From here?" He'd used the IV-pump excuse before.

"Twelve, eleven, ten … it's faster to take the stairs than wait for the elevator."

Not if he stopped to look for her on every floor. She pushed her cart to the next nursing station. Even as he joked and clowned, she kept a few steps between them.

"Hey, man." An orderly coming out of a patient's room touched knuckles with Kenny. "You cruising this babe on my turf?"

Rose ignored them. She waited for the coordinator to finish on the phone and sign her list. Only two bags of cans. Rose left her trolley at the desk and carried them inside the nursing station.

Kenny was gone when she returned, but an hour later she saw him on the fifth floor ambling down the hallway with a bag of blood.

"Don't you have to get that to the nurses?"

"It's got to warm up first. Think about it. Whammo! Ice-cold blood — direct from the fridge into the veins. You could kill a patient."

She clicked her tongue in disbelief.

"Some old geezer? You bet." Kenny liked to talk as if he understood anatomy and procedures simply from working in a hospital. She'd heard him once, explaining the risks of surgery to a man on a stretcher.

"Listen," he said now. "When are you taking a break?"

"I'm behind today. I'll just have time to get back to the kitchen." When she finished delivering tube feeding, she carried late supper trays to the patients' rooms.

"How about when you're done, are you free? I can take my supper late. I've got news for you, kiddo."

She stopped pushing her trolley. "About a place?"

He winked. "Told you I'd find one."

"Where?" She watched his face as if she could decode the answer in his freckles.

He held up his bag of blood. "Gotta get this upstairs. Meet me at seven-thirty at the Vietnamese place across the street."

The restaurant was small with tables pushed close together. People sat with their heads bent over noodles they poked and scooped with chopsticks. The air was damp and warm, and smelled of fried fat, bouillon cubes, and green onion.

Kenny waved from a table by the wall. As Rose sat down, the waiter slapped a plasticized page on the table before her. "Have a Tonkinoise," Kenny said. "It's good here."

She didn't know what that was. She'd never used chopsticks. And did she have enough money to eat in a restaurant? "I'm not hungry. I ate in the kitchen."

"Leftover mashed potatoes?" He groaned. "Rose, Rose, Rose."

He poured tea into tiny bowls and started complaining about the charge nurse who'd expected him to do four bed changes before he left for supper. Four! She wasn't the one who had to push the beds, the patients, and their belongings from room to room. He tapped a chopstick on the table like an angry finger.

Rose waited. He always talked in circles. Eventually he would land on what she wanted to hear.

A few weeks ago, when he kept asking where she'd lived before she came to Montreal, she told him about the cabin in the woods.

"Oh yeah? Where?"

"Near Rivière-des-Pins. About an hour north."

"A cabin in the woods." He whistled through his teeth. "By a river, eh?"

"More like a creek."

"I'll bet there's speckled trout." He began to talk about fish and lures and the best time of day to catch those babies. "We can drive up on the weekend. How far did you say, an hour?" Then he noticed her face. "What's wrong?"

"I don't want to go back."

"Why not? If I had a cabin in the woods, I'd be there all the time."

Rose hesitated. "I lived there with my mother. She died."

Kenny blushed and mumbled, "I didn't know. Sorry."

Except for her roommate, Yushi, Rose hadn't told anyone in Montreal about Maman. There was no one else to tell, but also no explaining how, without Maman, the air in the cabin was too still. Everything had lost its pulse. Maman's chair at the table. The spoons and knives and forks in the drawers. The wood stove. The dishes. The woven rag blanket on the bed in the attic where Maman used to sleep, and where her parents had once slept. Rose's bed was the sofa where Maman had slept when she was growing up. Rose had always felt comforted by these routines, repeated through the lives that braided around hers. She hadn't known what to do — alone, without Maman.

Even now, in the city, it hurt to think about her. Her wan cheeks and how she'd had to sit to catch her breath. Or in the night, when Rose heard her choking. In the morning Maman never mentioned it, so Rose didn't either. She washed the bed linen, scrubbed the blood spots from the pillowcases, didn't ask what they were.

Sometimes, though, Rose let herself remember the forest. The breathing silence between the boles of the trees. The gritty slide of pine needles underfoot. The warble and twitter of bird-call. The intense flavour of a single, wild strawberry. She held the essence of those memories deep inside. She didn't have to go back to relive them.

Where memory didn't help was with weaving. Her body missed the dance step of her feet on the treadles. The wondrous meld of the fibres — colour and texture — becoming cloth. Even here, in the city, across the distance, she could feel how the loom in the shed next to the cabin waited. Sometimes she dreamed that she sat on the bench before the span of hundreds of threads fed neatly, all in order, through the heddles. Or she walked down a street and stopped before the window of a yarn store, transfixed by the soft nests and skeins of colour.

If only she could bring the loom to Montreal. But even if she found a way, which seemed impossible, where would she keep it? A loom was all angles and frames, as wide as a double bed. It couldn't be pushed into a corner. She had to be able to walk around it — with added space for equipment. A loom needed a room of its own.

The apartment she shared with Yushi was already crowded. If Rose put the loom in her bedroom, where would she sleep? She had nowhere to keep a loom in Montreal, but once she started thinking about it, she couldn't stop.

For a few days after she'd told Kenny about her mother, he didn't mention the cabin in the woods. He clowned the way he always did, walking ahead of her down the hallway, hands cupped around his mouth. "*Mesdames, Messieurs!* Get your Osmolyte here!"

She was standing before the elevator with her cart when he sidled up, carrying a stuffed net laundry bag over his shoulder. "Hey, Rose, I was thinking ... I know you don't want to go to your cabin, but what if we went to the river and caught some trout?"

"It's not a river, I told you. I don't think there's trout."

"We could still look."

"There must be lots of places where you can go fishing."

"Where other people go. This is different. It's where you grew up."

"The only reason I'd go ..." she began.

"Yeah?" He hefted the bag on his shoulder higher.

"Would be to get my loom."

"A loom ... like for knitting?"

"For weaving. Making cloth."

"So let's get it." He jiggled his legs.

"It's too big. I'd need a van."

He grinned. "Van can do."

She couldn't tell if he was serious. A teddy-bear joker.

"My buddy's got a van."

She stared at a yellow poster for an EKG workshop. Getting the loom was only half the problem. "There's no point. The loom won't fit in my apartment."

"How big of a place do you need?"

"Right now it takes up the whole of a shed."

The elevator binged and the doors slid open. Rose wheeled her trolley on, expecting Kenny to follow. But he headed off down the hallway, the laundry bag on his shoulder swaying to the roll of his walk.

Rose hadn't eaten at the Vietnamese restaurant and now, in the bus on the way home, she was hungry. All she'd had since noon was a crumbled edge of shepherd's pie that was too small to serve a patient. She hoped Yushi had cooked.

She and Yushi lived on the second floor of a brick duplex. No matter how softly Rose climbed the outside metal stairs, her steps reverberated like a giant's trudge. *Kabunk-nk-nk-nk. Kabunk-nk-nk-nk.* She kept expecting the downstairs neighbours to burst out of their apartment and glare. After all these months in the city, she still wasn't used to hearing people talking, their music — and even more private sounds — through the walls and the floors.

She found Yushi in the front room sitting cross-legged on a chair at the table, a food magazine open beside her empty plate. The table was an enormous rosewood oval with a scroll-work apron and carved legs. Yushi had inherited it from her great-aunt, who'd brought it to Canada from India. Yushi's grandmother, the great-aunt's sister, had married and moved to Trinidad, where Yushi's mother was born. The elegant table didn't match Yushi's cropped hair and washed-out T-shirt, but she felt fierce about its *herstory* and that it was hers now. For lack of space, it was pushed against the wall across from the sofa.

Without taking her eyes from the page, Yushi said, "There's bean ragout."

Rose padded down the hallway to the kitchen. Even before she lifted the lid off the pot, she could smell fresh rosemary. Yushi had made a stew with fava beans, tomatoes, and mush-rooms. She used to work as a cook in a restaurant in Toronto.

Now she had a job as counter help in a patisserie at the Atwater Market. Rose wondered why she wasn't working as a cook but didn't ask. She'd never understood how people pushed for details beyond what was volunteered.

She ladled stew onto a plate, poured a glass of water, grabbed a fork and a placemat. She always sat at the short end of the table so she could see Yushi. Nudging out her chair, she said, "I'm coming to the market tomorrow. One of the orderlies at the hospital knows a place near there where I can keep my loom."

"One of the orderlies at the hospital." Not a question, a statement.

"You know I want to get my loom. I told you." With her fork she prodded the curved layers of an unfamiliar vegetable. "This is good. What is it?"

"Fennel." Yushi stretched against the high back of her chair, eyes on Rose. "How will you get your loom to Montreal?"

"He offered to get it. His friend has a van."

Yushi's level gaze and crow-feather hair. Thin and brown as she was, she in no way resembled Maman, but her precise, unhurried manner reminded Rose of how Maman always thought before she spoke. "He likes you," Yushi said now.

"He's crazy about fishing. He wanted to go even before I told him about the loom." Rose thought of the wayward hair that sprouted from the neckline of Kenny's blue uniform. How the hang of his tunic didn't quite mask his soft stomach. Sometimes her arm brushed against his. She never felt excited or wished he would move closer — the way she had when Armand strode through the trees toward her. Years ago, but she still remembered how her blood thrummed with expectation. How she'd longed for the slide of Armand's fingers under the edge of her clothes.

"I think you like him, too."

Rose didn't look up from her food, afraid that her memory of Armand's hands on her body might show on her face. Armand was a secret then. He was still a secret now.

Yushi flipped shut her magazine and unfolded her legs. "If you're coming to the market tomorrow, stop by and say hello. I'll sneak you a pastry." She took her plate to the kitchen. A moment later Rose heard the TV from her room.

She didn't think Kenny liked her — not in the way Yushi meant. He'd said he wanted to go fishing. Why shouldn't she believe him?

The trees, still leafless, stretched their branches to the sky. The buildings on the other side of the canal were reflected in the water. Kenny walked, oblivious to the cyclists whizzing by on the path, but Rose kept stepping behind him. Kenny always looked around in surprise and joined her again. He pointed out the train bridge that crossed the canal. He said the buildings, which were condos now, used to be factories.

"The canal looks great, doesn't it? They really cleaned it up. When I was a kid, it was one big polluted soup. The factories dumped all kinds of toxic junk. Factories and the ships. They stopped shipping before I was born, but my dad used to come down here and watch them — big ships with smoke stacks. He still talks about growing up along here with all the factories. My granddad worked in a nail factory, can you believe it? A whole factory just for nails!"

Kenny swept his arm through the air. "I'm giving you the big tour today. The scenic route. When you come down here, it'll be faster to cut through St-Henri."

Rose couldn't visualize the past he described, nor what he meant by the scenic route. She saw old brick buildings. Silos tattooed with graffiti. Banks of grass and trees hemmed in by asphalt. The canal, which didn't look wide enough for ships, was bordered by slabs of concrete. Somewhere, nearby, traffic roared along a highway.

Kenny stopped before a three-storey brick building with large windows of many panes. Some windows were curtained, some checkerboard-covered with squares of coloured foil or paper that spelled out words. *IMPRIMERIE JULES. CRÉATIONS BIX.* A man stood outside a loading dock before a block of pink stone. He crept his fingers across the stone's rough surface, set a pick at a spot he'd found, grasped the mallet that poked from his carpenter's apron.

"There's another artist for you," Kenny said. "You'll meet all kinds of friends here."

Rose followed him to the front of the building, puzzled by his words about artists and meeting friends. He pulled out keys knotted on an elastic band and unlocked the steel front door. The floor was concrete, the air dusty and cold. Doors along the hallway sported logos and posters.

Kenny used the second key to open an unmarked door. He bowed and motioned for Rose to precede him. She hung back, peering into the dimness. He strode past her and yanked aside a long curtain. Through its grid of many panes, the window looked onto the canal. The room was large but filthy. Scrap lumber and metal debris littered the floor. Spider webs drooped in long bibs down the walls, which were gashed with scars.

"What do you think?" Kenny grinned. "A great big room for your loom! You can make as much mess as you want."

What did he mean, make a mess? Weaving was orderly and neat. She couldn't imagine her loom here.

"And don't worry about the rent. The owner said it's all right. His uncle knows my uncle. He doesn't like these studios empty because people start to break in, and once you've got squatters, then you've got problems. Big time."

She felt uneasy with his talk about break-ins, the garbage in the room, how isolated it was from the streets of the city. Then she saw the porcelain sink against the back wall. She'd seen an old sink like this in a farmhouse kitchen. She approached with slow steps. The inside was splashed pink and green. The deep red of fresh blood.

"That's just paint," Kenny said. "I can try to strip it. But if you clean it, it'll be clean, right? Doesn't matter what it looks like."

His enthusiasm echoed dully against the gouged plaster and spatter of wreckage. She still didn't know what to say.

"Hey!" He opened his arms. "You've got a place now, Rose! We can get your loom. We'll set you up, you'll see."

"It's too —" she began weakly.

"It's perfect! And hey, if you need shelves, I can build them. I'm not an artist, but I can do that." He stood before her beaming, convinced he'd given her the best imaginable prize.

FARA

Through the month of May and into June, Frédéric continued to visit houses. Fara said she would come if he found a place with walls, roof, windows, and floors intact. *No* pond in the cellar. A bedroom large enough for their king-size bed. And please: no repeats of the last house, with the sullen adults grouped around the kitchen table, waiting to have their fate decided.

She still didn't see why Frédéric wanted a house, though with the freakish heat wave this past week, she could hardly stand to come home to the oppressive cage of their apartment at the top of a sixplex, a bull's eye under the scorching sun. The air baked. Sweat oozed. Garbage rotted. Travel by bus at rush hour was a stop-and-start nightmare.

Home from work, Fara stood under a cool shower and let the water sluice her. She patted herself dry, leaving wet tendrils of hair to drip down her back, and didn't bother to dress again except for a camisole and panties. Even that skimpy layer felt like too much. Groaning, she collapsed on the sofa. Their fan had broken last summer and they hadn't bought a new one yet. Who expected a heat wave in June? The balcony door was open, but the air didn't stir. She could hear the next-door neighbours having supper on their balcony. The chink and scrape of cutlery. Her breathless snicker, his monotone.

She sank into a doze, blinking awake to the click of the key in the door. Frédéric stepped around the corner, white shirt wilted, holding a baguette.

"Hi," she said, too depleted by the heat to sound anything but cranky.

"The balcony door's open. You're practically naked."

She rolled her head against the cushions. They'd had this discussion before. The windows of the building across the street didn't face their balcony door. Living in a box, above a box, between boxes taught you to calculate your angles of privacy.

"We need a fan," she mumbled.

"Us and everyone else in the city." He scuffed down the hallway to change out of his trousers and white shirt. She heaved herself off the sofa. Despite the heat, she was hungry. She would slice some tomatoes, add feta, olives, oregano, oil and vinegar. Lots of black pepper.

She slipped on a short, spaghetti-strap dress and they carried their plates to the balcony where they had folding chairs, though no pretty wrought-iron table like the neighbours'. Their door was closed now, their apartment quiet. They must have gone out.

"Supposed to rain tomorrow," Frédéric said. "The heat will break."

"I hope." Fara bit into a cube of feta. "How was work?"

"Marie-Ange twisted her ankle on the stairs today. She'll be off work for however long she can drag that out."

"She doesn't need her ankle to do data entry."

"She needs her ankle to get to work." Frédéric supervised the payroll technicians for a grocery chain with seven thousand employees. Most of the staff in his department used to be clerks who'd worked in the stores. They were his parents' age with parent-type tics and foibles. If they asked a question once, they asked five times. They granted that he was smart enough to have gone to university, which they hadn't, but still believed that they knew best. After lunch their eyes looked bleary like they needed a nap. Any change in routine met with astounded blankness — and resistance.

Frédéric wiped a chunk of baguette through herb-flecked juices and oil. "What can I do? Challenge her medical certificate? It's signed by a doctor."

Across the street a skinny man in low-slung jeans peered over the railing of his balcony at the apartment below. He'd moved in a month ago, strung a rope between the balconies and attached little bells. At first Fara had complained about the jingling jangling. Hadn't these buddies ever heard of *telephones?* Lately she'd noticed that, when the man upstairs tinkled the bells, the downstairs couple ignored him.

Just now Fara could see them inside, slouched on the sofa. "Must be a sauna in their apartment. They can't even open their door or he'll know they're home. What's that line — good fences make good neighbours? You'll have to remember that if you buy a house."

"Not *if*. When. I'm going to find one, you'll see."

High-rises blocked their view of the mountain, but their building was close enough that Fara felt the slightly cooler air that had begun to seep down its stone and earth bulk, through the trees, into the city. "Do you want to go for a walk? I want an ice cream."

They strolled in a lazy zigzag down one street, then another. Fara tutted when she saw a new block of condos on a lot that had been empty a month ago. Last winter, when Frédéric began talking about buying a place, they'd visited a few condos. The sales reps handed out pamphlets with statistics and cross-section diagrams demonstrating the superior quality of the windows and the insulation. Indeed, some of the details were pretty. A slim rail of crown moulding. Water-bright varnished floors. But the kitchens were derisory for anyone who meant to do more than microwave. Fara dared Frédéric to sit on a toilet snug up against a vanity. With his long legs, he had to twist sideways. She stood at one end of a unit while he jumped at the other. She felt the floor vibrate. How solid was that?

No condo, she'd said. She didn't want to live in a place that was smaller and more flimsy than their apartment, simply to have bragging rights that they owned it. She wanted real brick, not brick-look siding. She believed in walls constructed with hammer and nails, not prefab sections that came from a factory.

Fine, Frédéric said. Let's look at old houses.

Sunday morning, almost nine. Frédéric was still sound asleep. Fara eased out from the sheets and reached for her robe.

The coffeemaker growled and spit as she hulled strawberries into a bowl. Red juice on her fingers and the blade of the paring knife. Soft, wet fruit flesh against the porcelain. She heard flip-flops in the hallway, then Frédéric was beside her, scratching his chest through his T-shirt. She held a strawberry to his mouth. "Taste this. It's the best part of summer — fruit that doesn't have to cross two continents to get here."

He slid a hand into the opening of her robe and palmed her breast. "This is the best part of summer — no pajamas." His thumb stroked her nipple as he raised a questioning eyebrow.

She tilted her head. *Maybe.*

The phone began ringing and he dropped her breast to walk back down the hallway to answer. She retied her robe with a smirk. When they were first together, he would have ignored the phone. She could hear him from the front room, sounding brisk. At least it wasn't family. His mother or his sister would have kept him talking until the strawberries turned to jam.

Back again, he said, "That was Yolette."

"Who?"

"The real estate agent." Instead of pouring himself coffee in the mug she'd set next to the machine for him, he took a sip from hers. "She's got a house in Pointe St-Charles. It's empty — no tenants. I said I'd meet her at noon. Do you want to come?"

"To look at a house?" She scrunched her nose.

"That, too, if you want." He looped the ends of her belt around his knuckles and gently pulled her to the bedroom.

Yolette had given Frédéric the address. He and Fara walked from the subway, crossing a long, narrow park. From a distance, she heard a metal clunk that made her think of old movies with country fairs, pony carts, and candy apples. "Is that ...?" She heard it again. "Horseshoes?"

Past the trees they saw a man swing his arm. *Thud!* Even the sound was a miss. The man standing with him kissed his horseshoe before he tossed it. *Clang!* He hooted.

On the sidewalk sat a toilet planted with blowsy pink petunias. The row houses along the street still looked old and pockmarked, but this time Fara granted that they'd withstood the years. They were solid.

At the end of the street, against the sky, jutted the enormous metal letters of the FARINE FIVE ROSES sign. It was in the news just now, because the new owners of the building didn't want to keep it lit. Montrealers protested. The historic sign marked their horizon — which wasn't the horizon, Fara realized. Pointe St-Charles lay behind it.

The trees in the alleys were enormous branching patriarchs overlooking the houses. "Because there's been no development," Frédéric said. "No one's cut them down."

"No development means no cafés, either," Fara said. "No *boulangerie* with fresh baguettes. We'll have to eat sliced white bread from a bag."

"The Pointe's only a fifteen-minute walk from the Atwater Market."

"Where we live now, I can get a baguette in one minute."

"You're going to arrange your whole life around the availability of baguettes?"

They waited for Yolette on the sidewalk in front of a brick row house with a recessed entrance panelled in wood that had been painted beige. The paint was caked with grime, as were the windows, which were strung across with faded cloth. Frédéric crouched to examine the hewn blocks of stone that formed the foundation. Fara wandered over to look at the house next door. It had the same style of panelled entrance, but the wood had been stripped and varnished. "Come see this," she called.

He walked over but looked more skeptical than impressed. "That's a lot of work."

"You can't buy an old place and not expect a lot of work."

"You would still set priorities. I don't think stripping the entrance —"

The door swung wide. The woman who slammed it and bounded down the steps nearly collided with Fara. "Oops, sorry, I didn't see you."

"We were admiring your entrance."

The woman stared at the panelling as if she'd never seen it before. She raked her hand through her thick curls. She was Fara's age, maybe older.

"You didn't strip the wood?" Fara asked.

"Ages ago. Maybe ten years? I forgot all about it by now." She laughed. "Guess I could have left it the way it was. Listen, sorry, I've got to run." She fanned her fingers at them and hurried off down the sidewalk, the soft pummel of her broad buttocks ruffling the cloth of her skirt.

A car was pulling up. Yolette stepped out in a tailored white dress. To Fara, who hadn't seen her for a few weeks, the fixed arch of her eyebrows looked more incredulous than ever. "Wait until you see!" she trilled. "You'll *love* this place."

"We just met the neighbour," Frédéric said.

"Her?" Yolette nodded at the house next door. "I wish she'd sell. She's got a gorgeous stairway with the original banister and a tiger-oak newel. That's one good thing the hippies did. They stripped all the wood. Back in the seventies this was a commune."

"How do you know?" Fara asked.

"My aunt used to live a couple of streets over. Everyone around here knew about this house. Some old Woodstock hippie set himself up as a free-love guru. Kids from Westmount used to hide out and smoke pot — and who knows what else — until their parents hauled them home again. Sometimes the parents called the police. The bikers didn't like that. The guru got pushed out. Or maybe one of the parents laid charges. Some of the kids were minors."

"Bikers?" Fara asked.

"They're all gone now, don't worry."

Fara wasn't sure she believed Yolette. But the neighbour hadn't looked worried and she'd lived here for years.

Yolette dangled a house key as if it to hypnotize them with it. Just open the door, Fara thought. We're here. Why turn this into a game on the sidewalk?

Yolette still hesitated, seemed about to say something, then didn't. The door opened onto a hallway carpeted with filthy broadloom. Except for a mattress leaning against the wall, there was no furniture. Yolette strode across the large central room and tugged the chain for the vertical blinds. They stuttered open, flooding the room with light. The window was large, with a handsomely moulded frame in stained and varnished wood. Outside was a deck and a tiny backyard of weeds grown high as hay.

Weeds and dingy broadloom could be ripped up. The white-and-gold ceiling fan chucked. What mattered was the size of the room, the high ceiling, the large window, the stained and varnished wood. Fara dragged the toe of her sandal across the carpet. "What's under here? Wood?"

"Should be," Yolette said.

The room next to the main room was painted brown, walls and ceiling. The roll-down blind had been tacked to the window frame. The room was a cave. Fara felt a strangeness — that was somehow familiar? — but ignored it. She opened the closet, which was empty except for a pole and two hangers. She imagined the walls painted white. Or a pale wash of rose. A dining room or maybe a study.

Through the wall she heard Frédéric running water and flushing the toilet. Behind her Yolette was quiet. None of her usual chatter and pizzazz — for which Fara was grateful. She didn't like being told where and how to look.

The kitchen counters were buckled and would have to be replaced. There were square-edged gaps for a refrigerator and a stove. Dribbles of what looked like hardened molasses on the wall. But also two large windows, lots of cupboards, and a walk-in pantry lined with shelves.

Fara brushed her fingers down the deep moulding of the door frame and walked back to the main room. She could picture their sofa against the far wall.

Yolette said, "Do you ..."

Fara had turned to gaze out the window. The tiny backyard was large enough for a garden.

"Do you have a problem with suicide?"

The word was a blade that touched her, sharp and cold, but she wouldn't let it pierce her. She faced a window but felt herself standing in a dimly lit room. A bed with the duvet thrown back. Green plastic. Striped pajamas. A thin body. Socks balled on the floor. Clothes dragged off a chair.

Yolette cleared her throat. How much time had passed? Fara made herself look at her. The manic arch of her eyebrows. Her white dress smudged across the hip. What an idiot to wear white to walk through an old house.

"That's why the owner is selling. His son killed himself here."

"His son," Fara repeated.

Yolette skimmed a glance at the white-and-gold ceiling fan, and as quickly away again.

That wobbly fixture of gold paint and plastic? Fara nearly scoffed. It wouldn't hold the weight of a purse, much less a person.

"It happened more than a year ago but he still won't step in the house." Yolette tried to sound concerned, but Fara could tell she had no idea how suicide rent your life — how you were forever marked by the guilt that you weren't there when someone close to you chose death over life.

"He's selling as is," Yolette said. And more carefully, "His son's clothes and belongings are still upstairs."

Fara felt the cool edge of the blade again and willed herself not to. The clothes and belongings of a person who'd chosen to die were the detritus of a life that had been rejected. Winter boots and summer sandals jumbled at the bottom of a closet. A coffee mug that had been a gift. Fridge magnets. Photos. Mementos kept for years — but not worth staying alive for. Why should they mean anything to Fara if they'd meant nothing to Claire? *No, not Claire.* This boy.

"He's asking hardly anything," Yolette said softly. "Only a hundred and fifty."

"A hundred and fifty thousand for the house?" The condos they'd looked at last winter were a hundred and sixty. "What's wrong with it?"

"Nothing. He and his son started renovating, so the plumbing is all new and the wiring on the first floor has been redone." Yolette knocked on the wall. "This is drywall. Insulated. Upstairs you've still got the original plaster." She opened both hands like an emcee. "You won't find a house this size for this price anywhere else in the city."

"Why is it so cheap then?"

"People won't buy where there was a suicide. But you two are looking for an empty house."

Frédéric walked into the room and winked so Yolette didn't see. Fara could tell he liked the house. He crossed to the kitchen, where he gushed water into the sink.

"The counters need to be replaced," he said, leaning against the door frame.

"I was just telling your wife," Yolette began, then waited, as if Fara might want to tell him herself. Fara didn't. "The owner's son killed himself here."

Frédéric gave Fara a sharp look. Yolette glanced between them.

Still watching Fara, Frédéric said, "We don't want a house —"

"Can we see upstairs?" Fara cut him off. Daring herself. Not sure if she could.

Frédéric gave a small shake of his head.

"I want to see upstairs," she repeated.

He looked at her an instant longer, then motioned for Yolette to precede them. He cupped Fara's elbow and leaned close to whisper, "We can leave."

"I like the house. And he's only asking a hundred and fifty thousand."

"But won't it make you think about your sister?"

Fara didn't answer. No one thought about suicide until it happened. Then, once it had and your ears were attuned, you discovered that people were killing themselves all the time — among your friends, their families, at work, down the street. There was always someone who couldn't endure the despair of yet another day.

Yolette dropped them off at a diner to talk. She would return in an hour. Fara and Frédéric slid into a booth by the window. Orange vinyl seats and a chrome-edged table. "Holy 1950s," Frédéric said.

The waitress looked as if she'd worked there since the 1950s. Her posture was stooped, her neck wattled, but her hips were girdled tight and the remains of her bleached hair had been teased and pinned into a wispy beehive. Frédéric asked if she had espresso.

"Coffee." Her voice grated from the catacomb of a three-pack-a-day habit.

He ordered Pepsi. Fara asked for tea.

The paper placemat advertised hot hamburger with fries, club sandwich with fries, fish sticks with fries. "Do you think the spaghetti comes with fries?" Fara asked.

"The Plateau isn't far away. If we want to eat out."

In the upstairs of the house Frédéric had tested the taps and flushed the toilet. Fara had never before realized how obsessed he was with water pressure. The door frames canted, but the doors closed, and they were solid. All the condos they'd visited had hollow-core doors.

Fara had walked from room to room, gaze levelled high, trying not to see the bed with its turmoil of grimy sheets, the tangled clothes on the floor — legs and sleeves wrestling to be rid of themselves — the clutter of empty beer cans and the rubber mask of a devil's face in the kitchen. Those were all *things* that could be packed up and thrown away. They weren't the house. A house was a shell that, in itself, didn't carry memories. She and Frédéric would paint the walls, sand the floors, decorate. Make the house theirs.

Frédéric stirred his straw through the crushed ice in his glass. "Are you sure you're all right about the suicide?"

She heard how he kept it at a distance: *the* suicide. She should learn that trick. A horror you named but didn't claim.

"It's been years." The metal teapot dripped when she poured, soaking the white paper doily under her cup. What a time warp — doilies and beehive hairdos.

"What if the house reminds you?"

"You mean ghosts?" She blotted her cup on a napkin and sipped her tea. "If Claire's ghost never haunted me, why should this boy's?"

"As long as you're sure you're all right."

"Are you sure you're all right about cleaning up his stuff? I can't help you."

"I don't expect you to."

"His father ..." she began.

"What about his father?"

She remembered having to pack the clothes in Claire's closet. The flowered summer skirts. The black suede jacket with the pansy embroidered on the pocket. A metal hanger bent from the weight of a dozen pairs of jeans Claire would never wear again. Fara had punched the clothes into bags, arms rigid, face wet. Shoved the bags down the maw of a charity bin.

She made a face now. "His father's lucky you're doing it."

"*Am* I doing it? Have we decided to buy the house?" His wide-eyed trusting and trustworthy look. Ready to lead or follow. She had only to give him the sign.

Seven years ago she'd been trudging through snowdrifts down a sidewalk behind a man who leaped up the steps of the apartment building where she was headed. Through the glass she saw him batting snow off his sleeves and shoulders.

She opened the door, shook snow off her tam, eyeing him sidelong as she stomped her boots. "Ever seen such a snow?" What a silly thing to say.

"Crazy night to go out," he agreed. As if a snowstorm ever kept a Montrealer home.

Fara had crossed her fingers inside her mittens, hoping he was coming to Tom and Karin's party. She liked his boyish face, broad cheekbones, and lively eyes. He was taller than she was, too. She had nothing against short men, but it didn't feel as sexy when a man had to lift his head to kiss her.

When she began to climb the stairs and he followed, she asked, "Are you following me?"

"You're following me. I'm being polite and letting you go ahead."

Both stopped before the door with the music and laughter. Fara blushed that her wish had come true so easily. Hold on! she told herself. Just because he'd arrived at the party alone didn't mean he was single.

When he tugged off his brown toque, she asked, "Is that a helmet liner?"

"It only cost two bucks. I didn't know it was a helmet liner."

"I think it is."

"How can you tell?" He turned it inside out and squinted at the washing instructions.

"A *helmet*." She clamped a hand on her head. "Like soldiers wear. Inside, it's got a liner. You can buy them at the army surplus store."

"Ah!" He smiled. "I thought you meant a designer name — like Hugo Boss." And affecting a British accent, "Excuse me, is that perchance a Helmut Liner?"

Another point in his favour. A man who could laugh at himself.

They walked into the crush of bodies and noise where separate friends hailed them. From across the room Fara tracked him. She wasn't sure but she thought he did the same. No one seemed to claim him. They circled closer.

Et voilà, here they were, seven years later, married and about to buy a house.

"And you're sure you're sure?" Frédéric asked. "Because you weren't so keen on the idea of a house, and now this one, with a suicide ..."

"I like the house. I think I'm okay about the suicide. I should be, right? It's been seventeen years."

ROSE

Rose didn't have to start work at the hospital until two. In the morning she took the subway to St-Henri and walked past the discount stores, the pizza-slice and roti shops, the beer trucks unloading boxes. She turned down the wide street where a factory with a smokestack had been refurbished as condos. The brick had been cleaned but still looked old. The high, gleaming windows mirrored the sky. She had to take great steps over the converging and criss-crossing rails of the train tracks. Before Kenny explained that they curved north to skirt the mountain and south to the rail yards and downtown, she saw only a puzzle of parallel lines narrowing in the distance.

The first morning she unlocked the door by herself, she hung back. The dark room wafted with ghostly movement. Shadows hulked. She told herself it was only garbage. Planks and metal junk. She darted across the room to jerk aside the canvas curtain. Out the tic-tac-toe window she saw cyclists and the canal.

She'd been to the studio a few times now, and the view from the window was growing familiar. Between her and the bike path was a rusted chain link fence. Grey skies tarnished the water silver. Every few minutes a jogger or cyclist passed. If Rose craned her neck, she could see the sculptor near the loading ramp. Often he was working, bent over his stone with a chisel or a rasp, but just as often he had visitors and stood talking.

Rose banged the heel of her palm against the stiff catches on the lower panes of the window until she'd forced a few open. Fourteen panes across, four high: fifty-six panes of glass, each one filthy. She would need a ladder to get to the top rows.

She'd brought rags and a jug of bleach she'd carried from her apartment, on the bus and the subway. She was smarter when she realized she could buy a broom and bucket in St-Henri.

She couldn't find a stopper for the sink, so twisted a corner of rag into the mouth of the drain. She filled the sink and poured in bleach. Inhaled its good smell as she scrubbed the rusty tap and sink. The hardened dribbles of paint — the crimson splashes that looked like blood — had bonded to the porcelain, but the sink was clean now.

She swiped at the cobwebs she could reach. Stooped and lifted. Dragged the cracked boards and corroded spines of metal across the room to the door. Now and then she stopped cleaning to listen. She heard the tap and scrape of the sculptor's tools. A faint crescendo of drumbeats through the ceiling. The greedy keen of gulls. People on their bikes having a shouted conversation.

How her life had changed since she'd left the cabin in the woods and moved to Montreal. She no longer woke before dawn to birdsong, shoving aside her woven blankets to start a fire in the stove. Now she stayed up late to watch movies with Yushi. Life was both easier — a kettle that only needed to be plugged in — and stranger. Could she ever have foreseen claiming a room in an abandoned factory as her own? Or being a small yet necessary cog in the intricate network of a busy hospital? Sometimes, while she waited for the bus, she flipped through a circular rack of flowered dresses on the sidewalk. Yushi had made her taste mango, avocado, pomegranate, and papaya. Her life, once so austere, unfolded now with variety and sensation. It was all a surprise. All wondrous and new. Only, sometimes ... a moment yawned — when she sat on the bus, watching an elderly man grip his shopping bag between his bony knees — and she knew she was adrift without attachment or family.

Kenny always asked when they were going to the country to get her loom. Not yet, Rose said. She had a pile of garbage she didn't know where to take. She couldn't reach the top of the window, which hadn't been washed for decades, without a ladder — or get rid of the spider webs that drooped from the ceiling. Spiders, Kenny joshed. Don't tell me you lived in the woods and you're scared of spiders? Spiders, she said, get into the yarn.

She was coming down the street on the way to her studio, as Kenny kept calling it, and saw a man sitting on the front doorstep. She thought it could be him but wasn't sure until he lifted his takeout coffee in greeting. When she got closer she said, "Why didn't you tell me you were coming?"

"Didn't know if I was till I did. Come on." He heaved himself up. "See what I brought."

In the hallway stood a metal ladder. "Where did you get that?"

"I told you, I've got connections."

She unlocked the door and he carried the ladder inside. "Wow! You really cleaned up. This looks great."

"Except for that." She pointed at the heap of wood and metal. "I'll figure it out." He swung through the door.

The legs of the ladder opened easily enough, but Rose had to arm-wrestle with the mechanism to lock the legs. She wrapped a wet rag over the head of the mop and climbed the ladder to swab the corners of the ceiling. Kenny had propped the door open and was dragging away the garbage, sliding and bumping it down the hallway.

Rose pushed the ladder farther along, rinsed and wet her rag anew. She heard tapping she ignored until the person called, "Rose!" She looked around the room, then over to the window where she saw Yushi's tufted black hair.

"How did you find me?"

"The guy hacking at the stone said this was your window."
Yushi's green bike leaned against the chain-link fence.

"The sculptor? I've never even talked to him."

"Your boyfriend does."

"He's not my boyfriend."

"That's what the sculptor called him."

"Because he doesn't know he's not my boyfriend."

"How do you know he doesn't tell people he is?"

Rose wanted to say he didn't, but how did she know?

Kenny walked into the room and over to the window when
he saw Yushi. "Hi, I'm Kenny."

Yushi held up a paper bag. "I brought some brioches."

"I'll show you how to get in." Kenny pivoted and jogged out.

"He's not usually here," Rose said. "I didn't know he was
coming today."

"You didn't know — or you don't want to know?"

"He's helping me."

"He sure is," Yushi said dryly.

"Hey, Rose's friend!" Kenny called from the loading ramp.

"He's never" — Rose began, but Yushi was already striding
through the knee-high weeds toward Kenny — "tried to kiss me."

Rose steered her cart as close as she could to the wall, so
she and Kenny didn't seem to be walking down the hallway
together, though he kept pace step for step. He needed to
borrow a piece of equipment and had followed her to three
nursing stations already. The unit coordinator at the last one
told him it would be easier if he went directly to the Inhalation
Department. He thanked her cheerfully and stayed with Rose.

"You're not going to paint the walls?" he asked. "Because I
can help you with that."

She hadn't thought of painting. She shook her head. "No."

"Yeah, you'd have to plaster first. Those walls are wrecked."

An orderly, pushing a stretcher toward them, glanced at Rose and pursed his mouth at Kenny. Meaning what? Kenny was just being Kenny, wasn't he? She didn't believe he told people he was her boyfriend. The sparks and yearning weren't there. When he touched her, it was a game to get her attention. She couldn't explain why he was so willing to help her. Didn't friends help each other? She had too little experience of friendship to know.

"Basically," he said, "you're happy as long as your studio is clean, right? You don't want it all pretty and nice. You're going to be working there."

"I'm going to be weaving." She didn't think of weaving as work.

A woman walking past, swinging her stethoscope, said, "Hi, Kenny." And smiled at Rose. Everyone in the hospital seemed to know him.

Rose had only one bag of cans for the next nursing station. She carried it to the med room. When she returned, Kenny was gone. The unit coordinator signed her clipboard. "Your friend said he'd see you later."

Rose pushed her trolley to the elevator slowly, unable to pass two elderly women who scraped the floor with their walkers, legs swollen beneath the drooping hems of their gowns. The women didn't talk. It took all their focus to stay upright and keep moving. Had they become friends, Rose wondered? Both ill, lonely, and sharing a hospital room.

FARA

Fara had the phone to her ear, scribbling in her desk agenda. *28B Boucher GI lab NPO m/n. Med + INR.* The details weren't for her. She knew to send the med sheet and latest INR result and keep the patient fasting, but she didn't man the desk 24/7. With luck, if the patient left when she wasn't there, someone might glance at her agenda for directions.

Zeery, who was standing at the counter writing in a patient's chart, waited for her to hang up. "So, when do you get the house?"

"Next week." Between interruptions was the only way to talk at work. Fara grabbed the manila folder an ER orderly had slid onto the counter and began leafing the loose pages inside into the appropriate sections of the patient's binder.

"Already?" Zeery gaped. "You just saw the house."

"It's all happening so fast — except for when we signed the papers at the notary. *That* took forever. Two solid hours of signing. I thought my hand was going to fall off."

One of the nurses, Valerie, dropped a handful of blood tubes onto the counter. "Where is this place you bought?" And to Zeery, "Stamp me labels, will you? 28C."

"Pointe St-Charles." No one Fara had talked to yet had ever

been to the Pointe, though it seemed everyone remembered stories they'd heard on the news. A body found in a basement. Cars dredged from the canal.

Valerie smirked. "My sister used to date a guy who lived in the Pointe. She could never get a taxi to go there past midnight."

"That doesn't make sense," Fara said. "There's a cab stand around the corner from our house."

"That's what my sister said. Because of the bikers." Valerie scooped the tubes she'd labelled into a biohazard bag she set in the specimen basket.

"The bikers are gone now. And anyhow, what would bikers have to do with us?" Fara thought of the next-door neighbour who'd lived there for more than ten years. Yolette visiting her aunt as a child. Everyday people and ordinary goings-on. A neighbourhood where you could hear horseshoes, for Chrissakes!

She swivelled her chair around to reach for the lab results coming out of the printer. The patient in 40B had a potassium of 6.2. The level was panic high. Or, the patient was getting potassium in their IV and someone had drawn the blood too close to the IV site.

Fara glanced at the assignment sheet. Nahi's patient. Nahi wouldn't do that. Fara called into the intercom, "Nahi! I need to talk to you."

Zeery said, "When you have your first party, I'll get my mom to make butter chicken."

"Your mom's butter chicken?" Valerie hooted. "You'd better let me know when."

Fara threw her a look. "You're going to risk coming to such a dangerous neighbourhood?"

"For Zeery's mom's butter chicken? You bet! Anyhow, there'll be a gang of us. We'll all stick together."

Fara saw she was serious. A posse of nurses, armed with high heels and lip gloss, daring the dark and dirty streets of Pointe St-Charles.

The intercom was beeping. Fara stabbed a button. "*Oui?* Can I help you?"

"It's me." Nahi's deadpan voice. A patient could be spouting from an artery and Nahi would stay calm.

Fara wasn't supposed to give medical information over the intercom, but the patients didn't understand, and even the staff couldn't always make out the words the ancient sound system garbled. "40B, potassium of 6.2, not hemolyzed."

Against the muffled noise from the room, Fara heard, *"Crime de bine."* No one under eighty even said that anymore. It was the Québécois equivalent of *golly gee*. Where had Nahi picked it up? Then, louder, he said, "Call Surgery. I'll repeat the blood and do an EKG."

A porter from Radiology held a requisition slip across the counter to show Fara. "Is that my patient?" Zeery asked, following him to the room.

Fara wrote the patient's name and the test in the test book.

So far, she hadn't told people at work about the suicide in the house. Even nurses and doctors, who were familiar with the idea, the process, and the physicality of death, didn't like suicide. It was such a wrong way to die.

At the notary's, Fara and Frédéric had met the father of the boy. A man of about sixty with a narrow forehead and slick hair curled on his collar. His nervous eyes didn't once settle on them. He chewed gum with his front teeth — like a rabbit — as he waited for the pages to be slid his way. Pen gripped, knuckles a fence, he signed and pushed each page aside as if into a void. He ignored Frédéric, who sat beside him, the next to sign. At the last page he glanced at Yolette, asked if they were finished, and shoved back his chair. Frédéric stood to shake his hand, but he'd already slipped out the door. Fara wondered if he hated them for buying the house.

Fara grabbed the phone that was ringing. "Twelve Surgery."

"It's Mo. What's up?" There were three Mohammeds on this month's rotation of residents. The nurses had told them to decide who got called Mohammed, who Mo, and who by his last name — or whatever nickname he wanted to suggest. Fara gave Mo the potassium result and he said to repeat the blood test and do an EKG.

"Doing it as we speak," Fara said.

"So why call me?" he grumbled.

"Because you've got the fancy letters behind your name." They were both being facetious. If the nurses waited for a doctor's say-so to react to every budding emergency, the floor would soon be chaos. Especially on a surgery floor, where the doctors disappeared into the OR for hours at a time. Legally though, as Mo well knew, he had to be notified — because he had the fancy letters behind his name.

As Fara answered the other line that was ringing, she saw Brie, the charge nurse, coming down the hallway with a technician from Biomedical. Fara waved the page with the potassium result and Brie walked over to take it. Tall and chic in street clothes, Brie was all bones and angles, skinny and sexless, in nursing scrubs.

"*Oui,*" Fara said into the phone. "*Demain à huit heures.*"

"Whose patient?" Brie asked.

"Nahi's. He's repeating the blood." And into the phone, "*Oui, Madame.*"

When she hung up, she had to stare at her desk to remember what she'd been doing. No wonder, with a job like this, she felt tangled by the end of the day.

Fara and Frédéric stood looking out at the sun-bleached wood of the deck — *their* deck. "Happy?" she asked. "You got your house."

"No, no, no, no. Don't turn this into something that will be my fault if it doesn't work out. *We* agreed to buy the house."

"Of course it'll work out. Why wouldn't it?"

"Didn't you hear Eric?" Frédéric's cousin had stopped in when they were visiting Frédéric's mom a week ago. Eric was a class A handyman who carried a battery-operated screwdriver in one pocket, a Swiss Army knife in the other. He'd built his own two-storey bungalow, from the concrete basement floor to the shingles on the roof. According to him, with a new construction you knew exactly what you had, whereas an old house was an unknown mess of problems that might collapse on your head while you slept.

"Eric is anal. OCD with a tool chest." Fara bent forward to trace a scrape she'd just noticed running down the wall. Had that been there when they'd looked at the house?

Ever since they'd decided they were buying the house, they'd been revising their to-do list. Frédéric thought they should focus on getting the kitchen, bathroom, and a bedroom in order. The other rooms could wait. The living room could wait. They weren't going to be relaxing and watching TV for a while. Fara agreed — with the proviso that Frédéric's very first job would be to dispose of the dead boy's belongings. As long as his things were still in the house, he was. His stick of deodorant on the bathroom shelf. The beer bottles he'd drunk from. His jeans dropped on the floor like he'd just shimmied out of them. That weird devil's mask. Remembering the mask made her shudder.

Frédéric had stepped away to glance into the next room. "I'm thinking," he said. "We want to strip these floors, right?"

"That's what we said."

"Then that's the first thing we should do — all the rooms at once. It makes no sense to do one room, get sawdust everywhere, then bring the sander in again."

His voice sounded hollow because there were no furnishings to absorb the sound. It had nothing to do with a death in the house. And that strange feeling down her spine was the newness of being here. The idea of owning the house. No landlord to call if something happened.

"What do you think?" Frédéric said. And when she looked blank, "Sanding the floors."

"Sure." She nodded. The floors.

Had the doorway to the bathroom moved? She'd thought it was off the main room, not the hallway.

"Are you okay?" Frédéric asked. He slid his arm across her back and she relaxed against him. She would get over this uncanny sense of something just beyond her line of sight. It was the work, that was all. Overwhelming when you thought of everything to be done. Sanding, hammering, wiring, painting. Eric's sour predictions hadn't helped. Even Frédéric's mom, who was so happy that they were finally *settling down*, had started to look anxious.

But as Frédéric said, they would do one thing, then the next and the next, step by step. They weren't rushing headlong into anything.

He scuffed down the street — his old street — head lowered. He didn't want to talk to any neighbours with their big hellos and phony church hugs. Questions, clucking, and fussing made them feel better. Bad luck had dumped on him, not them.

He slowed when he saw the bags and furniture piled on the sidewalk. It was about time his dad started thinking about the house again, but why ...

Okay, the clothes were garbage. Who wanted to wear a dead guy's stuff? But why hadn't his dad kept the dresser? Or the vertical blinds that had been such a bitch to install? The louvres were tied and wedged between boxes.

He bent to flip open a box that wasn't tucked tight. Hair salon magazines, the shower curtain, all of it shoved over the dishes his dad had packed away in an upstairs closet. Thin cream-coloured plates with a border of yellow roses. His mom had bought them at a church rummage sale. Fancy plates for Christmas and birthdays, she'd said. But then she took off and his dad put the fancy dishes in a box.

He lifted a teacup. Yellow roses and a faded gilt handle. What were the chances his mom had heard? If she was still in Montreal, she might have read it in the paper. But he was pretty sure she didn't still live here.

He didn't want to look anymore at their belongings heaped on the sidewalk. He turned and walked away, the cup snug in his palm.

Fara had been on her knees all morning, tugging at broadloom. Some idiot had glued it to the floor. If she pulled too quickly, disintegrating fibres left a scabby crust on the wood. The wood had been painted mud brown, but close up, between the planks, she saw slivers of kelly green and peach. Earlier decorator statements.

From upstairs she heard the drag of furniture Frédéric was manoeuvring piece by piece down the stairs to the sidewalk. He'd brought boxes, expecting to salvage the clothes for a charity, but they were too filthy.

Claire's apartment had been messy too — but no messier than usual. When Fara had phoned her at work to ask if she would be going to their parents' for the long Easter weekend, Claire's boss said he hadn't heard from her for three days. She's getting a written warning, he said. She does this again and she's out. How am I supposed to staff this place when people don't even have the courtesy to call in sick?

In the middle of the day, in the middle of the week, Fara had expected Claire to be at work. Was she sick — too sick to call? They lived only a few blocks apart but didn't see each other often. They'd grown up with different groups of friends and different tastes, Claire with her rock music and boyfriends with muscled arms, Fara with her books and art films. A week earlier, when Fara had seen Claire at the small grocery store where they both shopped, Claire asked if Fara still had a key to her apartment. Fara said yes, why would she have thrown it away? She didn't wonder why Claire had asked.

After talking with Claire's boss, Fara tried calling her at home several times. Why hadn't Claire let her know if she was sick? Or was this some kind of game? She often pulled stunts without considering the fallout. She'd deliberately failed a college course because she hadn't liked the teacher. She'd taken a knife to her boyfriend's leather jacket when she saw him flirting with another woman. Fara had had to call the police when he'd tried to break down her door. Claire acted on impulse, never planning an escape route, spurred by a private, hyperbolic rationale that didn't alert her to danger.

Fara had no idea what might have happened this time. She felt more impatient than worried. Annoyed that — once again — she was going to have to haul Claire out of a mess of her own making. Was she even home if she wasn't answering her phone? Fara decided she had better go and see. After she finished work, she stayed on the bus past her stop. Traffic was heavy. The bus inched along.

It had snowed and the sidewalk had been scraped and strewn with gravel. In the years that followed, fresh gravel on a frozen sidewalk brought back the memory of that walk from the bus stop to Claire's apartment. The crunch of her heels on the gravel, the clumps of dirty ice around the tree trunks, the air cold with the smell of snow.

She buzzed at the outside door of Claire's building. No answer. A woman who was taking her poodle for a walk let her in. At Claire's door she rang again and put her ear against the door, but heard no music. Claire could play Guns N' Roses on repeat for hours, the thump turned low so the neighbours didn't gripe. Fara knocked on the wood and finally pulled out her key.

Claire! she called. Because there was Claire's parka tossed on the sofa, arms wide like a cartoon splat. It was her only winter coat. She had to be there. *Claire!*

Dirty dishes soaked in dirty water. Claire never washed them until there were no clean ones left. There were three full bottles of olive oil on the counter. On the table lay an income tax form, partly filled out and open.

Later, whenever Fara recalled Claire's kitchen, she hated how specific the details were. Three bottles of olive oil. Why buy three unless you meant to use them? Why bother with income tax if you were planning to die? Which led to the inevitable thought: maybe Claire hadn't meant to kill herself. Not *for real*. Maybe she was only ... pretending? Experimenting? Which meant that Fara, who had a key to her apartment and was supposed to have found her, got there too late.

Over the years, Fara had gone from berating herself to trying to imagine how Claire felt and what she was thinking as she waited to die. Or waited for Fara to find her. The end was always the same. Fara hadn't. Claire had. She was dead. And once she was dead, what did the questions matter?

More stuff heaped on the sidewalk, some of it still-good furniture he could have used if his dad had bothered to pick up the phone and call him.

He climbed the three steps and tried the door, but it was locked. He groped in his pocket for the key. It didn't fit. What the hell? Had his dad changed the lock?

He walked to the end of the street and around the corner to the alley. The back fence was too high to see over the top, but the weathered boards had shrunk with age. He could see through the gaps.

Someone was standing by the window — not his dad but a bigger man. And a lady pointing at the wall. Who were they? Had his dad decided to rent the house only half-renovated?

He was watching so hard he didn't hear the scrape of footsteps and the knock of the cane until old Coady said, "How about that? Your dad sold the house."

He pretended he hadn't heard, but the words ricocheted in his head. Sold? Sold? *Câlisse de shit de merde!*

Old Coady, the wizened turd, horked and said it again.

He shrugged as if he already knew and didn't care. He stepped past Coady and strode away.

MADDY

Maddy and Yushi always arrived at the market within moments of each other. One would cruise to the bike stand as the other was locking up. Today Maddy had already locked her bike and Yushi still hadn't appeared. Maddy scanned the bike path along the canal and the bridge that crossed it. A man cycled toward her, the hem of his trousers tucked in his socks. A woman walked briskly in a filmy blue dress and running shoes. People were cycling or walking to their jobs downtown — which from this perspective, below the hill of Montreal, was uptown.

Still no Yushi. Not good. Maddy jogged to the back of the indoor market, down the stairs to the basement. She slung her knapsack into her locker and grabbed a white apron from the starched and spotless stack. The staff were supposed to change their apron *tout de suite* if it became at all flecked or stained, though Madame Petitpois would then grill them. If one were handling desserts with care, each of the said desserts inside a fluted cup or cellophane band, how did one manage to get *crème aux framboises* on one's apron? *Hmm, how?*

As Maddy tied the strings of the apron behind her back, she glanced at the schedule posted on the wall. Yushi and Geneviève were on breads today. She was on pastries with Cécile. Cécile had to wear shirts with sleeves below her elbows to hide her tattoo of a skeleton. Cécile called Madame Petitpois "Pettypoo." Any more anal, Cécile said, and her hole would close.

The patisserie was among the best in a city where patisseries were competitive and highly vaunted. The dessert counter, where Maddy waited for a woman to finish conferring on her cellphone, was resplendent with concoctions of puff pastry, genoise, whipped cream, mousse, and marzipan. *"Du chocolat?"* the woman murmured. *"Ou plutôt des fruits?"* The woman could have made the call while she'd stood in line. Now that she was being served, she made everyone behind her wait. Bibbed apron taut across her breasts, clear plastic gloves on, Maddy had to wait, too. Haste was unseemly. Of course, once the woman decided, Maddy was expected to spring into whip-quick action. Urban fact #16: people who made you wait did not like to wait.

Past the dessert counter were the deep wooden shelves stacked with bread. Round, narrow, oblong, square, and braided; rolled, studded, and filled with nuts, seeds, olives, herbs, cheese, and dried fruit. Yushi hadn't arrived yet, and Geneviève still worked alone, shaking open bags, grasping loaves, tugging free her gloves each time to handle the cash. Maddy had heard Geneviève in the morning repeating the names of the breads to herself. She was a pretty young woman with a dimpled chin, the niece of one of the pastry chefs, but too timid to be working with an impatient public. Her cheeks bright with frustration, she'd just tried to shove a round *miche* into a baguette bag. More than a dozen people were waiting to buy bread, shifting their stance, looking past shoulders, checking the time on their phones. There was only a lazy queue of three people at the dessert counter.

"I'm going to help Geneviève," Maddy told Cécile.

"Pettypoo will kill you."

"She's downstairs." Maddy had worked at the patisserie longer than Madame Petitpois. Relations between them were cool but mannerly. Petitpois granted that Madeleine was the oldest and most experienced of her girls. One day Maddy was going to tell her that, at forty-three, she was no longer a girl. Also that Maddy was short for Madzeija. Her name was Polish — no relation to Proust's tea-soaked biscuits. She hadn't told Petitpois yet, because she liked feeling Petitpois was a fool, blinkered by ignorance and outdated values.

The next man in line for breads already held the exact change for a baguette pinched between thumb and finger. Maddy slid an olive *fougasse* into a bag and waited for the bread slicer to judder through a loaf of rye.

Beside her, Geneviève stammered when a customer asked if the flour in their breads was genetically modified.

"No," Maddy said. "Our flour is milled from heritage grain." She waved an imaginary wand across the rustic loaves, the rugged crusts.

Then Yushi's slender brown arm with its silver bangle reached across hers for a seed-encrusted bread, and there wasn't enough room for all three of them in the narrow space, added to which Madame Petitpois had appeared, solid and disapproving.

"Excuse me." Maddy manoeuvred behind Geneviève to return to the dessert counter.

When Maddy was younger, she'd despaired at her bottom-heavy hips and thighs she couldn't cram into jeans. Now she felt comfortable with — and comforted by — her padding. She liked the swirl of skirts around her thighs. *She* wasn't ever going to fall and break her hips. Though walking next to Yushi, she felt like a bowl next to a single-flower vase.

They were heading toward a picnic table beside the canal. When they'd passed the last fruit stall Pierre-Paul, who always winked and joked with Maddy, had flourished two peaches and bowed to present them. Obviously, his wife wasn't working today.

"What did Petitpois say?" Maddy asked. Yushi had been late because the pedals of her bike had stopped turning. Something with the mechanism inside had broken. She'd had to walk to the nearest subway station, which was nowhere near the bike path. Just before break time Petitpois had jerked a commanding finger at Yushi to follow her to the stairway.

Yushi bit into her peach. "Mmm ... Pierre-Paul knows his fruit."

"He's married." Maddy had played that game often enough. Whatever married men promised, for better or worse they stayed with their wives.

She sat on the picnic table bench as Yushi swung onto the tabletop. Both faced the water, where two teenage girls laughed as they steered a paddleboat in crazy zigzags.

"Petitpois?" Maddy prompted.

"My place of employment could not be expected to accommodate my personal mishaps." Yushi's tone was even. Only the spiked antennae of her hair radiated annoyance.

"Could not be expected to accommodate?" Maddy scoffed. "That's overkill. You've never been late before."

"She wanted to be sure that I understood never to be late again." Yushi leaned forward to eat her peach, juice dripping from her fingers.

"Petitpois is way too strict with you. Where does she get off?"

Yushi grimaced. "I'd better go back."

"Already? We just sat down."

"Pettypoo suggested I make up for my lateness by taking short breaks for a while."

"How long is a while?" Maddy pulled a tissue from her pocket to wipe her fingers.

"Who knows?" Yushi hopped off the table and headed across the grass. Peg-leg jeans and green sneakers. She was so slender she looked frail — until she moved. She had a toughness to her gait and narrow hips. A strange mix of reticence and temerity.

Yesterday, during a lull, Petitpois had tried to give them lessons on how to modulate their voices when pronouncing the names of the desserts. *Tartelettes aux fraises. Lingots. Pavé au chocolat.*

Yushi had stretched her lips and bared her teeth in a vicious grin. Ganache, she said with perfect enunciation and emphasis. Then added, Anyone with a bowl and a whisk can make ganache.

Petitpois flushed. She'd hired Yushi to slide baguettes into paper bags and set pastries in boxes, not to show off expertise Petitpois didn't have.

When customers asked about the pastries, Yushi could explain in detail. The genoise was moist because it had been drizzled with syrup. *Crème pâtissière* wasn't made with cream but milk and eggs. One day, when they weren't busy, Yushi had sliced a lump of pink marzipan into discs she flattened and curled like petals, one around the other, fashioning a rose. With skills like that, why was she employed as counter help, letting an officious snob like Petitpois bully her?

Maddy looked at her watch. Another minute and she should get back to work. Her eyes had been following the crazy trajectory of the girls in the paddleboat. Both had blond hair to their shoulders, but she saw now that one was older. Were they mother and daughter, having fun together? She watched, wondering what that felt like.

She sighed and glanced at her watch again. *Okay. Now. Move. Go.*

She sauntered back to the market.

"Enjoy the peaches?" Pierre-Paul called from behind his tables heaped high with berries and fruit.

She smiled her thanks but kept walking. He had a weathered tan as if he'd been in the fields, rototilling soil and watering crops. Undo a couple of buttons on his shirt, and she bet the skin beneath was pale and soft.

Stop that. She mentally slapped her hand. *No more married men.*

There was a shorter route home, but Maddy liked cycling along the canal. The water glimmered a rippled reflection of sky. The cluster of picnic tables where the embankment widened had a new batch of origami in bright red. In the spring, when the miniature centrepieces had first appeared, she'd ridden across the grass to see what they were. Someone had poked intricately folded paper between the slats. Grasshoppers, flowers, butterflies with antennae, stiff paper crowns. Maddy wondered if the artist was a man or a woman, young or old. Decorating picnic tables was such a sweet task. Good in itself.

She turned off the canal path, down a low hill to the Pointe, cycled past the side-by-side English and French Catholic churches, angled right at the hockey arena where people voted on election and referendum days. At Wellington she cruised to a stop at the lights. A hooker, her skinny buttocks moulded in a tight skirt, harassed the man on his kitchen chair outside the *dépanneur*. "A cigarette, *tabernac*! Give me a cigarette!" He perched at a tilt, as if his body had been rattled and the bones reset all wrong. She screeched at him and jerked her arm in the air. Maddy would be stoned, too, if she had to stick her face in strange crotches.

Across Wellington she turned into the alley and up ahead saw a man at her fence. Boy, oh boy! If that was one of the guys from the rooming house taking a piss, was she going to yell! How often had she told them the alley wasn't their personal, private latrine?

At the crunch of stones under her tires, the man began to walk away, his bandy legs stepping fast. Maddy slowed, recognizing the older of the boys who used to live in the house next door. What was his name? Ben. She'd been at the outdoor tap, rinsing a bucket, when he'd staggered onto the back deck carrying his brother, whose arms hung like deadweights, head lolling. She'd shouted, What happened? What's wrong? He hadn't answered and then she couldn't see what he was doing, because he'd stooped to the deck with the fence between them. Ben! she'd called, Ben! Sirens were howling down the street, careening to a stop before their houses.

She stood at her gate now, not sure if she should cycle after Ben to ask how he was. She hadn't seen him since the funeral a year ago. She wondered how he felt about his father selling the house. After the suicide, his father had moved away, leaving the house empty. People had assumed he would eventually return — or give the house to Ben.

That day, when she'd seen the couple on the sidewalk, she'd had no idea they were visiting the house. There was never a For Sale sign. Everyone along the street was surprised when they saw a stranger hauling bags and furniture onto the sidewalk, dumping out the house. Even if Ben's father had needed the money and Ben couldn't afford to buy the house upfront, families usually came to an arrangement.

Poor Ben, she thought. Exiled to the alley. How he must resent the new neighbours for living in the house that should have been his. How he must hate them.

She watched him walk to the end of the alley, unlocked her gate, and wheeled her bike into the yard.

Maddy woke, blinking at the slit of light between the curtains she hadn't fully closed last night. A bird was twittering in the tree outside her window and a car drove past, but the house sounded empty. No running water, no footsteps. Even though it was still early on a Saturday, Bronislav and Andrei must already have left. She didn't know if they'd gone to work or if they'd only stepped out. She belted her robe over the T-shirt she wore to sleep. If they came home, she would dress. In the meantime, this was her day off.

Coffee in hand, she ambled out to the deck. Many seasons of sun and rain had made the wicker chair swell and shrink, and the rattan creaked as she sat. The chair was still comfortable, still her favourite chair, but the armrest was wobbly, so she kept her fingers on the mug.

Jim was in the grass, a long-haired orange tom doing his sphinx act. Shoulders and spine regal, he kept his gaze on the distant horizon — which was, however, blocked by the wood fence.

"Jim," she said. A stone sphinx, he ignored her.

Saturday off ... what a treat. The air was warm, the sky a rich blue with fluffy, storybook clouds. A light breeze made the towering trees along the alley rustle. From inside the new neighbours' house, she heard, "Frédéric, come here!"

Maddy imagined him stopping what he was doing to see what she wanted. Six feet tall and obedient.

Again she heard, "Fred!"

Ah ... not so obedient. It would be a change, having a couple living in the house everyone along the street had gotten used to thinking was abandoned. *Abandoned* felt fitting after a suicide. Who would even want to live in a house where there had been a suicide? She hoped the real estate agent had told the new people.

In the grass Jim had grown yet more still. His ears were alert. A squirrel had scrabbled under the gate with a curve of bagel it now sat upright to nibble. The fur on Jim's back rippled the instant before he charged. The squirrel pounced up the fence, scampered a few bounds, and pivoted to scold the nasty cat for making it drop its piece of bagel.

"Jim," Maddy said.

He blinked at the dahlias, miffed that she'd witnessed his hunting interruptus.

"I don't want you catching squirrels." Bad enough when he brought her the mauled bodies of sparrows and mice. "No squirrels, okay?"

Maddy leaned forward in the lawn chair to snip the blowsy heads of the geraniums. Red petals fluttered to the deck. She'd changed into denim shorts and a peasant blouse she'd bought on sale and should have guessed wouldn't suit her. White puff atop big bum. It was fine, though, for sitting in the backyard.

She angled the shears into the leaves. Her father used to trim plants with her mother's sewing scissors. Heavy steel with black enamel handles. Her mother had brought them from Poland. As a child, Maddy had marvelled that the same scissors that bit through felted wool could take such delicate snips. Her father's blunt-boned knuckles and fingers so gentle among the flowers.

He wasn't a man of words — certainly not one for metaphors — but once, when she stood nearby as he snipped the fading flowers, he showed her inside the petals where the pistil was swollen with seeds. He said that when plants started to make seeds, they stopped blooming. So he was cutting the old flowers before they turned into seeds. Tricking the plants to keep them blooming. He called it a trick — a *sztuczka*. The explanation, indirect as it was, was the closest to sex education she'd had at home.

Her mother avoided all mention of the body and its functions. Maddy had found out about periods by listening to the older girls in the washroom at school. They said it only happened to girls — like growing breasts. Maddy's nipples had already started to swell. One of the girls told her periods would be next. Maddy wasn't sure what that was or how you could tell when it happened, but it excused you from gym. Some girls said it proudly. Others grumbled that it made them sick.

She didn't know what was happening when she started to feel nauseated from cramps low in her belly. When she saw the dark mess in her underpants, she thought she was dying — bleeding from the inside out. Crying, unable to keep it a secret, she told her teacher, who took her into an office and explained. At home, furtive and angry, Maddy showed her mother the extra Kotex pad the teacher had given her. She said she needed more. A bra, too. The teacher said she should be wearing a bra. Her mother, who lamented every expense and hoarded even pennies — each penny worth several *zloty* back home — went to the store for a box of Kotex and the Sally Ann for a bra. The pointed cups of the bra puckered over Maddy's small breasts but she wore it. Only years later did she realize how lucky she was that her mother had bought Kotex instead of making her wear the cloth rags she washed and reused herself. In this one respect, her mother allowed her to be Canadian. When Maddy finished the box of Kotex, which was kept behind the bucket of dirty laundry in the cupboard, her mother bought another.

But even after Maddy got her period, her mother still didn't explain about sex. She might not have known the words — or known you could speak about it. She hid behind her worries, her prayers, her scrubbing, her bread dough and jars of pickles, her great vats of cabbage in brine.

Maddy deduced what she could from the girls' talk at school about boys wanting to touch their breasts and begging them to rub their dicks. That part was disgusting — everyone said so — but then you had a boyfriend. If anyone said more than that, Maddy didn't understand. When Neil wanted to push inside her, even though it hurt, she let him. She didn't know what it meant when her periods stopped coming. She was hungry all the time and thought she was getting fat. She wore a large sweater, and over that a man's suit jacket she got at a church sale. She'd grown her curls into a shaggy mop she let hang across her face.

It was Mrs. Granville, the English teacher, who called Maddy to her desk and walked her from the classroom to the principal's office. The principal talked. Mrs. Granville, too. Maddy was fifteen. Their words blurred in the air. Why did they keep saying *baby*? She didn't want a baby. She blinked behind the hair that hid her face from view. The principal said she would have to call her parents. Her parents didn't have a telephone. Maddy was told to wait outside the office. When Mrs. Granville came out, she said she would walk Maddy home. She followed her up the steps and into the house, slipping off her shoes in the hallway as Maddy had. The floors shone, waxed and polished. Maddy knew her parents would be in the kitchen eating. They always ate before Maddy and her brother, Stan, came home from school, because her father had an evening job he went to after his work at the factory. Maddy's parents stared, appalled by the presence of a stranger in their kitchen. Mrs. Granville stood in her nylons on the linoleum tile, talking into a void. Maddy's mother spoke only Polish, her father only the most necessary words of French or English. *Pregnant* wasn't a necessary word. When Mrs. Granville finally realized that neither parent understood, she lay a hand on the high mound of Maddy's belly that was only partly masked by the loose sweater.

Maddy scowled, remembering, and dragged her chair across the deck to the next pot of geraniums. There was nothing to be done about the stupidity of the past. The mistakes and the ignorance. She angled her shears and snipped, dropped the spent leaves and petals by her feet. A *sztuczka. Huh.*

Behind her, through the kitchen window, she heard the clank of cans being set on the counter. Bronislav and Andrei must be home. They moved in tandem. They hadn't known each other before arriving in Montreal, but now they worked at the same factory, cooked and ate together, rented two of her upstairs rooms.

"I'm out here," she called, so they would know she was home.

Bronislav slid aside the door and stepped onto the deck. He was the more sociable of the two. "Hello," he said. For him, that was a complete sentence.

Her turn now. "The weather's nice. Are you off today?"

He nodded. He seemed to have nothing more to volunteer.

She heard the cans being slid across a shelf. She allotted tenants one cupboard each, the middle shelf and a drawer in the refrigerator.

"Feel free to eat out here." She waved her shears across the deck. "I'm just about done, then I'm off for a bike ride."

"We are going to a wedding."

"You know someone who's getting married."

"No."

Was it worth asking? She would only make him uncomfortable and he still might not tell her. "Enjoy yourself. Have a good time."

"Yes." He backed up, reaching for the handle behind him.

She scraped the heaps of dead flowers and leaves into a nest she carried to the composter. Pushing aside the lid, she squinted and held her breath against the insects that flew up. Her composter was a thriving stew of organic breakdown. In the fall she would shovel the rich black earth out the bottom and spread it around her bushes and plants.

In the kitchen she washed her hands, poured herself a glass of milk, and munched a few dates and tamari almonds. Through the ceiling she heard Bronislav and Andrei walking from their rooms to the bathroom, back and forth.

For hours after they left, the upstairs would stink of dollar-store cologne. Except for her own quiet movements, the house would be silent until dawn, when she might wake to their clumsy tiptoeing up the stairs, the lingering whiff of cheap cologne replaced by booze.

On sunny weekends the bike path along the canal turned into a pinball boulevard. There were speed-nuts in their Tour de France spandex; friends cycling in clots of six-way conversations; Daddy Bear, Mommy Bear, Kiddie Bear families; rollerbladers with their wide stride, pendulum arms, and overweight thighs hoping to lose weight overnight; and even pedestrians, some with strollers, some with dogs — not always on leashes. Urban fact #43: dog owners blamed cyclists when *their* brainless canines galloped into oncoming wheels.

Maddy waited until late afternoon, when the Pavlovian gong of suppertime called most of the crowd home. She turned onto the canal path behind a woman cycling with a milk crate strapped onto the back of her bike. Inside it sat a

Boston terrier with dejected eyes — reconciled to the ride but still unhappy. As Maddy passed, she made kissy noises. The dog's gloom didn't change.

Ahead, on the other side of the canal, rose the art deco clock tower of the market. She wondered if Yushi had worked with Cécile, who was good, or Elsie, who was new and needed help, or Régis, who was a shit. The dessert and bread shelves would be almost empty, though customers would still be waiting for the last baguettes, the last cakes.

She debated stopping and saying hello. Slowed as she approached the bridge to cross to the market but didn't turn. She was already in the trance of cycling.

Past the market extended a row of renovated factory-condos with sandblasted walls and large plate-glass windows. An ex-boyfriend, Brian, used to rage about this so-called revital-ization of old neighbourhoods. Revitalization, he spat. The real words are appropriation of cheap real estate. He was right. Someone was making a fat profit, and not necessarily — in fact, rarely — the people who currently lived in the neighbourhoods and would have to move elsewhere as the prices kept going up.

She crossed the next bridge to ride along the other side of the canal, where a hedge of rose bushes basked in the late afternoon sunshine. As a girl, she'd walked here with her best friend, Ginette. There were no rose bushes then, only Queen Anne's lace they'd picked to make lacy bouquets and pretend they were brides. Later, when Ginette had to go live with her grandmother in Rosemont, Maddy picked two bouquets so that Ginette would still get married one day.

Maddy's knees pumped. Wind cooled the sweat on her arms and her neck. She was approaching her favourite stretch, where the path twisted through the thick trunks of the cottonwoods. Shafts of sunlight dusted the grass, and the water in the canal gleamed green, reflecting the shade of the trees.

FARA

Fara took a deep breath. All she could smell was the varnish, which had hardened to a clear, if not quite smooth, gloss. The floorboards were uneven and Frédéric had had problems with the sander. The wood still showed scars of paint here and there — a stretched eye of brown, an abraded smudge of bright green.

Fara half-closed her eyes, still taking deep breaths as she walked to the kitchen. She'd become convinced she smelled something foul. It was too faint to identify or locate exactly, but she thought it came from here, in the kitchen.

Frédéric smelled nothing, but his nose was numb from working in the cellar. For the past year that the house had been abandoned, every cat in the neighbourhood had slunk in to piss in the cellar. Someone told Frédéric to spray vinegar on the walls and into the corners to neutralize the reek. Someone else had said bleach. First, he had to haul away the piles of rotten wood and corroded machinery. Movement was clumsy, because the ceiling was low — and made lower yet by the thicket of wires strung across it. He had to walk stooped, kept forgetting, and banged his head.

His build-a-house cousin, Eric, had arrived unannounced one evening. When he stepped into the cellar, he hissed,

Tabernac! It stinks down here! He poked around, then chuckled. Haven't seen an electrical box this ancient since I don't know when. A microwave will blow it in three seconds flat. In the kitchen he chopped a hand at the counters. Better replace those! As if Fara and Frédéric couldn't see that for themselves. He knocked on the walls of the second floor and tilted his head, listening. Winter'll be cold here. Don't think you've got more than newspaper for insulation. Fara followed the two men through the house, touching Frédéric's arm now and again, so he knew he wasn't alone facing the volley of Eric's opinions.

Fara stood in the kitchen, holding her breath then breathing again. The smell was definitely in here. She opened the cupboard doors and took big sniffs. They smelled musty and of mice, but not … whatever it was. She crouched to the floor. It was ugly beige linoleum with a fleur-de-lis pattern trodden to a dull ochre smear at the sink. They would rip it up eventually, but Frédéric said not yet. There was too much else that needed to be done before they tackled the kitchen floor.

Was the smell coming from *under* the linoleum? Something soaked into the wood? She shuddered, thinking blood, thinking …

The problem wasn't suicide. She could handle that. But she wished she knew how and where in the house. Like this, not knowing, she'd begun to imagine the worst in every room.

The boy's presence had become more real since Frédéric had found the album of photos upstairs. He'd been handsome, his body lean, with brown hair swept across his forehead. Often he had a pretty girl beside him — though never the same one. He didn't smile. His eyes were more connected to the camera than to the girl leaning against him.

Fara wondered if they should send the album to his father. He'd been so restless at the notary's, pen gripped in his hand, wanting only to be rid of the house. Rid of the house and everything that had happened here.

Her own parents acted as if they'd never had a younger daughter. All signs of Claire had disappeared from their house — the frame with her high school diploma, the cushion she'd knit, Claire's old bedroom renovated as a sewing room for their mother. Fara was sure she had the only pictures of her and Claire as children, not that there were many. Her parents took a yearly Christmas photo to send home to family, but otherwise saw no reason to take pictures of the girls. There were no birthday parties.

Fara put the photo album with the boy's pictures on a shelf in an upstairs closet. She wasn't sure if his father would want to see them, since he'd left them, but she also couldn't bring herself to throw them away.

The new people trusted that the fence that enclosed the small backyard was secure. They walked back and forth before the uncurtained windows, happy, prideful, and inviolate, so they thought, in their new home. They never noticed Ben spying through the gaps in the fence — the piecemeal outline of his body that they would have seen if they'd looked. The boards were so weathered and flimsy, he could have kicked them down.

He'd watched and heard them argue about the sander. When the man turned it on, it roared with a noise that meant it was blocked, but the moron kept using it until sawdust spewed out the top. He didn't even know enough to hammer down the nails sticking out of the floor so they didn't rip the sandpaper. Was he lazy or stupid? With money to waste.

Every evening Ben waited until the new people left. He still had his key for the back gate. Last night he popped a couple of nails off the deck and hauled out the winter tires his dad had stored there. Why leave perfectly good tires? His dad had already given away the whole damn house for next to nothing.

All his dad wanted was to forget how he'd fucked up — telling everyone big stories about him and Xavier fixing up the house so they could sell it for lots of money. Real estate was starting to happen in the Pointe. Xavier didn't give a damn about real estate, didn't give a damn about renovating, didn't give a damn about the house, didn't give a damn about much. But did he have to kill himself? Why didn't he just hand the old man a signed piece of paper telling him to drink himself to death? *Go for it, old man. Die!*

Not fast enough, though. Not fast enough for Ben to get the house.

Fara was painting the small front room white. She pushed the roller up and down, trying not to look when people walked by on the sidewalk. Their heads were at the level of the windowsill, their voices beside her. "That's what you said last time. You said it wouldn't happen again." The bounce of a basketball kept getting closer until Fara expected it to land at her feet. "You're getting a whack if you don't get your finger out of your frickin' nose *right now!*" Fara didn't hear the whack but the child began bawling.

Before they'd bought the house, she hadn't realized what it would be like to live almost on the sidewalk. People didn't seem to notice her painting the walls. They accepted there was a membrane, however invisible, between inside and outside — private and public. Fara supposed she would get used to it. Or never use this room.

"*Ostie!*" she heard from the bathroom, followed by the clatter of a tool dropped to the floor. Frédéric didn't usually swear, but every day in the house uncovered new problems. A light switch sizzled. One of upstairs windowsills had been pulled out from the brick. The washing machine drain wasn't connected to a pipe.

Fara leaned the handle of the roller against the window frame and stepped back to assess the wall. She thought she could still sense a shadow of green under the white, but that might be her mind playing tricks. It was bizarre how these small rooms had been made smaller yet by dull colours. Brown, khaki, green, grey.

She rubbed her knuckles into the small of her back and went to see how Frédéric was managing. He was on a ladder in the bathroom, poking his fingers into the light fixture hole in the ceiling. From inside the hole, wires dangled like cartoon punctuation. "How's it going?" she asked.

"Nothing but black wires. How am I supposed to tell which is which?"

"How about you take a rest? Come sit outside for a minute."

"Do you want a light in here or don't you?"

Didn't he intend to use the light, too? She decided not to say that out loud. She couldn't help with the wiring, nor with his mood.

From the deck she gazed at her modest domain of hacked weeds and grass. Next spring she would plant tomatoes, green beans, maybe even strawberries. She glanced across the fence at the neighbour's yard, which was larger. There were bushes and leafy plants, but no garden as far as Fara could tell. Along the edge of the deck stood large ceramic pots bursting with pink and red geraniums.

A movement closer to the house startled her. The neighbour, legs curled on a basket-weave chair, lifted her hand in a slow wave.

Fara was embarrassed to be caught gawking. "Sorry. I just wondered how big your yard was and if you had a garden. I can't wait to plant one next year."

The neighbour had twisted her thick curls up and poked them in place with geisha sticks. "You might have too much shade — because of the maple and the fence. Your yard's pretty small, too. Have you ever had a garden?"

"No."

"Well, then." She smiled. "You won't miss it."

Fara smiled in return. Polite but not giving way. She still meant to try.

"So, you bought the house. I saw you coming and going. And I heard you sanding."

"Did we make so much noise?"

"Renovation is all you hear in this neighbourhood. Everyone's buying up the old houses."

"Isn't that better than letting them fall apart?"

The woman shrugged. "I'm actually surprised how long it's taken people to discover the Pointe. We're closer to downtown than Outremont or the Plateau, but it's like Montreal doesn't even know we exist."

"You must have discovered it. You moved here years ago."

"I was born here — not in this house, I bought it later. But in the Pointe, yeah. My name's Maddy and this is Jim." She scratched the head of the orange cat who was rubbing against the chair leg.

"I'm Fara. And that's Frédéric." Fara waved inside the house.

"When are you moving in?"

"This weekend. We took time off to fix up the house. It's still nowhere near ready, but we have to go back to work and we already booked the movers. We've got a couple of rooms where we can sleep and eat."

"Must have been a mess. The owner …"

"We know. The real estate agent told us about his son."

Maddy tilted her head, her geisha sticks like antennae. "Not everyone would live there. It doesn't bother you?"

"I work in a hospital. Somebody's always dying. You get used to the idea."

"That people get sick and die? Sure. But that's not the same as hanging."

Hanging. The word settled like an object between them, daring Fara to touch it. She remembered how the real estate agent had glanced at the ceiling fan. Frédéric had already taken it down — more plastic than metal and attached with only three screws. No way had the boy hanged himself there. She thought of the house. The ceilings were high.

Maddy clasped her arms. "Do you know where?"

Fara gave a small shake of her head.

"Between the hallway and the big room on the ground floor. He and his dad had just made the opening wider and finished it with a wood frame. He screwed a hook for the rope into the wood. You'd think ... I don't know. You'd think drugs would be easier."

Fara had thought the same about Claire, but over the years she'd realized that people who were serious about suicide didn't care about easy or pain-free solutions. They wanted to be sure it was final. Done. No recourse.

"Who found him?" Fara asked. "His father?"

"His brother."

Fara's skin prickled. The real estate agent had never mentioned a brother.

"He called the police but didn't want to let them in the house when they came."

Fara had called 911 too — in a panic — then tried to stop the ambulance drivers from coming inside the apartment. She'd yanked at their arms and screamed they should go. She didn't want them to revive Claire if she was already brain-dead — or whatever happened when you tied a bag over your head. She hadn't been able to touch the bag herself. Rigid with horror, staring at the plastic knotted and tucked around Claire's neck, remembering Claire's question about the key. She'd known Fara would find her.

"Are you all right?" Maddy asked.

Fara blinked. "... I'm thinking what it must have been like for his brother to find him."

"His brother ... I guess so. It must have been ..." Maddy gave herself a shake. "I think most people wonder about Xavier. Why he wanted to kill himself."

Neither woman spoke for a moment. "I should get back," Fara said. "I'm painting the front room."

"I'll have you over once you're moved in and settled."

"Great. We'll look forward to it." Mechanical words. Fara wasn't even aware she'd spoken.

She walked into the house, through the kitchen, to the wood-framed opening between the main room and the hallway. And there, above her head — how had she never noticed? — she saw the hole bored into the wood. A deeply gouged cone in the middle of the frame. Every time she'd walked in and out of the room, she'd stepped through the air where his body had hung.

No wonder his father had sold the house. At least Claire had ...

Fara checked herself. Was any form of suicide *nicer* than another?

The grey light of dusk. Ben could make out shapes but no colours. The house was dark. The couple had gone back to wherever they lived. He'd followed them once, at a distance, as they walked to the subway.

He unlocked the back gate. He could creep across the yard by feel. His hands found the deck boards that he hadn't hammered down again after he'd pulled out the tires.

That morning he'd remembered that the cellar window under the deck had never had a lock, only a hook on the inside frame. He shimmied into the narrow space and used the blade of his jackknife to ease the window open. They hadn't even hooked it shut. Didn't they realize that anyone could crawl under the deck and get into the house?

He fished the pliers from his jeans pocket and tugged the hook off the inside frame. He didn't have a plan. He didn't know what he wanted to do. Nothing to *them*. He wasn't a criminal. But he also wasn't finished with the house yet.

He slid the window shut again. Now he could get in if he wanted.

Fara didn't like standing so close to the top of the ladder. The metal trembled as she reached over her head. She imagined crashing and Frédéric finding her unconscious, neck broken, sprawled under a tumble of aluminum geometry. She shouldn't be doing this while she was alone in the house. She dipped the scraper into the bucket of putty and reached up again. A million-umpteen things they still had to do before they could move in, but first she had to hide this hole.

She'd shown it to Frédéric, who asked if it bothered her. No, she said, I'll just step aside so I don't bump into his body. He assumed that, if she could joke, she was fine. He didn't understand that she wasn't joking. She didn't believe in ghosts and didn't worry about the house being haunted. But as long as there was a hole for the hook where his body had hung, she saw his body hanging. She wasn't even sure if filling the hole would help, but she had to try.

At least now she knew where and how. She could stop sniffing the air in the kitchen. Or peering at the grout around the tub for bloodstains. He'd killed himself here.

So what? A hole was a hole was a hole was a hole. She repeated it the way she'd once told herself a bag was a bag was a bag was a bag. You recited a word until you reduced it to a meaningless nothing. Even so, how many years had passed before she could use a green garbage bag? She'd kept remembering Claire in bed, hands folded over her chest, her matted, eyeless teddy bear tucked in her elbow, green garbage plastic knotted over her head. How could she have done that to herself? Like saying, look, I'm garbage. Fara hadn't wanted to believe it was Claire — except that no one but Claire would have hugged that ancient, discoloured teddy bear.

Fara scraped putty into the ugly gouge in the wood. When the putty was dry, she would paint the frame with a darker stained varnish to disguise the patch. Except then she would have to paint the skirting boards to match. The window frame, too. Hiding a hole was work.

Making one, too. He'd drilled through the wood into plaster. Bought a hook long enough to hold his weight. He must have done it secretly over several days so his father and brother wouldn't notice. Screwed the hook in place, then waited, wondering when to stage his death. Once the hook was in place, he could do it any time. Every time he walked into the room, he knew it was up there. The steel curve of a beckoning finger.

She stepped off the ladder and looked at her work from the floor. The patch of putty was only slightly paler than the wood. Maybe when it dried she wouldn't even see it. She would still stain and varnish it — get another layer between herself and the hole.

ROSE

Rose had said Kenny should pick her up on the corner of Parc and Villeneuve. She'd thought it would be easier than having him look for her address. She also wasn't sure she wanted him to know where she lived.

Though she was early, she found him already parked in a white van with red letters along the side: FENÊTRES FAVREAU. He wagged a bag of doughnuts at her through the window. "I got you coffee."

It wasn't yet seven. Traffic was sparse, moving easily past stores, Chinese restaurants, pizza shops, apartment buildings. Kenny jabbed the radio button until he found music he liked. He asked if she liked it. She shrugged then said she remembered it from when she was in high school. He grinned, assuming that meant yes. She felt she was still asleep, dreaming she was sitting in a van and leaving the city to return to the cabin in the woods.

Kenny said he was pretty sure he knew where to find Rivière-des-Pins. "Near Rawdon, right? But why don't you get out the road map?" He pointed at the glove compartment.

She unfolded the map across her lap and legs. A network of lines tangled thick around Montreal, thinning as they headed north. The occasional town was a hard knot.

"Why don't you fold it in a square with the part we want to get to on the outside? You don't have to hide under it."

She wished she could hide. She hoped no one would recognize her. *Thérèse's daughter. Crazy Thérèse. Imagine living in a cabin the woods in this day and age! Her poor daughter. Poor Rose.*

Rose hated how people always used to feel sorry for her. She didn't feel sorry for herself. She knew she wasn't like the other girls at school, giggling about TV shows and makeup, whispering their silly, made-up secrets. Rose knew that when you had a real secret — like meeting Armand in the woods — you kept it to yourself.

No one except Armand ever came to their woods. Even the roaring ATVs stayed away since the accident with the Bilodeau boy. The trees grew too close. The ground heaved with their roots. When the boy fell from his ATV, his brother couldn't stop it from rolling back and crushing his head.

Kenny sang a few lines along with the song on the radio. He was always in a good mood, but he was especially happy today. Even if she told him that people in Rivière-des-Pins believed the forest around her cabin was cursed, he would still want to go. His green tackle box and fishing rod lay on the floor behind them.

Yesterday he'd shown up at her studio with his fishing rod. *Isn't it a beaut?* He swirled it in the air like a wand. *I'm going to practise outside.* She'd seen the odd person standing along the canal with a fishing rod. She didn't think there were fish. Certainly nothing one should eat.

She was painting a dresser she'd found in a furniture shop in St-Henri. Three large drawers with two small ones on top. Twenty dollars, no tax, and the man had delivered it. He was an older man with an eye dulled by a cloudy spot she hardly noticed because he kept winking as he talked, turning every sentence into a possible joke. He had leaned against the counter in his shop, surrounded by shabby, scuffed furniture he'd cleaned up and repaired. He had a rhythm to his voice that reminded her of Yushi when she talked about food or her mother. Rose wondered if the man in the furniture shop came from Trinidad, but she was too shy to ask.

She would use the dresser to store yarn, shuttles, bobbins, and combs. When she finished painting the drawers and set them on their backs to dry, she peered out the window along the canal. Where was Kenny? She finally walked down the hallway to the loading dock. The sculptor waved her around to the side of the building, nowhere near the canal.

Kenny stood on a bank of grass, swinging his rod back smoothly, then forward, abruptly stopping short. The rod formed an elegant arc of movement tethered to his stocky arm. Sunlight caught the long glint of string slithering through the grass as he reeled it in. She backed away, not sure if he would be embarrassed to be discovered fishing in the grass. Though anyone cycling by could see him.

Today he planned to go fishing while she took her loom apart. She wanted to tell him not to mention her name if anyone stopped him or asked how he got there. She'd taken care to disguise herself, getting her hair cut to frame her face, wearing a new pair of capris.

She sat in the van, staring straight ahead, pretending not to see the outlying houses of Rivière-des-Pins. Modern pre-fab bungalows, the bank, the pharmacy, the Corvette where Maman bought clothes, the IGA. Once a month she and Maman came to Rivière-des-Pins to buy flour, oats, rice, molasses, lentils, and potatoes.

"The old hometown," Kenny said.

She wanted to say no, home was where she lived now, with Yushi — except that she knew this place and its stories. The stone church with the steeple. The street to Lisette's house. Maman used to bring Lisette the rugs and shawls they wove, because Lisette knew a woman who distributed to stores that sold Québécois crafts.

In Montreal Rose had seen the price of hand-woven goods. Four cotton placemats cost more than Lisette used to give Maman for a whole woollen shawl with a braided fringe. The placemats weren't even hemmed properly. Rose understood that stores needed to make a profit, but Lisette must have taken a hefty cut as well. Rose didn't ever want to see her again.

"Here," Rose said as they approached the gas station. "Turn."

She felt disembodied, sitting high up in the van with Kenny, driving through a landscape she recognized but where she no longer felt she belonged. The horizon of trees. The dip in the road. The Tremblays' yellow house. Jacques Tremblay collected disability for his back and worked under the table for a buddy of his who was a plumber. Madame Burns stood on her porch shaking out a mat, her periscope head following the van as it passed. Madame Burns lived for bingo, driving not just to Rawdon for a game, but as far as Joliette and Mascouche.

With surprise Rose saw that the land Armand used to rent from Maman had been planted with corn. The plants were almost waist-high, shading the long furrows of rich brown earth. Where and how did he pay rent? Maybe there was an account at the bank. She'd never thought of it, though she knew Armand was honest to the last clod of earth for any detail related to farming.

A windbreak of cedar trees hid his white clapboard house. She jerked her head away, not wanting to look, but she'd already seen the car set on blocks beside the driveway — another of Jerome's projects he'd begun and never finished. Jerome was six years older than she was, Armand's youngest son who still lived at home. No one understood how a hard-working man like Armand could have fathered such a useless son. When Rose was in high school, Jerome often sat in his car at the back of the school parking lot. He wasn't in school anymore, just hanging out with the older boys, selling whatever it was they smoked. She never told Armand. They didn't talk about his family. Nor about Maman. She couldn't actually remember a single word Armand had ever said to her, though they must have talked to arrange meetings. When, if not where. Where was always the same. Deep in the woods by the lean-to where Armand stacked the wood he cut in the winter and fetched with the trailer in the summer when the ground was dry.

"Are we there soon?" Kenny asked. The fields and few houses had given way to densely wooded land. Thick cedar and pine, the smooth white trunks of birch trees, the grey bark of maples.

"Soon."

He drove slowly on the dirt road. "You really did live in the sticks, didn't you?"

Rose didn't understand the admiration in his voice. "Here," she said. "Slow down."

"Stop?"

"Not yet." They passed the dead tree where, at the top, an owl nested. The pine with a tuberous growth on its trunk. "Here. Stop."

The weedy edge of the road dropped to a deep ditch. Rose stared out the window into the shady depth of the trees.

"Wow. We're really in the middle of nowhere."

Madame Burns had seen their van. And who else? Kenny had to leave before someone drove by and saw where he'd stopped. She pointed down the road. "You continue to the end, then turn right."

"Aren't you going to show me your cabin?"

"I need to go alone."

"Because of your mom, eh? I thought it might be easier if I came with you the first time."

Nothing would be easier. With or without him. But she wanted the loom.

Kenny leaned between their seats into the back of the van to snatch a red hazard rag from the floor, hopped out, and crashed through the weeds.

"No!" Rose clambered from the van when she saw him reach for a branch to tie the rag. "If someone sees it —"

"*I* need to see it. I'll never find this spot again."

She couldn't think of another way. "Okay, I'll meet you here."

"Around four?" He jiggled his legs, anxious to get going. "Wish me luck! We'll have trout for supper!"

The canopy of trees grew so dense that only puzzle pieces of sky could be seen high above. It was cooler in the woods than in the city. Fern brushed against Rose's legs. A chickadee dipped in flight across her path and landed on a branch. She and Maman used to hold out handfuls of seed in the winter. She remembered the grasp of thin claws on her finger. The greedy black eye and quick peck on her palm. The air smelled of cedar, pine trees, and resin.

The trout lilies should have finished blooming long ago, but here was one late yellow flower poised like a lantern over the sleek, speckled leaves. Maman had taught her the names and habits of the flowers. The puffed jowls of the *orchidées* that grew under the maple trees. The intricately pleated crowns of wild columbines.

There was the story, too, that Maman used to tell about the five roses. *There once was a girl who lived in a cabin in the woods with a garden of five magic roses.* The story changed with each telling, because the roses told the girl different secrets about the woods. How bees lived in decayed tree trunks where they made their honey. How the owl swooped through the dark to catch mice. The biggest secret was about the girl's name. She didn't have one so the five roses named her. They called her Rose.

Rose walked slowly, remembering. Another chickadee flitted past — or maybe the same one — sending her a questioning chirp.

Through the trees she glimpsed the slap of sunlight on the metal stovepipe. The tarred black peak of the roof. In the clearing she stopped. After only one winter empty, the cabin seemed to have sagged into the earth. The blank window stared at her. *Who are you?*

She wasn't going in the cabin. She only wanted the loom. She followed the short fieldstone path through the cedars to the shed, but when she saw it she was startled. She'd remembered it as white. She'd forgotten she'd painted it blue last summer. She'd worked alone because Maman kept losing her breath. Rose had thought she was tired. She hadn't understood why she was so tired, but she also hadn't asked. And Maman never said.

She grasped the doorknob but — of course — it was locked. The key was in the cupboard in the cabin. She had no choice. Move, she thought. Get it. You need the key. Go.

The key to the cabin hung on a nail in the shelter where they stored wood. There were no more than a dozen logs left — pretty well advertising that the place was abandoned. She wondered if anyone had used the key since she'd last touched it. It slid into the lock of the cabin door and turned, but the door had swollen in its frame. She had to shove hard with her shoulder, each ram thudding through the cabin and her body.

When she burst through, she stumbled over the doorstep into the box of her past — the sofa where she used to sleep, the enamel-top table, the chairs, the wood stove. The faint stink of a squirrel nest or mice. How had she ever lived in such a cramped and dim space? Except that it had felt different with Maman there.

She had to step on a chair to reach the top shelf of the cupboard, tapping her fingers along the shelf until she found the key. She kept her eyes on the task and didn't glance around the cabin. She slammed the door behind her.

She felt calmer as soon as she unlocked the shed and saw the squat angles of the loom and the warping frame hooked on the wall. They were old friends waiting for her to fetch them. The loom was still dressed with a runner in brown linen that was only half-finished. Rose had wound the warp and put it on the loom, but Maman had tied it. Rose lay her hand on the width of threads that spanned from the back beam. She felt the give of strung linen against her palm and fingers, and wished she could keep the sensation to remember Maman.

She straightened. She had to get started. No choice but to cut the runner off the loom. The linen would be ruined in any case. Left on the loom all winter in an unheated shed, the tension would be stretched and uneven. She grabbed the heavy steel scissors and rasped long, sharp bites across the threads. Tension chopped, they collapsed against the heddles in sloppy twists. She unrolled the cloth that was already woven off the front beam and rolled it again, carefully folding the unfinished edge inside. She would hem this half-piece and keep it. Maman's last weaving.

Moving more quickly now, she unknotted and bundled the remaining threads off the back beam. What a waste. Though maybe not completely wasted. If she scattered the threads outside, the birds would tug ends free for their nests. The *marmottes* and the chipmunks could line their holes.

She realized she should have brought boxes to carry the shuttles, bobbins, hooks, and extra heddles. The harnesses lifted off the loom, though each one swayed with the weight of three hundred heddles — too heavy for her to carry through the woods. She tried to open the frames to remove the heddles, but the clips were jammed. She squeezed and pulled, then tapped with a hammer until the metal began to bend, but it still wouldn't release its hold.

She would have to undo the bolts that joined the parts of the loom. She clutched the wrench tight, but the first bolt wouldn't budge. She tried another, leaning her weight against the wrench, and sent it flying, smashing her hand into wood. "Ow! *Merde!*" She squeezed her hand in her armpit, then took up the wrench again, more gingerly. She tried another bolt. Crawled beneath the breast beam. Each bolt seemed to have been fused in place.

She stood with her hands hanging useless, unsure what to do next. She'd expected to take the loom apart and carry the pieces through the woods to the road by four o'clock. The harnesses were too heavy and the loom wouldn't come apart. It was a wide-legged skeleton, too unwieldy to manoeuvre out the door.

Her stomach grumbled. She'd made lunch for herself and Kenny but had forgotten it in the van. She knew there would be some food in the cabin — in the Mason jars on the shelves by the stove. She couldn't wait until four o'clock to eat. She strode to the cabin and shoved against the door. She ignored the sofa and the table, looking only at the jars. Kidney beans, split peas, rice, oats.

She didn't want to light a fire but she was so hungry. If she didn't eat, she wouldn't be able to carry the heavy harnesses through the trees. She grabbed the axe from behind the door. A tree stump served as a chopping block. She propped a log upright, her hands and arms remembering the movements. She wedged the axe in the log, knocked the log on the stump. One more knock and the log split in half. She split the pieces again, gathered the kindling, scooped twigs off the ground. Dry pine needles, yes. That would start a fire.

Rose waited in the trees by the road. She'd staggered along the path with a harness on her shoulder — only one. There were four.

She needed Kenny to help. Where *was* he? She'd already waited so long that she could have walked back to the shed for the wood crate she'd stacked with reeds, shuttles, and bags of yarn. She bit the skin around her thumbnail. The loom was still in one awkward piece. If they turned it on its side, maybe they could angle it through the shed door. Or maybe not. She couldn't tell.

She heard a car in the distance and leaped across the ditch to wave, then scrambled back into the trees when she saw two vehicles. She hid behind a cedar, but they still slowed and stopped. A door slammed and she heard Kenny. "Hey, thanks, I appreciate it. She should be here soon. Why don't you wait and say hi?"

Through the cedar branches Rose saw a red car in front of the van. She didn't recognize the driver until he turned his head to peer into the trees. Jerome. Armand's do-nothing son — who had, however, spotted her. He opened the car door and stepped out. "Hi, Rose."

Kenny still scanned the trees. She walked out from behind the cedar, surprising him. His jeans were muddy, his thick hair raked to one side. "Sorry, Rose, I know I'm late, but I couldn't find the place. Did you take down the rag I tied?"

Rose had forgotten about the rag. But he was right, it was gone.

"Yeah," Jerome said. "Your friend here was lost."

Rose expected Kenny to object that he hadn't been lost, but he only grinned. She saw him as he would appear in a story Jerome would tell over supper tonight: a soft-fleshed city boy trying to fish minnows. Not even smart enough to stay out of the mud. Armand would be sitting at the table, listening. Jerome would describe her, too — in her silly capris, ankles scratched, hoping no one would notice she'd come to Rivière-des-Pins. How stupid could she be?

Kenny said, "Man, was I lost! I'm lucky Jerome helped me. He knew who you were right away. Even though you left, Rose, people still remember you."

Remember *her*? People in Rivière-des-Pins still remembered how Maman's parents died — one coughing to death without even the benefit of oxygen, the other in a field under the wide open sky. When Rose was a child, people had told her. Had told her, too, how Maman left for Montreal and returned with a baby. Not for a minute did anyone ever forget that Rose was that baby. When she was four years old, then fourteen, then twenty-four, she would always be the baby Maman had borne in secret in Montreal. And who was her father? Who? People squinted at Rose as if she must know but was too stubborn to volunteer the details.

Kenny was explaining how he'd driven up and down the road looking for the rag.

"I would have seen you," Rose said. "I've been waiting for a while."

"When I couldn't find the rag I went down some other roads. Then I couldn't find this one again. There aren't any signs."

Of course there weren't signs. Strangers didn't belong on these back roads. Rose wished that Kenny would stop talking — and that Jerome would leave.

Jerome peered past her into the woods. "So you came to get your loom."

What else had Kenny told him? Everyone in Rivière-des-Pins would know before nightfall.

"Is that it?" Kenny pointed at the harness she'd leaned against a maple.

"That's a part," Rose said. Could he try any harder to look stupid?

"How are you going to carry your loom all the way out here?" Jerome asked.

"We'll manage," Rose said. And to Kenny, "We should go while we've still got light." He was such a city boy that he might not realize there weren't streetlights hanging off the trees.

"I'll put this in the van." Kenny hopped across the ditch for the harness but didn't expect the heavy sway of the heddles when he lifted it. "Jee-zus!"

"Need help?" Jerome asked.

"Thanks, bro. I've got it."

Jerome leaned against his car. "I can't figure out why you're in such a rush to drive back tonight. You've got a cabin."

"That's what I was telling Rose —"

"No. We're not staying here."

Still hopeful, Kenny said, "My buddy said I could have the van for the weekend."

"It's not yours?" Jerome gave it a slow once-over.

"Nope." Kenny obviously didn't know that, in the country, not owning your own wheels meant you were socially retarded.

"Come on," Rose said, turning to head into the woods.

Kenny slammed the van doors. "Got my marching orders. See you around, eh?"

Rose heard Jerome start his car and the crunch of gravel as he drove off. She walked quickly, impatient to get the loom and leave. Her steps were quiet, but Kenny scuffed and stumbled as if there weren't even a path. The sun wouldn't set for three hours, although here among the trees, with the light filtered through the branches, shapes were already beginning to lose definition. The trees grew close. The loom would be bulky and difficult to carry.

"Rose ... don't you like Jerome?"

"He's not a friend."

"He sounded really interested when I said who you were."

"What did you say?"

"That you used to live in a cabin in the woods with your mom, who passed away. He knew right away who I meant."

"What else?"

"Nothing."

He wouldn't have had to tell Jerome much. Jerome would have enough of a story describing Kenny. Even if he didn't tell his father directly, Armand would hear. There would be gossip in the village or his wife might tell him. Rose had always believed it was his wife who found out about her and Armand. Or maybe one of his sons. Someone who'd been walking in the woods and had glimpsed the unlikely movement of bodies among the branches and foliage. She couldn't bear to think it might have been Maman.

Kenny lumbered behind her, huffing. "There's perch in that lake, did you know? I caught a couple, but they were so little, I threw them back."

The path opened into the clearing of tall maples that circled the cabin.

"Wow," Kenny breathed. "Cool."

The cabin was not cool. There was no toilet or electricity. You had to pump water from the well, light a fire to cook and to heat.

"Come." She crossed the clearing to the shed. "I'll show you the loom."

They tipped the loom on its side and tried with one edge, then the other, butting its splayed wooden angles against the unyielding rectangle of the doorway. Kenny suggested they carry the pieces they could to the van — the remaining harnesses and the beams. Every time they stepped from the woods onto the road and he unlocked the van doors, Rose imagined someone spying through the trees, though there wasn't a house close enough and they would have seen a parked car.

"But what about the loom?" she asked Kenny.

"Let me think."

The sun had already dropped behind the trees. Above the clearing the sky was still blue, but at ground level dusk was grey. Mosquitoes whined around their heads, though they'd sprayed themselves with the repellent Kenny had brought.

He squinted at the loom with its front corner thrust from the doorway. They'd managed to detach the treadles, which he kept calling pedals, but that hadn't made the boxy frame of the loom any smaller. Inside the shed it was already dark. "I don't know, Rose. Nothing's moving tonight. Either we head back to Montreal or we sleep here and figure this out tomorrow."

"I don't want —" she began.

He raised a palm. "I know you don't want to stay in the cabin. I'm talking about your loom. How badly do you want it? Tomorrow ... I don't know. We'll figure out something. But it makes no sense to drive all the way to Montreal and come back tomorrow. That'll just waste time."

Rose stared at the obstinate loom stuck in the doorway. She'd already bought the yarn for her first project — a gold-and-brown herringbone bolster to match the satin cover on Yushi's bed. She hadn't thought it would be so hard to move the loom. She'd imagined having it in her studio, with its view of the canal, as early as this evening.

Barely moving her lips, she said, "You have to sleep on the couch."

"Sure." Kenny tilted his head. "Is that what's bothering you? Hey." He lifted three fingers. "No monkey business. Scout's honour."

That meant she would have to sleep in Maman's bed — as Maman had when she returned from Montreal, sleeping in the bed where her parents had once slept. The hypnotism of patterns repeating.

Mouth tight, resolved now, Rose strode to the cabin and shoved the door open. She knew there was no gas left in the Coleman lantern. She'd finished it last fall. She reached behind the cutlery in the drawer of the table for the emergency candles. As she dripped melted wax onto two plates to fix the candles, Kenny said, "What can I do?"

"Chop wood." She pointed at the axe behind the door.

She held a candle to the Mason jars. Rice. And a can of tuna. She grabbed a pot for water and followed Kenny outside. The metal hee-haw of the pump screeched, but the water spurted fresh and cold. When she stopped, the woods were so silent she realized that anyone listening would have heard the rusty cry of the pump and Kenny's blows with the axe.

Back in the cabin, she stared at the rocker with the rope seat. The plank steps that led to the hole in the ceiling that opened into the small attic bedroom. On the wall hung a crucifix Maman had kept in memory of her parents. Rose had never seen her pray. More useful, she'd said, was the fly swatter hooked on a nail by the door.

Here I am, Rose thought. Though it wasn't the same. She would sleep at the head of the stairs where the roof slanted close over the iron bedstead. She would sit in Maman's chair at the table and let Kenny sit in hers.

The door crashed open with Kenny breathing heavily, clasping an armload of wood. He tumbled the long wedges onto the floor by the stove. "You want more?"

"Yes." She bent to the stove.

At supper Kenny said little. His hair was still raked at a slant. Either the silence in the cabin — only the sounds of their eating and the snapping of the fire — kept him silent or he was too tired to talk. When he asked about a toilet, she directed him to the outhouse behind the cabin. "But if you only have to pee, go in the trees."

She'd forgotten how much longer it took simply to cook rice when you couldn't turn on a tap or a stove dial. After they ate, she washed the dishes in the water she'd heated on the stove. Kenny dried. Each gesture was exaggerated by wavering shadows and light.

She opened the chest where she kept her sheets and woven blanket, and tossed them on the sofa for Kenny. He fingered the ribbed blanket. "Wow, this is real old-timey Quebec. My grandma had blankets like this. They're made from rags ripped into strips."

"I know, I made it." She turned to the stairs, the flannel pajamas she'd taken from the chest under her arm. She didn't want to think about him sleeping on the couch. Alone in the cabin together was already closer than she wanted them to be. Eating in the silence, handing him the plates and forks to dry, hearing the stream of his pee against a tree outside.

"Rose, stop." He waited until she looked at him. "I want to thank you. I love sleeping in the woods. It's one of my absolutely favourite things to do."

Was it the candlelight or emotion? His eyes gleamed bright. "Okay," she breathed, not sure what else to say. Was he really that excited about staying in the cabin?

She carried a candle up the stairs. Each step creaked. No one had walked here since she'd left last fall. Light yawned up the slant of the gabled ceiling. Heat from the stove had risen, so the attic was warm. She undressed quietly. Didn't answer when Kenny called, "G'night! Good dreams!" She didn't want him to hear how close they were in the small cabin. She could hear a spark pop in the stove. His body shifting on the sofa.

She blew out the candle and slid between the sheets onto the sagging mattress. She'd been afraid that being in the cabin would deepen the emptiness she felt between its walls, but the weight of Maman's blanket comforted her. In the pillow she could smell the faint scent of Maman's hair. The anxiety of the day came to rest under the steeply angled ceiling.

She felt more at ease now that the cabin was dark and no one could see in. While she and Kenny were eating at the table, she'd sensed how easily someone could be standing outside among the trees, spying through the window. Maman had never hung a curtain because she wanted as much light as possible in the cabin. It never occurred to her that a person might sneak through the trees and watch them.

Rose had been thirteen, alone in the cabin, examining her newly swelling nipples in the light from the window, when a furtive movement outside caught her attention. Armand, the neighbour who rented land from Maman, stood under the trees closest to the cabin. Legs braced. The bristle of his moustache. His mouth. He didn't move away, didn't hide that he stood there watching. The glass between them was no barrier. She hugged her arms to her chest and turned her back — but not before she'd felt the rove of his eyes on her skin and seen how the lines of his cheeks deepened.

After the first time, she watched for him watching from the shadows of the trees. Sometimes he was there. Sometimes he wasn't. Sometimes Maman was in the cabin. When Rose was alone, she stood in the window and unbuttoned her shirt. She let him look at what she could tell from his expression he craved to see. His hands hung loose at his sides as she touched her small breasts. He watched, then pivoted and strode off so quickly she worried she'd frightened him. She couldn't remember if she'd left the cabin to run after him, deeper into the woods, or if he'd coaxed her outside.

When Rose was younger, she sometimes saw Armand waiting in the car in the IGA parking lot while his wife did the shopping. She used to wonder if he was Maman's boyfriend, because he was the only man who ever came to their cabin. For a while she even thought he might be her father. But he never even glanced her way. He stood at the door to talk to Maman about wood and land and planting corn.

Later, when Rose began meeting him in the woods, she tortured herself imagining that he used to touch Maman the way he did her. That they'd lain on the same grey blanket. That Maman, too, had opened her legs or crouched beneath him — until she was pregnant *with Rose*. It couldn't be true! A man would betray his wife but he wouldn't desire his own daughter. Would he? *Would* he?

Maman had had a baby in Montreal. Rose's father must be there. Though Rose had also heard that Maman hadn't been in Montreal long enough to have had a baby. She must have been pregnant when she left Rivière-des-Pins.

Rose couldn't bear to think of Armand with Maman, or that she might be his daughter. Except that, if she were, then that was a bond that held him in a way nothing else could. Even if he'd done *this* and *this* and *this* with his wife or Maman, his pleasure wasn't as deep as with Rose because Rose was his very flesh.

Rose squirmed her head into Maman's thin pillow. Armand was so long ago. The last time she'd seen him he moved liked an old man with a sore back. Hard to imagine that he'd ever kneeled between her thighs. Still, after Maman died and Rose was alone, she'd thought he might return. In the silence of the cabin, grieving for Maman, she'd waited. When weeks passed and he didn't come, she decided to leave — as Maman had. To go to Montreal.

In the hush of the night Rose woke again. She lay, listening to detect any sounds from outside. Was that a mourning dove? Armand used to call with a mourning dove's long, yearning coo to let her know he was waiting. She sat up, convinced he stood outside in the dark, watching the window. She could feel his longing envelop the cabin, as commanding as ever.

The iron bedstead rasped and groaned as she eased her legs from under the blanket. She crept down the stairs and stepped softly to the window. She squinted, then widened her eyes, staring into the dark haze of trees. Their thick shadows.

Behind her, embers in the stove crumbled. A man breathed in sleep. Her foot touched his jeans on the floor. She turned to the sofa, stooped, and brushed her fingers down the ribbed weave of the blanket, down his stomach to his sex. Armand had shown her how to caress him, sliding his hand around hers on his penis.

Up and down, up and down. It worked even through the heavy blanket. She felt the animal thickening, and slid her hand under the blanket into his underpants.

His breathing changed. She jerked the blanket away and kicked off her pyjama bottoms to straddle him.

"Rose?" he croaked.

"Shh!" She batted his hand away, rocking into him hard when — already? — he gasped a light, feathery cry. She ground her teeth, her hunger still bottled, and fumbled off him.

"Rose —"

"Quiet!" she cried harshly, snatching her pajamas from the floor and sprinting up the stairs.

Rose surfaced once from dreams when it was still dark. Already the birds were calling to each other about the kingdom of their nests, the fat insects they would snap from the air, the clouds the sun would send to decorate the sky for them. Strident, confident melodies.

She woke again to the round metal bars of the bedstead outlined by the angle of light from the stairway. She was immediately alert to danger, but didn't yet know why. Then she heard the rumble of voices outside. She recognized the cadence of Kenny's, but who was he talking to?

She pulled on her T-shirt and capris, and tiptoed to the stairs. The air in the cabin was chilly. Kenny hadn't made a fire, though he'd folded his sheet and blanket, and set the pillow on top. She pressed her forehead to the window but still couldn't see. She tugged the doorknob softly, but the wood squeaked and the voices stopped.

Jerome. Of course. Beside him stood Kenny, his hair even more like a woodpecker's. Didn't he ever touch it or pat it down? He lifted a mug toward her, though his glance slid away. "Jerome brought us coffee."

"Mom sent it. We didn't know what you had out here since you weren't expecting to spend the night."

We. Did that include Armand? Husband and wife discussing Rose in the cabin. Rose and her supposed boyfriend from the city.

"There's bagels too." Jerome nodded at the Thermos and bag propped on the fieldstones that bordered Maman's small flower bed. Greenery had snaked as best it could through last year's tangled stalks, which no one had cleared away. Jerome and Kenny, who still didn't look at her, turned back to the loom that blocked the doorway of the shed.

Jerome's mom had even included plastic camping mugs. Rose sipped the coffee, grateful for its milky warmth, though it was too sweet. The bagels were all in a row in a plastic bag. Grocery-store bagels.

Last winter she and Yushi were coming home from a walk on the mountain. It was cold and snowy, which Yushi said was perfect bagel weather. Rose had never had a bagel. They waited in line beside refrigerators packed with jars and large, flat packages. Lox, Yushi said. Rose recognized the smell of bread baking in a wood fire. A man in a turban slid a long paddle into the oven to scoop out hot rings of dough he flipped into a bin. Yushi asked for six black, and the woman tumbled fresh, seed-encrusted bagels into a paper bag.

"Rose," Jerome called, "why don't we undo the bolts?"

"They won't. I tried."

"Got any machine oil? Or just oil."

She headed to the cabin, not sure if there was oil, then remembered the can Maman kept with the tools. "In the shed," she said. "On the shelf on the right. By the hammer."

Kenny rummaged about inside. "Found it!" He and Jerome bent over the loom.

"This'll do it. Just a question of ..."

"Yeah. Give it a minute."

"Grease up the works."

Rose didn't want to remember what had happened in the night. Nor, from the way he was acting, did Kenny. She walked over to the chopping stump and sat with her coffee and grocery-store bagel. She wondered if Jerome knew that a real bagel tasted a lot better than this. She hoped he'd seen that Kenny had slept on the sofa. Alone.

"Hey, Rose, it's working!" Kenny sounded more like himself.

"Grab that part," Jerome cautioned.

She watched the two men ease the wooden structure apart. Above her, pine branches swept the morning breeze gently. A chickadee flew to a branch and cocked its head at her. There were only a few polka-dot poppy seeds embedded in the shiny dough. She scraped a fingernail to pick loose the seeds, then crumbled a bit of bagel, and held out her palm.

The chickadee darted to another branch. Not wanting the men to overhear, Rose whispered the singsong call. "Chickadee-dee-dee-dee." She lifted her arm higher toward the bird. "Chickadee-dee-dee-dee."

The bird fluttered from the branch. The weightless pincer-grip of its skinny claws gripped the fleshy edge of her palm. The jab of its beak. She wondered if chickadees in Montreal would come if she called them. Here was something she could show Yushi.

MADDY

Monday morning, as Maddy coasted across the bridge to the market, she saw Yushi's green bike and Yushi sitting nearby on a bench, knees splayed. Was she waiting for *her*? Maddy felt a happy prick of surprise. She liked Yushi, but up until now hadn't been sure whether Yushi singled her out from the others who also worked at the patisserie.

Maddy swung off her bike. "Got your bike fixed already?"

"I wish. I worked this weekend, remember? I wheeled it over here yesterday because it's too far to get all the way home, but I don't know where to get it fixed around here." Yushi sounded indifferent, but her expression, considering her bike, was glum.

"There's a great place." Maddy waved east. "They're cheap and I trust them. I can take you."

Yushi peered at the buildings that lined the canal, the trusses of the Charlevoix Bridge, the skyline of silos. The gel in her hair gleamed in the sunlight.

"I can take you," Maddy repeated. And after they went to the bike shop, maybe she could invite Yushi back to her place for supper.

"Okay. But not today, I've got something after work. How about tomorrow?"

"Tomorrow's good." Maddy tried to sound as casual as Yushi. She felt she'd scored a point — like taming a wild creature — and didn't want to scare her off.

"I'd better get in," Yushi sighed. "I'll bet Pettypoo's waiting with a stopwatch in hand."

That afternoon, before Maddy left the market, she bought eggplants, tomatoes, mushrooms, and zucchini to make ratatouille. That way, supper tomorrow would be ready if Yushi agreed to come. At Pierre-Paul's stall she saw his wife, a big-shouldered blonde, easing a basket of strawberries into a bag for a customer. Pierre-Paul gave Maddy a discreet nod she ignored. If he couldn't be friendly in front of his wife, forget it.

She cycled past her usual exit, heading toward Griffintown. She wanted to make sure her bike repair place hadn't closed. It wasn't a shop, only the open steel doors of an abandoned warehouse, staffed by a few ad hoc guys who were handy with a bike wrench.

The man with the bushy red ponytail who'd tuned her bike in the spring was leaning against the sunlit brick. She smelled the joint before she saw his cupped hand. She cruised to a stop. "Hi. Are you here tomorrow?"

His eyes pondered her wheels, brake pads, cables, handlebars.

"Not for my bike. My friend's broke — something with the pedals."

"Pedals ..." He shifted against the brick. "Gotta see it."

"We'll come tomorrow."

She pushed off from the curb and cycled home along Wellington, which was faster than heading back up to the canal. In the Pointe, A to E could be shorter than A to B. The streets spoked willy-nilly off each other. Maddy imagined that once upon a time they'd been farmers' paths skirting marshes, aimed at stables, pastures, home, the church. Now they were paved and had street signs. St-Patrick, Mullins, Sébastopol, Bourgeoys — which was pronounced *Bourgeois* in French and *Burgess* in English.

She turned down her alley and saw Frédéric on a ladder, reaching across his back fence. She slowed and swung off her bike. "Hi! How did the move go?"

"Fine, thanks. We're still upside-down in the house. I thought I'd try some yardwork for a change. Get some fresh air."

Maddy couldn't tell what he was doing, with his arms poked deep into the vines that grew in profusion whether they were helped along or not.

The gate scraped open. "Fred —" Fara stopped when she saw Maddy. "Hi."

"Congratulations," Maddy said. "You moved in."

"Trying to." Fara rolled her eyes. And to Frédéric, "Can you bring some of those boxes that I marked 'kitchen' into the kitchen? The movers left them in the front room."

He climbed down the ladder and walked through the gate Fara let slap behind him. She explained, "I pulled my back. Talk about timing. Did Frédéric ask if your boyfriend has a —"

"No boyfriend," Maddy said.

"Sorry. I saw two men going into your house."

"They're tenants."

"Do either of them have a drill? Frédéric's stopped working."

"I doubt it, but I can ask."

"The people here ..."

Why did Fara say *here* as if she'd moved to a land overrun by troglodytes? "What about them?"

"Do they stand outside your fence and stare at your house? Is that normal? I'm used to living in an apartment four floors up. I like to know I'm alone at home when I'm alone at home."

Maddy had seen Ben only once, but how often had he come? He didn't go into the yard, did he? She shook her head. "Must be one of the guys from the rooming house at the corner.

They're harmless, don't worry — except sometimes they take a leak in the alley. I yell at them when I catch them."

Fara grimaced.

"Yeah, I know." If Maddy saw Ben again, she would talk to him.

The gate creaked and Frédéric stepped out. "There were only two boxes."

"There should be more."

"Not in the front room." He climbed his ladder again.

Maddy wasn't sure if they were arguing and didn't want to get pulled in as a witness. "Bye then. Good luck!" She rolled her bike to her gate.

From her yard, she heard the stomp of Fara's feet on the deck. Frédéric's silence.

She unlocked her back door, set the vegetables on the counter, and trudged upstairs, unbuttoning her shirt to change into a tank top. She wondered why Ben — if it was him — was hanging around the house. She remembered what Fara said the other day when she'd told her about Xavier's suicide. She asked who'd found him.

What a horror story, coming home and kicking off your shoes, looking up, and ... hullo? Was that a body hanging in the hallway? What had it felt like to cut him down? Grabbing scissors or a knife to saw the rope, holding the weight of his slack body close. Maddy shuddered.

Fara's question had shifted the focus. Maddy saw what she meant now. Once Xavier had killed himself, he was dead. Story over. Ben was the one who had to go on living with the memory of finding his brother — the kind of memory that crept like a festering disease through the gut. Maddy knew it wasn't ghosts that haunted people. It was memories.

Bronislav stood at the kitchen counter, eating a wedge of bread smeared with *cretons*. Among Québécois who'd grown up with it, the ground pork fat and onion spread was a favourite. Maddy's mother used to make a Polish version called *szmalec* — pork drippings mixed with chopped fat and crackling. From Bronislav's thoughtful chewing, Maddy guessed there was a Russian version, too.

"Hey, Bronislav. What's up?"

He scrunched his eyebrows. "Nothing is up."

"What do you mean?"

He gestured at the empty plastic container on the counter. She hoped he would throw it in the recycling bin. She hoped he would rinse it first. She hoped ... whatever was reasonable to hope when you allowed strangers to share your living space.

"No more *cretons*?" she guessed.

He shook his head. "I am living."

"Living?"

"Living," he confirmed. "In two weeks."

"Ah, you're leaving. And Andrei?"

"Yes." Bronislav's truncated English served the purpose.

"Are the two of you renting an apartment?" An apartment would be a step up from rooms. After that, a washing machine, a car, a house. Her parents had left their families and homes — all they'd ever known — to come to Canada to climb the rungs of Western opportunity.

Bronislav looked sour. "In Gatineau."

"Why Gatineau?"

"Our job is moving."

"You don't want to live in Gatineau?"

"We like Montreal."

"Can you change jobs?"

He shook his head.

She wondered if he didn't want to look for a new job or if he was only allowed to stay in Canada as long as he worked at that particular job. Immigration was more complicated now than in the 1950s when her parents had come.

"But you ..." He wrinkled his brow.

"It's okay. I'll get someone else. But I'll miss the two of you." They'd been good tenants, mostly gone from the house, working double shifts, keeping to themselves.

"Yes."

Was he agreeing that she would miss them or was he saying they would miss her, too? He set his knife in the sink and tossed the empty container in the recycling bin.

"Please rinse it or it smells." And at his puzzled look, "Never mind." She waited until he left and rinsed it herself. Dropped it back on a sheaf of flyers, a flattened box of rooibos tea.

She didn't actually need to rent out rooms. She'd long ago paid off the mortgage and didn't have expensive tastes, but the house was too large for one person. Space yawned around her. When she was alone too long, she began to hear feet on the stairs. The pluck of guitar strings. She remembered the kids who used to live here, sprawled on sleeping bags, lighting joints off candles, barefoot in long skirts ... those hazy weeks when she'd let Stilt convince her that losing the baby was a solution. Hey, he'd crooned, you're only sixteen. What do you want with a baby?

At sixteen, no, she hadn't wanted a baby. She'd had no idea what to do with her, why the baby mewled and cried when she'd just been fed, how to make her stop. She'd thought of leaving her under a tree in the park and hoping someone kind would take her. She'd squeezed a pillow between her fists, daring herself to stop the crying once and for all. She'd felt so overwhelmed by despair and helplessness. What was she to do with a bawling, stinking baby? Her parents spat words at her — *kurwa*, *dziwka*, *flejtuch* — words she'd never heard before but knew were ugly. Was this why they'd crossed the ocean? For this shame she'd brought upon them? Let her take her bastard child and go find the father.

But then, when the baby was stolen and she told her parents the most likely story she could think of — that she'd given her up for adoption — her father walloped her so hard across the head that he knocked her to the floor. Her mother wailed, How could you? How could you? Your own child! Your own blood! Her father made as if to kick her but kicked a cupboard instead. Her mother kept shouting, her voice strained and high. In the doorway, Maddy saw her brother's terrified face.

Her parents brought the priest to force her to say where she'd taken the baby, but he'd already damned her when he saw her big belly and she refused to go to confession. Let him damn her again. She clenched her teeth, feeling the pain of the bruise on her face. It was too late now to tell the truth.

For her parents, accustomed to hiding inside ignorance, the silence closed again. They acted as if nothing had happened. They never spoke of it. But they also didn't encourage their Polish friends to bring their sons to visit as they'd used to. Maddy was no longer a nice girl.

Only she herself — and the crazy woman with the braid — knew that Maddy had once had a baby. And perhaps her brother, though in all the years since, he'd never mentioned it.

Yushi gazed from the hallway into the double front room then up the broad stairway. She'd already had a tour of the backyard and the kitchen. "And this whole house is yours?"

"All mine." Maddy waved for Yushi to precede her up the stairs, where there were more rooms and a skylight in the hallway to brighten the core of the house, even on gloomy days. In her bedroom, the large sash window looked onto the leafy branches of a beech tree, the brick house fronts across the street, and above the long, carved row of their cornices, the sky. She'd had the foresight to put away the clothes that were usually heaped on the settee.

Yushi walked to the window. "No offence, but how did you afford a house bagging croissants? Did you rob a bank?"

Maddy sat on the bed. "I inherited some money when my parents passed away."

"Both of them?"

"Years ago. My father had pancreatic cancer. He went fast. And then my mother, four months later."

Yushi picked up one of the mussel shells scattered along the window ledge. Mementos of a vacation in the Gaspé. "Your mum followed him."

Maddy was surprised at such a romantic interpretation from Yushi. Nor did she believe it — her stodgy mother pining for her gloomy husband. "She had an aneurysm. She'd had it for a while. No one knew. It could have ruptured before he died."

"But she let him go first."

Again Maddy arched her eyebrows. "I think it just happened that way. I mean ... okay, she didn't know what to do with herself once she didn't have him to take care of anymore. I tried to get her to go with the other Polish ladies to Goplana for a slice of poppyseed roll, but she wouldn't. She went to church and she prayed. Or she sat in her chair with her rosary." Maddy mimed how her mother sat with her fist closed with the rosary wrapped around it. "My brother and I thought she was depressed. We assumed it would pass. It wasn't like our parents were happy together. Then her aneurysm burst."

Yushi was stroking her thumb along the water-worn edge of the shell. She'd turned while Maddy talked, a slim figure in silhouette against the light from outside. "Do you feel guilty?"

"About them dying? Why should I feel guilty?" Maddy could have felt guilty about the fiasco of her pregnancy, but Yushi didn't know about that. And over the years, she'd grown to feel that her parents had failed her as much as she'd failed them.

Yushi tilted her head. "I don't know. Sometimes ..." But she didn't continue. She set the shell on the ledge again. "So you got a big inheritance."

"Hardly a big one — but enough to make a down payment. Houses in the Pointe were really cheap back then."

Yushi was staring out the window again. "My mum would have been like yours. If he'd gone first. She would have wanted to be dead, too."

Maddy didn't move, waiting to hear if Yushi would say more. She so rarely mentioned her private life and her past.

"My mum waited on him hand and foot. She got up every morning to make him fresh roti before he went to work. Laid out his clothes on the bed so he just had to step into them — his underpants, his socks, his shirt, his pants. Even his belt. Every day she did that. Even for his factory clothes, not just weekends. He liked to get dressed up. He's a real *saga boy*, my dad. He had this other woman he used to visit. He took her dancing. My mum knew about it, but she didn't say anything. She believed that no matter what a man did, a wife did her duty."

Why was Yushi speaking in past tense? Her mom couldn't be much older than Maddy. "Where is your mom now?" she asked gently.

"She died. A year and a half ago."

Maddy let out her breath. "I'm sorry."

"That's partly why I left Toronto. It's easier not to see him. My sisters and my brother can't harass me about my *duty*." She said the word with a Trinidadian lilt. And after a pause, her tone even again, "I hate the life he gave her. I hate how she put up with it. I hate how he didn't even wait three months to bring the other one to live in our house."

Her controlled monotone reminded Maddy of how she used to clamp her arms to her ribs when women handed around babies. Everyone wanted to hold them and coo. Not her, thank you.

Yushi leaned away from the window, looking off down the hallway. "What are these other rooms?"

Maddy followed her. She was awed Yushi had told her as much as she had. She guessed Yushi probably didn't have many friends.

She tapped on the first door. "This room's for storage. It's just boxes and junk." The next room was self-explanatory. The bathroom.

"Skylight in here, too?" Yushi glanced up at it. "Lucky."

Maddy opened the next door onto an ironing board and a table with a sewing machine.

"You sew?" Yushi asked.

"It's my mother's old machine. She taught me, but I never liked sewing. If I have to, I can hem a skirt. But the machine and the scissors are the only things of hers I kept. She didn't have any jewellery — and I did *not* want her rosary. I think of this as her." She opened her hand at the sewing machine. "Meet my mother."

Yushi hefted the large steel scissors. "This is some serious hardware."

"Polish make. Hard and heavy. Potentially lethal."

Back in the hallway Maddy raised her chin at the remaining closed doors. "Those are the tenants' rooms. Two of them."

"Aren't tenants trouble?"

"They take care of themselves. I just rent out the rooms. So far I haven't had problems, knock on wood." She touched the door frame. "These two are leaving in a couple of weeks. I'm going to paint before I get someone new. The rooms could use some freshening up. I should tear down the old balcony, too. It's a fire hazard. I don't even know what's still holding it up. I think it's practically solid pigeon shit by now."

Yushi traipsed behind her down the stairs. Again she looked around the kitchen with admiring eyes. "This is the best room, so big and bright."

"You should see it in the morning with the sun shining in." Maddy lifted the lid on the pot of ratatouille, releasing a moist cloud of good smells — roasted eggplant, red peppers, garlic, oregano. Plates and a basket of pita stood ready. On the deck, she'd pulled the plank table from the wall, wiped away the spider webs, and flapped out a red tablecloth.

They carried their plates, the pita, a dish of grated Parmesan, and bottles of beer outside. Maddy clinked her bottle against Yushi's. Yushi said it was nice to be there. She tasted the ratatouille and pronounced it good. She scooped a mouthful of stew with a torn piece of pita and said, "This would be really good with roti. I could show you how to make them — or we could get fancy and make buss-up-shut."

"I'd like that." Maddy had no idea what buss-up-shut was, but she liked the idea of Yushi teaching her to cook something new.

A furry orange bomb catapulted over the fence into the backyard. Yushi was startled, then laughed. Maddy didn't think she'd ever heard her laugh before. "Is she yours?" Yushi asked.

"*He*. Definitely a he. Tarzan of the alleyway. This is Jim."

Jim stepped onto the deck, the curled tip of his tail questioning that Maddy had invited a guest. Yushi held out her hand for him to sniff.

"You like cats?" Maddy asked.

"More than some people I've met." Yushi's bangle slid down her wrist as she scratched Jim's skull and around his ears. He squinted, seemingly indifferent, then butted his head against her fingers in obvious command.

FARA

Fara snapped shut an empty binder and slid it onto the pile in the corner of her desk. Zeery walked past the counter, eyes on her phone, thumbs busy. She'd changed from nursing scrubs into snug jeans and a form-fitting top. Her breasts, hips, and ass were outlined, her knees, shoulders, and cleavage covered. Her wardrobe was an object lesson on meeting her culture's guidelines for modesty in a world where she wanted to be seen as attractive.

"You could say bye!" Fara called. If humans were to adapt, then the next generation should be born with insect eyes on double-jointed thumbs — to keep people from falling on their heads while texting.

Zeery stopped moving but still finished her message before she looked up. "Why aren't you gone yet?"

"Tiff had an appointment. I said I'd wait. She came in early for me a couple of times when we had stuff with the house. Anyhow, go. Don't get stuck in traffic." Fara waved her off as she pulled the mail basket toward her and started opening envelopes.

From down the hallway she heard the trundling and rattling of a cart. The sound belonged to a medieval costume drama, but it was only the young woman who delivered the tube feeding. She looked the peasant part with her solemn face, no makeup, hair tidy in a hairnet.

"Noisy cart," Fara said. "I think it's got square wheels."

The woman glanced at her cart. She didn't seem to realize Fara was joking. She handed Fara her clipboard to sign.

The stairwell door swung wide and one of the surgery residents strode out. The nurses would tackle him with questions, but Fara wanted him first. "Oscar!" She grabbed a patient's chart from farther along the counter. "Dupont's got a bed at Rehab tomorrow. We need an exit script."

"Sure thing. Any food here?" He'd been in the OR all day. He took the chart from Fara as José nabbed him to co-sign an order and Guang twisted around in her chair to get him next.

Tiffany scuttled past, hips wagging, sandals swishing. "I'm here, I'm here. Let me dump my stuff."

Fara snapped a rubber band around the stack of filing she'd sorted, pushed off her chair, and went to the med room to wash her hands.

"Beds are full," she told Tiffany, who was fanning an infection control booklet at her neck and down between her breasts. "You should have a quiet evening. Don't let Oscar leave till he writes exit meds on Dupont."

Tiffany groaned. "Why didn't you ask him?"

"I did. You're going to have to remind him every five minutes till he does it." Fara grabbed her knapsack and escaped the nursing station. She ran down the stairs to the parking lot exit, saw a bus coming, and jogged to the stop.

Getting home now took longer. It was her night to cook, too. Shopping was more complicated now that they lived in the Pointe. She and Frédéric had been spoiled by having two greengrocers, a small supermarket, a bakery, and a fish store around the corner from their apartment. In the Pointe they had a twenty-minute walk to the nearest grocery store, where, even in the middle of the summer, peppers and tomatoes were shipped from Mexico, apples and pears from South Africa. If she stopped at the Atwater Market — also a hike — she could buy apples and pears from Quebec, but they cost even more. And this was during the summer. Money aside, shopping for supper every evening on the way home took up too much time.

She and Frédéric had to have a talk about groceries. And getting patio furniture, even if that was yet another expense. They obviously weren't going on vacation this year. Couldn't they at least sit outside while the weather was nice? Enjoy having a backyard.

The bedroom, too, needed to be moved. They'd painted, bought curtains, and put their king-size bed in the spacious upstairs room that seemed so perfect for a master bedroom. They hadn't realized it was impossible to sleep facing the street. Every night she was woken by revved-up cars blasting music, or some lone drunk having a garrulous monologue under their window. Last night she'd snatched her pillow and stomped downstairs to the sofa. That wasn't why they'd bought a house, was it? To end up sleeping in separate rooms on separate floors?

In the subway Fara stood with her hand clamped on a pole. Bodies and shoulder bags brushed her hips and back. She kept her chin high, glad that her head cleared the crowd. Especially now, during *armpit season*. She smiled, remembering who'd first called it that. Claire.

Fara had made a tortellini salad. She and Frédéric sat at the table that they'd placed before the window so they could see the deck and the backyard. On his way home from work, Frédéric had stopped at the Éco-quartier and picked up a composter. He wanted to put it in the far corner of the yard.

"Won't it smell?"

"It's not supposed to."

Fara leaned at an angle to check that they wouldn't see it from the window and noticed the outline of a man through the slats of their fence. "He's out there again."

"Who?"

"I told you. One of the guys from the rooming house. Maddy said they're harmless, but I don't like how he stands there. He's not watching anyone else's house, just ours."

Frédéric leaned forward to look. "He's not doing anything."

"He's watching us."

"Don't get paranoid."

"I don't like it." She slammed down her fork and shoved back her chair.

"Fara, I don't want you fighting with the neighbours!"

"Standing there like that isn't neighbourly." She yanked open the back door. By the time she'd loped across the yard to the gate, he'd sprinted down the alley and was turning the corner. A thin man with dark hair. What was his problem? Did she have to hang a sign? *This is not a bus stop. NO panoramic view. Keep moving. Get lost.*

She trudged back inside. "Don't you mind that people watch you?"

"What can he see through the cracks in the fence? Not much."

"Not much is still way too much. I don't like people gawking at me."

Frédéric spit an olive pit into his hand and dropped it on his plate. "If he comes back, I'll talk to him."

"I wish you would." She stabbed her fork into tortellini. "Listen, you're not going to like this, but I want to move the bedroom."

Frédéric widened his already wide eyes. The bed would have to be taken apart again. The brown-and-cream curtains had been bought specifically to fit the large double window.

"I *know*," she said. "I'm sorry. I didn't know the street would be so noisy."

"You'll get used to it."

"The noise? You should know me better than that by now." When they'd lived in an apartment, she'd rung doorbells the instant it was 11:00 p.m. and music disturbed her. She'd waged war with the neighbour who did bel canto exercises on the other side of an adjoining wall, telling him he sounded like a bullfrog having an amplified orgasm. She'd called the police to complain about the restaurant that shared their back alley, where the staff slung bags of garbage, including wine bottles, past midnight.

"So, you want to move the bedroom where?" Frédéric didn't bother to hide his exasperation. "The room next to the bathroom is too small and the room at the back isn't painted yet."

"The room at the back. I'll paint it."

"Are you sure that's where you want the bedroom?"

"It's not as big, but it'll be quieter. And we'll be in the same bed."

He'd saved a piece of artichoke for his last bite. He always kept a morsel of what he liked best for the end of the meal. "What will we do with the front room?"

Now they half-smiled, both hearing the absurdity of having so many rooms that they didn't know what to do with them.

When the doorbell rang, she got up. So far this week they'd had Jehovah's Witnesses; a boy collecting cans and bottles to go to summer camp, though he couldn't tell Fara where the camp was; a man who offered to paint their cornice for a hundred dollars; another selling posters of the *Sacré-Coeur de Jésus*. Did people actually buy glossy illustrations of a melancholy man pointing at his glistening heart wrapped with thorns? No thank you, Fara said over and over again.

This time there was no one. "Another prank," she said as she returned to the table.

"Why do you do that? Every time you walk to the hallway you move to the side."

She knew she did it sometimes, but not every time.

"It's the suicide, isn't it?"

"Not the suicide." She gave a small shake of the head. Filling the hole hadn't helped. "The body. It's still ..." She waved toward where it had hung.

He looked but saw nothing. Still, he considered the air as if he could. "So ... what do we do?"

She appreciated that he said *we*. Some men would have dismissed it as craziness. Her problem and hers alone. Let her figure it out. "I don't know," she admitted. "I'll eventually get over it — I have to."

"How about you walk through that space over and over again? I could do it with you."

She saw he wasn't joking and touched his hand. "Thanks, but it doesn't work like that."

The doorbell rang again. "I'll go." He strode to the door — right through the body.

She heard a man's voice. Then Frédéric was saying, "That's okay, we've finished supper."

Eric. She gave him a push-button smile he returned with barely a glance. He wasn't visiting *them*. He'd come to see the house.

He kicked the toe of his shoe against the floor. "Have you decided yet what you're doing here?"

"We did it," Frédéric said. "Sanded and varnished."

Eric's head bobbed back with surprise. The floor obviously wasn't what he would call sanded and varnished. "A floor buckled like this? You should rip it up and put down a new floor."

"We like this one," Fara said. "You know, there are people who drive up from New England to buy these old pine boards."

"Americans." Eric seemed to feel that single word sufficed. He stood with his hands on his hips, still peering down at the floor. "What are you doing about the draft?"

"What draft?" Frédéric asked.

"You don't feel it? Don't worry, you will in the winter. Did you insulate the ceiling in the cellar like I told you?"

"We just moved in," Fara said. "Give us a chance. Fred's still hauling out junk from the cellar."

"Better do it before the winter. I'm telling you." He rotated on his feet. "What are you doing about that?" He jabbed a finger at where the boy had hanged himself.

Fara stiffened. Frédéric glanced at her. "About what?" he asked.

"That great big space where all the cold air is going to suck up and down the stairs. What you need here is a set of French doors. You won't lose any light and you'll block the draft." Eric outlined the entrance to the room with a knowing finger.

Fara began to stack the plates and cutlery with as much noise as possible. Was he determined to drain their bank account? "You just said to insulate the cellar. We can't start buying French doors, too."

"It'll save on heating. The doors will pay for themselves."

"Fred." Fara gave him a look that meant get your cousin out before I push him out.

Frédéric was ignoring her, gazing where Eric had pointed. "He's right, Fara. Doors will change the way everything looks."

"That's not what I said," Eric interrupted. "It will still look open. French doors are glass, right? Even when you keep them shut, you can see through them."

Fara sighed. Did he think they didn't know what French doors were?

"Look, Fara," Frédéric said. He held his hand flat in the air and glided it across the entrance. "*Doors.* All along here." He drew his hand back and forth.

Oh. Now she understood. Doors to block the body.

"That's right," Eric said, mocking their slowness. "What you need here is doors."

Fara stood at the fax machine waiting for the confirmation that her pages had been sent. The counters in the nursing station were messy with charts, stray medication records, an armload of towels that had been forgotten, an empty box of chocolates with its paper cups tossed willy-nilly. Why didn't someone throw away the empty box? Here and there a nurse sat writing. An orderly pushed a bin of isolation gowns down the hallway.

"Fara!"

She heard but didn't answer. Even leaning against the wall, she was taller than anyone else in the nursing station. All Brie had to do was lift her head and look around. But no, she preferred to bellow.

"Fara!"

The fax machine groaned and thrummed as it disgorged its wobbly page. Poor thing, it sounded constipated. Fara skirted the chairs wheeled against each other, spied her three-hole punch farther along the counter — where it *didn't* belong — and grabbed it.

"There you are." Brie tossed a quadruplicate form on her desk. "Evenings wants to make an incident report against the kitchen. They were missing a tube feeding yesterday. Tiffany said you signed for them."

"I signed for them because they came."

"There wasn't any Vivonex for Labranche."

Fara remembered Labranche's name on the list. Still standing, she reached for the phone that was ringing and listened for a few seconds. "Your husband is gone for a test. Yes. Probably another hour. Yes. Yes. No, the doctor will have to give you the results, not me." She hung up, and though the intercom was buzzing, walked down the hall to the kitchen.

"What about that incident report?" Brie called after her.

Fara flapped a hand in the air. It wouldn't be the first time she was told something was missing when it was only misplaced. The tube feeding had probably been shoved behind a carton of chicken soup. How often had she said that the tube feeding shouldn't be kept where family members stored food?

Ricardo, the housekeeper, cautioned her. "Watch out, I just washed the floor."

Fara stooped before the refrigerator. The light had burned out years ago and never been replaced. One day she would buy a bulb at the dollar store and screw it in herself. She shoved aside juice and plastic bags. There were a couple of containers of tube feeding but none for Labranche.

She stood again and scanned the kitchen. Stainless steel cupboards. A box of plastic spoons. The ice machine. A large garbage bin. The garbage hadn't been emptied yet, and she saw noodles slithered across a white Styrofoam container.

She leaned out the door to snatch a pair of gloves from the box on the railing. Grimacing, she dislodged the container from the noodles. LABRANCHE. VIVONEX.

She set the container in the sink and asked Royal, who was carrying a clutch of urine bottles down the hallway, to tell Brie to come to the kitchen. Ricardo still leaned against the wall next to his housekeeping cart. "That stuff's sticky, man. I had to wash the floor two times."

"Someone spilled it."

"And didn't clean up right." He mimed lazy back and forth wiping. "Big puddle under the fridge."

Brie walked toward them briskly. "What's the fuss?"

Fara showed her the food-smeared container. "Ricardo had to wash Vivonex off the floor. I've told you the tube feeding shouldn't go here."

"There's nowhere else."

"Well, don't be surprised if someone knocks it over."

"Jesus."

"Probably not him." Fara dropped the container in the garbage again. She remembered the young woman who'd delivered the tube feeding. Her solemn expression. Her low, grave voice. She didn't look like someone who only half-did her job.

Ben slouched on the sofa in his boxers. The TV was on loud, but he wasn't watching it. Some police drama. On the coffee table, next to a few empty drink cans and flyers, sat his mom's teacup with the gilt handle.

He couldn't believe the new people had already moved in. He'd thought they would keep renovating the house the way his dad and Xavier had planned. Knock out the wall of that small room. Rewire and insulate upstairs. He'd expected to have months to sneak into the house, walk around, and remember. Even if the house didn't belong to him on paper, the space was still his — the shape of the rooms, the doors, the corners, the closets. He could walk to the fridge in the dark with his eyes closed. *That* was knowing a house.

Damn his dad for selling it. For not even asking if Ben wanted the house. Or was Ben the stupid one, thinking anything had changed? Ben was never the son who mattered to his dad. Only Xavier, who was always doing crazy things and taking risks, no matter how reckless or dumb. There was no telling if the rope around his neck was just another stunt. Maybe he was counting on their dad to come home in time, find him hanging, and freak out. Or maybe he thought a bruise around his neck would look cool — like the time he stabbed his ear with safety pins and had to take antibiotics for a month.

Ben hadn't been watching the show on TV, but when a commercial came on he lurched from the sofa to get a can of Pepsi from the fridge. He scratched his back because the nubbly upholstery made him itch. When Anouk lived there, she'd thrown a bedspread across it.

He still missed Anouk. Almost two years and no steady girlfriend since. They'd had an argument — he couldn't even remember about what — and she'd walked out. It wouldn't have been the first time she'd crashed at her sister's for a few nights. He was still expecting her to come back when one of the guys at work said he'd seen her in Verdun with her arm around someone new.

She'd always warned Ben that she liked to move along. He was the sucker who'd thought she would stay — not just because of the sex or because she made *pâté chinois* with creamed corn the way he liked it, but other crazy things he bet no other guy let her do. Like the manicures.

He stretched his fingers and frowned at the oily black rims of his nails. Except to cut them, he'd never paid attention to his nails before Anouk. First she scoured his hands with a scrubber until she almost tore his skin off. Then she soaked his nails in a jellied liquid. He had to sit still, but he could watch TV. Or the neat side part in her hair and her small, sleek head bent over his hand as she poked and snipped.

Through the shock and unreality of Xavier's death, Ben had clasped the smallest hope that Anouk would come to the funeral, if only to say how sorry she was. He'd scanned the crowd at the church, and later at the graveside. His dad had been drunk since before the funeral started. And his mom ... he hadn't thought about his mom in years, but when Xavier died, he wondered if someone might have told her. He hadn't been looking just for Anouk at the funeral.

Ben clanked his empty can on the coffee table, picked up his mom's teacup, and walked to the bedroom. When Anouk used to live here, she'd kept a china shepherd girl her grandma had given her on the window ledge. In the morning the sun gleamed on its shiny arms and curly head. There, exactly there, he set the teacup.

Fara, nestled against Frédéric's chest, could smell soap and the soft musk of his skin. He'd showered when he'd come upstairs after working in the cellar.

"You've got to admit ..." he began.

"Yeah?"

"Eric knows his stuff. He figured out those orange wires."

Fara had no idea which wires Frédéric meant, but if Eric had helped, well, good.

"And the French doors. That's a really good idea, don't you think?"

Fara rolled onto her back, staring at the ceiling that was only dimly lit by the bedside lamp. "I wonder what it's like for him."

"For who?"

"For his brother — the boy who killed himself. He found him hanging."

"Fara ..." He turned toward her and cupped her shoulder.

"Sorry," she said. "I can't help it. I think about it."

"Maybe we shouldn't have bought this house."

She remembered her immediate attraction to the room and the window facing the backyard. The real estate agent yanking aside the blinds and light flooding in. "I'll get over it," she said. "I love the house."

Ben didn't like standing in the shadows along the street because now and then a neighbour walked by whom he recognized — and who might recognize him. No one addressed him, though, as long as he kept silent. People in the Pointe knew to ignore what didn't concern them.

He had to wait a long time until the upstairs light was turned off. He waited longer and decided they must be asleep by now. He walked around the corner to the alley and through the darkness to the gate. Strange how they'd changed the lock on the front door and never thought about the gate.

He lifted the deck boards, set them aside, and eased himself under. So far, so good. This much he'd done before. He pushed against the window that swung inward on hinges. The frame was clumsy to hold open as he wiggled in. It wasn't much of a drop, but he scraped his arm against the stone wall.

Even in the dark, he could tell that the cellar was different. There was more space. He took careful steps to the stud he knew was on his left and felt along the wood for the light switch his dad had wired. The angle of light made the packed dirt of the floor look bumpier. Shadows leaned in around him. Weren't those his dad's tools on the workbench? His dad never tried to teach him to build things, but he sometimes helped Xavier. Ben had watched once as their dad showed Xavier how to fit two mitred corners together. Their dad held the wood, Xavier the bottle of white carpenter's glue.

Ben picked up the hammer, wondering how he could tell if it was his dad's. Suddenly, water gushed down the drain in the cellar, startling him. He shrank back, groping to turn off the light. *Shit! Were they still awake?* He strained to hear movement from upstairs.

He waited until the cool cellar air made the shirt on his back feel like a cold hand. He crept softly to the frame of dimness that was the window. Clicked on his flashlight just long enough to spy a crate he could set below the window. He pulled himself out as quietly and quickly as he could, listening all the while for sounds from inside the house.

ROSE

Rose helped Kenny carry the pieces of her loom from the van into the warehouse. The breast beam, the beater, the treadles, the harnesses. He still wouldn't meet her eyes. On the drive back from Rivière-des-Pins he'd hummed with the radio, made random comments about the traffic and the weather, swerved his glance away from her — as if *he* were embarrassed. Wasn't sex what men wanted?

For her, the memory was more dreamlike than true. A command she'd obeyed in the night, hypnotized by the cabin, the whispers of the trees, the nearness of Armand, the reawakened longing of her body. She, too, would sooner forget what had happened. But she wished Kenny would stop acting as if she had a disease he was afraid of catching.

He set the warping reel against the wall and stood back. His hair was still raked upright, which he'd finally noticed in the rearview mirror and tried to tug flat. "I should go. I've got to return my friend's van."

"I'm staying. I want to start putting the loom together."

He frowned at the different lengths and shapes of wood ranged along the wall. "You can't do that alone."

"I can get started."

"I'll come help you tomorrow — before work, around eleven."
He shuffled to the door without waiting for an answer.

"Kenny."

He half-turned in the doorway, shoulders reluctant, wary of
whatever she meant to say.

"Thank you for helping me — for getting my loom. I really
needed it here." She hoped he understood how truly grateful
she was. Everything else should be forgotten.

One side of his mouth almost lifted. "Told you I'd get it,
didn't I?"

He shut the door behind him and she was alone in her studio with the loom. It was in pieces — dismembered — with no
diagram to connect the parts, but it was here. By tomorrow or
the next day it would be whole again. The cranks and ratchets
attached. The heddles on the harnesses. Since she'd had no
boxes, she'd taken the drawers from the dresser in the cabin
to pack the shuttles, bobbins, and lease sticks. She opened the
drawers of the dresser she'd bought in St-Henri and began to
fit the hooks and shuttles side by side in an order Maman would
have recognized. Like Maman, whose hands could heft an axe,
skin a rabbit, or re-thread a heddle when the yarn snapped,
Rose's movements were deft and practical.

Several times she glanced at the window. She'd bought two
lamps but had always preferred daylight for weaving. In the bare,
white light, she could examine the row-by-row texture of the cloth
and immediately spot any flaws. Her studio was large enough to
place the loom in whichever relation to the window she wanted.

She looked at the pieces along the wall for the breast beam.
She carried it to the line she'd mentally drawn on the floor. She
stood back and considered. Here was where she would begin.

"Ho-ho-ho!" Rose heard as she closed the apartment door
behind her. "Is that *Santa Claus*?"

Rose peeked around the wall. Yushi sat on the sofa with one foot in a basin of water, the other propped on a towel on her knee. With both hands she kneaded her instep, toes, and heel with a pumice scrub. Her weekly foot treatment.

"So, who was that guy who called?" Yushi asked.

"Let me put this away." Rose carried the pillowcase she'd stuffed with sweaters she and Maman had knit to her room. She'd asked Jerome to call Yushi to tell her Rose wouldn't be home. She'd stressed the word *home*. She wanted him to hear that Montreal was home now, and that she had a roommate and a life in the city. Though she hadn't liked giving him the number. She should have asked Kenny to drive her back to Rivière-des-Pins so she could call herself. She didn't trust what Jerome would say. Or imply. The other option — not to call at all — wasn't fair to Yushi, who would have worried. Or might have worried. Rose wasn't sure. Her years of living isolated in the woods hadn't given her much sense of what people wanted.

Rose poured herself a glass of grapefruit juice and headed back down the hallway. "We got my loom."

Yushi peered at her toes. "I figured."

From where Rose sat at the table she could smell eucalyptus. "I asked the neighbour to call you."

"He said he was a friend."

"That's just his way of talking."

Yushi lowered her foot into the water in the basin and lifted the other to her lap. "I guess it was just his way of talking when he said ..." Yushi squirted exfoliating cream onto her palm and rubbed it around her heel. "When he said that you and your boyfriend were staying in your cabin."

"He slept on the sofa." Rose set her glass on the table.

"Rose!" Yushi pointed at the glass.

"Sorry." Rose lifted it and wiped her arm across the wood.

"On the sofa? That must have been cozy."

"I slept upstairs."

"You never mentioned an upstairs."

"It's an attic. There's just enough room for a bed and a dresser. There isn't even a window."

Yushi's fingers rubbed and pressed and circled. Since Rose had seen how Yushi took care of her feet, she'd begun smoothing cream on at night so her skin wasn't as dry.

"My loom wouldn't come apart. Then it got late and we figured we'd stay and try again in the morning."

"Who's the guy who called?"

"I told you — a neighbour."

"You always said you and your mom lived in the woods. You never mentioned neighbours."

"He lives past the woods, a couple of fields over."

"How did he know you were there?"

Rose shrugged. "He saw the van."

Yushi lowered her foot into the basin, scooped water across the tops, wiggled her toes. "Are you happy to have your loom here?"

"Yeah."

"That's all that matters, right?" Yushi squeezed the towel around each foot.

Rose hoped the questions were over.

"Tell you what. Take this bowl and get some fresh water. Sprinkle in some of my bath salts and soak your feet. Then I'll do them."

Rose felt the unusual kindness of the offer at the same time that she stiffened in refusal. No one had ever touched her with the attention and care Yushi applied to her feet. Not even Maman. It was too intimate. Rose was too shy. Especially now. She hadn't had a chance to wash since last night — since Kenny.

"I have to take a shower. My loom was really dusty. I ..."

"Suit yourself." Yushi stooped to the basin and carried it down the hallway.

Rose heard the great splash of water as Yushi emptied it in the sink. She felt she'd missed an opportunity — and that it was her loss.

Yesterday, when Rose saw Kenny in the hallway at work, she smiled and said hi. He blushed, ducked his head, said he was busy, and hurried away.

Two mornings earlier, when he'd come to her studio to help her finish reassembling the loom, he'd been careful to keep his distance. When Rose leaned across his arm to show him how to attach the ratchet, he held his back stiffly. She'd always thought that when he jiggled he was excited or nervous. She saw now that rattling his bones signalled an easiness in his body that he no longer had with her.

Because they'd had sex? It had hardly even been sex!

He had been so eager to spend a night in the cabin. She remembered how contented he'd looked during their candlelit supper of rice and canned tuna. But he hadn't once mentioned the cabin since. He acted as if ... as if he didn't want to know her anymore. He'd promised to help bring her loom to Montreal, and now that he had, he meant to disappear.

Today, when she wheeled her trolley off the elevator on the twelfth floor, he was ambling down the hallway, slapping a white plastic package against his thigh. He saw her and his hand stopped. "Hi," he mumbled and would have kept walking except that she blocked his path.

"Hi," she said. "How's work?"

"The usual." He jerked the package that dangled from his hand. "They run out of oxygen tubing and I have to play gofer."

"I'm getting ready to start with my loom. I chained a warp and I've got it on the breast beam — you know at the front?" She levelled a line in the air at hip level. "Tomorrow I'll start hooking the threads through the reed."

"How many threads?" That had impressed him when she'd first described weaving.

"Five hundred and seventy."

His lips pursed in a soundless whistle.

"This part is called dressing the loom — sleying the reed, pulling threads through the heddles, winding the warp. Weaving is easy. It's the setting up that takes time. You should come see what it looks like when I'm weaving. You did so much to help me get the loom here."

He backed away. "Sure." But it sounded more like "I don't think so."

He'd been listening as long as she talked about weaving. As soon as she'd mentioned him visiting, his face had changed. She pushed her hip against the cart to get it rolling again. Kenny was her only friend in the hospital and she didn't want to lose him. Not just because he was a friend, she realized, and she had almost none. Because she liked him.

At the desk on Twelve South, she handed the clipboard to the unit coordinator with the shaved skull who always signed without checking.

"You there," said a tall woman behind the counter who leaned forward to read her hospital ID. "Rose, is that your name? I saved your ass the other day. The nurses were going to write a complaint. It would have gone in your file."

Rose had no idea what she meant.

"I don't know who the culprit was, but it wasn't your mistake. Not mine, either. I know what you left and what I signed for. People are always looking for someone to blame."

Rose remembered the tall woman now. She'd been at the desk and signed Rose's clipboard. Rose waited for her to explain what she meant, but she'd already forgotten Rose, turning to slap a doctor on the arm. "Where's that chai latte you promised me?"

Rose wheeled her cart to the kitchen, where she had to edge aside juice cans and bags of food in the refrigerator to make room for the Styrofoam containers of tube feeding. Whatever the woman was telling her, it seemed to have been solved. Why had she even told Rose? Was Rose supposed to thank her? She wished she could ask Kenny, who understood the complicated etiquette among hospital support staff. Maybe she would see him again on another floor. Or when she returned to the kitchen, she would check if there were any trays to deliver to Six South, where he worked.

Rose had put her chair inside the frame of the loom to sit as close as possible to the harnesses. She'd bought the chair in the furniture shop in St-Henri. When the man saw how she sat in each one, testing the exact height so her knees were slightly raised when her feet were flat on the floor, he laughed and called her Goldilocks. But then he took her down into his cellar workshop where he had more chairs. She didn't care about the shape of the legs, the state of the varnish, the style of chair. She had to sit correctly, since she'd be sitting like this for hours.

In addition to the light from the window, she'd turned on a lamp and angled it close. Halfway along the top of the first harness was a wispy knot of scarlet wool Maman had tied to mark the middle. For Rose, reaching for thread after thread, it helped to have a signpost. Five hundred and seventy divided in two was two hundred and eighty-five. Rose hoped to get halfway through before she had to leave to go to work.

She tugged the slipknot that held the next bundle of threads, fingered free the first one, and angled the hook through the eye of the heddle to grab it. Glance up, glance down. Make sure she had the correct heddle. If she made a mistake, the herringbone pattern she'd planned would be ruined. Glance up, glance down. Her guide was the long metal edge of the harnesses. The heddles themselves swam in an indistinguishable forest of long, skinny needles.

A light rain had started to fall, pattering on the weeds outside. The sculptor hadn't come today. From somewhere in the building she heard someone fingering guitar strings. The person wasn't playing a song — not yet — only repeating a sequence. Fingers and strings. Almost the same as what she was doing but with sound. *Huh.*

Yesterday Yushi had stopped by with a friend from work. They'd locked their bikes to the fence and come into the building. Yushi wanted to see what Rose had done so far on the loom. She introduced her friend, Maddy. Maddy lived close by. She and Yushi were going to head back to her place after cycling. You should come over sometime, Maddy said. Rose didn't answer. Why would she go to Maddy's? Or did she automatically become Maddy's friend because she was Yushi's? Maddy had hardly looked at what Rose was doing on the loom, though she'd hefted Maman's large steel scissors. I've got scissors like these, she said. They were my mother's. Rose almost said that these were her mother's, too, but she didn't. There was something about Maddy she wasn't sure she trusted. She watched Yushi and Maddy cycling off and thought how odd they looked together — especially on their bike seats. Yushi's bum was like a boy's. Maddy had great, fleshy haunches. Maddy was older, too, wasn't she? But maybe people did that: older friends, younger friends.

Rose hooked another thread. Glance up, glance down. Once she'd finished with the heddles, she would be ready to wind the warp. Maman knew how to do it alone, but Rose had only ever done it with Maman turning the crank while Rose stood at the front of the loom and held the warp taut.

She had known she would need someone to help and was going to ask Yushi, but now she wondered about asking Kenny. The last few days at work he'd seemed more comfortable with her, acting almost like his old teddy-bear self. Yesterday he'd walked into the kitchen. "Hey Rose! I'm picking up a tray so you can cool your feet."

They seemed to have regained their easygoing camaraderie — except that it was different. He no longer poked her on the shoulder. He didn't come looking for her on her tube feeding rounds. He didn't want to be alone with her.

But if she asked him to help her, would he? He'd always helped her before.

The grass along the canal had been cut yesterday. Large city mowers had swept in broad swath, circling the lampposts. Sharp edges of grass tickled Rose's legs. She sat watching the water in the canal gently lip the shadowed reflections of the poplars that grew along the bank. The blocks of concrete that formed the wall of the canal were worn and cracked. Out of one crack grew a rogue bush dotted with straggly pink roses. Rose remembered Maman's story of the five roses who were the girl's only friends. If she picked five roses and put them in a mug in her studio, she would have her five friends. She would have to cross the canal, and how would she reach the bush? Better to leave the roses in the sunlight.

Kenny had said he couldn't come help her wind the warp. He'd said he was too busy, but she'd seen he didn't want to. It made her feel sad — even more sad because she didn't know how to change his mind. Last night she'd asked Yushi if she would help. Yushi said she would cycle over after she finished work at three.

It must be close to three now. Behind her, cyclists whizzed by on the path. A couple on a tandem were arguing, his voice querulous, hers matter-of-fact. A rumbling of wheels crunched stone. The two women who pulled the cart with its load of toddlers sang about the days of the week. *"Jeudi bleu vient à son tour, Vendredi vert le suit toujours."* Maman hadn't taught Rose the days of the week before she started school. The days of the week didn't matter in the forest. Rose knew which plants she shouldn't touch. The three-leaf flag of poison ivy.

Rose unfolded her legs and brushed away a spider climbing the mound of her knee. From a distance she heard the thunk of a great weight being dropped onto concrete again and again. Some of the factories along here were still functioning — if not at their original trade of a hundred years ago, then at some form of noisy, mechanical labour. When the weather was nice, men in stained overalls hiked across the grass to lunch at the picnic tables that bordered the canal. The factories where they worked looked much like the one where she had her studio.

The buildings around the silos farther along the canal were abandoned, their windows ragged holes, the glass long knocked away. When Kenny had first pointed them out, she'd seen only the decrepit shells of empty buildings, but slowly the urban metamorphosis of reclaimed and deserted buildings was growing familiar. She'd begun to pick out details — the gears and pulleys atop a shaft where bales or sacks must once have slid to a loading dock. The ten-storey zigzag of a rusted metal stairway against a brick wall. On top of the highest tower perched what must have been a watchman's shed. The corrugated metal walls were stained with rust, but the peaked roof and the shape of the shed reminded her of her cabin in the woods.

She frowned, remembering her ignorance when Kenny had first brought her here. He'd talked and talked, but she hadn't understood how his stories from the past explained the present.

She didn't hear footsteps behind her until the man spoke. "Look at your face. What bad thought attacked you?"

She looked up at a man in a woolly hat that hung in twists to his shoulders. "May I?" he asked with a formal sweep of his hand, but didn't wait for an answer to cross his legs and drop next to her in one smooth movement. His skin was an even brown like Yushi's. His eyes were lighter, more brown than black. And his hat, she now saw, was *hair*.

"Leo," he said.

"Excuse me?" She was still wondering about his hair.

"My name is Leo. *Je me présente: Léo.*"

She hesitated. He was a stranger. But everyone in the city, except for Yushi and Kenny and a few faces at the hospital, was a stranger. And they, too, had been strangers a few months ago. "Rose," she said.

"Why are you sitting by the canal, Rose, meditating on the water and looking so unhappy?"

His lips were full. One of his front teeth was chipped at the corner. What did those woolly bunches of hair feel like? And *how* were they bunched like that? She realized she was staring and looked away.

"Hmm, Rose? What's up?"

"I was thinking of a friend — or he used to be a friend, but I don't think he wants to be friends anymore."

"A boyfriend?"

"No."

He looked down his nose at her. "Are you sure?"

"He never kissed me. He never even tried."

"He was like a buddy."

"Yes." It was true, she was thinking. Kenny had never even tried to kiss her. He wasn't interested in sex.

"How come he's not your buddy anymore?"

She frowned at her knees, no longer listening to Leo. She shook her head to make him stop. She had to think this through.

Leo stood. "I'll talk to you another time, Rose. You work out your problem with your friend. You'll figure something out, don't worry." He ambled off to wherever it was he'd come from.

Rose was trying to remember exactly what happened that night in the cabin. She'd woken, convinced that Armand was outside. She'd crept down the stairs, haunted by her longing. Touched Kenny in his sleep. Took what she needed — or tried to. She didn't know when he woke or what he thought. Next morning she'd thought he was embarrassed, but that wasn't it. He was afraid of her. The craziness of what she'd done to him.

She tucked her knees to her chin and closed her eyes. The more she remembered the details, the more she knew this was true. Look at how he acted now, shying away from her, always keeping a distance between them.

The grass rustled beside her. A bicycle tire and Yushi's foot. The thin red straps of her sandal. "Here I am." She dropped a paper bag with something Rose knew would be buttery and delicious — that Kenny would love — next to Rose.

Rose stood, brushing bits of grass from her shorts, and waited for Yushi to lock her bike to the fence. The abandoned complex of buildings and silos farther along the canal blocked a geometrical silhouette against the afternoon sky.

"All set," Yushi said. "Show me how to weave."

They had to go around to the front of the warehouse, because the loading ramp doors were locked. The sculptor had wrapped his marble in canvas and plastic, and gone on vacation.

Rose steered her cart of tube feeding off the elevator. She saw Kenny with a stack of towels clamped under an arm, talking to a housekeeper. She'd been watching for him. She'd planned what to say.

She slowed her trolley and the housekeeper, a heavyset man with a bird's-beak ponytail, interrupted his story. "Check."

"Check what?" Kenny asked.

"You've got company." He winked at Rose and backed away.

Kenny glanced behind him and blushed. "Doing your rounds, eh?"

"I wanted to tell you I started weaving. My roommate, Yushi — you remember her — she helped me with the warp and I'm ..." She motioned swinging the beater toward her.

"You're off."

"I'm really grateful for all your help."

He took a step away. "That's okay. Don't worry about it." Another step.

"There's something else." She spoke quickly to keep him there. "You always talked about going to my cabin. I thought you might want —"

"I'm really busy these days. No time to go anywhere."

It hurt to hear how determined he was to avoid her, and she looked down at her trolley. "I didn't mean go with me. I don't want to go. There are too many ghosts there for me. I start to act crazy." She wanted to say it more directly but couldn't. Kenny wasn't stupid. He would understand what she meant. "But you can go if you want. You can try fishing again. Maybe you'll catch something." She didn't think so, but that was what he wanted. "And you can stay in the cabin."

She sneaked a look at him. He was listening.

"I'll tell you where the key is. You don't even have to let me know when you're going. But you should take food because there's not much left there. If you can't get a car, there's a bus. You can go up any time."

He shifted his feet and hitched the towels under his arm higher. "You're sure about this?"

"Positive." She wanted to say she was his friend, but what if he thought she meant girlfriend and backed away again?

He had to move aside to make way for a patient on a stretcher. He and the orderly wheeling the stretcher nodded at each other. She wondered if she would ever learn the cat's cradle of words and gestures that seemed to link everyone but her.

Kenny waited until the stretcher had passed. "A cabin in the woods," he said under his breath. "I could ... hang out there?"

"Yes."

"That's practically the best thing anyone's ever done for me."

"You found my studio. And you got my loom here."

"I've even got a friend out there — Jerome."

She righted her clipboard, which had slid at an angle between her bags of tube feeding. She didn't want Jerome in the cabin. Or Kenny stopping at Jerome's house and meeting Armand.

Armand would see a city boy with clean hands who'd never ploughed a field.

But she'd decided to let Kenny stay in the cabin. With no conditions.

"You'll really let me go stay there?"

"I told you. I want you to go."

Kenny lifted his palm at her. To her surprise, Rose understood she was supposed to smack her hand against it. She hit his thumb instead, but it was close enough. She felt herself smiling to match his grin.

MADDY

Maddy and Yushi crossed the bridge from the market to the other side of the canal carrying trays of sushi. They sat at a picnic table decorated with an origami flower in stiffly pleated yellow paper. "I love these," Maddy said.

Yushi tilted her head, looking at it, but didn't comment. She popped a tiny avocado roll into her mouth.

"That —" Maddy poked her chopsticks across the canal at a condo complex with round porthole windows. "That's such a farce. Twenty years ago — *ten* years ago — you couldn't pay people to live down here. The canal was full of toxic crud and who knows what else. When they started to clean it up, you should have seen how many car skeletons they dragged off the bottom. I'll bet you there were bones inside a few of them. And now we've got condos with fancy windows to make people feel like they're cruising along in a boat, having a martini."

Yushi smeared wasabi on a piece of mackerel. "It's a canal. There must have been boats once upon a time."

"Barges filled with sacks of grain on the way to the mills." Maddy nodded farther along the canal at the Farine Five Roses sign.

"Five roses," Yushi intoned. "It makes your neighbourhood sound like a garden."

"If there are only five of them? Some pathetic garden." Maddy dabbed a ball of rice in soy sauce. "How's your bike riding?"

"My Irish stallion."

"Irish because it's green?"

"Irish because it's mine and I'm Irish."

Maddy wondered what she meant by that but decided not to ask. Since Yushi had told her about her mother, Maddy trusted that Yushi thought of her as a friend, though she still had that aura of indifference, as if at any moment she could stand up and walk away.

Then Yushi added, "On St. Patrick's Day everyone's allowed to be Irish. So I figure, why not every day if you want to?"

Maddy couldn't tell if she was joking. Maybe not saying she came from Trinidad had to do with her family. Maybe saying she was Irish was a smartass answer for people who asked where she came from.

"What was Petitpois on your case about this morning?"

Yushi shook her wrist with its silver bracelet. "This. She says it's not hygienic to wear it while I'm serving food."

"And you said ..."

"I said I wear it for religious reasons and my family is already upset because I'm not wearing my bindi." She poked a finger between her eyebrows. Maddy snorted.

"And while I was talking to her I stared at the crucifix she's got around her neck."

"It's not right, the way she harasses you. You should talk to Zied." Petitpois was their boss, but Zied was her boss. Zied was the head pastry chef, a big-chested man with a regal nose who sent an underling upstairs when he wanted an espresso. Whoever made it was supposed to add three packets of sugar and stir well.

"Pettypoo I can handle. She's a menopausal tyrant. Him, he's a temper tantrum set on instant explode. Even if you're not the target, the fallout could leave you with scars. Believe me, I had to work close up in a kitchen with a chef who threw whatever he could grab — a zucchini, a crepe pan, a wineglass, a glop of roux."

"Is that why you don't work in a kitchen anymore?"

Yushi aimed her chopsticks at Maddy's tray. "You don't eat ginger?"

"Take it if you want it."

Yushi scooped the translucent petals. "Chefs ... owners ... all the politics. I just wanted to make desserts. I wasn't interested in being a minesweeper in a daycare centre for misfits shrieking about their *brochettes de lapin*. And I tell you, we worked like crazy — way busier than it's ever been over there." She flicked a haughty glance in the direction of the market. "And where did all the money go? To pay for the owner's coke habit and his fancy car."

"You mean ... you were a pastry chef!" That explained Yushi's knowledge and expertise.

"I never had a fancy title. I made the desserts, that was all. Whisky chocolate ribbon cake, Paris–Brest, hazelnut mocha torte, caramel pecan tart, brioche for Sunday brunch — and cheesecake. *No es posible* to have a restaurant in Toronto and not serve cheesecake."

"So why are you working at a counter now, bagging bread?"

"Why are you?"

"Because I don't know how to make a marzipan rose — or Paris–Brest or brioche."

Yushi looked into the distance. "If you can't do what you want to do, it's better to do nothing at all."

"That doesn't sound right."

"It's what I'm doing." Yushi snapped shut her empty sushi tray. "Time to go back."

Maddy wanted to say more, but clearly not now.

Maddy slid the baguette and vegetables onto the counter in the kitchen and ran upstairs to change into shorts and a tank top. In the hallway stood cans of paint.

On her way back through the kitchen, she stopped to tear off the end of the baguette. Working at a patisserie had made her immune to sweets, but bread was a constant temptation. Her Polish genes craved starch.

She opened the gate onto the alley and there sat Jim, a tangerine demigod too grand to jump over a fence if a human was going to open the gate. He rose off his haunches and blinked for her to roll back her bike so he could pass. "I beg your pardon," she said, which he acknowledged by grazing his tail across her leg.

She rode along Wellington, attentive to nervous rush-hour traffic. Urban fact #22: automobile drivers were territorial about their cars, the space around their cars, the road in general. At the Canadian Tire she could cross to the bike path by the river. A light breeze rustled through the poplars, flipping the silvery skirts of their leaves. Purple martins swooped in and out of the holes of an apartment birdhouse. A man standing by the path shouted, *"As-tu l'heure?"* She lifted her arm to show him she wasn't wearing a watch.

Her heart opened with the view as the river widened. She loved its blue lizard-skin ripple and the frills of foam from the rapids in the distance — the same rapids Jacques Cartier had thought were the Northwest Passage. He'd had no idea how large the world was.

She passed a woman who was power walking with her hair still tucked in a French twist from her day at work. She wore running shoes and shorts, yet her hips moved with the memory of heels, clacking down the hallway of a downtown office.

Maddy cycled at a good speed, gaining on a woman pulling a trailer buggy. As Maddy passed, she peered into the canopied shadow of the buggy. Bare knees relaxed in sleep. A polka-dot sun hat hiding the child's face.

At first, when Maddy had lost her baby, she thought she'd been saved. She'd believed Stilt when he said she was lucky the crazy woman with the braid had taken her baby. She'd thought she was lucky, too. She'd thought she could forget. The baby was a mistake she didn't want to remember.

Except that she'd felt the baby's kicks against the taut skin of her belly. Her body had split wide, giving birth. Even if in her head she didn't want to remember, the clock in her womb kept time. When she walked through parks and past playgrounds, where two-year-olds and three-year-olds clambered onto their mother's laps, she felt how her own lap was empty. No little girl clutched at her hand or nuzzled a hot forehead against her neck. Somewhere in the world her child was two and three years old. Then four and five, careening on a bicycle.

Since she didn't know where her child was, why couldn't it be this one, singing to herself as she drew stick people in blue crayon? Or this one, with her mouth agape before a sandwich board with an ice cream cone? Maddy had clenched her hands by her hips, not allowing herself to step closer.

The little girls grew into tweens in training bras. Teenagers who swung long hair over their shoulders, pretending they knew how to hold cigarettes. Young women with skirts stretched so tight around their thighs their steps minced.

Her daughter would be twenty-seven now, more than ten years older than Maddy was when she'd had her. Impossible numbers. Nonsensical math. *How* could she have a twenty-seven-year-old daughter and not even know who she was?

And *yes*, it had occurred to her that Yushi must be close to her daughter's age. But ... so what? Couldn't she like Yushi simply for who she was? Maddy didn't want to keep living under this cloud of self-blame. To what end? There was no changing what had happened — except to bear it in mind, see how she'd messed up, try not to mess up again.

She veered off the bike path, bumping her tires across the grass toward a bench. She dropped onto it, unsnapping her helmet and raking her fingers through the hot, bunched mass of her hair. Far off, across the water, the horizon stretched in a bristle of matchstick trees.

What she should have done, she knew now, was call the police. Too bad if Stilt didn't want them in the house, smelling pot in the air, noticing how many underage kids belonged to his free-love harem. Her baby had been kidnapped, damn it! The police would have put out an alert for a woman with a braid that hung to her waist, carrying a baby that wasn't hers. They would have blocked the airport and the train station. Checked the buses. Asked the ticket agents and drivers. No one else had a braid that long, a baby that young, and breasts that didn't leak. They would have found her.

You had to act, she knew now. Not wait on what anyone else thought you should and shouldn't do. Decide for yourself what needed to be done and do it.

The doorbell rang. Maddy dropped her brush into the plastic tub of paint, and wiping her hands on an old T-shirt, traipsed down the stairs. "Coming!" she hollered. She wore a pair of pink shorts so ancient the corduroy had rubbed bald, and had tied a head scarf around her curls.

Fara stood below the steps on the sidewalk. "Hi. Am I disturbing you?"

Maddy held up green-spattered fingers. "Painting one of the rooms upstairs."

"I can come another time." Fara backed up. "I just wanted to say hi."

"Come on, then, if you don't mind me facing a wall." Maddy had already turned away, assuming Fara would follow.

"Your banister is gorgeous. The real estate agent told us about it."

"What real estate agent?"

"The one who sold us our house. She said hippies used to live here and they stripped all the wood. She said she'd love to sell your house."

"Real estate agents." Maddy blew a raspberry. "They keep pushing cards through the mail slot. I *know* they can sell my house. But tell me, if I sold it, where would I live that wouldn't cost me just as much to buy as I'd make on the house? I'd be no further ahead." She stooped for her brush and stood back to survey the corner where she'd left off.

"But this is such a big house and you're all alone. You could buy a smaller place."

Maddy smoothed the brush in slow up-and-down strokes. She found painting relaxing. "What if tomorrow I meet the love of my life and get pregnant with triplets?"

"I didn't mean —"

"It's okay. I'm joking." Actually, only half-joking. She wished people with partners would think before assuming that people who were single were fated to stay that way.

Fara said nothing for a moment. "I like this pale green. It makes the room look fresh. Maybe I'll use it for one of our upstairs rooms. We're shuffling everything around again. We had our bedroom in the front, but the street's too noisy." She peered down the hallway. "You sleep in the front?"

"Always have. I'm one of the original hippies — that's how long I've been here. Why don't you grab a chair? There's one next door." Maddy pulled the ladder toward the corner and climbed a couple of rungs.

Fara returned with the chair from the sewing room. "This would make a nice bedroom."

Maddy sucked in her lips. For nothing in the world would she sleep here. It was the woman with the braid's room. At the beginning, after the other kids had left and Stilt had moved to Vermont or B.C. — wherever it was hippies retired — she'd kept the door closed. She'd never even looked inside. The pigeons and squirrels could have been having a party. For her, the house didn't exist in that corner of the hallway. She'd rented out the other upstairs room, and after a year that tenant asked if her cousin, who was moving to Montreal to study at Concordia, could have the empty room next to hers. They would fix it up themselves. When they left, Maddy rented out both rooms again. It was still the woman with the braid's room, but Maddy could bear it now. Look, even paint it.

She heard the chair squeak and remembered Fara, who'd said nothing since her comment. "You still there?" Maddy asked.

"Yeah ... I wanted to ask you about the people who used to live in our house."

Maddy lifted an eyebrow at the wall. "You mean the suicide."

"Not the suicide," Fara said so sharply that Maddy glanced at her. Fara sat twisting a thread that trailed from the hem of her shirt round and round her finger. "I was wondering about his brother. Was he living there when it happened?"

"He moved out a couple of years ago. He didn't get along with his dad. It was like his dad thought Ben wasn't his kid. I heard him a couple of times yelling at Ben, saying his mom should have taken him when she left."

"She wasn't living there either?"

Maddy dipped her brush and began painting again. "She took off years ago. I don't know if they ever heard from her again. Ben was maybe eight or so. Xavier was younger. He hadn't started school yet, so one of the neighbours up the street used to mind him along with her own kids. When Ben finished school, he would get Xavier. You'd see him coming down the street, hardly tall enough to push the stroller in a straight line, but he wouldn't let anyone help. I saw them out on the back steps once — there used to be steps where you've got a deck now — eating ravioli from a can. They both had a spoon and took turns, handing the can back and forth." She had to stop talking to concentrate on not touching the brush to the ceiling.

Fara said, "Sounds like they were really close."

"That was when they were little. Xavier turned into a bit of a wild boy. He did all kinds of crazy things. Once — the story was in the paper — he climbed up under the Victoria Bridge. You know, across the St. Lawrence? And he was always getting into trouble at school. I don't think it was easy for Ben, being his brother."

"I wonder what it's like for him now that he's dead."

Maddy climbed down the ladder. "What do you mean? Obviously he knows his brother is dead. What should it be like for him?"

"I think losing a sibling is a very specific kind of loss. It's not like a parent who was in charge and took care of you. Your sibling is the other kid who was there while you were growing up. Even if you didn't have a good relationship, your sibling is part of you in a way no one else is — and probably even more so if your parents weren't around or not really there for you."

Maddy had crouched to begin painting the bottom of the next corner. She thought about her brother, Stan. They only saw each other twice a year, though they lived in the same city. "I guess," she said. "I never thought about it. When we were growing up, my brother and I were more antagonistic than friendly. Our mother was always running interference, making sure I did all the chores and he got the biggest piece of *babka*."

"Do you and your brother get along now?"

Maddy had painted as far up as she could reach and turned now to get the ladder.

"Let me." Fara said. She manoeuvred the ladder to the corner and rattled the legs in place.

"We're not friends but we're not not-friends, if you get what I mean. If he needed help, I'd do what I could. And him for me, too, I think. Mind you, we haven't actually tested that theory." She looked at Fara. "What about you?"

Fara shrugged but said nothing.

Meaning what? Maddy wondered. Didn't her theories about siblings apply to herself? Or was she an only child?

"Suicide," Fara muttered. "It's such a definitive way to die. I know, all death is final, but suicide isn't just dying. It's choosing death. His brother must blame himself that he never noticed something was wrong. Do you know if there was a note? If he explained why?"

"No idea." Maddy waited a beat. She didn't want to keep talking about suicide. "How's Frédéric? Have the two of you been getting to know the Pointe?"

"Mostly we're still working on the house. But you were born here, right?"

"This is where my parents headed when they got off the boat. Their only contact in Canada was the Polish priest at Holy Trinity on Centre Street."

"So you know a lot about the Pointe."

"When you're a kid, I think you take most things for granted. You don't have any perspective. Most of what I learned about the Pointe came later, when I took courses at Concordia. I had this sociology professor who was big on oral history. He came to the Pointe to interview people and collect photos. He told me a lot."

Brian had interviewed her, too. She'd told him about the neighbourhood boys walking to Verdun for a street fight, and how the *dépanneur* three streets over had a horse for deliveries up until the nineties. She'd never told him about her baby — at first because she was too shy to admit how stupid she'd been to have a baby and then lose it; and then, when he became her boyfriend, she worried that he wouldn't approve if he found out. So naive he was, too, tracing the stretch marks on her stomach and believing her when she said they were from a vitamin deficiency when she was growing up. Even though at other times, she'd told him her parents had kept a garden with carrots, onions, tomatoes, and green beans. Later, after she and Brian split, she was glad she'd never told him about the baby. He would have included it in an article or a book, and blamed it on poverty and poor living conditions in the Pointe.

Fara shifted on her chair. "The signs along the canal call it the Cradle of Industry. *Le Berceau de l'Industrie.*"

"My professor said that, too. The history of Pointe St-Charles is the history of Montreal is the history of Canada. The Lachine Canal, the railroad, the factories, and the workers from the Pointe were the link between the Great Lakes and the Atlantic — the rest of the world."

"You don't sound like you believe it."

"Sure I do. But history isn't just the part that sounds glorious. It's everything." Maddy poked her brush into the top corner. "Why aren't there any signs saying that the Pointe was Canada's first industrial slum?"

"Not a slum," Fara objected.

"People living twelve in a room with no running water and open sewers in the street? I'd say that was a slum. In the early 1900s the Pointe had the highest rate of infant mortality in all of Canada." Another of Brian's statistics. She used to accuse him of making his career from slumming, and listen to how she echoed him.

"But it's not like that now," Fara said.

"Not like that, no." Though if Fara opened her eyes, she could see a few things for herself. The women in tight skirts standing at the corner of Wellington, leering at the traffic, weren't waiting for the bus. And those teenage boys who hung out at the house on the corner. Maddy had been cycling down the alley and saw the mom in the open back door, giving one of the boys a blow job. And though the family who used to send their toddler onto the sidewalk to exchange drugs for money had been evicted, Maddy had seen them since living only a few streets over. Wait until that kid got to kindergarten.

She climbed down the ladder. Her neck and arms ached from stretching. "I want a beer. How about you? We can sit outside."

Maddy peered at every building as if the numbers might suddenly skip or somersault backward. 4437, 4439, 4441. They were fixed to the top of door frames or screwed into the brick. Some walls had a glazed ceramic tile with a faded saint's head next to the door. This used to be a Portuguese neighbourhood. Urban fact #11: Ethnic communities formed inner-city ghettos around churches, temples, or mosques, and grocery stores stocked with vegetables and meats they liked to cook. As soon as they could afford to, they moved to houses with lawns and indoor garages in the suburbs. Another kind of a ghetto.

For her parents, leaving Warsaw had exhausted their daring. They stayed in the Pointe, scrimped and saved, until they could buy a narrow brick row house. Another Polish family lived upstairs and paid them rent. Maddy's family had four rooms on the ground floor, as well as the dirt cellar lined with shelves filled with jars of vegetables, jam, sauerkraut, and pickles her mother preserved. Maddy's mother did the laundry by boiling their sheets and clothes in a large kettle on the stove. Maddy remembered the excitement when her father salvaged an ancient wringer washer. The rollers squeezed the wet clothes into flattened pancakes her mother shook open and hung outside, even in the winter when they didn't dry but froze. Maddy had many household chores but was forbidden to touch the washing machine. Only her mother lifted the dripping clothes from the tub and fed them into the rollers. Maddy used to watch with growing dread mixed with guilty longing. Those were the same hands that slapped her on the head and boxed her ears. What if they got snatched by the rollers and crushed, spewed out flat as the squished pillowcases? She knew these were wicked thoughts, and that thoughts were as evil as deeds, but she still never told the priest when she kneeled in the confessional. If it ever happened, she would tell him. *Bless me, Father, for I have sinned.*

Maddy checked the napkin where Yushi had printed her address. There, on the second floor at the top of a curved metal stairway. Each step echoed with a tremor.

She pressed the buzzer and turned to survey the neighbourhood. As in the Pointe, she saw mostly brick, but the brick wasn't as old, and the buildings were wider, the cornices more ornate. The horizon felt closer, too: spreading roofs and skylights, with high-rises just beyond and the mountain nearby. Here, you were *in* the city, not on the edge of it, by the river.

Behind her she heard the door open.

"Sorry." Yushi was drying her hands on a dishtowel. "I was cutting mango for pickle."

"I thought you were going to wait till I got here so I could watch." Maddy followed Yushi down a scuffed oak hallway into the welcoming smell of warm curry. Yushi wore a chef's apron, folded at the waist, with the strings wrapped twice around her small waist. The front and sides were blotted with smears of yellow, green, and brown. It was a working apron, unlike the pristine bibs they donned to serve pastries.

Yushi dropped the dishtowel over the back of a chair. "If you wanted to watch from the start, you'd have had to sleep here. I soaked the *channa* last night."

"*Channa?*"

"Chickpeas. *You canna do buss-up-shut w'out channa,*" she half-sang. And in her usual voice, "Let's do one lesson at a time. Today you'll see how I make roti."

At one lesson at a time, Maddy could look forward to several visits. She sucked in her lips to keep from smiling too broadly.

On the counter was a bowl of chopped mango, a larger bowl covered with a cloth, a chopping board, a plate upended over another plate, a scattered handful of green chilies. On the stove two large pots bubbled softly. Though orderly, the space was cramped for cooking. Maddy's kitchen was so much larger. She could have suggested Yushi cook at her place, but she'd wanted to see where Yushi lived.

"Here's the *channa.*" Yushi lifted one of the lids on the stove and stirred the thick, turmeric-yellow stew. She prodded a few chunks and squished them against the sides of the pot with the back of the wooden spoon. "Potato," she explained. "It *t'ickens* the sauce. We call it *aloo*."

"*Aloo* is the sauce?"

"*Aloo* is potato."

The stew in the next pot was darker. "*Baigan*," Yushi said as she stirred it. "Eggplant." She rapped the spoon against the pot and set the lid at an angle. "Just before we eat, I'll add shrimp. That's not Trini, that's how *I* make curry shrimp — with *baigan*."

Channa, aloo, baigan. The vocabulary of getting to know Yushi. "What do you call shrimp?" Maddy asked.

Yushi threw her a look. "Shrimp."

Maddy was embarrassed — as if she'd been caught on the lookout for exoticism. But she, too, came from a culture with its own food. "I never ate shrimp growing up. It would have been too expensive. Also, I don't think my parents even knew what shrimp were. We lived on cabbage rolls. *Golabki*." She patted her hips as if that explained why they were so wide.

"Cabbage rolls filled with ...?"

"Rice, sometimes hamburger."

"There's more interesting stuffing you could make. Let me think about it." Yushi lifted a heavy, flat metal round from a cupboard. "Seen one of these before?"

It looked like the bottom of a cast-iron pan. "No sides?" Maddy asked.

"You need to press around the edges of the roti while they're cooking so they puff. It's hard to do that with sides. It's called a *tawah*."

"Can you buy them here?"

"In Montreal? Probably. I got mine in Toronto."

Yushi began clearing as much space as she could on the counter, setting the bowl with the chopped mango on the toaster oven, sliding the chopping board behind a canister.

"What's this for?" Maddy pointed at the two plates, one upended over the other.

"Nothing. I'm finished with that." She lifted the plates apart. The bottom one had a green smear along the edge, a tiny mash of minced garlic, bits and flecks of leaves. "My mum always chopped her garlic and herbs before she started cooking, and put them on a plate —" Yushi dabbed pursed fingers in spots around the plate. "When she was cooking, she had everything ready. But you had to cover the plate to keep *de nasty flies off*. Keeps the herbs fresh, too. She always covered plates and bowls with plates or a damp cloth. I don't think she ever bought a roll of plastic wrap. She wouldn't have seen the use."

Yushi rinsed the plates and left them in the sink. "I already made the roti dough because it has to rest. Any kind of bread dough, you want the gluten in the flour to ..." She rubbed her finger and thumb together. "Get elastic."

She plucked the cloth off the steel bowl to reveal a ball of white dough.

"What's in it?" Maddy asked.

"Flour, baking powder, water, bit of yeast. Pinch of salt if you want. What's important is the texture. Wash your hands and feel."

Maddy dried her hands on the towel on the chair and poked a finger into the dough.

"No, *feel* it." Yushi scooped up the ball and smacked it into Maddy's open hands. "Pull it apart and make me eight *loyas*."

"*Loyas?*"

"Balls."

Maddy felt the resistance and stretch of the dough as she pulled it in half, twisted those halves apart, then again.

Yushi rolled each of Maddy's chunks into smooth balls, lined them up on the counter, and draped the towel over them. "So they don't dry up," she explained. "The Indian name for these breads is *paratha*. *Buss-up-shut* is Trini for burst-up shirt. You'll see why. When I flip one off the *tawah*, you'll slap it up." Yushi demonstrated by clapping her palms. "The layers get all torn and lovely — perfect for sopping up sauce." She pulled a small steel bowl toward her. "This is ghee. Clarified butter. You know what that is, right?"

"Isn't it just melted?"

"More than melted. The foam gets skimmed off, you let the butter cook a while, then you strain it. That gets rid of the milk solids. You're left with ..." She swirled the bowl of clear yellow liquid. "Pure butter."

She grabbed a pastry brush off a rack of spatulas, whisks, and ladles, took a rolling pin from a drawer, set a canister of flour on the counter. She poured ghee into a dish, sprinkled flour on the counter, scooped one of Maddy's balls from under the cloth.

"What did you call the balls?"

"*Loyas.*"

Channa, aloo, loyas, tawah. She'd forgotten the word for eggplant. Maybe when they ate, Yushi would say it again.

Yushi had rolled the dough into a circle. She nodded at the dish of clarified butter. "Take the pastry brush. Cover this. Don't skimp. The ghee is what makes the layers."

Maddy squinted to catch the reflection of wetness on the dough, trying not to miss anywhere, especially with Yushi watching. Then Yushi said, "You know, you don't have to go to the doctor. You can get glasses at a pharmacy."

"I can see. It's just hard to tell where I've already brushed."

Yushi smirked. "My mum used to squint like that. I got her glasses at the pharmacy — with leopard print frames. They were cool."

"Do I ..." Maddy wasn't sure she wanted to ask.

"Act like you need glasses? Yes. The other day you had to ask Geneviève to read a bill for you."

"No, I wondered if ... I'm probably the same age as your mother was. Do I remind you of her?"

"My mum?" Yushi's voice rose in surprise. "You're not at all like my mum! Except that you're as vain about not needing glasses when you obviously do."

Vain? Maddy nodded. She would stop at the pharmacy and buy a pair of glasses.

Yushi touched the tip of a knife to the centre of the dough circle and sliced a radius. "Now we roll it up." She lifted one cut edge and began to roll it around the circle, forming a cone. "The ghee keeps the layers separate. It's the same principle as puff pastry — when you make croissants." She tucked the tips of the cut edges inside both ends of the cone, flattened the top, and slipped it under the towel.

"Want to make one?" She held up the next *loya*.

"I'll stick to this." Maddy lifted the pastry brush. She wouldn't be able to handle the dough as deftly as Yushi. She was glad she'd asked if she reminded Yushi of her mother. If it didn't matter to Yushi that she was the same age as her mother, why should it to her?

From down the hallway she heard the outside door open and close. It must be Rose, the roommate with the studio and the loom.

Rose's steps neared the kitchen, then stopped. Maddy had turned to say hello, but didn't when she saw how blankly Rose stared at her.

Yushi said, "Hey."

"Hi." Very quiet.

"You remember Maddy?"

No answer. As if she hadn't heard or didn't understand the words.

Yushi seemed not to notice. "I hope you didn't eat. I've got a feast on the go here. It'll be ready in about an hour."

"I'm going to lie down for a while." Rose slipped away and Maddy heard a door close. When she and Yushi visited Rose's studio, she'd noticed how low Rose's voice was. A mezzo register — but without any trace of song.

"Is she ..." Maddy began. She didn't want to sound rude. When she'd first met Yushi, she'd found her behaviour strange, too. Except that she'd felt curious about Yushi. She didn't feel curious about Rose.

"She grew up in the country — in the woods in a cabin. She doesn't always feel comfortable with people. She's a bit shy."

More than just shy, Maddy thought.

Yushi stepped away from the counter and held out the rolling pin. "You're going to make one now. And remember, it's not a cabbage roll. It's a buss-up-shut."

ROSE

Rose had left her trolley at the nursing station since there was only one Styrofoam container to carry to the kitchen. Ahead of her an orderly was pushing a woman in a wheelchair. She was complaining because the test had taken so long and her intravenous hurt. Did the nurses remember to order a meal so she could eat now? Probably not. They starved you in this place.

As the orderly turned into the room, he raised his eyebrows at Rose. Once again she was glad she hadn't gotten a job working with patients. They were too peevish in illness. Cranky and demanding. The woman in the wheelchair didn't even look sick.

Maman's face had been pale, her cheeks wan. Her breath had kept failing so she had to stop and sit. Yet never once had she complained. Rose pressed her lips tight with pride. She would be stoic like that, too. Not make a nuisance of herself.

Then Rose had a thought, so sudden and surprising it made her steps slow. Maman might still be alive if she had complained. If she had told a doctor — or Rose — how her heart stumbled and bounded. Her heart could have been fixed with an operation. The coroner had said so. Of all Maman's symptoms, the most dangerous had been her silence.

———

With one hand Rose tapped the shuttle across the taut span of threads. With the other she swung the beater toward her to tamp down the yarn. She was weaving a vein of crimson bouclé into zigzags of brown to echo the glint of red in the warp. Secret accents made the cloth richer, gave it depth.

She snipped the red bouclé and reached for a spool of gold. Already the cloth stretched over the breast beam. Even though she had executed each workaday step — preparing the warp, winding it, dressing the loom, tying up the treadles — it still felt like magic to see the hundreds of threads meld into a pattern and become cloth.

She slid her feet from treadle to treadle. Held her arms wide to catch the shuttle. Through the open panes of the window she could hear the tap of the sculptor's mallet followed by the clang of the chisel on stone. Thuds punctuated by scrapes and pauses.

Yesterday she'd had to rush off to work at the hospital, and the day before she'd had a dentist appointment. Today she had the whole wonderful day to herself and could stay through the afternoon and into the evening. She'd stopped at the market and bought a piece of cheddar, two tomatoes, a cucumber, a baguette. A feast! Yushi would have added a more exotic flavour — spiced Moroccan olives or a jar of baba ghanouj — but Rose looked forward to the simple farm vegetables. She would sit outside on the grass by the canal to eat her supper.

She was so hypnotized by the dance of hands and arms, the glide of her feet from treadle to treadle, that she was startled when the end of the yarn flipped from the shuttle. Already time for more.

She dropped a bobbin onto the winder she'd braced on the edge of the work table. As she cranked the handle, she gazed out the window at the grass, the bike path, the trees on the other side of the canal. A cyclist in red spandex and a gleaming insect-head helmet careened past. An Asian man shuffled along, pulling a metal shopping cart. Earlier in the summer she'd seen him crouched to the ground, picking dandelion leaves he collected in a small burlap sack.

Then a young man with hair to his shoulders ambled past with his head turned to her window. An instant later he ambled by again from the other direction, still staring. Rose drew her elbows in, instantly alert — until she recognized the long twists of hair. She'd wondered if she might see Leo again, but had expected it would be outside, by the canal like last time.

What was he doing, parading back and forth in front of her window? Now that he saw she'd noticed him, he stopped, smiling broadly.

Four of her bottom windowpanes were open. As she crossed the room, he scuffed toward the chain-link fence. "Hey," he called. "What's that contraption?"

"A loom!"

"What's that?"

Did no one in the city know what a loom was? "Wait." She walked out of her studio down the hall to the loading dock. The sculptor was crouched at the bottom of the ramp, scraping a rasp across an indentation in the marble. He'd told her the shape wasn't supposed to *be* anything, but her mind still grasped for a similarity that made sense. A fat fish upright on its tail. A misshapen vase.

She waved for Leo to come up the ramp. The sculptor acted as if he didn't notice, but she caught his smirk. He was as much a gossip as the self-righteous women of Rivière-des-Pins.

Leo played along, sneaking through the weeds on tiptoe past the sculptor and up the ramp. In the hallway he said, "You really concentrate. I've been waiting for you to notice me."

The coils of his hair looked fluffier than she remembered. "How did you know which window was mine?"

"I've been watching you since you were up on a ladder, washing the walls. I made sure you didn't fall." He grinned, showing off his chipped tooth. "I've got powers, you know."

Her hand was on the doorknob, but she didn't turn it. His words nudged a memory she didn't like. "You were spying on me."

His grin fading, he said, "No. Not spying." His eyes were serious. "Anybody could have seen me standing right there. The sculptor saw me. All you had to do was turn your head and look. Like today."

It was true that when she was weaving, she completely forgot to look out the window. She wasn't sure why, but she decided to believe him.

She opened the door and let Leo walk in. He walked right up to her loom, peered into the shaft, then down at the treadles and the brake. He took soft steps around the wooden geometry of angles and beams, the heddles and reed that held the threads in place. He was curious, more curious than anyone else had been. "I'm guessing you've got to know what you're doing," he said.

"My mother taught me."

"But you do it because you like it."

"I love weaving." In the bare room the simple words sounded like a vow.

"Do you sell what you weave?"

"This piece? No."

"You could."

"I know. My mother and I, we used to sell." She stopped. She didn't want to explain about Maman. Not right now. "I'm making this for a friend." The bravado of the claim surprised her. Was she a person who had friends? "My roommate," she added, as if that sounded more proper.

"You live around here?"

"No."

"Too bad. I could see you more often." He smiled.

She felt herself smiling back. Mirror effect. The pleasure, too, of hearing that he wanted to see her again.

He noticed the baguette and tomatoes on the dresser. "Are you expecting company?"

"Are you hungry?"

He shrugged. "I could eat. All I had for breakfast was an apple."

She dropped the vegetables that she'd washed and dried into her cloth shopping bag, tucked the baguette under her arm, and grabbed a small serrated knife. "Will you get water?"

He reached for two of the three mugs she'd bought at the dollar store in case Yushi or Kenny visited. A third guest was more than she could imagine just yet, but some hopeful instinct had made her buy a third mug. She felt giddy with the surprise of hosting a lunch.

Leo walked ahead, balancing the mugs of water he'd filled to the brim. Following him down the hallway to the loading ramp, she looked at his body more closely than she had yet. His narrow shoulders. The loose hang of his jeans.

"This way." She led them away from the sculptor's curiosity toward a tree that cast shade and partly hid them from view.

She sat on the grass, emptied the bag of vegetables and cheese, and spread it between them. Leo set the mugs at opposite corners. He took the knife and cut pieces of cheese, sliced the cucumber in chunks, sawed through the baguette. He sat close enough that she could smell him. It wasn't a dirty or a sweaty smell, but as if he'd just woken from sleep and hadn't washed yet.

He asked how she'd met her roommate and if they got along. He wondered what kind of name Yushi was. Rose said it was Indian and short for Ayushi. He told her that he sometimes worked in a garage in St-Henri. The job wasn't regular but they were teaching him. He began explaining how a carburetor worked. Rose listened, happy to have him talking to her, watching the play of interest on his face.

They'd finished all the food except the cheese, and had sat so long that the shade from the tree had moved and Leo had to squint against the sun when he looked at her. Rose shook the crumbs off their ad hoc tablecloth and put the cheese in the bag. Still they sat in the grass next to each other. Leo hummed a song, mumbling words she couldn't follow. He broke off and lifted his hand toward her face. Without touching her, he traced a curl in the air. "Your hair," he said.

She curved her hair behind her ear. Was that what he wanted?

"Your ears are pretty."

She lowered her eyes, happy yet embarrassed. No one had ever said her ears were pretty.

"You should wear earrings."

Yushi had earrings — a porcelain dish of gleaming lozenges, crescents, drops, and hooks, all tangled together. Maybe she would let Rose borrow a pair.

Leo had lain back in the grass, hands crossed on his chest. "What's the deal with you? You show up first thing in the morning. You take off after lunch. Today you're hanging around. I can't keep track of you."

"I don't have to go to work today."

He squirmed his head to look at her. "You've got a job — like a real place where you go and punch in?"

"I've got a schedule, yeah."

"Okay. So I need to find out when your next day off is."

She felt herself blushing and didn't know whether to look out at the canal or at Leo. She wanted to see him again, too, but hadn't expected that they could simply plan to get together. Well, why not? He wasn't a married man, years older than her, who had to sneak through the woods.

And bravely, despite the flush on her cheeks, she said, "I'm off every second weekend, and when I work weekends, I get Monday and Thursday off."

He rolled on his side to face her, crooking an arm under his head to pillow it. "You'll be here again Thursday."

She nodded, daring herself not to look away.

Rose rinsed the saucepan she'd scrubbed, and dried it. In her mind she was still by the canal with Leo. She had wondered if he would move closer. Though she hardly knew him, she wished he would. Another part of her marvelled at his lazy appreciation of time. How he assumed there would be more days like this in the grass under the trees with the sun on the water — that they had time to get to know each other. Leo had finally yawned and said he had to go to the garage to see if they wanted him tomorrow morning. 'Cause I don't have a phone, he explained. Rose thought everyone in the city had a phone. She and Yushi had one, though it rarely rang.

From Yushi's room came the choreographed dialogue of a TV show. Rose flapped out the tea towel and hung it on the back of a chair. In the doorway to Yushi's room she asked, "Do you want a drink?" Their latest favourite cooler was cranberry juice spritzed with club soda.

Yushi, who lay propped on her bed, sat upright and aimed the remote at the TV to shut it off. "Bunch of dumb shows."

Rose glanced at the dish heaped with jewellery on Yushi's dresser. "I wanted to ask you," she began, but stopped when she saw how Yushi was watching her.

"Am I supposed to guess?" Yushi asked. "Is it about food? About clothes?"

"Earrings. Will you let me borrow a pair?"

"Just like that? You've decided to wear earrings?"

Rose didn't answer. Yushi would probably figure it out soon enough, but until Rose knew more about Leo, she wasn't telling. She peeked at the earrings again. Yushi hardly ever wore them, though she kept her bracelet on all the time, even to sleep.

Yushi slid forward off the bed and, with no warning, reached up to pinch Rose's earlobes. "You don't have holes."

Rose didn't know what she meant.

Yushi snatched an earring from the dish and waggled the hook at Rose. "Look." She pulled at her earlobe, where Rose saw a slashed pucker in the flesh. "We've got to make holes. Then you can wear as many of these as you want."

"I didn't know ..." Did everyone who wore earrings have holes in their ears?

"It's easy. I saw my mom do it for my little sister. I was a baby when mine were done." Yushi had opened the top drawer of her dresser and was rummaging through underwear and socks. From the very back of the drawer, she fished out a small box. Inside, on quilted cloth, nestled two tiny hanging bells in rich yellow gold. "These were my mom's."

Rose drew back her shoulders. "Don't give me your mom's."

"It's the only gold I have and you need gold at the start so your holes stay clean."

Yushi strode past her to the kitchen. Still unsure, but hearing the freezer door slam and a drawer being rattled open, Rose followed. The ice cube tray was on the counter. Yushi was filling the kettle. "Get a sewing needle," she said.

A sewing needle and boiling water. Ice on the earlobe to freeze it. It didn't hurt when Yushi stabbed her with the needle and pushed the earrings through, though later that night her ears felt sore when pressed against her pillow.

But that was okay, Rose thought, because now she could wear earrings.

As Rose pushed her cart down the hallway, she heard how each movement made the tiny gold bells that dangled from the earrings tinkle.

That morning, when she arrived at the studio and drew back

the curtains, she found a yellow page, folded and tucked against one of the windowpanes. It wasn't a pane she could open, and she'd had to go back down the hallway and outside through the weeds. She was curious about the paper, half-guessing, half-suspicious. She hadn't forgotten Kenny's tale about squatters.

Still standing in the weeds, she unfolded the paper. *Hi, I'm a working stiff today. I wish I could see you instead. L.* The precise edges of the printing were so unlike Leo's casual, ambling walk. Yet she could hear his voice in her mind as she read and reread the two lines.

She, too, wished she could see him, but almost better at that moment was the lovely surprise of a letter on her window. Anyone could have seen it. Cyclists on the bike path. The sculptor, if he'd come early. Leo wanted people to see he knew her. The feeling was so precious and wonderful she wanted to hug it close. She held the page between her fingers as if it were a bloom. This was how people were supposed to come together. Not like Armand with his stiff-lipped mumble no one but she could hear.

She propped the page open like a card on the dresser. She glanced at it while she was weaving, and once, when she had to get up from the bench to advance the warp, she crossed the room and picked up the page to read the words again.

She always had to clip her hair back before she started work at the hospital, but today she thought about how she was showing off her *pretty ears* with the gold earrings.

Behind her someone called, "Rose!" She turned, saw Kenny jogging toward her.

"Hey, I wanted to tell you. This weekend? I'm renting a car. And that cabin in the woods — here I come!"

She'd told him where the key hung on a nail in the lean-to, where to find the sheets, to make sure he opened the flue before he started a fire in the stove. "The Coleman lamp," she said now. "Unless you want to keep using candles, you should buy naphtha. Or more candles." She felt she had to remind him that if he ran out of supplies in the woods, he couldn't just step out the door to get more.

"I'll have enough food," he said. "I'm bringing a box."

"A box will be hard to carry through the woods. Pack a knapsack."

"Yeah ..." Kenny bobbed his head. "The woods. I was thinking about that. What if I can't find that path?"

When he'd helped her carry pieces of the loom through the woods, he'd thrashed through knee-high bushes, not seeing the trail between the leaves where he could have walked more easily.

She stopped at a nursing station and handed her clipboard across. Kenny followed her to the kitchen. "What if I get lost?"

The woods were an hour's drive from Montreal — isolated in themselves, but hardly the great uncharted North. If he were to walk in a straight line in any direction, he would come to a road or a fence he could follow. Although he'd already gotten lost on the roads, hadn't he?

"I don't know," she said. She could offer him the use of her cabin. She couldn't give him eyes he didn't have.

"I was thinking Jerome could show me."

Rose jerked the trolley forward. On the sound system, an operator droned a licence plate number. Someone's blue Jetta was blocking the ER entrance.

"I could call and let him know I was coming."

She imagined the phone ringing in Armand's kitchen. White counters with white cupboards. When Rose was younger, Maman sometimes sent her to Armand's house with a question about the fields he ploughed or to order another cord of wood. His wife always insisted Rose sit at the table for a glass of milk and a brownie that was chocolatey moist.

Kenny shifted from foot to foot. "What do you think?"

What she thought was no. She wanted nothing to do with that family. But: she had also decided she wanted to let Kenny stay in the cabin. "It's up to you," she said finally.

"I need his phone number."

"I don't have it. We never had a phone to call anyone."

"We can look it up." He'd stopped walking, so she had to stop, too.

"How?" she asked. "You'd need a phone book for Rivière-des-Pins."

"Here." He walked into a visitors' lounge where a woman slept on a plaid sofa with a crocheted afghan draped over her hips and legs. There was a drinks machine and a computer on a table. Kenny sat and began jabbing at the keyboard.

Rose hung back. She didn't know what he was doing.

"What's his last name?" Kenny's two index fingers aimed at the keyboard. When she didn't answer, he peered at her. "Jerome's last name?"

"Villeray."

He poked the letters one by one and a list appeared. "There's no J. Villeray."

"Is there an A? Villeray?"

"Yeah. That's where he lives?" Kenny groped for the roll of hand towel farther along the table and tore off an edge to scribble the number.

Rose had said more than she'd meant to, but Kenny looked so pleased, flushing through his freckles as he shoved the scrap of paper towel in his tunic pocket.

FARA

Fara got off the subway one stop early to walk home through the market. Mounds of chubby tomatoes, tables heaped with corn, green beans, yellow beans, carrots, new potatoes.

At the patisserie she looked for Maddy, but couldn't see her. White-aproned staff bustled with boxes and pointed at loaves with gloved fingers. She asked for a baguette and the diffident young man who served her asked which kind. *"Ordinaire? Bio, tradition-nelle, trente-six heures ...?"*

Fara didn't want to be *ordinaire*, but she guessed each variation cost a bit more.

Weren't the French smart? The baguette fit exactly in her grip and the crust kept it from getting squished. You could stride along, with a baguette wand leading the rhythm of your steps and hips.

She crossed the canal that separated the moneyed from the poor of the city. Maddy's talk was changing how she saw the Pointe. Here, close to the market, the once-upon-a-time fac-tories that lined the canal had been sandblasted and renovated as high-end condos. Maddy said a small one cost six hundred thousand — in the same year that Fara and Frédéric had bought a house in the Pointe for one hundred and fifty. The Pointe was still mostly streets of brick row houses that had been built for the workers who'd dug the canal and supplied the labour for shipping, the factories, and the rail yards — who'd kept the manual side of industry moving. Since then, the industries had been shut down and the head offices moved to Toronto. The Pointe had one of the highest percentages of unemployment in the city. Enter people like herself and Frédéric who were looking to buy a cheap house. The real estate agent had called it revitalization of a crumbling neighbourhood, but as the new residents moved in, what was going to happen to the people who played horseshoes in the park and reclaimed an abandoned toilet for a flower box? Who sat on kitchen chairs outside the *dépanneurs* watching the goings-on in the street?

It had been over a month since Fara and Frédéric had moved into the house, but she still unlocked the door as if play-acting. Did this whole big structure of walls and floors truly belong to them? Her steps in the hallway echoed. They needed more furniture. Their square oak table, which used to be crowded into the kitchen of their apartment — so close to the refrigerator that she could open the door and grab the mayonnaise without getting up from her chair — now stood by itself in the dining room, which would fit a table twice its size. And there was still room for a cabinet for wineglasses, maybe even a side table against the wall.... What else did people put in dining rooms?

When she walked from the hallway, she still veered to the side. The idea of a hanging body didn't spook her as much, but she was still aware it was *there*. She glanced up at the hole she'd puttied, sanded, and varnished. This weekend Eric was coming to install the French doors they'd bought. Frédéric wasn't sure how to build the frame. He'd called a few carpenters and discovered that they made more per hour than he did as the manager of a payroll department. When Eric offered, Frédéric was grateful.

They'd decided that the small room off the dining room would be a guest room — another bed, another dresser, more furniture to buy. But why had Frédéric left the door closed again? She'd told him to leave it open. Why shut up the room? He said he wasn't closing it, but who else was there except for the two of them, huh?

She gave the door a push, but it knocked against something behind it. She hesitated. *Don't be silly.* She looked behind the door and saw it had banged against the door to the closet, which was open. Was Frédéric planning to use it? He could have told her. But why leave the door wide open? *And* close the door to the room again? He could blame the shut door on a draft, but the closet door wouldn't open by itself. Another mystery in the house. Like the odd knocking noise she sometimes heard in the walls. The creep of soft steps at night.

She shook her head. She did *not* believe in ghosts. If Claire's ghost hadn't haunted her, why should this boy's? She might see a hanging body where there had once been a body hanging, but that was her imagination. Not a ghost. She made the distinction.

She slid the baguette onto the counter in the kitchen and stepped out the back door. On the deck lay Maddy's orange cat. He was a fat fur sickle ending in white-tipped paws. His ears swivelled, but he didn't lift his head until she crouched next to him, keeping her hands on her knees. She was allergic to cats.

"Hey," she murmured. "You like it here?" He was so comfortably sprawled. Cat of the manor. She hesitated then pressed a finger along the curve of his spine, furrowing a groove in the thick hair, feeling the nubs of bone beneath. He flicked her a cool, green look. *Is that the best you can do?* Now that she'd touched him, she would have to wash her hands anyhow. She rubbed around his ears and scratched under his chin.

Claire had a cat when they were children. Their mother wouldn't allow it in the house, not even during the winter.

Claire built it a shelter near the back door and salvaged bones and gristle from the table. One day the cat disappeared. Claire had a tantrum, shrieking at their mother that she'd killed it. Their mother slapped Claire so hard that she fell against the corner of a chair and got a black eye. After that, Claire kept the creatures she caught — frogs and snakes, field mice and, once, a turtle — in a box hidden behind the garden shed. Some escaped, some died. She accepted that it was natural. As long as their mother didn't find her pets, Claire felt they were safe. When she left home, she got herself a cat, a small tabby she called Tiger. Fara asked her, Why Tiger? He's not orange. Claire said all cats believed they were tigers.

Before Claire killed herself, when she asked Fara about the key, she also asked if Fara could take Tiger for a few days if she went away. Where would Claire have gone? She had no friends outside the city. But Fara didn't ask. Didn't even wonder. Haven't you got anyone else? she asked. You know I'm allergic.

Later, when she found Claire, she never even thought of the cat. Only afterward, when she called Claire's few friends to tell them Claire was dead, did she hear that Claire had asked each one if they could take Tiger for a few days. Her ex-boyfriend had brought the cat to his mother, who wanted Fara to come get it. Fara was in shock, grieving — and angry at what Claire had done. What she heard about the cat made it sound as if Claire was more concerned about the cat than her own life.

Exactly, Fara thought now. Claire had loved that cat. She'd felt closer to Tiger than she had to her own family. Which said what about their family? And what kind of sister was Fara not to have seen that?

She sighed. No way to change what was done and gone. She'd done her best to pick up the pieces and keep moving.

Jim was purring with a leisurely stop-and-start rhythm. His eyes were half-slit, ignoring the sparrows that hopped across the yard. She smoothed her hand down his head and back. Her eyes were starting to itch. "That's it, buddy."

As she stood, she glanced at the back fence. No one.

Ben looked over his shoulder down the alley. The new people would be off at whatever jobs they did, but in daylight the neighbours could see him at the back gate. Except that people no longer sat on the stoop or looked out the windows the way they used to, keeping an eye on comings and goings. They stayed inside, watching TV. Even old Coady, poking along with his cane, only left his house every few days.

Once Ben shut the gate behind him and was in the backyard, no one could see him, unless the hippie next door looked out her upstairs window. His dad called her the hippie. She was the last of the free-love commune that used to live there. They had all finally left — except for her. Love must have gotten too expensive. He always said that, too.

Ben lifted aside the boards of the deck to crawl under. He was getting better at wiggling through the window. He just had to be careful not to scrape himself on the crusty edge of mortar. In the daytime, with the new people gone, he didn't have to tiptoe around. He could be alone in the house. That was all he wanted — to be able to walk through the rooms. He didn't give a damn about the new people's stuff. He wasn't a thief.

Here in the front room was where he and Xavier had slept on a mattress on the floor. Their dad had said that one day they would get bunk beds, but that never happened. Ben crouched to his knees to look out the window at the gigantic cottonwood tree behind the house across the street. A two-storey building with a great, leafy crown twice as high as the house. Looking out, low down the way he'd used to when he was little, made him feel small again — small, with Xavier curled on the grubby sheets beside him. They always forgot to close the curtains at night and when he woke in the morning, he imagined the branches in the sky had kept watch over him and his brother while they slept.

Ben ignored the sofa that was in the room now. The stereo system on a low set of shelves. He needed to take a leak and walked to the bathroom, which he could have found in his sleep — and had often had to. But this was a strangers' bathroom with a blue shower curtain, and bottles and tubes of lotions stacked on a wicker corner unit. Only when he stood at the toilet and faced the wall did the old sense of the room settle around him ... the memory of Xavier jostling next to him, the arcs of their piss splashing together. Ben tucked himself away, still staring at the bright yellow piss in the bowl. He leaned to flush, then didn't.

In the room they'd always used as a living room, the new people had a table. French doors leaned against the wall. Where did they plan to put French doors?

He smelled fresh paint, but that must be from upstairs. He never went up there. Didn't even want to. Downstairs was where they'd lived. His dad had tenants in the second floor flat up until he and Xavier decided to renovate. Why they wanted to renovate, Ben never knew. Did they plan to sell or get new tenants at a higher rent? Turn the two duplexes into a single house? Here, on the ground floor, they'd smashed through the old plaster walls to rewire and insulate and put up drywall. They'd knocked a big, wide entrance between the hallway and the main room. *Why?* To make it easier for Xavier to hang himself?

The kitchen looked much the same, with the cupboards and counters and sink. The new people's fridge and stove were fancier — brushed steel with black handles. The dishes were done and put away, the counters wiped. Their own kitchen had never been that clean.

Yesterday, before he fell asleep, he'd remembered his dad's secret panel under the corner kitchen cupboard. He slipped his finger into the hole and tugged. The hinged door opened, still full of his dad's keys for locks that no longer existed. Ben dropped the loose jangle of metal in his pocket, and left the door hanging like a dropped jaw.

Fara stood chopping cucumber at the counter. The magazine with the recipe was on the stove, folded open to the page. The phone rang and she wiped her hands on her hips. "*Âllo?*" she asked. There was silence, then a click.

"Same to you," she muttered, turning back to the counter.

The front door opened and she heard Frédéric drop his shoes, then the slap of his flip-flops.

"How goes?" he asked as he came into the kitchen and kissed her.

"I wish you'd flush the toilet when you use it."

"I do."

"Are you telling me I'm dreaming in yellow?"

"Maybe *you* forgot."

"I ..." She pointed the tip of the knife at her chest. "I use toilet paper."

He gave a shrug. "Sorry." He reached for a chunk of cucumber he popped in his mouth.

"Did you know about that?" She lifted her chin at the corner cupboard, where a hinged flap hung open.

He stooped to look under the cupboard, examined the flap and snapped it shut. "How did you find it?"

"It was open."

"Must have come undone."

"How?"

He opened and closed the flap a few times. Each time there was an efficient magnetized click. It didn't make sense that it would just drop.

When the phone rang, Frédéric moved to answer, but she held out her arm, knife still in hand. "Let me. Someone just hung up on me." Into the receiver, she barked, "Hello!"

A man laughed softly. "Someone didn't eat her cornflakes today." The English was smooth — colloquial — but the vowels were tugged tight like elastics. He was a foreigner used to speaking English. "It's me, Georg." *Gay-org*. The way her parents would have said it.

"I don't know any Gay-org."

Again that soft laugh. "Sure you do. Remember ..." He didn't sound at a loss. He wanted to pick the right memory. "My motorcycle? Up in the woods behind your dad's place?"

She'd never called her father Dad. He'd been Papa up until she was ten or eleven, then something had happened — she couldn't remember what — that had made her so angry she'd vowed to call him Father. If they'd noticed, they gave no sign. She'd never called them Mama and Papa again. She'd also never called them Mom and Dad, names that in no way fit who they were. Nor had she ever been on a motorcycle. "You've got the wrong number."

He repeated her number.

"It's still the wrong number. I don't know who you are."

"This is the number your dad gave me."

"I'm going to hang up now."

Frédéric, who'd started to walk out of the kitchen, turned when he heard her tone.

"Your dad and me," the man said quickly, "we both come from Brimberg."

She grimaced at his continued repetition of the ridiculous word, *dad*. "Even if you did, that's got nothing to do with me. I was born here."

"I know you were, sweetie."

"Don't call me that!"

He chuckled. "You liked it before."

"Listen, buddy, I don't know you and I don't care where you came from!"

Frédéric gestured for the phone but she flapped his hand away. Anything to do with her family she would deal with herself.

"Calm down, okay? Your dad told me you got married. I just wanted to say hi for old times' sake. Your dad knows we went out for a couple of rides on my bike. Don't tell me you don't remember — up in the woods by the pond."

The pond was a neglected marshy puddle at the back of her parents' land. Only her parents called it a pond. "I don't —"

"Don't you dare," he cut her off. "Don't give me that I-was-a-virgin-before-I-got-married act. Maybe your husband buys it. I don't. You had your ass in my face, begging me to eat you out."

Fara stared before her, remembering the story Claire had told her about a man on a motorcycle with the engine running. He'd revved it when she came.

Her hand with the phone slid to her breasts, muffling the voice still coming from the receiver. Frédéric watched her with concern. Again he gestured for the phone. "I'll get rid of him."

She shook her head. "He knows Claire." And after a beat, she said, "Knew."

The confident rumble of his voice. The insinuating leer of a question. She'd known Claire was more sexually adventurous than she was. The men she went out with weren't gentle. Sometimes she had bruises on her arms. Once, Fara saw what looked like a ridged soother on Claire's dresser. Curious, she'd reached for it. Claire said, Leave it. It's a butt plug. It puts me in the mood.

Maybe Fara should have listened to Gay-org's stories. Yet more details to add to her memories. But this wasn't how she wanted to remember Claire — this jerk from her father's village reminiscing about how much fun Claire was.

The voice against her breasts had stopped and she lifted the phone to her ear again. "When you called my father, who did you ask for?"

"You," he said as if she were being thick.

"I'm asking what you said. Exactly."

"I told him how everyone back home was doing. You know, the village news. Then I asked about you. He said you were in Montreal and you were married. I thought maybe you —"

"No. *Who* did you ask for?"

"I told you!"

"You still haven't said my name."

"Your name?" He blew into the phone. "I don't remember, okay? So what? You don't even remember *me*! And that was the best tail that bike ever saw, and believe me, I put miles on it. Rode out to Prince Rupert and down to Oregon. You were the best."

All these years, Claire was dead and the myth of her sexual appetite had lived on in his imagination. She wondered if Claire would have been pleased. "Not me," she said slowly. "My sister."

A beat. Then a laugh exploded. "No wonder you don't remember me! Because your sister, there's no way she forgot me. We really hit it off."

Had her father even suspected that this Gay-org was looking for Claire — or had he forgotten that he'd once had two daughters?

"So, yeah, how about you give me her number?"

"She's not in Montreal."

"Where is she?"

"You'll have to call my father. Ask him for his other daughter's number." It was cruel, but he deserved it after making her hear how Claire had begged this Gay-org to ... whatever. Let her father tell his own lies.

"What's her name again?"

Fara hung up. Stared hard at the phone, daring him to call back. When nothing happened, she stepped forward into Frédéric's arms and leaned against him.

His hand found hers and released the knife she still gripped and set it on the counter. "He didn't know she was dead?"

"He's from Germany." Her parents' families in Germany hadn't been told Claire was dead. Suicide was a sin and a shame visited by God as punishment. Her parents explained Claire's ongoing absence by saying that she'd moved to Australia to work. Fara had protested. The very least her parents could do was admit Claire was dead. It was ghoulish to pretend she was working in Australia! Her mother said Fara didn't understand how the people back home would judge them. Sometimes Fara wondered if that was the bottom line for her parents: not losing Claire, but how that loss reflected on them.

Past Frédéric's shoulder Fara saw the French doors leaning against the wall in the dining room. Doors made of wood and glass that would open when you wanted to step through them and otherwise be closed. A solid barrier, not this gauze between life and death and unwanted memories.

Two days in a row felt risky, but next week Ben worked the day shift and wouldn't be able to get into the house. He reminded himself to walk slowly down his old street. Just another guy on his way to the *dépanneur*. He wasn't doing anything wrong. He didn't take anything. He only wanted to get into the house. In the house he could remember Xavier — the shy, snickering boy he'd grown up with, not the crazy daredevil he'd become.

At the fence Ben stood close to the shelter of the overhanging vines, key in hand, glancing quickly behind him to make sure he was alone. The lock was rusty, and he had to jiggle the key. Then he heard the oncoming crunch of gravel — too fast for anyone walking — but he took the chance that he could slip through the gate unnoticed.

"Hey! What are you doing? Ben!"

The bicycle braked hard, so close to him that the front tire nearly pushed him through the gate. He was face to face with the hippie, with her wild frizz of hair poking from under her helmet, her legs braced as if to charge him.

"What are you doing?" Her voice had dropped to an insistent whisper. "I'm sorry your dad sold the house, Ben. I'm *sorry*. But you can't go in there anymore. It's illegal. If they find out, you'll get arrested."

His lips twitched to retort, but no sound came out. He didn't give a shit about her being sorry, but the word *illegal* made him bristle. Did she mean to call the police? Her face was concerned like a teacher's or a social worker's — useless concern that never made anything happen. He'd seen enough of that look when he was a kid.

"Why do you even want to go in there? What are you doing?"

He had to scrape through the vines to sidle past her tire. He hated that confidential, wheedling tone people used. Face rigid, he strode off down the alley.

"Ben!" she called after him.

Great. Now anyone with half an ear would know he was there.

"Ben!" Same as the day he'd found Xavier. Carried him outside, dead in his arms, head an inhuman colour, body limp and lolling — and all the while she wouldn't stop screeching on the other side of the fence. *Ben! Ben!*

He spat his disgust onto the pavement.

Eric had come to install the French doors that morning. When Fara left the house, he was setting up a table saw in the dining room. The table and chairs had been pushed against the wall and covered with drop cloths. Frédéric was lugging in the lumber Eric had brought in his truck. When Fara called bye, both men looked surprised she was still there at all.

She was meeting Karin downtown. Karin couldn't often get away now that she and Tom had two children. The first, Julia, had been easy enough to pop into a stroller. But Julia, who was now an ingenious three-year-old with Houdini powers, *plus* the imperious Charlie, who believed anything within reach was a javelin to be hurled, were impossible. Fara thought Tom should have been able to manage by himself for a day, since Karin spent each day of the week with the volatile duo, but Tom insisted on his mother for backup. Grandma duly fetched and ensconced for the day, Karin had been set free. Even so, she checked her cellphone constantly. Fara hardly recognized her friend, who used to know the doormen of the dance clubs along Saint-Laurent by first name, in this woman who spilled a Winnie-the-Pooh diaper and a Ziploc bag of wipes from her purse while groping for her wallet.

Fara shouldn't be buying clothes — and had told Frédéric she wouldn't — but what a treat simply to walk into stores that didn't sell light fixtures, tools, paint, and faucets. Had she even been anywhere except a hardware store since they'd bought the house?

Karin fingered a tunic. "What do you think?" She was still plump from pregnancy and favoured tops that covered her hips.

Fara knew that the thigh-length tunics, which were the fashion this season, wouldn't even cover her crotch. But she let herself be tempted by the shirred and crisp fabrics, the insistent beat of the look-cool, feel-good music. She and Karin gathered an armful of clothes and joined the lineup for the change rooms.

Her first misgiving was the boxy little cubicle that made her feel like a football player in a bra. Second, the stark light in the cubicle. No hiding any bulges. Third, the way the clothes that draped so elegantly on the hanger pulled awry on her. She fiddled with straps and tiny buttons. What kind of body did you need for clothes like these to fit?

"How's it going?" Karin called from the next cubicle. And when Fara didn't answer, "Fara?"

"It's not." Fara smirked at a neckline that gaped across her bra. "Yeah ... I guess I'm not this size anymore."

Karin kept only one of the many tops she'd taken into the change room. When she saw the long lineup of women waiting to pay, she groaned.

"It's okay," Fara said. "I don't mind waiting."

"Nah." Karin slung the top over the closest rack. "I don't really love it. I'm not into this anymore."

"Me neither," Fara admitted. "At least not today."

"I buy clothes for the kids."

"I buy boxes of screws."

Karin slid her hand in her purse to check her cellphone. That neither Tom nor Grandma had called seemed to bother her more than if they had.

Fara strode down the hill, feeling how she was leaving the manic bustle of the city, the urgent grumble of voices and music, the dense crawl of traffic. As she waited for a light to change, she looked back at downtown — which, from this perspective, was uptown: the jut of skyscrapers stacked close around the mountain with its trees and mansions on the slopes. She was heading down, down, down ... to where the castle serfs lived.

She'd never before walked from downtown to the Pointe but guessed that eventually she would reach the canal. She oriented herself by the Farine Five Roses sign in the sky.

She wondered how Frédéric was managing with Eric. When Eric had arrived that morning he'd announced that they had to be finished by suppertime because he'd dropped Chantal and the boys at her sister's. It was already late afternoon.

She found Eric standing with his hands on his hips, scowling at the frame he was building between the hallway and the dining room. Frédéric mimicked his pose, though his expression was more mystified than upset. The opening was too large for the French doors. Eric had fit panels of glass along the top and to one side.

"Is something wrong?" Fara asked. "It looks great."

"Against building code," Eric muttered.

"Why —" Fara began, but Frédéric shot her a warning look. Right. Let Mr. OCD fantasize about a building inspector barging into their house to slap them with a fine.

She backed away and went upstairs to get her novel from the night table. She'd finished painting the new bedroom and had hoped that Frédéric would still have time to move the bed today. Probably not.

In the living room, she dropped onto the sofa and stretched her legs. It felt good to come home and relax. She caught herself thinking the word *home*. It was true, every day the house felt more and more like home.

She hadn't opened her book yet, still listening to the men. "Hold it steady," Eric said, followed by the grinding of the drill.

Would she be allowed to walk through to the kitchen to make herself a cup of tea? Eric was on the ladder. Frédéric stood waiting for instructions. "Does anyone want tea?" she asked.

"Beer," Frédéric said.

"Yeah," said Eric.

Sawdust had drifted from the table saw across the floor. Fara debated sweeping the floor, but it would only have to be swept again later. She grabbed two bottles of beer from the refrigerator and set them on the drop sheet on the table.

"Thanks." Frédéric winked and gave her a quick grin. What a trooper. Still able to smile after a day of playing underling, admirer, and audience to Eric.

Fara lay on her side in bed, waiting for Frédéric. He'd been so long, she wondered if he'd fallen asleep, upright under the shower.

Eric had fussed over the French doors well into the evening, even though Chantal called twice to remind him that her sister had made supper. He'd told her he was still working and to go ahead and eat. After the second call, he turned off his phone.

At seven, Fara decided to order a pizza. She asked the men what kind they wanted. Eric, stooped over one of the doors, sweeping the planer with exact, smooth strokes, didn't answer. Yet he ate a few slices when it came — still standing, a level hanging from one hand. He only finally packed up his tools and left at nine-thirty. The doors closed perfectly. They made the dining room look elegant. The hallway too. Imagine once she'd stained and varnished them.

Only now, as she lay in bed, did she realize that she'd admired the doors, leaning back on her heels in the hallway to take them in, and not once had she thought of the hanging body.

She heard the bathroom door open and the floor creak with Frédéric's slow steps. He shuffled into the bedroom. "Oof." He sat heavily on the bed, swung one leg up, then the other, and fell back on his pillow. "Eric doesn't stop," he groaned.

"But you got it done." She nestled close. "I think it's worked too — the doors."

"Good." But he was already falling asleep and might not have heard.

"Tomorrow you'll move the bed into the back room?"

"Sure ..."

She leaned over to kiss him and lay back on her pillow.

Over lunch today, Karin had said that now that they owned a house, they would have a baby. Fara let her talk. People who had kids didn't understand that you simply might not want to. She and Frédéric had agreed on no children before they'd married. Why would a house change that?

She glanced around the large room, wondering what they would do with it once they moved the bed. It used to be a bedroom. Frédéric had had to drag out a futon and twisted debris of blankets, and break apart a platform base built of plywood and painted black. It must have been the boy's. Maybe this had been his bedroom all his life. Maybe when he was little, he'd slept here with his brother.

She and Claire had shared a room up until Fara had left home. Two single beds pushed into opposite corners. The closet was divided with a line of masking tape Fara had stuck to the floor. Her shoes and Claire's shoes. Claire's clothes and her clothes. Of the six drawers in the dresser, three were hers, three Claire's. Once, Fara had walked in when Claire was changing her sheets and had thrown her pillow and comforter on Fara's bed. Galvanized with rage at the trespass, Fara had whipped Claire's bedding to the floor.

In her body she could still feel how angry she'd been. The righteous stiffness in her arms. She closed her eyes, wishing she didn't remember so clearly, turned in bed, and curled against Frédéric, pressing her forehead to his shoulder.

She knew she'd been a terrible sister to Claire. But what else would she have learned growing up in that family? They were all terrible to each other. A younger sister wasn't a companion but a burden Fara hadn't asked for. *Where's your sister? What is she doing? Was macht sie?* The eldest was supposed to watch out. No one ever spoke of sharing or love or kindness. Obedience was the expectation, punishment the threat. Fara knew her parents blamed her for Claire's suicide. She was supposed to have realized Claire was going to do something stupid. *Didn't she live close by in the city?*

For years, too, Fara had blamed herself. It had taken her that many years again to understand that the longing to die was irrational. Sure, she could imagine circumstances that might lead a person to consider suicide — the wickedness of others, desperate loneliness, emotional starvation, mental health, altered consciousness, fear of the future, even chance. But she would never have an answer for that final, definitive why. There was no explanation for a wish that was stronger than the instinct to draw breath.

And yet, Claire and this boy had killed themselves. That was the only ugly yet knowable fact. Fara had come to believe that the only meaningful gesture those left behind could make was to acknowledge that, not make excuses or pretend it hadn't happened. She wished she could tell this boy's brother that and save him years of asking himself a question that had no answer.

Ben pointed a pistol finger at the waitress to signal for another bottle. On the TV at the head of the room, men in bulked-out uniforms trotted across hyper-green turf. Before the TV was installed, there used to be a moose head. Ben remembered the head from when he used to dart into the murk of the tavern to get his dad. Years had passed, but the men scattered across the room at the tables still sat in the same poses. Backs stooped, legs splayed, arms on puppet strings hooked to boozer heaven. Lift the bottle to the mouth. Glug. Lower it to the table. Lift again. Short, stubby brown bottles in his dad's day. Long necks came later. Even skinny men were deadweights glued to the seats of their chairs.

Ben had hated when his dad sat too near the moose head. It was an enormous hulk, dry with dust and dead flies, scraped patches on its neck, its blunt snout withered, eyes dead glass. Only the great, branching rack of its antlers belonged to a fairy-tale about a moose roaming the forests. Here in the tavern, the only story was the owner's. He bragged about how he'd killed the moose with one clean shot, gutted it in the woods, and needed four men to drag it to the trailer. He was a backwoods hero in his own eyes — but too cheap to have the head stuffed properly. Kids used to dare each other to sneak inside the tavern and sling their toques onto the antlers. If the bartender caught you, he shoved you out the door with his boot. What was his name? *Gros* ... *Gros* something. Thickets of hair bushed out his ears and up the neck of his shirt. He had arms like shaggy clubs, with the sleeves always rolled up. The men liked the show of a boy being booted across the tavern, so they always gave a holler to alert him.

Ben always had to slink in alone to get their dad. Xavier stayed by the door, too afraid of the bartender, the grizzled moose head, the sullen men at the tables — but just as frightened of the older boys who might saunter along the street. So he crept in after Ben and hid by the door. Tagalong kid brother. He hadn't started his crazy stunts yet.

Ben tilted the bottle to his mouth and downed the last swallow. The waitress, walking by, scooped the empty from the table. He nodded. How many had he had already? Four or five? Who was counting?

He'd waited for a couple of days to see if the cops were going to bang on his door to ask why he was stealing into other people's backyards. Backyards weren't B and E, were they? Damn lucky he was that he didn't get caught inside the house. Whatever the story with that hippie lady, she didn't seem to have called the cops. He'd still better not go back to the house.

He glanced at the door that had swung wide on shrill laughter and had to quell his gut instinct to slouch lower in his chair. What in hell was Anouk doing here? She and her friend were scanning the men at the tables, wondering whom to bless with their giddy presence — who was flush enough to pay for their rum and Cokes.

"Ben!" Anouk sashayed to his table. Touched a turquoise fingernail to the back of a chair. "You don't even say hello anymore?"

"You just walked in," he managed. His lips were dry. Her flowery perfume held the scent of déjà vu. That hazy feeling of knowing this had happened before, but not what would happen next. The coy mounds of her breasts framed by a scalloped neckline.

Anouk pursed her lipstick mouth. "Grump." She swung her tight hips between tables and sucked dimples at Henri, who'd moved to Ville Émard but still worked on houses in the Pointe. Windows, doors, cement, plumbing. People had to call someone when their basement pipe started pissing puddles and they couldn't afford anyone listed in the Yellow Pages.

Anouk's friend joined her at Henri's table. Henri was a moron, hoisting himself up in his chair, trying to puff out pecs he didn't have. So what, he had two girls at his table? Every other man in the tavern knew what that meant: Henri would go home that night with an empty wallet.

Still. To have that bubbly laughter in his face. To breathe that perfume. Her smooth arm next to his on the table. The energy in her slim, agile body. Lots about Anouk had bothered Ben when they'd lived together, but he'd always loved how he could gather her close inside his arms.

He scowled at his beer and lifted it for a swallow. Down the long cannon neck of the bottle he saw that Anouk was watching him. Grinning at Henri, but with her eyes on Ben.

MADDY

Maddy shuffled upstairs, yawning. Rain drummed on the skylight in the hallway. She clicked on her bedroom lamp, unzipped her shorts, and tossed them with her foot onto the settee that was scattered with clothes she'd worn yesterday and the day before. An ex-boyfriend, Winston, had given her the settee. He'd said the antique carved legs and satin upholstery, though faded, would look good in her house. She'd been pleased, believing it was a sign he was going to leave his wife and wanted to move in. Only later did she discover his wife was redecorating and had told him to cart the settee to the dump. Oh boy. What was the message there? But by then, she'd grown used to dropping her clothes onto the settee, which *was* a handsome piece of furniture. Why blame it for Winston's sloppy disregard?

She yawned again, so hard that tears squeezed out. Why had she stayed up past midnight to watch such a meandering, pointless movie? The characters were so pathetic. No backbone, no sense of imperative. They weren't even prompted by the basic selfishness that kept an animal alive.

At least her excuse was that she'd been young, with no idea what to do and no help from her parents. They'd shouted at her to get help from the baby's father. She hadn't even known what that meant until the school nurse explained. Even then, what the school nurse explained about boys and penises had happened months before. Neil and his family had already moved away. It didn't make sense to think of him as *the father* — any more than that she was *the mother*.

She'd thought the worst that had happened was that she'd embarrassed herself when she'd followed Tonya, the new girl, home after school. Tonya had a deep voice — like someone who should sing in the church choir, but on the boys' side. Tonya walked next to her, brushing against her arm, showing her the coral lipstick she kept in her jacket pocket. She said Maddy could try it, but Maddy was afraid people watching from the windows of the houses would see.

Tonya said to come in and see if anyone was home. Her older brother was watching TV with a friend. Her brother had red hair. He said his name was Neil. He looked right at Maddy the way the boys at school never did. Up and down, smiling. He said, How about a game of cards. Maddy played euchre at lunchtime at school. She liked cards.

In the kitchen Neil rummaged under the sink until he hooked a bottle. He lined up four Mickey Mouse glasses and poured. Only a bit, he said, and added ginger ale. Maddy's father sometimes let her have a swallow of beer. It made her feel tipsy. When you were tipsy, it was easier to laugh and feel comfortable.

But no one laughed as they sipped their drinks. Mickey Mouse glasses in hand, they trooped downstairs to the cellar, where a bulb was screwed into a fixture that hung from wires. The floor was part concrete, part dirt, with an area covered with sheets of warped plywood. Tonya shook out a blanket so it settled on the wobbly squares. Everyone sat across from each other like they were at a table. The air was damp with the smell of earth and spiders. A mushroomy stink. It wasn't nice down here, but maybe it was the only place they were allowed to play.

The boys said strip poker. Maddy didn't know that game. No sweat, Neil said. We'll show you. Maddy expected Tonya to explain because Tonya had invited her, but Neil hitched himself closer. Show me what you've got, he said, which made the other boy laugh. I know what she's got, he said. Shut up, Neil said. Maddy liked that he helped her and told the other boy to shut up.

Maddy giggled when they started playing for real and the other boy lost and had to take off a sock, but no one else laughed. Neil gathered up the cards, shuffled, and dealt again. No one spoke. The light bulb shone on their hair, casting their mouths and eyes in shadow.

Maddy lost the second hand. She followed the boy's lead and slipped off a sock, flattening it on the blanket beside her. Then she lost again. Next sock.

And again. What now? Did they really mean she had to take something else off? She only had her blouse and her skirt. If she took them off, the others would see her underpants or her bra. In her deep voice, Tonya said, That's why it's called strip poker.

Maddy tried to remember what underpants she was wearing. Any pair had to be nicer than her church-rummage-sale bra that didn't fit. She unzipped her skirt, pulled it off, and sat with her legs tucked close, her blouse yanked low.

Then Tonya lost, but instead of pulling off a sock, she peeled off her blouse. She sat across from them, her back straight as a model's, in a pink bra. You can take off what you want, she told Maddy. I keep my socks for last.

For last? How far were they going? It wasn't a question Maddy could ask. Without understanding, she'd stumbled from the schoolyard into an adult world. A game with risks. Liquor in their glasses. She felt nervous, but bold, too. Ready. The expectant silence of the others pressed against her. She thought of a trick now — like Tonya's. If she lost again, she wasn't going to take off her blouse, but her bra underneath. The bra with the cups too big for her breasts.

Neil lost a few times and was down to his Y-fronts. Maddy didn't want to look, but then she peeked and had to look again.

He had something shoved inside his underpants, poking out the cotton. He held his cards as if unaware. It couldn't have been comfortable, though he sat cross-legged as if at any other game — as matter-of-fact as his sister in her pink bra.

The other boy snickered. *She wants it. She keeps looking.*

Maddy blushed. Didn't they all notice? She kept trying not to look, but across the edge of her cards, she could see the bulge in his green Y-fronts.

She lost and — calmly, she thought, proud of herself — reached under the back of her blouse, unhooked her bra, and slid the straps out her sleeves and over her hands.

Hey, Neil said.

She took something off, Tonya said. That's how she wants to play.

Maddy felt pleased she was getting the hang of the game. Pleased, too, that she'd bunched her faded and ugly bra under her knee so no one could see it.

Tonya lost the next hand. With a sly smile she daintily tugged off a sock. She sat poised, her pleated skirt smoothed to her knees, her breasts in her pretty bra perked on her chest.

Maddy tried to copy how she sat, angling her back and her hips.

Neil's friend had shuffled and dealt. Maddy picked up her cards. She had no pairs. Her highest card was a six. Was she going to sit before them with her bottom or her top naked? That was the choice. She could feel how, under her blouse, her nipples were soft, blind eyes butted against her shirt.

Maddy shuddered in bed, wide awake now. Why hadn't she realized she could have stood up, put on the clothes she'd taken off, and left that house? She curled on her side and tucked the sheet closer to her cheek with her fist. She'd never in her life — ever — played cards again.

Maddy and Yushi cycled side by side along the path above the marshy shoreline of the river. A wispy cloud cover dulled the gleam of light on the water. Poplars rippled leafy coins in the breeze.

"This is great," Yushi said. "I had no idea you could get so close to the water."

"A lot of people don't." Urban fact #6: people tended to stick to their own hoods.

Their knees — Maddy's tanned from a summer of cycling, Yushi's more slender — pumped up and down in tandem. They'd cycled as far as the marina and were on their way back to Maddy's for another cooking lesson.

"It doesn't help," Maddy went on, "that there's a highway between the city and down here. Makes you wonder if it's deliberate or just dumb city planning. The highway's like a mini Berlin Wall between the beautiful people and the grubby hoi polloi." She heard herself and stopped. A concrete line of non-stop traffic like the Berlin Wall was one of Brian's metaphors. He'd always thought city hall councillors sat around a table plotting how to further isolate the already disadvantaged southwest sector. With luck, the old rotten houses would slide into the river and disappear.

"That could be okay," Yushi said. "I think I'd like to be so close to the city but separate from it, too."

"Nothing's stopping you. You can move to the Pointe any time. Then you wouldn't have to cycle all the way down from the Plateau to get to work." She'd said it lightly — half a joke, half the logical follow-up to Yushi's comment — but as she said it, she thought, yeah, it was a good idea. Yushi *could* move to the Pointe.

Yushi had to drop back now that they were leaving the river path to cycle along Wellington. Under the overpass, past the factory that recycled glass, past the park with its great, baronial poplars. Maddy waved an arm at the trees so Yushi would look, then wished she hadn't because there stood a man, leaning against a tree trunk for balance, bobbing with the violence of his coughing as he horked great gobs of phlegm.

They turned into the alley, getting a view onto the back sides of houses. Some sagged like faces without teeth — the mortar between the century-old bricks crumbling. Weeds thrived around abandoned, sun-bleached toys and boards left to rot. Here and there, new people like Fara and Frédéric were trying to revamp their scrap of ground by installing a deck or planting a garden.

"It's so green," Yushi said.

"This all used to be swampland. The water table is still pretty high."

Maddy coasted to a stop at her gate. She felt a little guilty — but only a little — to have asked Yushi come to her house for the next cooking lesson. She'd said that her kitchen was larger, which was true. Also true was that she hadn't felt comfortable with Rose when they'd had supper at the apartment. Rose seemed not to know that she could pretend to be listening, even if she had nothing to say. Without a word she'd dabbed pieces of buss-up-shut through the chickpea stew on her plate. Maddy couldn't recall the name of the stew, but she remembered the fanciful burst-up shirt name for the roti. And *aloo*. She remembered the word but not what it meant. Eggplant, chickpea, or potato?

Maddy had bought all the ingredients Yushi had told her they would need. Flour and eggs, baking powder and yeast, turmeric. She'd set out steel cooking bowls and put the new wok on the stove.

Yushi had Maddy slice green onion while she minced garlic. Chopped green chilies, parsley, and coriander were already dotted in separate heaps around the rim of a dinner plate. Yushi's mother's system.

"Okay." Yushi rinsed her hands and lifted the wok. "Is this brand new?"

"You said you needed a wok."

"You didn't have one?" An incredulous look.

Yushi twisted her silver bangle off her wrist and dropped it on the table behind her. She shovelled scoops of flour into the largest bowl and added a spoonful of baking powder.

"How much of which?" Maddy asked, though she could see Yushi hadn't measured.

Yushi didn't answer, not even to squint her eyes at her. She stirred the flour and baking powder with her hand then doused them with some water from the bowl she had ready.

"Did you mean what you said about living in the Pointe?" Maddy asked.

"That it would be a good place? Sure, why not? You're comfortable, aren't you? You've got this big house."

"That's what I was thinking. I'm going to be looking for a tenant. And it would be so much easier for you to get to work."

"You mean for me to live here?" Yushi shook her head slightly. "I've got Rose."

"What about Rose?"

Yushi shrugged but didn't explain. She had both hands in the dough now and nodded at the bowl of water. "Throw it."

Throw it?

"*T'row it*," Yushi said again, her intonation more musical.

Maddy dribbled water across the dough Yushi kept punching and squeezing.

"More. Okay. Bust the eggs now. *Swizzle 'em to take de skin off.*" She smiled but looked sad. "My mum always said that. *Bus' de eggs an' swizzle 'em.*"

Maddy cracked the eggs into a bowl.

"I always think that," Yushi said quietly, "when I'm beating yolks to make mousse or *crème pâtissière.*"

Maddy showed her the eggs she'd *swizzled*. She would think that too now, whenever she used a whisk.

"*T'row it.*"

Maddy scraped the eggs onto the dough Yushi was still squishing with her hands. It was thinner than roti dough, more a thick batter.

"Yeast."

Maddy sprinkled some yeast.

"More. Where's the cod?" Yushi looked along the counter.

"In the fridge." Maddy went to get the bowl. Yushi had told her to buy salt cod, soak it, and drain it for one whole day as often as she remembered. Then she had to squeeze the water out and shred the fish with her fingers.

"Add it," Yushi said.

"You don't want me to throw it?"

Yushi frowned. "Why would you throw cod?"

Perhaps only liquid got thrown.

Yushi folded the cod into the batter with her hand. She'd told Maddy she was going to fry it in the wok to eat with the tamarind chutney she'd brought in a jar. Cod fritters, Maddy thought. She'd forgotten the Trinidadian name Yushi had told her.

The kitchen smelled of fish and Maddy kept expecting Jim at the screen door. He could smell fish from beyond the gate in the alley. Fish always called him home — the fish *she* ate, not the adulterated by-product served up as cat food. Jim assumed she would share her fish with him as he shared his mice with her. Quid pro quo.

"That." Yushi lifted her chin at the plate of chopped herbs.

"How much?"

"All of it."

Maddy scraped the fragrant mounds of greenery and garlic over the batter. She forbore asking why they'd kept the mounds separate only to mix them together.

"Now turmeric."

"How much?"

"You always ask how much. Don't you have a gut feeling?"

"For something I've never even eaten? No."

Yushi sniffed. "That's no excuse. You should still have a sense. I'm not Viennese but before I ever baked a hazelnut torte, I knew how the batter should turn out from reading the ingredients."

"That's why you should be working in a kitchen, not boxing pastries and putting up with Petitpois."

Yesterday Yushi had been waiting to serve a woman who kept asking her friend which of the crème fraîche, mousse, whipped cream, and chocolate desserts she thought had the fewest calories. Yushi, head lowered, had muttered, Buy an apple. The woman hadn't heard, but Régis, working next to Yushi, tittered and stage-whispered, Did you say buy an apple? This time the woman heard. Régis cleared himself by protesting that he'd only repeated Yushi's words. He was Pettypoo's favourite. Cécile called him her yappy French mutt. Yushi had been scolded and warned yet again about her *comportement.*

Yushi scraped batter off her hands. "Cover this with a towel. We let it sit till it's risen. Then —" She nodded at the stove.

Cod fritters, tamarind chutney, cold beer.

Maddy turned on the outdoor light to make sure nothing had been left on the deck. Racoons and skunks nosed along the alley at night. She didn't want any beasties to get the impression her backyard was a place to find snacks.

She'd said she would clean up the kitchen and had sent Yushi home, since it would take her an hour to cycle up to the Plateau. Maddy hadn't said what she itched to mention again — that if Yushi lived closer, for example, upstairs, then she wouldn't have to cycle anywhere.

Maddy had tumbled some of the leftover fritters into a plastic container for Yushi to take home to Rose. Funny, their relationship — whatever it was. She'd wondered if they might be lovers, except then Yushi had said she thought Rose had a boyfriend at the hospital where she worked. The other day, when Rose stopped by the patisserie, Yushi had slipped her a bag. If Petitpois had seen, Yushi would have been fired on the spot. Why take such a risk? Sure, the staff were allowed to help themselves from the basket of damaged goods — with the strict understanding that only the pastry chefs would decide what was damaged and that the damaged pastries were to be consumed on the premises. *No* doggy bags.

Maddy wiped down the stove as the dishes soaked in hot, soapy water. Why did Yushi feel so responsible for Rose? Maddy had asked if they'd known each other before they'd become roommates but they hadn't. Maddy clicked her tongue, impatient with herself. How could she feel jealous of a social misfit like Rose?

ROSE

Rose couldn't weave properly with Leo on the bench beside her, blocking the movement of her hand and distracting her with his nearness, but he'd wanted to watch close up and she was pleased he was so interested. He leaned forward, peering at how the slits in the reed kept the threads evenly spaced. She'd explained how the pattern was controlled by the heddles. His hair hung forward, the straggly ends grazing the cloth.

Two days ago, when they were walking and had stopped to lean on the railing by the canal, he'd leaned forward and kissed her. She wished she could feel the soft pressure of his lips on hers again. The melting, electrifying fizz along her skin. When he finally pulled his head back to look at her, she did what she'd wanted to do since the first time she'd seen him. She reached up and squeezed a loc. It felt like uncarded wool.

"Watch out," she said now as she pulled the beater forward, "or I'll snag your hair."

"You'd like that, wouldn't you?"

"Mmm," she mused. "It would make a nice bumpy bit." She traced a finger across the cloth, showing where.

"Is that the nicest you can say, a *bumpy bit*?" He sounded

offended, but he was smiling, his glance lingering on her ears, where she still wore Yushi's gold earrings.

Rose tapped the shuttle across with one hand and reached to grasp it with the other when Leo's hand cupped hers. He took the shuttle from her fingers and smoothed them open. "Such smart hands," he murmured. He kissed each finger.

The gentleness of touch was new to her. His lips on her eyelids. Her hand on his chest. Both were still careful of each other, fingers exploring the edges of clothes, mouths soft.

She marvelled at how he paced the slow unfolding of desire. Each caress along her arm tingled. His warm breath on her neck. The tip of his tongue.

She'd thought she'd known desire with Armand, but it was only the ravage of his appetite. After the first few times, when he'd led her deeper into the forest to the woodpile and hesitated, not knowing if she would bolt when he showed her what he wanted, their rendezvous were matter-of-fact and rapid. He unzipped his fly as soon as he saw her between the trees. He sat on the chopping stump so she could kneel between his legs. He'd already spread the blanket — his one concession to nicety — on the ground. His breath grew quicker as she kneeled, until he gripped her shoulder. Then she stood, shucked her pants, and lay on the blanket. The rest of her body or undressing didn't matter. She'd thought he would want to see her breasts because of how he used to watch her through the window. When she understood he didn't — her breasts were too small, still growing — she felt embarrassed and kept them covered. He only wanted her mouth and the hole between her legs. Before he pushed into her, he unrolled a rubber on his *sexe* so they wouldn't make a baby. Rose couldn't remember how she knew about rubbers stopping babies, but she did. When he finished, he folded the blanket and pushed it high under the eaves of the lean-to where he piled the cut logs.

Now, remembering, she wondered why she'd simply obeyed
him the first time in the forest when he nudged her head to his
crotch and said, *Ta bouche*. Your mouth. She didn't protest or
question his commands. She didn't even find what he wanted
strange — no stranger than anything else people did or expected.

She soon guessed that what she did with Armand was what
the other kids at school wanted to do with each other. She felt
proud that she was doing it already — and with a grown-up.
She was doing it for real. She knew Maman could never find out.
Armand's wife or the people in the community, either. When
Armand saw her in Rivière-des-Pins, he acted as if he didn't
know her. The meetings at the woodpile were secret. Everyone
had secrets. Maman, too.

As a fourteen-year-old, having a secret so important had fed
the pulse of her thoughts and all her imaginings. She ached
when a few days passed and she hadn't gotten a signal to come
to the woodpile. She needed Armand to need what she gave
him. She thought about when she would be older and Armand
could marry her. His wife would be dead and she, Rose, would
live in the farmhouse.

Even when it all stopped and Armand never spoke to her
again, she didn't question the rightness or wrongness of the
longing she still felt for him. She believed it was love, and didn't
everyone set a high value on love?

But if that had been love, then what was this feeling she had
with Leo? She leaned against him and felt embraced. As they
walked along, she snaked her arm around his waist and tucked
her hand in his back pocket. Felt the rhythm of their hips walking together. Leo didn't make her feel desperate, but happy.

Rose was wheeling her trolley around a cluster of blood-pressure
pumps when she noticed an elderly visitor creeping along the
wall ahead of her. The woman seemed to know where she

wanted to go but couldn't make herself get there. The silky folds of her dress drooped off her scrawny frame. Her swollen feet were crammed into low-heeled pumps. She clenched a white handbag.

Her steps tottered, then she swayed. Her handbag dropped. Rose sprang forward to catch her in the cradle of her arms, her legs and back braced to keep the woman off the floor. Stick bones inside a slippery dress, the skeletal grimace of dentures in a papery face.

Burly arms slipped under Rose's. "Let her drop, let her drop. Let go!"

Rose heard but didn't move.

"It's okay, let go! I've got her!"

Rose slid her arms away and watched the orderly lower the woman to the floor. Steps pounded from every direction. Rose's cart was shoved aside as a nurse came running with an emergency cart stacked with equipment. An oxygen mask was strapped to the woman's face, a blood-pressure cuff wrapped around her skinny arm. Sharp voices called, *"Madame! Madame!"* Hands probed her neck and yanked wide her eyelids. Nobody straightened the indecent splay of her legs. Rose wanted to, but she stood outside the circle of backs and arms in lab coats. The bodice of her dress had been ripped wide to expose the woman's flattened brassiere.

Arms jabbed under the woman's limp body to lift her to the stretcher an orderly had careened down the hallway. Tubing trailed from the oxygen mask, the blood-pressure cuff, a machine on her finger. A nurse loped off, shouting, "I'll get the elevator!"

Where were they taking her? Rose wanted to follow but couldn't abandon her tube feeding. She stepped in front of a doctor who'd hung back to read a message on his phone. "Where are they taking her?"

He glanced at her hospital uniform and said, "Resus. ER."

"Will she be okay?"

"Are you a family member?"

Rose shook her head.

He shrugged. "Don't know yet."

She wanted to clutch his lab coat and insist on a halfway intelligible answer. He must have some idea! He was a doctor! But she watched him walk away, feeling that she hadn't acted quickly enough either. She should have rushed forward when she saw how the woman's steps wavered. Made her sit and called for help.

The handle of the trolley felt solid after the tumbling collapse of the woman's frail limbs. She had to glance at the room numbers to remind herself where she was. Seven South. She blinked at the list on her clipboard as she reached the nursing station.

An orderly, a short man with a broad, smiling face, said, "You caught her, right? You're Kenny's friend."

She couldn't recall having seen him before. He was still talking. "Most people are too scared to get involved. Not my job, they say."

He was the kind of man who would talk whether she was listening or not. She read down her list. Two Styrofoam containers and three bags of cans. She pushed her cart to the kitchen.

When she returned, the orderly was telling the unit coordinator and the nurses how Rose had saved the woman from cracking her head on the floor. He pointed at Rose. Flustered, she kept steering her cart past the nursing station.

The unit coordinator waved. "I didn't sign."

Rose walked back with her clipboard.

"You're all in a flap, eh?" The coordinator, an older woman with glasses, laid her arm across the clipboard.

Rose didn't know what she meant by a flap. "I hope she's all right."

The coordinator pursed dry lips. "What's all right at that age? Every day she comes to see her husband, but he doesn't know who she is anymore." She reached to answer the phone and Rose retrieved her clipboard.

Pushing her trolley to the next nursing station, Rose thought of how the woman had worn a pretty dress with white shoes and a matching purse to visit her husband. Even if he didn't know she was his wife, maybe he recognized a woman who dressed nicely and came to see him. Maybe the coordinator was wrong.

Rose was one floor down when she heard someone calling. Kenny trotted down the hallway, out of breath. "Hey, you're a hero." His elbow jostled hers.

"Who told you?"

"Renzo, when I got laundry."

She slowed as she reached the nursing station and handed the unit coordinator her clipboard. "Just this." She lifted the brown paper bag of cans to show him the label. He never signed unless he saw what she brought. A nurse walking past held out her hands. "Is that mine? I'll take it."

Kenny hovered. "So how does it feel to save someone's life?"

Rose shook her head. All she'd done was react.

"That was great, Rose. Hey, do you want to hear about the cabin? We cooked up steaks on the stove. "

Steak would be a first for that ancient wood stove. And who did *we* include? Jerome?

"When it gets dark out, the stars, man! And it's so quiet in the woods." Kenny had dropped his voice to a whisper. "It's creepy but good creepy, just the cabin and the trees all around." He shivered and grinned. "And the owls. Jerome stood outside hooting like an owl. From one part of the woods, then another, you could hear the real owls coming closer. They couldn't figure out who this new owl was."

Jerome hooting like an owl? She couldn't picture it. Not the same Jerome who used to hang an elbow out the window of his rundown car with a joint pinched between his fingers.

An orderly, ambling down the hallway, tipped an invisible hat to Rose.

"Told you," Kenny said. "Everyone knows you caught that lady."

She didn't believe him, but then she thought that if everyone knew, then anyone could find out what had happened to the woman. "I want to know if she's all right. I asked one of the doctors, but he wouldn't say."

Kenny's face sobered. "You know where they took her?"

"Recess?"

"Resus. Layton works in Resus. I'll find out." He pivoted on his heel and jogged off.

When Rose finished delivering her tube feeding and returned to the kitchen, the supervisor told her to sit down and rest. The others would deliver late trays. She wanted Rose to tell her what had happened.

Rose climbed the metal stairs to her apartment, feeling sad, not even trying to walk softly. Kenny had come to the kitchen to tell her the woman had died. Was it any comfort to think she'd been on her way to see her husband? Rose wasn't sure.

She unlocked the door and began to slip off her running shoes, but was startled when Yushi bolted into the hallway. "I've been waiting for you!" She nudged Rose aside so she could strap on her sandals. "Come on."

"Where?" Rose followed her down the stairs again. She hadn't eaten yet, but it was unusual for Yushi to be so excited.

"Puppet theatre at the park."

"Aren't puppets for kids?"

"Don't be such a snob." Yushi strode past the carpet store; the second-hand appliance shop; a bar where, late at night, old-fashioned-looking men in black coats and ringlets rolled up their sleeves and played pool. The sun was already setting, its fuchsia glow warming the staid fronts of the brick and stone buildings. For those few moments, grimy balconies were transformed into elegantly worked gilt baskets.

A woman with blond, ropy hair like Leo's walked out of a *dépanneur*. Rose nudged Yushi. "How does she get her hair like that?"

"I don't know how white people do it. I think African hair will just grow like that if you let it."

"Can you do it?"

Yushi snorted. "I'm not African. I'm Indian. Don't get your coloureds mixed up or you'll step on some toes that'll stomp back hard."

Yushi cut across the park to where a wooden stage had been erected. The curtains were still closed. They were dark blue and painted with glittery zigzags, suns, stars, and moons. Behind the back structure of the stage, legs in baggy pants and sneakers stepped back and forth. They moved in such a tight knot that Rose kept expecting them to trip. Out front on the grass, children sat cross-legged on blankets, facing the curtains with perfect trust that the magic would soon begin. Parents stood farther back. Some had brought folding chairs.

Yushi scurried up behind the children. "Sit!" She patted the ground next to her. Like the children, she stared at the curtains. A bump of movement against the cloth made some children giggle with nervous anticipation. Others asked high, clear questions and craned their necks to search out their parents under the trees.

A horn blared and the curtains jerked open on a brightly lit backdrop of painted clouds and trees. As the box stayed empty, some children wondered out loud what would happen. Then, from the bottom edge, antlers wiggled into view. They were attached to the round head of a puppet boy. *"Tu sais quoi?"* he cried. "It's not my fault I've got antlers. I was born like this. It's just the way I am!"

The children shrieked with happy laughter. Rose slid a look at Yushi, who grinned.

Other puppets cajoled the boy not to be upset that he looked different. His antlers were unique. Because of them, he could do special things other little boys couldn't. He could hook objects from high off a shelf. He could block a ball with his antlers. All the other kids would want him on their team. His mother, his older sister, and his teacher listed reasons why he should be happy about his antlers.

The children squirmed on their bums and shouted. The little boy next to Rose cried, "I love you!"

The horn sounded a deep bass note of threat, and a new crowd of puppets bumbled into the frame. Mean boys with square shoulders and nasty, drawling voices. "What's that on your head? What are ya, some kinda reindeer? Why don't you go up north and look for Santa, see if he likes you? Ha-ha-ha!"

The children in the audience grew still. The puppet boy with the antlers was confused by the taunts and couldn't defend himself. Rose stared in disbelief. What kind of show was this?

"Yeah! Go on! No one wants any weird antler-boy around here!"

"Stop it!" some of the children in the audience screamed. "Leave him alone! Go away!" Rose's hands closed into fists.

The mean boys kept jeering, but as the children in the audience kept shouting to defend the boy with the antlers, the puppet boy grew taller and the mean boys smaller until they disappeared below the edge of the box. The children laughed in triumph. The puppet and his good friends ended with a song.

Yushi brushed her jeans as she stood. "Good, wasn't it? I love puppets." Around them children abandoned their blankets in a mayhem of small milling bodies to run back to their parents and tell them what they'd seen.

Rose and Yushi headed across the park at an angle. Rose said, "What if none of the kids say anything? How does it end?"

"I don't know. I guess the boy gets beaten up and has his antlers ripped off his head."

Rose's steps slowed.

"I'm *teasing*." Yushi knocked her arm. "One of the kids always starts. And if no one does, I guess someone prompts them. Why were you late today?"

Rose frowned, remembering again. "An old woman at the hospital fell down."

"Did she break anything?"

"No, I caught her. But she died."

"Not because of anything you did."

"No, but I was thinking about getting old like that. She had no one with her or to help her. I just happened to be there."

"In death we're always alone." Yushi's tone was matter-of-fact, but Rose saw how she looked at the ground and guessed she was thinking of her mother. Sometimes Rose wondered if that was what drew them together, both losing their mothers.

They climbed the curve of stairs to their apartment. Rose had begun to feel hungry. She hadn't eaten at the hospital — hadn't even thought of it. She kicked off her shoes and went to the kitchen to saw a bagel in two and drop the halves in the toaster. As she waited, she licked a dollop of peanut butter off the knife.

Yushi followed and leaned against the side of the refrigerator. The door was covered with magnets Rose had discovered at the dollar store. Purple eggplants, red tomatoes, yellow bananas, green peppers. The plastic foods were fake, but she loved the idea.

"Don't you ever wonder about your father?" Yushi asked.

"No." Rose popped the toaster and flipped the hot bagel on the breadboard. She smeared on peanut butter and took a big bite.

"Why not?"

Rose shrugged.

"Aren't you even curious?"

Rose had thought about it. Of course she had. She wasn't sure she could explain. "He never tried to see me. What does it matter if he's my father if he never acted like one?" And what if Armand was her father? Which was worse, an unknown father or Armand as her father? The question was far more confusing than Yushi could guess.

"Maybe he didn't know about you. Maybe your mother never told him."

Rose, her mouth full of peanut butter, opened the refrigerator to grab the milk. She'd thought of that too — how Maman had never told her about her father and maybe hadn't told him either. She'd come to Montreal and left again, never to return. Maman and her secrets.

"What about that?" Yushi insisted. "What if he doesn't know about you? That's hardly his fault."

"He knew about her. He never tried to find her."

"Come on, Rose. Cut the guy some slack. You said yourself you lived hidden in the woods."

"Where would I even look for him? I don't know where she lived when she was here."

"You could put an ad in the paper. Or post online."

"For someone who had a girlfriend called Thérèse in 1978?" Rose smirked at her. Now Yushi was being ridiculously naive.

"Okay," Yushi admitted. "Maybe you're right. An invisible father might be better than some of the ones out there."

Rose had overheard Yushi a few nights ago arguing on the phone with her sister. Yushi refused to go to Toronto to visit their father. Let him disinherit her. She didn't care.

Rose was close enough to finishing the bolster for Yushi that it was time to start planning a new project. Decide what to make — and for whom.

From outside the window she heard a rustle of movement in the weeds. Leo appeared, holding up a bag. "Apples! Can you wash them?"

She reached for the bag through the pane.

She and Leo met every day now, except for when they had to work. If Rose didn't live so far away, they could have seen each other in the evening when she finished work. She had begun to wonder if it was possible to sleep in her studio.

She hung back when she stepped outside with the apples and saw Leo talking with the sculptor, who turned at the sound of her steps. *"Mademoiselle,"* he said graciously.

"Would you like an apple?" Leo offered. The sculptor declined. Leo moved away to join Rose, slinging an arm over her shoulder as they walked to the canal. They sat, half-collapsed against each other, in the grass. Rose told him about the puppet show in the park.

"Your roommate sounds like fun."

Rose shook her head. Yushi had a sense of fun, but *fun* wasn't the word to describe her.

Leo had taken out his knife and was cutting an apple in pieces. "These are the best — Lobo. First of the season. Do you like them?"

What she liked was being with Leo, but there was so much she still didn't know about him. Whenever she asked where he lived, he nodded at the canal. Over there.

Over there were abandoned factories and grain silos. A concrete and brick wasteland where no one had worked for forty, maybe fifty years. The watchman's shed at the top of a tower, against the sky, was a shell of rusted metal.

Leo was reaching for the bag. "Want another apple?"

"No, no apple. I want you to show me where you live."

His face grew still. "You won't like it."

"Maybe I will."

He shrugged, slowly unfolded his legs, and stood.

She expected him to head to the road, but he kept following the path through the grass by the canal. He didn't talk. His hand brushed hers but he didn't try to hold it. How poor could his place be? Didn't he remember that up until last year she'd lived in a cabin without running water or electricity? She knew he didn't have much money. He wore the same jeans every day. He'd never mentioned a roommate or family.

As they approached the chain-link fence around the deserted complex of towers and silos, Leo glanced behind them. He waited until a string of cyclists passed, then pulled aside a ragged curl of fence for her to step over.

This close, the hulking buildings looked more empty than ever. Eerie and dangerous. Leo and Rose skirted broken chunks of concrete and brick that must have fallen from higher up. The tough stems of weeds scraped at her bare legs. Shards of glass in the dirt winked reflections of sky. Rose gazed up the length of a shaft as high as the silo it had once serviced. The rusted metal was still in place but biscuit-crumbly with decay.

It didn't feel safe to creep around these dank-smelling ruins. Was it a shortcut? She kept hoping they would turn a corner, step through another hole in the fence, and stand before a yellow-brick duplex not so different from the one where she lived.

"Leo?"

"Shh." He motioned for her to flatten herself against the cool wall of the silo. He leaned back too, waiting in silence. People shouted to each other as they cycled along the bike path, which was out of sight from here.

When it was quiet again, Leo reached into a crevice to dislodge a slender rope. He gave it a jerk, and from higher up, a knotted mass unfolded and dropped. It swayed then hung still, becoming a ladder.

Rose craned her head back, squinting at the knotted rungs that scaled the wall.

"It won't take our weight at the same time," Leo said. "You go first. I'll keep an eye out. They can't see the ladder from the bike path, but sometimes someone stops to have a piss."

"Up here?" Rose's mouth stayed open as she gazed up the ladder.

"Are you afraid?"

Not afraid, but puzzled. People thought that growing up in a cabin in the woods was strange, but this was even stranger.

"When you get to the top, sling yourself on the floor. I'll be up as soon as you're off."

Rose didn't understand, but she grabbed hold of the rung over her head and started climbing. The tightly coiled rope dug into her instep. It was some form of nylon, strong but slippery. She fixed her eyes on the wall before her. Metal abraded by the weather. A bubbled map of rust. Up she went, hand by hand, step by step. Progress seemed slow until she glanced down and saw how far she was from the ground, which was strewn with rubble and wreckage, jagged edges. Don't look, she told herself. Don't slip. Bolts large as monster eyes bugged out from the corroded wall. A breeze fingered her hair. She heard a squawk offside and glanced at a crow that had settled in disdainful profile on a pulley contraption. Birds had their eyes on the sides of their heads. When they seemed to be looking away was when they watched you. Watch me, she thought. Watch me climb this ladder. She trusted the coiled and knotted nylon more than the rusted metal wall. Rope was yarn in a heavier guise.

When she reached for the next rung, her hand bumped wood. She was at the end of the ladder, her head level with a platform. Leo had said to sling herself onto it, but how could she get her leg high enough? At the far end of the platform she saw a crate with a mug on top. If this was Leo's place — if he did this every day — she could do it, too. She scrambled as well as she could, grunting from the effort, banging her leg, and propelled herself headlong onto the floor. She lay still, getting her breath. Above her, a simple geometry of metal struts braced the ceiling. Three walls looked solid, but this wall, where Leo had strung his ladder, had crumbled. Past the hacked edge of the ceiling, she saw the watchman's shed — higher even than she was. This close, it was a shell splotched with holes and rust. No one had sat there for a long time.

She rolled over to look at the city below. The flat ribbon of the Lachine Canal nosing toward the port and Old Montreal.

The converging gleam of rail lines. She guessed which of the blocks along the canal was the building where she had her studio. From this angle the sculptor was hidden. The tower of the Atwater Market where Yushi worked looked like a toy.

She looked toward the high-rises of downtown and there, poking up from a building between the canal and downtown, were the gigantic metal letters of a sign. FARINE FIVE ROSES. The red lights that outlined the letters flashed on for a few seconds, then off for a few seconds, and then on again.

She heard a scrape of movement and Leo's woolly head appeared. He grabbed a handhold she hadn't noticed and hauled himself up. Still on his knees, he began to tug on a string attached to the ladder. The string scrunched the ladder into a tight accordion of rope.

Leo sat back and looked at her. "Just us now. And the birds." He swept a hand across the view spread before them. "My penthouse."

She swivelled away from the view, more curious now to see where he lived. A rolled mat and a sleeping bag hung from strings hooked to the struts. Another hook held a canvas bag crammed with clothes or food. Of course. Anything left on the floor would get chewed by whatever rodents foraged in deserted factories this high off the ground.

"Does anyone know you're up here?" she asked.

"Just you. And probably a few other squatters, but they've staked out their own places. They leave me alone. The only real problem is the graffiti acrobats. They can climb anywhere. But no one bothers to graffiti these old silos anymore. That" — he waved at the boxy blue letters sprayed across a brick wall higher than the one they'd scaled — "that's already years old."

"But you don't want anyone to find your ladder."

"Damn right I don't. I'm not supposed to be up here — no one is. I'm trespassing. So are you now."

His shoulder was close to hers. He questioned her with his eyes. She watched his face, letting him understand her answer. When he tilted forward with his mouth parted, she met him.

Leo's hand lay on her ribs. His rhythmic breath warmed her ear. The sleeping bag was thrown across their hips and the narrow mat he'd unrolled. They'd kicked free their clothes.

Her eyes traced the struts that criss-crossed the ceiling. Against the far wall, by the crate, leaned a whisk broom. She thought of Leo climbing the ladder with a broom so he could sweep the floor, and she smiled. The solitude of his aerie was as close to the solitude of her cabin in the woods as she had ever felt in the city.

The open wall faced the sky, where clouds drifted lazily. Leo stirred against her. His hand slid to her breast and cupped it. "Rose." It was like a purr deep in his throat.

She whispered, "What's that sign, Five Roses?"

"It's flour. You've never seen the bags in the store?"

"My mother used to tell me a story about five roses. A little girl who lived in the woods, and her only friends were five roses. They told her things. They ..." How could she explain why the story felt so important? "They gave her her name. They called her Rose."

"Perfect name." Leo rubbed his nose up her neck, nibbled around her ear, and kissed the earring. "Your mom liked to tell stories?"

She turned so they lay forehead to forehead, their breath mingling. "That was the only story she ever told."

Leo kissed her. "She made up a story about roses just for you."

She liked the thought and that Leo had said it. She liked how surely his hand slid to her hip.

MADDY

Maddy was sliding a rectangle of mousse and cake into a box. Off to the side she sensed a bustle of movement. Sharp steps and Pettypoo's high-hipped rump, then a savage slap that would have been offensive in private, and in a workplace was probably illegal.

Maddy glanced and saw Pettypoo and Yushi glaring at each other. "What the fuck," Maddy muttered.

"Pardon me?" The woman waiting for her cake was holding out a platinum card.

Yushi spat words at Pettypoo, who whirled off with flushed cheeks. Yushi stared after her, shoulders stiff, mouth grim. Angry spikes of hair.

Maddy's next customer asked which desserts had no nuts.

"There are several, but all of the cakes come from a kitchen where nuts are used. We cannot assure you that a cake that does not contain nuts has not come into contact with nuts." The nut spiel was a jingle Maddy recited at least twice a day.

"Oh, it's not for an allergy." The woman leaned across the counter as if to confide a great secret. "I think I've got fibro-myalgia, and when I looked online, I saw I shouldn't eat nuts."

Why didn't the woman go to a doctor and get herself tested? In her place, Maddy would eat every nut in sight — before it was forbidden. With no expression, she pointed out the desserts that featured chocolate, fruit, mocha, whipped cream, caramel.

As the woman debated out loud with herself — because Maddy had no intention of being drawn into a dietary consultation — Maddy leaned toward Cécile, who was setting *macarons noisettes* on a tray. "What got into Pettypoo?" she whispered.

"Did you see her? She's crazy. Yushi was fixing a sign that slipped and Pettypoo thought she was reaching for a bread without gloves on."

Maddy looked across at Yushi. Her face seemed calm, even indifferent, but she shot a baguette into a bag with such force that Maddy expected it to tear through the paper.

Maddy followed Cécile downstairs. They untied their aprons and crumpled them into balls they lobbed into the laundry hamper inside the locker-room door. Yushi was sitting on a bench, knotting her green running shoes.

Cécile said, "We all saw that upstairs. We're witnesses. That was an act of aggression. You should charge her with assault."

Yushi didn't lift her head.

"Come on, Yushi," Cécile said. "You have to stand up for yourself."

"She's right," Maddy said. "If you don't do anything, she's going to keep bullying you."

"Sure, she's right." Yushi scowled. "So what? Pettypoo is nuts. I don't want to get sucked into her crazy vortex."

"No," Cécile said. "She's nuts with everyone. With you, she's ballistic." She'd pulled off the shirt with three-quarter sleeves she was obliged to wear to hide her tattoos and stood before them in a tiger-stripe push-up bra, her stomach lean and tanned.

Maddy had a fleeting instant of envy. Never would she look that young and fit again — if she ever had. She looked at Yushi. "Pettypoo's out of control. Even for her. You have to talk to Zied."

Yushi snatched her knapsack from her locker. "Or quit this funny farm and find a new job."

Maddy bit her lip. That was another option, yes.

Cécile had squeezed into a ribbed tank top. "You could do way better than counter help. You could work in a kitchen."

Yushi shrugged and asked Maddy, "Are you coming?"

Maddy grabbed her helmet and slammed her locker shut. "Bye, Cécile. *À demain.*"

At the last of the fruit stalls, Pierre-Paul stood behind his bins of apples. His wife wasn't there, but he gave them only a distant nod. He'd finally got the hint that Maddy wasn't playing. She still felt his eyes on her back. On her ass.

Fog had crept across the city and along the canal. The buildings of downtown had been swallowed by a duvet of grey.

"What do you think you'll do?" Maddy asked.

"About what?"

"Pettypoo."

"I don't want to talk about it right now." Yushi bent to unlock her bike. Her movements were so brisk, her bike already wheeled from the rack, that Maddy thought she was going to cycle off without her. But Yushi waited until Maddy had her bike free. And though Yushi didn't speak again, she cycled with Maddy as far as the turnoff to the Pointe.

"Bye," Maddy called as Yushi continued along the canal into the mist.

The fog thickened, but Maddy didn't think it would rain and decided to go for a cycle by the river. She stopped at home first to change into shorts. On a day like today she would be alone on the path. Urban fact #42: people only remembered they had bikes when the sun shone.

She liked this sense of cycling into nothingness, not able to see farther than the asphalt before her, a damp bristle of grass, the trees shrouded in fog, an edge of grey water. It felt as if *she* were making the path unroll before her.

She grinned when she saw the woman in baggy shorts with her hair tucked in a French twist, the decided motor of her hips and legs stomping the stress of the day underfoot. Maddy passed her with a silent mental salute. *Hey-ho, sister!*

As she cycled, her brain whirred to come up with a solution for Yushi. She didn't want her to leave the patisserie, but the patisserie wasn't a good place for her to be — and if you were someone's friend, then you wanted the best for that person, not what happened to suit you.

Her knees pistoned up and down. Fog breathed thick and cool around her. Even the birds that usually squawked and called were silent.

The mist over the river thinned just enough that she made out a narrow shape gliding along ... a canoe with one figure at the bow, another at the stern. She slowed, lightly squeezing her brakes, to see more clearly — but knew she shouldn't stop or the vision, which was what it seemed, would disappear. The upright grace of the two figures. The tent of long hair to their shoulders. The canoe slipping low through the water. Iroquois used to hunt and fish along these shores when the land was called Teiontiakon.

As Maddy thought the words, the mist closed again, obscuring the mystery of the river.

The day at work had been long and dull without Yushi. Maddy was paired with Régis, which always put her on edge. She wasn't surprised Yushi had called in sick after yesterday's scene, but she wished Yushi had let her know. She would have called in sick as well. One down, the counter could manage. Two down and Pettypoo had to tie on an apron and serve customers.

She pulled her bike onto the sidewalk by the *dépanneur* and said *salut* to the man who sat tilted on the kitchen chair. She said hello so he would know she knew he was there and expected him to watch her bike, which she leaned against the storefront.

"Thalut!" His greeting was slurred by his toothless, frilly lips.

Walking into the store, she nearly tripped over a man on the floor, reading aloud from a book that looked like the Bible — columns of dense print with numbered verses. His performance was earnest, if tortured and difficult to follow. Yet, chin in hand at the cash, the Korean store clerk listened. The stumble of words followed Maddy down the aisle to the beer refrigerator, back to the cash, out the door again. She slipped the man on the kitchen chair a loonie.

At home she opened a beer and walked onto the deck. It was still warm enough to sit outside, but autumn was coming. The maple tree against her back fence was still green, but high up it sported a single tuft of crimson. It did that every year — her own personal harbinger of winter.

From across the fence she heard Fara and Frédéric's door open and saw Fara step out.

"Hi!" Fara called. "How are you?"

"Good, thanks. And you?" Maddy heard how fake her friendliness sounded. She should have told Fara and Frédéric about Ben trying to get through their gate.

"Busy day at work. Nice to come home."

But what if they'd called the police? That was all Ben needed, added to everything else that he'd already gone through. She'd told him to stay away and hoped he'd listened.

"It's starting to feel like home, too." Fara was still talking. "We've got the furniture in place and all the big problems fixed. You know what really helped?" Fara lifted her chin at the house behind her. "Frédéric's cousin installed French doors between the hallway and the dining room. You know, where the ... It changes the look of the room and the hallway completely."

"I shouldn't have told you."

"No, I'm glad you did. It's better to know than not know. If you don't, you keep wondering *where* ..." She bugged her eyes dramatically.

"But it bothered you —"

"No, no, no!" Fara said too quickly. And again, "No, no." Even shaking her head.

Maddy recognized a woman who could be stubborn in denial past her own best interests.

"Once we're completely settled, we'll have you over for supper. We might even have a housewarming party. The people where I work really want to see the place. I'll let you know when."

"Great," Maddy said, hearing again how glib she sounded. If she saw Ben again, even just standing at the back fence, she would tell Fara and Frédéric. Alert them, too, that he might still have a key.

Fara turned on her heel. "My phone's ringing. See you!"

Maddy opened her palm in a flat wave at the now empty backyard.

Maddy hunkered before a small hibachi, brushing balsamic marinade across rounds of eggplant and halved red peppers. Drips hissed on the hot grill. Yushi sat behind her in the rattan chair. No cooking lesson today. Maddy had planned a simple supper of grilled vegetables and couscous salad.

Jim posed in haughty disbelief on the corner of the deck, not convinced yet that the delicious odours of grilled meat seared into the metal were truly no more than ghosts of past suppers. He stared without blinking at Maddy, as if that might make her change the menu.

"Sorry, Jim. That's life." Maddy reached for her glass of wine on the table.

"You don't have to watch the barbecue all the time," Yushi said. "It cooks by itself."

Maddy pushed herself up from her knees and groaned. "My old knees can't take it."

"You could have put the grill on the table."

Maddy shrugged. She could have and should have. She hadn't thought of it.

The cowl turtleneck of Yushi's bulky sweater made her face look smaller — but no less resolute. She'd told Maddy she would be quitting the patisserie as soon as she found another job. Work at the moment was only bearable because Pettypoo was keeping a frigid distance and never addressing her directly. Zied had given Pettypoo a spittle-flecked, operatic dressing-down that everyone in the kitchen had heard from his office. Not that Zied cared if an employee was spanked with a red-hot spatula — *but not in view of the customers.*

Maddy realized Yushi had no choice but to leave. Even if Pettypoo could be made to behave, who wanted to work for a boss who loathed you? "Have you applied for any jobs yet?"

"I hate interviews, with their stupid questions — like if I know how to crimp a pie crust. A pie crust!" She huffed. "I'd like to see them make a sour cherry buttercream without it curdling."

Maddy piled the grilled eggplant and peppers on a plate. They were going to eat inside at the table by the kitchen window. "Can you bring my glass?" she asked. "Sour cherry buttercream sounds delicious. Tart and rich — great combo. What would you put that on?"

"Anything. A genoise, a chocolate torte."

"You should be working as a baker." Maddy poured more wine as Yushi helped herself to couscous.

"This is Montreal. You've got French cooks *de la France* applying for kitchen jobs. I'm a Canadian Trini who masquerades as Irish. Who would believe I can make a *croquembouche?*"

"Anyone who's tasted your cooking."

"That makes a sum total of you and Rose."

"How's she doing?" Maddy asked. She still wondered why Yushi, who'd cut so many ties with her family and her past, felt responsible for her sullen roommate.

"She's devoted to weaving. Some days she doesn't even come home. She sleeps at her studio."

Maddy, about to bite into charred eggplant, stopped her fork in mid-air. "Maybe she wants to move out."

"We've got a lease. She can't just take off."

"You could sublet. On the Plateau, it would be easy."

Yushi wasn't listening. "You should see the fabric she weaves. She made a bolster for my bed in this really intricate design." She zigzagged a finger in the air. "I think she should quit her job and weave all day long. She could sell her pieces." It was rare for Yushi to sound so enthusiastic. "She could," she repeated. "She used to sell when she lived with her mom. That's how they made a living. And you can tell she loves doing it."

Maddy's lips parted as an idea began to form.

"She's a real pro, too. Before we stuffed the bolster, she showed me how she finished all the edges on the inside — where no one even sees them, but they're all smooth and tucked away."

Maddy grabbed her wineglass and raised it to the fairy dust of fantastic ideas — wherever they came from. "That's it! That's what you'll do! You don't have to work for anyone. You'll make your own desserts and sell them to restaurants. Your tortes and your genoise and your marzipan roses. Once people taste them, they'll be gung-ho. They won't even ask where you trained."

Yushi gave a curt shake of the head. "You don't know what's involved. You need a big kitchen. You need equipment — bowls and cake forms, an industrial mixer, a processor to grind nuts.... And then how do you get the cakes to the restaurants? It's not like selling Girl Guide cookies door to door. If you've got cakes layered with mousse and whipped cream, you need a van — a refrigerated van."

"You sound like you know about it."

"Where I worked in Toronto, the baker before me left the restaurant and went into business for herself."

"Did it work?"

"Yeah, but that's Toronto. This is Montreal."

"I beg your pardon? You've been working in a patisserie for almost a year and you aren't aware that people here have a serious sweet tooth?"

"What about the van and the equipment? And a kitchen. I'd need a kitchen."

"Here." Maddy swept an arm at her stove and counters. "That room, too." She tossed in the large double front room off the kitchen. "You want a bigger stove? More counters? I've got a whole *house*, Yushi! And I'm living here by myself. I can do what I want."

Yushi considered the length of the room.

"We can rent a van to start. A refuelled van — I mean, refrigerated." Maddy's words tumbled in her excitement. "I'll talk to my hotshot brother. He knows how to start a business. He'll help us out. He'll invest." Maddy wasn't sure about that, but it sounded good. If he wouldn't invest, he would tell her how to borrow.

"I can't drive."

"Why would you drive? *You're* the pastry chef. You bake. I'll drive."

Yushi was listening — not believing her yet, but she was listening. Maddy would show her this could work. Because it *could*!

ROSE

Rose folded the blanket over the sleeping bag, stuffed the pillows over the blanket, and closed the lid of the chest. Then she propped the sponge mat against the wall. Tidying away the bedding reminded her of life in the cabin — how she'd stripped the sofa of the sheets and her blanket every morning, turning her bed into a sofa again.

She and Leo had bought a chest at the furniture store where she'd bought the chair for sitting at her loom and the dresser for her shuttles and spools of thread. When the man in the store met Leo, his always warm intonation grew even more rich and relaxed. Leo's voice changed, too. The man said he was from Jamaica, Leo that his grandparents lived in Barbados. Rose had never seen Leo act so boyish, cocking his head and looking aslant at the man as if he were much shorter, peering up at him, slapping his leg and laughing.

Later, after they'd carried the chest to her studio and were sitting on the sponge mat drinking tea, he told her about his grandparents, whom he'd visited when he was four and eleven. He talked about flying fish and the sea. Running between the men, who drank rum in the shade of the palm trees, and the women, who sat in groups scraping vegetables they cooked in huge cauldrons.

He started to say, Once when my ma ... But his face grew still and he stopped. Rose wasn't sure what his expression meant. He'd never before spoken of his mother — or his father. And though she felt shy about prodding, she wanted to know. What about your mother? she asked gently. Leo closed his eyes. Is she ... Rose decided she could say it because her own mother was dead. Is she dead? No, he said dully. But she doesn't want me around. She made it damn clear. Rose waited, but he didn't say more. She sat closer and touched his face to stroke the hurt away.

The bedding packed out of sight, Rose surveyed the studio. Leo had cautioned her against anyone discovering that they slept here. It probably wasn't legal — though, as she pointed out, they were more equipped here than she and Maman had ever been in the cabin. They had a sink for water and washing, and the toilet in the hallway on the second floor. They were only missing the wood stove.

Not every night, then, but some nights she and Leo slept here. With the canvas drawn across the window, no one knew they were there. In the morning he made them tea before he left for the garage. She washed at the sink. Her hair had grown long enough that she could scrape it into the stub of a ponytail. She worked at her weaving until it was time to go to the hospital.

Rose wished they could stay here always. She had to stop herself from buying a table and two chairs and a hot plate. She'd wanted to make a key for Leo and had gone to four hardware stores. Each place said they could make a copy of the key to her studio, but not the main door. That key had a security code. Rose hadn't asked further, not wanting to excite suspicion. Leo couldn't always return during the day to get into the warehouse while the main door was still unlocked. When she worked, she couldn't be here before the evening. They were both conscious of being seen sneaking in and out at night. She didn't want to lose her studio. What if Kenny's uncle's friend decided she was a squatter?

Leo, too, held to his tower aerie. The same man who slept pressed against her still felt most at home in an abandoned factory, high up over the city where no one could get to him once he'd pulled the ladder up after himself. She didn't understand, but she accepted it was what he needed in the same way she'd needed to flee the woods and her cabin and come to the city.

Rose glanced at the dollar-store clock on the dresser. Outside the window, a pod of cyclists in yellow-and-black Lycra — wasps churning their legs — streamed past. On the floor she had balls of purple, blue, and red wool she was feeding onto her warping reel. She was going to make cushions for the studio — to toss on the sponge mat, for leaning against the wall.

Rose looked up from the sidewalk as she approached the duplex. There was a light on in the front window. She hadn't been home for the last two nights. Yesterday she'd called before Yushi got home and left a message on the answering machine. She unlocked the door as softly as she could and slipped off her shoes. She heard no music, no TV, no slide of pots from the kitchen. Light spilled from the front room into the hallway.

Yushi sat cross-legged on a chair at the large table, head bent, writing. Loose-leaf pages were scattered almost halfway across the length of the table. On the chair next to Yushi was a ripped plastic package of paper. Yushi snagged another few pages and kept writing. Lists, it looked like. Some pages with no more than headings across the top. Here a line, there a line.

She looked so absorbed, Rose didn't want to interrupt, but it didn't feel right to keep watching. "Hi."

"Hi." Yushi kept writing. Then, "Did you eat?"

"At the hospital."

Yushi sucked her teeth. Even intent on whatever had her so engrossed, she was present enough to scoff at hospital food. She grabbed a fresh page, wrote another word at the top, then reached across the table to push all the pages together. She straightened the stack and dropped it on the package of paper. "I didn't eat yet. How about I make us an omelette?"

Rose loved Yushi's fluffy omelettes, with their creamy ooze of melted cheese and herbs. In the studio she and Leo ate bread and cheese and vegetables, or ramen noodles that only needed boiling water. She was happy because they were together, but she wished she could cook Leo a real meal. She'd invited him to the apartment, but he wouldn't come. He didn't explain, except to say he felt safe in St-Henri and along the canal.

Rose washed her hands and joined Yushi in the kitchen. Yushi had set the skillet on the stove and was cracking eggs against the edge of a bowl. "You want to slice those tomatoes? And there's basil in the fridge."

Rose slid the cutting board out from beside the canisters and took a plate from the cupboard.

"I've got to thank you, Rose."

Was Yushi teasing her?

"I'm impressed with how committed you are to what you're good at — to weaving. You *are* really good at it, too."

Rose looked at Yushi sidelong. Yushi had said she liked the bolster but she wasn't usually so insistent with her compliments.

"You showed me," Yushi said.

She'd shown Yushi the inside of the bolster before she'd stuffed it, but that couldn't be what Yushi meant.

The melted butter bubbled as Yushi poured beaten egg into the skillet. "Maddy wants to help me start a dessert business. I'd make cakes to sell to restaurants. I've been" — she lifted her chin at the hallway — "thinking of recipes and ingredients. Things we'll need."

Rose stopped slicing tomatoes to look at Yushi. She didn't for an instant doubt that Yushi could make exquisite desserts, which could — and should — feature on restaurant menus. "That's wonderful."

"Yeah." Yushi sounded calm but then gave a nervous shiver.

Suddenly Rose felt bad that Yushi had told her this great good news while she'd been keeping secrets. "I've met someone," she blurted.

Yushi stopped running the spatula around the edge of the omelette. "Are you serious?" She ogled Rose then grinned broadly. "Do tell."

Rose raised her arms high over her head and laced her fingers in a peak. She had to remember to stretch now and then while she stood bent over the loom with her hook.

The raspy caw of a crow made her glance at the window, but it was a real crow settling itself on the post of the fence. What was she thinking? Leo didn't have to pretend to be a crow when he wanted to see her. They weren't trying to fool anyone — like Armand calling from the woods with a mourning dove's long, yearning coo. As himself, as a man, he'd never sounded so tender. She tightened her lips and bent again to the reed. All these years she'd hoarded memories of Armand, reliving and refurbishing them, believing they were wondrous in the way that a person assured herself a mirror made a room larger, ignoring the hard, flat wall it hid.

She heard shouting close by outside, but it wasn't at her window. She pulled the lamp closer, having to pay attention to her sequence of blue thread, red thread, purple, then red again.

Now someone was shouting at her window. "Hey, Rose!"

She was surprised to see Kenny and circled her arm in the air to show him to come around to the door.

"I didn't remember which was your window!" he yelled.

She pointed at the door again.

"I banged on your neighbour's window! Do you know she makes jewellery?"

Rose had finally met the woman in the studio beside hers. She had white hair, cut short like a boy's, and wore a cook's apron over a long, loose shirt. She worked with silver she twisted around chunky stones. To Rose's eye, the necklaces and earrings she fashioned were so heavy and large they no longer looked like jewellery. The woman said, Don't worry, dear, it's an age thing. These aren't supposed to be sweet. They're armour. On her breastbone rested an amulet the size and colour of a robin's egg.

Rose hadn't known Kenny was coming, but she expected Leo. She'd told Leo about Kenny having found the studio for her and helping her get her loom, but she'd never told Kenny about Leo. Nor that she sometimes slept here. Quickly, she surveyed the room. The sponge mat was propped against the wall. The chest with the bedding could be just another place where she stored yarn.

Kenny rapped on the door, then opened it. "I had some stuff to do thisaway and thought I'd come see your weaving. What are you making?" He peered at the thick chain of threads hanging down the breast beam.

"Cloth to make cushions — a few of them. But I'll attach the treadles a different way for each one." She pointed at the treadles, which he'd called "pedals" when they'd taken the loom apart. "So, it'll be the same yarn for each pillow but a new pattern."

"Neat." He stepped away and gazed around the studio. She held her breath, hoping he wouldn't ask about the sponge mat. "You're really set up here. You've got a kettle, a table, chairs ..."

"Most important is my loom."

"Your loom." He nodded, crossing to the window and looking out. "Did I tell you I'm not renting a car anymore when I head up to the cabin? I take the bus and Jerome picks me up. We go to the IGA and buy groceries and we're all set for a couple of days."

She couldn't picture Kenny and Jerome with a shopping cart in the IGA. Even if it was only partly true — another of Kenny's exaggerated stories — it would be enough to trigger the gossips to brew a pot of coffee and get on the phone.

"Yeah ..." He turned around and leaned against the window ledge. "That's what we were wondering about. It's ... um ... getting cold and up till now we've been collecting old wood. You know, dead branches and stuff like that to burn. Is that all right?" He peeked at her.

"You're cleaning up. That's good." Though decayed branches wouldn't make a very satisfying fire, especially as it kept getting colder.

"Jerome was saying you've got some spots where the trees grow really thick and he could get his dad's chainsaw and cut down a few."

Maman had asked Armand about that a few years ago, but he'd never come with his chainsaw.

"The wood won't be dry for this winter," she said. "You'll need to buy some."

"But you'd be all right with that?"

"Go ahead." She wondered what Armand — and the people of Rivière-des-Pins — made of Jerome spending whole weekends, from the sound of it, in Rose's old cabin.

Behind Kenny, through the window, she saw Leo, pulling an exaggerated funny face — jaw dropped, eyes wide — at the presence of a *man* in her studio. She waved him to come in.

Kenny looked to see why she had waved.

"That's my boyfriend." Rose felt herself blushing. Last night, when she was talking to Yushi, was the first time she'd said the word out loud.

Kenny appraised her head to toe with a pleased smile. "Didn't I say you'd be hobnobbing with all kinds of *artistes* and interesting people down here?"

She felt an impulse to hug him for being so ready to accept Leo before he'd even met him. The sensation was so new that her blush deepened, and she lowered her face to hide the strange fluster of emotion.

She slid off her bench to fill the kettle at the sink, because here was another first: using all three mugs at once.

It was too cold to undress in Leo's tower. They lay snug in his sleeping bag, his arm around her waist, his hand under her sweater, cupping her breast.

Rose loved to listen to how alone with each other they were up here. It wasn't like being alone with Maman in the woods with only the chirp of birds and shush of wind in the branches — theirs the only human voices for many acres all around. Here, above the city, she never lost the sense of human presence. The susurration of traffic was audible like a motor that kept the city running. There were always punctuated thumps from the rail yards or a factory. But no one knew where they were, or could have followed them had they known, with the ladder pulled up after them. Up here, they were above and beyond the city, cushioned by the quiet of distance and willed isolation.

Here was where Leo had found refuge when he'd fled the foster homes where he'd been placed because of his mother's rages. He'd run away and run away again, until he was too old for the social workers to make him stay. It wasn't family or friends who had helped him, but strangers who'd shared what little they had. An elderly man with cracked glasses patched with hockey tape had brought him to the food kitchen. A girl in a pleated skirt gave him her scarf. The woman in the food kitchen snuck him into the church basement at night so he had somewhere to sleep. Her husband ran the garage where Leo was learning how to repair cars. Rose too, he said. She was the kindest of all. She had trusted him and let him love her.

Rose didn't realize, until he told her, that he was almost ten years younger than she was. But what did that matter? She stroked his face, touched his eyelids and lips, and under his locs, the soft nape of his neck, hoping with the gentle brush of her fingers to anoint him with every tenderness she could offer.

The wind that swirled around the tower was cooler than on the ground along the canal. The walls exuded cold, and the open side with its penthouse view, was frigid. Rose had found a spot where they didn't lie too close to the wind but she could still see the Five Roses sign past the edge of the platform, and behind it, the congested sprawl of city buildings.

"You like your sign, don't you?" Leo teased her. "We can go look at it close up if you want."

"No, I like it like this."

"It makes you think of your mom's story."

"Yeah. It makes me wonder if she lived around here. If she knew about the sign."

"How would you find out?"

"I don't know."

His hand, under her sweater, shaped her nipple, made it hard. His mouth puffed moist heat as he nuzzled her ear and the flat lozenge of her earring. She shifted against him and turned her head, mouth parted. They could have waited until they were in her studio where it was warmer. From Leo she'd learned the luxury of patience. Except that, sometimes, the right time was now.

FARA

Traffic careened along the curve, racing to beat the stoplight. The long-angled rays of the setting autumn sun spotlit the clock tower of the market. The pumpkins heaped around the stalls affirmed their own orange rotundity. *They* were their own suns, thank you.

Fara waited at the curb to cross to the market. That morning they'd run short of coffee and Frédéric had made half cups. Cute, but no cigar. She needed a full dose of caffeine to withstand the upstream jostle of the subway, the standing-room-only bus ride to the hospital, the first sight of her desk buried under every colour of requisition used in the witchcraft of medicine.

She bought half a kilo of French roast and held the tightly packed bag of beans — her favourite perfume — to her nose as she threaded past shoppers. A woman cradling a huge paper cone of flowers, friends having a delighted, isn't-this-incredible reunion over a mound of kale.

Her steps slowed when she glimpsed a woman waiting for a vendor to root through his leather apron for change. Where did she know her from? The stalwart back and shoulders, yes. The serious young woman who delivered tube feeding. Fara tapped her arm. "Hi! Remember me from the hospital, Twelve South?"

The woman didn't answer, but Fara saw the shutter-click of recognition on her face. "You live around here too?" Fara asked.

"No." She hesitated, then lifted her chin in the direction of the canal. "I have a studio in an old factory." She'd spoken with such gravity the words sounded like a confession.

"You're an artist."

"That's what I keep telling her," a skinny woman with spiked hair interjected. "She's got a loom. She weaves."

Fara arched her eyebrows as if impressed, though she knew nothing about weaving. The skinny woman looked familiar. "Do you work in the hospital, too?"

"Making stew for four hundred patients? You couldn't pay me."

But the woman didn't explain what she meant and Fara wasn't about to start guessing.

As a loose group they strolled past the stalls, to the end of the market. Fara, flipping through the kaleidoscope of faces in her head, suddenly said, "I know where I've seen you before. At my neighbour's — out on the deck. You know Maddy."

"Maddy." The woman smiled. "Yeah ..."

"I'm Fara."

"Yushi."

Had she said Yooshi? Or Looshi? Fara didn't want to ask her to repeat her name and get branded as an ignoramus white person who could only say Susan and Mary.

Yooshi, if that was her name, turned to her friend. "I have to get back to work. If I see you at home later, I'll see you. If I don't, have fun." She glanced at Fara as she left, which Fara supposed was a curt version of goodbye. Not overly sociable, was she, this Yooshi?

The tube feeding woman still stood next to Fara. "You know," Fara said, "I don't think you ever told me your name."

"Rose."

"Ha!" Fara pointed into the distance at the Farine Five Roses sign. "You should take a picture of yourself with that sign behind you."

Rose glanced over her shoulder, but her expression stayed indifferent.

Fara had thought it funny. An interesting coincidence, if nothing else. "I guess I'll let you go. See you at the hospital."

She strode to the pedestrian bridge, which was painted the bright green of oxidized copper she thought of as Montreal green — the colour of gables and cupolas. The water in the canal had a dark, oily flatness. The nights had been cool enough lately that the trees had started turning. Someone had stuck posies of gold and crimson leaves between the slats of the picnic tables near the canal. Every time Fara crossed into the Pointe now, she felt the drop in bustle, money, and upscale edginess. At the market, you bought duck breasts and bluefin tuna. In the Pointe, you stopped at the *dépanneur* for canned food and beer. Though, sure, with the advent of people like herself and Frédéric, the Pointe was changing. Brick was being repointed, old windows and doors replaced. The air smelled of tar. Cement mixers sat on the sidewalk. The new residents complained to the city about the hookers, the graffiti, the garbage rotting in the alleys. She and Frédéric had gone to the community meeting with the mayor to demand more police presence. They'd met others who'd also recently moved to the Pointe.

The old Pointe was still here. Witness the man in his crooked pose on the chair outside the *dépanneur* on the corner, the guys who played horseshoes, the elderly man hobbling along the alley with his cane, looking for gossip. He'd accosted Fara one day and asked if she knew about the crime that had happened in the house. Were there still people who thought suicide was a crime? I work in a hospital, she'd said coldly. I'm used to death.

As she unlocked her front door, she eyed the grimy beige panelling of the entrance. She'd washed it, but decades of city dirt had fused with the paint. She'd debated stripping the wood the way Maddy had, but boy, oh boy, what a lot of work for what they only saw when they were coming home or leaving.

She stooped to pick up the mail from the mat. A pizza flyer and an envelope from the bank. The hallway was dim in the dusk. She kicked off her shoes and hollered up the stairs. "Frédéric?" No answer.

The French doors were closed because they'd had the heat on yesterday evening. She'd stained and varnished the wood and Frédéric had added a scrolled brass handle. The gleam of wood and glass changed the look of the downstairs, made the hallway elegant. And yeah, in whatever bizarre way the mind worked, she no longer saw the body hanging. She thought of the boy in the house less often. The reawakened memories of Claire's suicide were fading, settling into the old hollow sense of loss she would sooner leave undisturbed.

She slung her knapsack on the table in the kitchen, unlocked the back door, and stepped onto the deck. The fence paraded the patient innocence of wood that had withstood rain, sunshine, and snow. The man who used to stand out there seemed to have disappeared.

Over on Maddy's deck, her orange cat huddled next to the basket-weave chair, as if waiting for Maddy *there*, where she often sat, would make her appear. Fara clicked her tongue. One ear swivelled in her direction, but otherwise he ignored her. Cats, she smirked. So unto themselves.

"How about ...?" Anouk stood as if undecided before the shrink-wrapped mounds of ground beef. Then she winked at Ben. She hadn't forgotten how he loved her *pâté chinois*. She'd already hefted potatoes, apples, celery, and a head of iceberg lettuce into the cart he was pushing.

A few days ago he'd opened his door and there stood Anouk. My bag's downstairs, she said. He'd tripped down on light feet, couldn't get back upstairs fast enough, lugging the huge and heavy suitcase. She showed him the bruises on her arm where her boyfriend had grabbed her when he heard she'd had some fun for a change. *What a total a-hole!*

She was so upset — and Ben so keen to show off that she'd come *to him* for refuge — that he'd taken her out for smoked meat and spaghetti. She'd had four Bloody Marys. Back in his apartment, she threw a blanket over the scratchy upholstery of his sofa and straddled him with all her clothes on. He knew this game, where she didn't get undressed but squished her breasts out of their cups and twisted her skirt up her hips. He had to finger aside the crotch of her panties to get in. Sex with no clothes was easier, but Anouk was always wilder when he had to wrestle with elastic and lace to get at her good parts.

The next day at work, Mathieu asked if it was true Anouk had moved in with him again. News didn't take long to get around the Pointe. Ben shrugged. He didn't know what Anouk meant to do and didn't dare ask her.

That evening, when he came home, she had pork chops fry-ing and a can of mushroom soup open on the counter. That was her trademark fancy dish: pork chops in mushroom sauce.

He went to the bedroom to change his oil-streaked shirt for a T-shirt. Anouk had glared when she'd seen the teacup on the window ledge. Who's is that? she demanded. He thrilled at the snap of her jealousy — but didn't want her to smash the cup to the floor. My mom's. Her eyes narrowed. He wasn't sure if she believed him. Then she pulled him to her. You poor baby.

Today the teacup shared the ledge with her grandmother's shepherd girl. The light from the window made the china crook gleam like the handle of the teacup. He looked around the room, but Anouk's huge suitcase had disappeared. He eased open the top drawer of his dresser. His underpants had been pushed aside to make room for shiny twists of frilled nylon and lace.

He walked into the kitchen, brimming with a sense of great, good luck. He gathered her close in his arms, feeling how per-fectly she fit against him, smelling the perfume of her hair. We should get married, he murmured. She pulled back her head to look at him. For real? You can get a white dress, he promised. And walk down the aisle. She snuggled her head under his chin again. Don't be silly, she whispered. I don't need the jokers around here laughing at me in white. Let's do it fast at city hall. She gripped her arms around his waist tighter. Let's do it, Ben.

Since then, because he'd been at work all week, she'd made the phone calls and booked a date. They had to wait three weeks, but three weeks was okay if he thought that, a week ago, he didn't even know he was going to be married at all.

Anouk wanted to visit her parents in Shawinigan to tell them. He'd already met them when he and Anouk used to live together. He didn't care for her old man, a short bully with a mouth on him. Hard to believe he hadn't had his face broken yet. Her mom looked like an older, more tired, fatter version of Anouk, but Ben bet that even when she was younger, she didn't have Anouk's spunk.

Ben hadn't decided yet if he was going to tell his dad or let him find out — the way Ben had found out about the house. It would serve him right to miss his own — his only — son's wedding.

Anouk had asked about the house and swore when he told her. *Crosseur!* What a bastard, your dad!

Yeah, he was. But now Ben had Anouk on his side — soon to be his wife.

They talked about Xavier, too. She said she'd always thought Xavier was over the top. A bit crazy. Had she told him Xavier tried to get her in the sack once? His own brother's girlfriend, what did he take her for? Ben already knew the story — she'd told him before — but he let her tell him again. He remembered how Xavier was like a firecracker that could burst in your hands at any moment.

He didn't tell Anouk about sneaking into the house where the new people lived now. He hadn't been back since the hippie caught him. It didn't feel safe anymore — especially now that he had Anouk to think of and was about to get married. No way did he want to get into trouble.

Still. He should go back and fix the boards on the deck. He could look through the gaps in the hippie's fence and check if her bike was there. He would walk through the house one last time, then throw away the key.

Anouk pinched his arm, recalling him to the important task of grocery shopping. "Ben! We're not even married yet and you're not listening. I asked if you wanted crackers."

He leaned forward and pecked her on the mouth. She turned her face away but he saw how she'd made dimples. She liked finding fault and bossing him around. He, too, felt content, pushing the cart down the aisle with Anouk beside him. She dropped a box of Special K onto the cans of creamed corn, peas, soup, foil wrap, and other necessities she claimed were missing from his kitchen.

He had a good job and a credit card. She radiated that wifely, proprietorial air that would have made him feel shoved into a corner a couple of years ago, but that warmed him now from head to toe. If he hadn't already asked her to marry him, he would ask her at this very moment in the aisles of the grocery store.

Spanish guitar plucked from the CD player. Fara sat in one corner of the sofa with Frédéric's feet in her lap, massaging them through his thick socks. She had her head tilted back, eyes on the ceiling.

Suddenly, she frowned. This was the first room she'd painted. When she'd bought the paint, she'd thought all whites were white — and that words like *ecru*, *linen*, *ivory*, and *eggshell* were marketing gimmicks. In the store she'd grabbed cans of white, regardless of their fanciful names, knowing only that she had to paint coat upon coat to cover grim brown, green, and grey. Only after she'd finished the front room did she notice how the light from the street picked out stripes in the paint. *What the …?* She looked at the cans again. She'd begun with Linen and finished with Du Jour. Weren't they all *white?* What a dumb lesson to learn the hard way! She had had to repaint the room in a single tone of white. She hadn't bothered with the ceiling because who looked up there? Well, she could see it now. A brighter swath across a more sedate white.

Head still tilted back, she swallowed, wondering if she was getting a sore throat. She swallowed again. Definitely an itch there. She could use a couple of days away from the Alice-in-the-madhouse circus at work.

And what was that noise? A light, intermittent scratching through the mournful music. She looked at Frédéric, who lay with his eyes closed. It was coming from behind him — behind the sofa along the floor. "Do you hear that?" she whispered.

"A papaya." He sounded half-asleep. "It's trying to get in."

"A what?"

"You don't remember?"

She had no idea what he meant.

"I'll get a trap."

"Is it a mouse, do you think?"

"Or a papaya."

"Stop it." She gripped his toes. Whatever the joke, she could tell she was the butt. "I saw Maddy today. She wants to start a business in her house — making cakes and delivering them to restaurants. She's got a friend who's a pastry chef."

"Maybe they'll need a taste tester."

"I doubt that'll pay enough that you can quit your job."

"I wasn't going to charge. I'll do it for free."

"Free, my eye. You'll get fat."

"We married for better or worse, remember?"

"Why do people always pull out that better-or-worse line when all they mean is worse?"

He pushed himself up from the cushions. "I'm falling asleep. If you want me to rub your back, you'd better come to bed." That was the deal. His feet, her back.

He trudged up the stairs. She wanted to follow but felt too lazy — or was she getting sick? She swallowed again. No doubt about it, her throat was swollen.

Fara woke, rolled onto her back, blinked at the curtains. Her mouth was dry, her throat sore. She'd called work in the night to tell them she wasn't coming. Frédéric had gone ... minutes or hours ago.

She dozed, then woke again. She should get up and make herself tea or drink some juice, but the kitchen was all the way downstairs. So far away. She glanced at the clock. Almost noon. If Frédéric called, she would tell him to buy lozenges on his way home. Come home earlier. Make her soup. Her stomach growled. She hadn't eaten breakfast. Which was it, feed a cold or feed a fever? She thought she had both.

She propped herself upright and let her legs dangle. She felt woozy. Where were her slippers? The floor was cold on her bare feet. She groped for yesterday's socks and had to sit again to pull them on.

She shivered as she walked to the stairs and grasped at the rail for balance. Her stocking feet were so quiet that she felt unreal, not like herself at all. She pressed her palm to her forehead and swallowed. Maybe she was really sick and needed antibiotics.

She stepped into the hallway and saw ... the hanging body! *No.* She widened her eyes, disbelieving. The body wasn't hanging! *It stood against the light!* Legs on the ground, head lifted, staring at the French doors. She shrank back, expecting it to wheel around and accuse her of ... of what? Not letting it hang?

She swayed, heart thundering, and must have gasped, because it turned to face her, but against the light she couldn't see its face. She didn't have to. She knew it was the boy. It staggered away from her, charged to the kitchen, banged the back door open, and ran out. Through the window, she saw it leap off the deck — and only then understood it wasn't a ghost but a man who'd been in the house while she'd been sick upstairs!

She flailed, scrambling to the door to lock it, grabbed the phone, and punched in Frédéric's number at work. "Fred!" The force of the word scraped her throat, made her start coughing.

"How are you feeling? I didn't call because I didn't want to —"

"Home," she choked out. "Come home now! There's — there's a man in the house. He was —" She recalled how he'd been standing, staring at the French doors. He hadn't heard her on the stairs, hadn't known she was there until she gasped.

"What do you mean, a man? Who? Is he still there? Fara!"

"I think he broke in. A thief, I don't know. He ran away."

"Call the police. I'm coming." He'd already hung up. She still clutched the receiver. An inert piece of plastic that linked her to the world.

Out the window she saw the gate ajar. She had to lock it so he couldn't get back in.

She fumbled Frédéric's jacket off the hook and shoved her feet into his clogs. She stepped out the back door, then froze when she saw the boards lifted off the deck. The hole into the dark beneath.

Frightened again, she stumbled back inside. Was she even safe in the house? Maybe someone else was in the cellar. Suddenly she realized she hadn't called the police. The police! She snatched the phone and called 911.

MADDY

From Wellington, Maddy saw the police car angled across the head of the alley. She cruised to a stop. "What happened? I live here." She pointed. "The house with the balcony."

The officer asked if she'd seen any suspicious activity at the house next door.

"Suspicious?" She immediately thought of Ben. What had he done? Why hadn't she warned Fara and Frédéric? Damn, damn, damn!

Then Frédéric stepped out of their gate, and though he didn't look happy, he also didn't look as if he or Fara had come to harm. He told her they'd had a break-in through the cellar window. He was going to have to get bars on the windows. Fortunately, nothing was missing. Fara had interrupted the thief because she'd been home sick and had surprised him. He didn't know if it was her fever or the shock, but she was still trembling.

"I'm really sorry this happened." More than sorry, Maddy was appalled.

"Have you heard about other break-ins along the street? Do you think it's because we're new here?"

Maddy shook her head. The police wanted to talk to Frédéric again, so she said goodbye and wheeled her bike to her gate.

Through the fence she could hear the police telling Frédéric they'd found a handful of screws under an upstairs window. "That's me," Frédéric said. "I dropped them."

She didn't want to talk to the police, but she felt she should tell Frédéric and Fara about Ben. They might — or might not — understand. Ben wasn't a thief. He only wanted ... who knew what he wanted? She guessed he felt something confused and impossible about the house.

The subway slowed as it entered the station. Maddy had to manoeuvre a path past a man transfixed by his phone, and a clot of teenage girls transfixed by themselves. She was careful of the small pastry box she held, making a shield of her arm when the doors slid aside and a woman tried to barge in, determined to get a seat. Urban fact #4: you had to let people *off* the subway before you got on. To Maddy that seemed such an obvious basic rule of civilized behaviour, but all too often she felt she needed to shout, Make way!

She'd taken the subway rather than cycle so she wouldn't arrive at her brother's sweaty and dishevelled. Stan would *not* be impressed, and today's visit was all about making the best possible impression. He was a cautious, easily skeptical man. Even as a boy, he could only be attracted by a tangible sense of advantage. She and Yushi had drafted concrete plans with figures, percentages, and demographic profiles. The pastry box held a tiny cake called a *nouméa*. Circles of baked almond meringue were layered with mango mousse and toasted, slivered almonds. From the top pillow of whipped cream poked three fingers of caramelized pineapple. The meringue was crisp, the mousse velvety. Maddy thought there were too many steps involved in making this single small cake, but Yushi said the leftover mousse, toasted almonds, baked meringue, and glazed pineapple would be put to good use in other desserts.

As Maddy walked, she eyed her reflection in the glass store-fronts of the flower shop, the kosher deli, the pharmacy. She'd had her hair cropped in a style she'd let the hairdresser convince her looked neater. *Plus propre.* She should have known from past experiments that when her hair was this short, the curls bobbed crazily. The explosive mop made her look wilder, but younger, too. She wore her short leather jacket and dress pants. She had to look the part, if she wanted Stan to listen.

She turned the corner onto his street, heels treading purpose and decision. For twelve years she'd been serving glazed and filled cakes, chocolaty creations adorned with chestnut purée, berries, more chocolate, and whipped cream. Hadn't Stan asked her more than once if she didn't want to do more with her life? *Well, okay, brother dearest, are you ready to invest?*

Stan had a mock Tudor townhouse with half-timbered gables. Out front were stone pots of pink and white asters. Their parents would have been so proud of his success. She had a house, too, but hers was yet another brick row house in the Pointe. Stan had moved up in the world. Oh yeah, parents didn't have to be alive for the old triggers to kick in — which child had pleased and which disappointed. To do Stan credit, he rarely mentioned the past. It suited him to behave as if he'd been born complete and installed among his beautiful, expensive possessions.

Stan had told her Gaylene wouldn't be home. This was her ... something or other night. Pilates? Knitting? Books? Maddy liked Gaylene well enough, but they never seemed to speak the same language. Gaylene said *sweater* and Maddy thought of a garment that kept her warm. Gaylene meant a circular needle, Italian hand-dyed merino wool, stylish ribbing, and bone buttons that cost three dollars each.

Stan opened the door and Maddy handed him the pastry box. "I brought you dessert." Stan was taller than their father, though still not tall. A daily battle at the gym gave his naturally squat solidity a tight-fleshed, hungry, even predatory look. He still wore his dress shirt from the office, though he'd loosened his tie.

As she stepped in, they kissed cheeks, which was funny since they'd never kissed as children. But as adults, the social convention of living in Montreal had overtaken family habits. Now, not kissing belonged to pickled beets, rosaries, unheated bedrooms.

"How are you doing?" she asked.

"Good, good. Nothing new. We redid the breakfast nook since you were last here."

She followed him to the kitchen with its butcher block island and granite countertops. Copper-bottom skillets hung on the wall. All the appliances were in brushed steel.

She and Yushi planned to redesign her kitchen to maximize space and utility. Broad stainless steel counters and cooling shelves. The size of the stove was more important than its design features. A larger refrigerator would be necessary, though white was fine. Theirs would be a working kitchen, not a magazine showpiece.

The new breakfast nook was styled in oak with a granite-top table. A window the exact width of the table faced the garden out back. She slid onto the bench, which was upholstered in faux suede. Or maybe it *was* suede. "Nice," she said, as he seemed to be waiting.

"Do you want coffee? A glass of wine?"

"I'll have what you're drinking."

"Scotch?"

"Sure."

She heard him take glasses from a cupboard, the churn of the refrigerator plonking ice cubes into glass, Scotch being poured from a bottle. With so much stone and metal, the least sound echoed. He set coasters on the table, then her glass and his. If he was curious that she'd asked to see him, he didn't show it.

"Do you want water or soda?"

"Ice is fine."

One side of his mouth lifted. "Like me."

Maybe not like him, because she couldn't recall when she'd last had Scotch, but if it made him feel brotherly, all the better. She looked around for her pastry box. "I want you to taste the cake I brought."

"I'll have it later with Gaylene."

"No, I want you to have it now. That's why I'm here."

That got a quizzical look. She pushed herself off the bench, too impatient to wait any longer. She had to open a few cupboard doors before she found the plates. He'd put the box in the refrigerator. She undid the string and lifted out the *nouméa*. It looked perfect. She scanned for drawers until, enjoying her puzzlement, he said, "Next to the stove." She grabbed a fork, tore a piece of paper towel off the roll, brought the plate, ad hoc napkin, and fork to the table.

"From your patisserie?"

"Nope."

"What's the occasion?"

He might be able to restrain himself while Gaylene was around, but she knew he loved sweets. "Taste it and I'll tell you."

He nudged a baton of pineapple with his fingers, dabbed it deeper in the cream, bit into it. "Mmm."

"You should try the cake."

The tines of the fork crunched through meringue, then slid into the rich mousse. He tasted it, feeling the textures on his tongue, raised his eyebrows. He took another bite. "Wherever you got this, you should work for them."

Maddy grinned. He couldn't have said it better if he'd cracked a fortune cookie and read the message out loud.

"Why don't you tell me what this is about?"

"My friend makes these. She used to work as a pastry chef in Toronto. I want her to start a business here — as an independent, selling directly to restaurants."

"Why doesn't she?"

She wanted to reach across the table and knock on his forehead. *Hello in there?* Since *he* had investments and capital, he assumed everyone did. She restrained herself and said calmly, "We need funds. She's a pastry chef. I want to use the downstairs of my house for a kitchen."

He set his fork on the plate and put his hand on his glass as if to lift it, but didn't. He twisted it half a rotation on its coaster, twisted it back again. "Before you start anything, you should approach some restaurants. Get a list of customers."

"Okay. And then?"

"You start small. Get a reputation. You've got a product. No doubt about that." He took up the fork again, swiped it through mousse, and put it in his mouth.

"But the ..." She wished he would say it first.

"The what?"

"The money."

"You'll need money," he agreed.

Exasperated with how easy it seemed to him, she blurted, "Will you lend me some? Will you invest?"

"I thought you told me you paid off your mortgage."

"Ages ago."

"So you're sitting on three hundred K of home equity. Even in the Pointe. It's inner-city real estate. Property prices are going up. The bank will give you money against it. Didn't you know?"

She stared at him. "No."

"Just don't get yourself in too deep. Ask for a hundred and see if you can stretch it."

She and Yushi had calculated that it would cost forty thousand, including the renovations to her home, to get underway.

"Start by finding customers. Get papers drawn up. If this woman —" He pointed at the remaining morsel of meringue and mousse. "If she isn't bringing any cash in, she only gets a small share."

"She's bringing her expertise."

He nodded. "You work that out. I'll give you my account-ant's number."

From his tone she could tell that he believed this would work. She felt excited and proud — and useful in a way that was new to her. "You'll have to meet her," she said, though she'd always taken care to keep her odd assortment of friends to herself.

"Why didn't you bring her along today?" He, too, had never been interested in meeting her friends.

"I wanted to talk to you first."

"Is she younger? Older?" He smeared his fork across the plate to collect any last crumbs.

Maddy hesitated. He would see soon enough. "Younger."

"Good. More initiative and energy. This" — he tapped his fork on the china — "is worth gold."

In the stillness of the night Maddy woke to a voice deep in her ear. The cadence was low, yet a girl's — a girl taunting her with her pretty pink bra. Maddy opened her eyes, not wanting to fall back into a dream about those long-ago, stupid times.

As soon as she'd come home that evening, she'd called Yushi. Rose had answered in her slow, deep voice. Maddy asked for Yushi but then couldn't tell if Rose had gone to get Yushi or if she was still there. Should Maddy remind her who Yushi was? *Remember Yushi, your roommate?* The girl had a few neurons missing. Yushi made excuses for Rose, saying she grew up iso-lated and then lost her mother, but Maddy thought that if a person knew how to pick up a phone when it rang, then she should learn how to use it. *Hello? You'd like to talk to Yushi? Just a moment please.* Yushi had lost her mother, too. That didn't make her comatose.

Maddy was about to hang up and call back when Yushi said hello. Maddy was so impatient and excited to tell her how Stan had advised them to proceed, she forgot about Rose. Yushi had

had more ideas, too. A cake made with blood-orange glaze, marbled with bitter chocolate. A stacked shelf system she'd seen in a restaurant kitchen. A menu of petits fours to appeal to the cupcake crowd.

So why, Maddy groaned, with her life finally getting on track and everything dovetailing so beautifully, were her dreams dredging up that damp dirt cellar? So sick with shame and fear she'd been. So sick she could have thrown up. One minute she'd felt bold, with her bra tucked under her leg, her shirt still covering her underpants, sipping the whisky or rum or whatever Neil had poured, and then she saw her cards. With these cards she would lose and have to take off her blouse or her underpants. Let the others see her breasts or down there.

Both were too awful. Neither was possible. She tried to keep her voice from trembling and asked where the bathroom was.

The other boy, the one she didn't like, grumbled, Gimme a break. In the middle of a hand she wants to pee.

Neil cut him off. Upstairs, he said. Past the kitchen, down the hall.

She closed her cards and set them face down on the blanket. By now she'd realized that Tonya wasn't on her side. She'd played this game before. She'd known to wear a pretty bra. Her low voice rose from deep within her own self-assurance.

Maddy tiptoed up the stairs. The dirt on the steps stuck to her damp feet. She felt air on her thighs because she wasn't wearing a skirt. The kitchen looked strange because she was standing in her underpants. You were supposed to be dressed when you were in a kitchen. She found the bathroom, where yellowing grey towels and dirty clothes sagged off the back of the toilet and were kicked along the floor. Didn't Tonya's mother clean the bathroom? Nervous, Maddy peed. Then what? She stood, not touching the sink, which was grimy with streaks of old toothpaste. A pebble of soap melted in a scummy pool. She didn't know what to do. She couldn't even

leave the house without her skirt. She couldn't make herself
go back to the cellar, where the others waited with that weird,
eager tension she'd thought she understood but knew now
she didn't. They *wanted* to take their clothes off. She wanted
to keep hers on.

A double knock on the door startled her.

Maddy?

One of the boys. Probably Neil. The other one wouldn't
have come.

Are you okay? You don't have to play anymore if you don't
want to.

The relief of not having to take off more clothes made her
forget she was already missing her skirt and bra.

Open up. I've got something for you.

She trusted Neil because he'd been nice to her. She opened
the door and nearly closed it again when she saw him in his
Y-fronts with that bulge in the front stretching the cotton, but
he stood as if so what, he was in his underwear? She was, too.
He held two Mickey Mouse glasses he'd filled again. Come on,
he said. We don't need to play cards. Let's go to my room.

His room sounded safer than the cellar. She took a glass from
him and sipped as she followed him down the hallway. The
drink tasted stronger than the last one. There was nothing in
his room but his bed, with the sheet and blanket kicked against
the wall. There were clothes strewn across the floor. He waved
at the bed. Sit. Are you cold? He pulled the rumpled sheet and
blanket around her. She was glad of the blankets to cover her
bare legs. She tried not to look at his underpants. Maybe boys
always looked like that. How would she know?

Comfy? he asked.

Yeah. She sipped again. The drink made her face feel funny.

Push over. Make room. It sounded so casual. There was space
to sit side by side and finish their drinks. It felt all right, too,
when he nudged her and whispered, Hey, look at me.

He kissed her, which felt nice. His hands had crept under her shirt to squeeze her breasts. In his room with the door closed, both of them under the covers, no one could see. He told her to drink up so he could put her glass on the floor. He kept kissing her and she kissed him back. Then he put her hand under the blanket onto — she didn't know what. A single hard muscle. She tried to pull her hand away. No, he said between his teeth, grab it! He wasn't kissing her anymore. When she wouldn't hold it, he started butting against her with his hips, twisting off her underpants, thrusting and pushing. She cried out in fear and he told her to shut up. He climbed on her, kneeing apart her legs, poking and shoving where there was nowhere to go, *hurting* her! She squirmed, trying to get away. Lie still, fuck you! His hands gripped her shoulders, then he groaned and collapsed on her. It hurt where he'd pushed. Wetness trickled down her legs. She wanted to get out from under him but was afraid that if she moved he would start again.

In a normal tone, he asked if he should get her clothes.

Her clothes! She had to get home! She was way too late. Her mother would yank her hair and pull her ears. Maddy wiped the sheet down the wetness on her legs. The smell made her feel sick. It wasn't yellow like pee. There was blood, too. What had he done? She hurt between her legs. Her underpants were ripped.

When he came back with her skirt and bra all bunched together in his fist, he said, Are you okay? She didn't answer, twisting her skirt up her hips, wishing he wouldn't watch her dress.

The next day at school, Tonya pretended she didn't know her. When Maddy finally walked over to Tonya's locker, she squinted evil eyes and told Maddy to get lost. Because she hadn't kept playing cards? There was no way to ask.

Then Tonya disappeared from school. Maddy dared herself to sneak past the house, but when she finally did it was empty. The cellar windows were dark. When she next walked by, a family with all the women wearing saris was living there.

Months passed and Maddy got fat. When the principal and the English teacher asked if Maddy was having relations with a boy, she didn't know what they meant. "Relations" sounded deliberate and ongoing. The only boy she'd had contact with was Neil, but that was months earlier, it only happened once, and she never saw him again.

It was the nurse at the clinic who showed her a line drawing of a woman and a man. The man had a prod at the top of his legs that the nurse called a penis. The woman had a place in her stomach where a baby could grow. The nurse said that if a penis went between a woman's legs, it made a baby. Maddy remembered Neil's clumsy thrusting that hurt her.

The drawing of a woman's parts only became truly — horribly — real for her during the day-long torture of birth, when she was split wide to expel a baby.

From a window Maddy saw Frédéric changing the lock on his gate and went out to ask how Fara was feeling. He said he'd stayed home for a day because she was feverish and anxious about staying alone in the house. Maddy should have told him right then about Ben, but she wasn't sure how he would react. Despite what Ben had done, she didn't want him to get into trouble. She would feel more comfortable telling Fara.

She waited another day before going over and ringing the doorbell.

Fara looked wan — and wary. Her shoulders relaxed when she saw Maddy. "I thought it was another ex-con selling rosaries. I think they pick on us because we're new here." She stepped back so Maddy could come in.

"They come to my place, too, don't worry. They do the whole street. Guys with strawberries, kids with chocolate bars, Jehovah's Witnesses, people selling calendars, you name it. Maybe because our houses are on the sidewalk. Or Pointers are gullible." She'd stopped in the hallway, admiring the French doors. "These look great!"

Fara slid a glance, as if she didn't trust what she'd see. "Yeah. That's where the guy was standing the other day."

"Frédéric told me. You must have been …"

"I nearly had a heart attack. I wasn't sure if I was hallucinating — if it was a ghost or what. I don't even believe in ghosts, but at that moment —" She shuddered.

"Scary. Especially if you were already sick and feeling woozy."

Fara had squeezed shut her eyes and turned her head away from the French doors.

"How are you now? Are you up for a visit?"

"Please. Frédéric's got retirement cocktails for one of his employees. He doesn't care about the party, but he's glad she's leaving so he can hire someone younger who won't faint at the sight of a computer." Fara had walked through to the kitchen and opened the refrigerator. "Do you want a beer?" She handed Maddy a bottle. In the dining room she clicked on a tiffany lamp, motioned for Maddy to sit, and pulled out a chair for herself.

A painting hung on the wall across from Maddy — a large pale abstract of horizontal stripes. The soft light from the lamp warmed the grain of the wood furniture and stroked gleams on the wineglasses in the buffet. "Nice what you've done in here," Maddy said, not that she'd ever seen the room before. Ben's father didn't invite people in, and she'd been too young when Ben's mother still lived here.

"It's best when the sun shines in. That's what made me want to buy the house — before I knew people crawled in under the deck."

"That's how he got in?"

"There's a window under the deck. Frédéric never noticed it wasn't locked." She smirked and took a swallow of beer.

So Ben hadn't broken a window. Maybe not for the police, but for her it was a point in his favour. "I wanted to tell you,"

Maddy began. "I think the guy who broke in was Ben — the brother of the boy who killed himself."

Fara's rueful look faded.

"I saw him hanging around in the alley ... near your fence."

"You told me the guy in the alley was from the rooming house."

"That's who I used to see. Ben only recently started coming around."

"And you think he ...?"

"I think he was upset his dad sold the house."

Fara considered this. "Yeah, I can see he might be. But we didn't know anything about him and his dad. We bought the house fair and square."

"I don't think he blames you. He knows this is about him and his dad, not you." She didn't actually know what Ben thought, but she didn't want Fara and Frédéric to view him too harshly. "I think he only started to miss the house after his dad sold it. And ... maybe he wanted to see it again?"

Fara tilted her beer bottle at the French doors. "He was standing right there when I came downstairs. Right where his brother hanged himself."

Maddy looked where she pointed. Though she'd told Fara about the hanging, she hadn't expected Fara to identify the exact spot.

"It's not the house," Fara said now. "It's his brother. That's what he's trying to figure out. Why his brother killed himself. Except it doesn't work that way. He'll never find out." Fara paused then added, "I know. My sister killed herself."

Maddy gave a jerk of surprise. Even disbelief. Fara had said it so calmly.

She continued in an even voice, "That's the thing about suicide — even harder than the loss is the guilt. You beat yourself up because you didn't notice in time to stop them. It's probably even worse for him than for me. Remember? You told me how he used to pick his brother up after school and take care of him when their father was at work. My sister and I, we weren't close."

Maddy was trying to remember if Fara had ever hinted that she'd had a sister.

"When you're the eldest, you always feel responsible. You feel like you should be keeping an eye out. There's this weird connection — and you hate it, but it's there, too. Always there."

Fara was picking at the edge of the label on the beer bottle. "I know exactly what he's going through — probably better than he knows himself. The not being able to figure it out, the anger.... *They* end their lives, but they leave you with a life's worth of knowing they chose nothingness over anything you could offer." She rolled her head from side to side then dropped it forward again. "Sometimes I got so angry at what she did that I thought if she wasn't already dead, I would kill her. It takes you years to get past that, and even then, you don't forget."

"How long ago was it?" Maddy asked quietly.

"Seventeen years. She was in her apartment. I should have known something was wrong when she asked if I still had a key. They give you little messages, you know. Little last chances to see if you're paying attention. I guess I wasn't. I mean, I heard her, but was I supposed to be second-guessing a motive behind every word she said? Anyhow, she knew I had a key and I'd be the one to find her. She planned it down to that detail. It wasn't an accident."

Maddy recognized the circling logic. How often had she replayed the night when she woke with leaking breasts, and her baby and the woman with the braid were gone? What should she have done differently? What should she have noticed but didn't?

Fara took a swallow of beer. "I knew right away something was wrong. She didn't answer the door and I had to use the key to get in — and there was her coat on the sofa. She only had that one coat so I knew she had to be there. I called but she didn't answer. Then I looked in all the rooms. Where do you look for someone when you know she has to be there but you can't find her? The bathroom door was closed, but I couldn't make myself go in there. No way, I thought. She wouldn't do that to me — one of those bloody bathtub scenes. Exsanguination." She pronounced each syllable then set her bottle hard on the table.

As Fara sat silent, staring at the bottle, Maddy guessed that was what had happened. "I'm really sorry, Fara —"

"Yeah, so am I." Fara sounded more dry than sorry. "Most of the time I don't even tell people I had a sister. Just those words — *had a sister* — screw me up completely. Because obviously I don't have her anymore. She's dead. But that feeling of having a sister doesn't go away just because she dies. I didn't grow up alone. I'm not an only child. I still have that sense of a bond. But where is she then? If she's dead." Fara sniffed. "Not *if*. She is."

Maddy gave a slight nod. She knew this, too. Once you had a baby, you always had a baby, even when the baby was gone. The feeling was deeper than absence or logic.

Fara scraped her hair off her forehead. "It was the hardest thing I've ever done in my life, opening that bathroom door. And then —" She snorted. "It was just an ordinary bathroom!" She thrust a hand out, pointing. "Sink, toilet, tub, shower curtain, towel ... no blood. No Claire."

She paused, as if waiting for the rest of the story to reveal itself — as if she, too, was hearing it for the first time. Maddy felt uneasy, not sure what was coming next. Not sure either that talking about her sister's suicide was good for Fara. Her eyes glittered.

Strangely, then, she smiled. "I was so glad I didn't have to see blood. I figured I could handle whatever else I was going to find. Stupid, eh?" She glanced at Maddy. "I walked back through the rooms again. I looked behind the furniture and opened the closets. I even looked in the bottom cupboards in the kitchen. She used to do dumb stuff like that when we were kids. Always hiding. She was thinner than me and not as tall. If she really wanted to, she could have squiggled in. It was crazy to look in the cupboards, but I didn't know what else to do. I knew she had to be somewhere in the apartment because her coat was there." Fara wagged a hand, pointing beside her at the invisible, yet incontrovertible fact of the coat.

"But I couldn't find her and then I started to think maybe she was doing the laundry in the basement. Or she was in someone else's apartment. I didn't really believe it — she didn't have friends in the building — but I had to think something. Your mind tries to make sense."

"Yes," Maddy murmured. The mind was a great rationalizer.

"I wasn't even looking for her anymore, just walking from room to room. Waiting for her to show up. Starting to get pissed off at whatever game she was playing." Fara paused, as if watching herself walk from room to room. "Then I was in the bedroom and I saw an edge of green garbage bag sticking out from under the sheets. I thought, what stupid thing has she done now, leaving garbage in her bed. So I flipped back the duvet."

Maddy waited. Fara didn't speak. She'd started scraping her fingernail down the edge of the beer bottle label again.

Finally, Maddy asked, "What was in her bed?"

"She was."

Maddy flushed with shock. The bald words tingled on her skin.

"She'd tied a bag over her head. She didn't have any drugs or alcohol in her system. The coroner told me. She suffocated herself stone-cold sober."

"That's ..." Maddy began but had no idea where to go.

"He said it's a peaceful death. The person keeps breathing and slowly falls asleep."

"But for you ... to find her like that."

"Yeah. On a shock level, it ranks right up there. And as a statement, it's gross. It's like you're no better than *garbage*." The accusatory sharpness of the word rang clear. But who was she accusing, her sister or herself?

Maddy didn't know what to say. Even though it had happened years ago, when Fara talked about it, she seemed to relive the details as if she were still in her sister's apartment. "Do you know why she did it?"

"Why?" Fara scowled. "Everyone wants to know why, but I don't think why matters. Even if you find a reason, that's just an excuse. The fact is the person did it. They ran up against a wall or they were depressed or they couldn't face something or ... whatever. We all have those times. Haven't you?" Fara shot her a look, and as she seemed to be waiting, Maddy nodded.

"But there are only certain people who choose suicide. That's what I wonder — why was suicide an option for her? It's not *even* an option. It's the end of all options. What makes a person decide to do that? To people who are still alive that kind of decision just doesn't make sense."

Maddy had had times, during those anguished months of living with her parents' hatred, and not knowing what to do or where to turn with her baby, when she'd thought about jumping off a bridge — but never to the point of deciding which bridge.

Fara leaned back in her chair. "That's what Ben is feeling. He knows his brother's dead, but he doesn't believe it. He blames himself because he didn't realize his brother was so desperate. He's kicking himself in the head. So there's guilt, but there's grief, too. And what do you do with the grief? Because you lost them, right? They're *dead*. You're in mourning. You grieve for them. But you're angry, too. Because they didn't just do it to themselves, they did it to you — and everyone they left behind. Suicide is such a fucked-up mess."

"I'm sorry," Maddy said. "I had no idea ..."

"It was a long time ago." Fara's voice was cool now. Matter-of-fact. "I've been thinking about it more since we've been living here. I knew a boy killed himself in the house but not that he had a brother. I feel sorry for him. He's going to have to figure all this out. The guilt, the grief, the blame. Do you really think it was him I saw?"

"One of the neighbours told me they saw him with a key to your gate." Under the table, Maddy crossed her fingers for her white lie.

"Recently?"

"I think so."

Fara tapped a finger on her empty bottle. "Nice if they would have told us."

Maddy tightened her lips. "Well, you scared him off for good now. He won't come back."

"We should still tell the police."

"Do you have to?"

Fara gave her a narrow look. "He knew we were living here when he broke in. Why should I trust him? Maybe we won't press charges, but he should be warned. That seems pretty obvious to me."

Maddy nodded quickly. "Of course. You're right."

"I think you have to go now. I need to lie down for a while. I probably shouldn't have had a beer."

This was too abrupt. They should have had a few moments of quiet talk — of consolation — but Fara had already risen from her chair and was walking to the door. Maddy grabbed her jacket off the wall hook and thrust her arms in the sleeves. Fara waited. Her cheeks looked drawn, her mouth sad. Maddy wanted to say something, but what? Fara's story about her sister was still too raw between them. Fara had already opened the door.

"I'm sorry about your sister," Maddy said as she stepped past Fara.

Fara's pose — one arm on the door frame, the other holding the door — made her look awkward and graceless. Maddy wasn't the huggy type, but she wished now she'd hugged her. Fara closed the door.

In her house Maddy stood for a few moments, thinking about Fara. How strange that she'd chosen to live in a house where there had been a suicide.

ROSE

Early November. A lowering sky, the light too dim to penetrate even the many panes of the windows. Rose had clicked on both lamps, angling their heads to shine on her loom. She pulled the beater toward her and stepped on the next treadle, closing the mouth of the threads, then opening it again. With each bite, the cloth grew in huckaback stripes of violet, poppy red, cerulean, and aqua.

She swayed as she wove, with a gentle, back-and-forth bob of her shoulders. She loved hearing the pull of thread rattling the spool in the shuttle, the silvery jangle of the heddles, the paddle-knock of the treadles. Beneath the percussion of her loom, she heard an undertone of ghost looms thumping, the faint clangour of hundreds of harnesses dropping. Leo had tried listening but never made out the echo. Yet he believed her. Years ago this building had been a textile factory where men and women worked at enormous looms, weaving great bolts of cloth. Children stood at either end, throwing the shuttle across, or crawled under the shafts to fix tangles and free the heddles when they caught. When the children were hungry, they chewed the scraps of threads that had dropped to the floor.

Next to the sponge mat propped against the wall were Leo's two canvas sacks of clothes and belongings. When the wind had whipped the last leaves from the trees and the stars glinted like chips of ice in the night sky, Rose had finally convinced Leo to move to her studio. She could no longer climb the ladder because her hands were too frozen to trust her hold. Where are you going to spend the winter? she'd asked. You have to find somewhere warm. I'll worry too much about you. But this is your space, he said. She touched his face with her fingers. It can be yours, too.

At the triple knock on the door, she set aside the shuttle and crossed the room to let in Leo, who held a bag of food. The graze of his hair was cold on her cheek. She could taste that he'd eaten an apple on his walk from the market and smell the faint, wet-dog scent of his parka.

He swung the bag onto the small table. "You're expensive, girl."

"Because I wanted olives?"

He shrugged off his parka. "It starts with olives. Then it's fancy shoes, diamonds, and a little Japanese car so you can zip around the city — and trips to a four-star hotel in Cuba in the winter."

"Barbados." She sat on her bench again, leaning forward to flick two heddles apart. "I want to go to Barbados to meet your grandparents." Barbados sounded magical, but she was even more curious about his grandparents. Imagine having grandparents.

"Wouldn't that be something?" He'd joined her on the bench. "These are new." He touched her earlobe. Yushi had given her a pair of silver hoops, her first earrings.

"From Yushi," she said shyly, still awed by gestures of affection and friendship.

Busy as Yushi was these days, she'd insisted on meeting Leo. Rose had brought him to the market, where they'd shared a slab of spinach and goat cheese pizza. Leo had been easy and friendly. Yushi watched him closely. To Rose she said, So that's why you were asking me about dreads.

Rose's hair hung to her shoulders now, but she almost always wore it clipped back or gathered in a short ponytail.

She hadn't known she could be so vain, but she liked showing off her *pretty ears*.

"It started snowing," Leo said. "Did you see?"

She turned her head to the window, where bits of fluff drifted down from the endless duvet of sky. The day she'd answered Yushi's ad for a roommate, flakes had twirled through the air as she'd climbed the metal stairs. That meant she'd been in Montreal for a year. Dates on the calendar never felt as real to her as the markers of the seasons. The first trillium in the woods. The first ice in the morning. The first snowfall.

She relaxed against Leo's chest, eyes on the almost invisible flutter of snow against dusk. She'd met him in the summer, with the smell of freshly mown grass in the air.

She was wheeling her trolley down the corridor when she heard, "Hey, Rose!"

Kenny waved a small box he was holding and shuffle-jogged toward her. "Hoo!" he exhaled. "You move fast. Guess where I was yesterday? Up at your cabin, when it started snowing. The trees getting all heavy with snow and the fire in the stove? I was like ..." He held out both his arms and beamed at the ceiling.

"I'm glad." She remembered how desolate the cabin looked when she last saw it. The reproach of its blank window. "Someone should stay there."

"Why don't you take Leo? He'd love it."

"Leo likes the city. Me, too."

"That's it, eh? Bright lights, big action."

That wasn't what Rose meant, but she wouldn't have known how to explain.

"You just let me know if you change your mind. It's your cabin, eh?" He backed up a step, tapping the box against his leg. "Doctor can't go into the room till I get her these masks."

Rose leaned into her cart again, steering it close to the wall as an orderly passed with a patient on a stretcher.

She was pleased to see Kenny so happy. And how easy it had been for her. The same cabin she'd fled was the castle he'd dreamed of. She still wondered that he and Jerome seemed to have become friends, but maybe she'd never understood Jerome. The people in Rivière-des-Pins called him useless — so different from his hard-working, upstanding father — but those were the same people who had disapproved of Maman. And she herself knew Armand wasn't the man everyone thought he was, either. She remembered how Jerome had helped Kenny carry her loom through the woods. She'd kept expecting a sneer, which, she had to admit, she never saw.

People and how they acted were still a great mystery to Rose. Maman had been so alone and furtive. Even though she was close to Rose, there was so much she never told her. School had been an exercise to be endured. And how was Rose ever to understand a man like Armand?

Her life among people had only truly started when she'd moved to Montreal and met Yushi and Kenny and Leo. They were her friends now, but she didn't understand how they had known they would like her. She'd watched animals in the woods — rabbits and deer — freeze with their snouts lifted, smelling a stranger. Friend or foe?

But how did people know? How did they decide?

Rose climbed the metal stairs to her apartment with her hand on the railing. The snow that had fallen two days earlier hadn't collected, but the steps were frozen and slippery. From the street she'd seen the light in the window and was glad Yushi was home. Since she'd started planning this dessert business, Yushi was spending most evenings at Maddy's, whose kitchen she would be using. Even so, the hallway of their apartment was stacked with the bowls and cake tins they'd been buying, odd-shaped paraphernalia made of silicone, glass, plastic, and stainless steel ... a pastry blender, a sifter, a dough scraper, piping tubes, a zester. Yushi had explained what they were. The only one Rose recognized was the rolling pin, except it wasn't wooden like Maman's but grey-and-white marble. Stone stayed cooler, Yushi said, which was important when working in the heat of a kitchen.

Rose opened the door onto the smell of sautéed garlic and herbs. From the kitchen she heard voices, then a hoot that didn't sound like Yushi. The rosewood table in the living room was strewn with papers and manila folders. Yellow sticky notes dotted the folders and the table.

Rose hesitated, then walked down the hallway past the knee-high towers of baking equipment. Yushi was at the stove. Maddy leaned against the counter, her hips and thighs outlined in burgundy tights and a short denim skirt. Rose still felt they looked odd together, Yushi so elfin and Maddy so broad. The oddness wasn't a criticism, but the only way Rose could formulate to herself that there was something about Maddy she didn't trust.

"Here she is," Maddy said.

Yushi glanced over her shoulder. "We've been waiting for you."

"Do you want me to serve the rice?" Maddy asked. Three plates stood ready on the counter.

Yushi nudged her away. "I'm cooking. You two go sit. Take placemats. Or no — wait. You can carry your plates."

Rose lifted her hands. "I haven't —"

"Go wash your germy hospital hands," Yushi ordered. And to Maddy, "You take her plate."

They waited for her at the table, where they'd pushed aside the manila folders and papers. Yushi had made a cashew and vegetable stir fry. There was a bottle of wine on the table and a juice glass at each of their placemats.

Maddy said, "We're celebrating. As of today, we've got twelve restaurants who will take four desserts a week." She raised her glass.

Rose followed Yushi's lead when she leaned forward to clink. "You'll make forty-eight cakes a week?" she asked.

"Cakes, flans, tortes, and brioche." Yushi bobbed her head. "Maybe quiche. I haven't decided yet."

"Isn't that a lot?"

"Not if that's all I'm doing."

Maddy stabbed her fork into a chunk of zucchini. "Rose is right. It adds up to a lot of hours in the kitchen. It would make more sense —" She stopped and looked at Rose. "I've been trying to convince Yushi that it would make more sense if she moved to the Pointe. So she wouldn't be travelling across the city every day."

Rose knew what she meant. She, too, wished she lived closer to her studio and Leo.

But — oh! She turned to Yushi, forgetting about Maddy. "Are you moving?"

"I sort of thought," Yushi said slowly, "that *you* might be moving. You've been spending quite a few nights at Leo's."

Rose had never explained about Leo's penthouse suite that was missing a wall, windows, furniture, electricity, a bathroom, and running water. In turn, Yushi had been so preoccupied with starting her baking business that she hadn't visited Rose's studio since Leo had begun sleeping there. Caught between two secrets, Rose didn't know how to answer.

Yushi watched her. "It's too soon to say? You're not sure about him?"

Rose was sure that she and Leo belonged together, but she didn't know if he knew, and they couldn't both live in her studio all the time. They would get caught. Softly, she said, "We've never talked about getting a place."

"If Yushi moved to my house," Maddy said, "you could get a place with him. Or he could move in here. You could stay. You wouldn't even have to move."

Rose kept her eyes on her food. These were things for her and Leo to talk about, not Maddy and Yushi.

"Stop," Yushi told Maddy. "You're talking too fast. You mentioned it, now let Rose think about it."

"Okay." Maddy took a swallow of wine. "I'm just saying that —"

Yushi held up her palm, and Maddy closed her mouth.

Rose thought about having a place with Leo — not the studio with her loom and sleeping bags, but a real apartment like she had with Yushi. He'd told her he'd run away from rooms and apartments and houses. Rooms could so easily become cages where people snapped and snarled. Even people who loved you got nasty, hugging you one minute, weeping and slamming you hard against a wall the next. He'd grown up more frightened of his mother when she was happy than when she was sullen and depressed. The higher her spirits soared, the more demonic the crash. He remembered being locked in a room for so long he peed on the floor because there was nowhere to go, and wiping the puddle with his socks so she wouldn't find it and hit him. Leo didn't trust the way people turned monstrous behind the closed doors of their homes. Rose thought of how that hadn't happened in her studio, even though they were more or less living together. She tried to imagine him in an apartment, taking a carton of milk from the refrigerator. Sitting on a sofa. Getting into a bed with sheets and blankets. She couldn't picture it. Leo was a cheese-and-apples, wash-at-the-sink, sleeping-bag kind of guy.

Yushi and Maddy were talking desserts again. "A nutmeg grater," Yushi said, flipping open a folder and adding it to a list. "Nothing like fresh nutmeg in *crème pâtissière*." Her silver bracelet jiggled as she mimed sprinkling nutmeg.

She looked across at Rose. "Hey." She laid her hand on Rose's wrist. "Stop thinking about it. Everything will fall into place. It serves no purpose to worry about what hasn't happened yet."

Maman would have said that.

Rose had an hour before she had to catch the subway to work. She'd asked Leo if he wanted to go to a diner in St-Henri for soup. The booths had green Arborite tables with powder-green vinyl benches. The walls were the same sickly green. Under the stark white lights even Leo's brown skin looked wan. Rose focused on the warmth of his eyes, his chipped tooth that made his smile endearing, the soft jute of his locs.

Both leaned over the bowls of pea soup the waitress set before them. The smell reminded Rose of Maman returning from a trip to Rivière-des-Pins with the extravagance of a small ham. When they finished the meat, they used the bone to make pea soup.

Then Leo said, "My ma used to make pea soup — with cow heel."

She waited to hear if he would say more about his mother. She wondered if, by cow heel, he meant a cow's hard, black heel. Though was that any stranger than Maman's Christmas meal of pig's feet in gravy?

The restaurant phone rang every few minutes. The man at the cash, who answered, shouted orders to the two cooks working at their grills and fryers behind the counter. *"Deux grosses frites! Une pizza, large, all-dress!"* She was getting used to the mix of English and French — Franglais — in Montreal.

The counter was piled with Styrofoam trays and foil tins. Men walked in, stamping snow off their boots, and left again with armfuls of paper packages and pizza boxes. The diner was busier with deliveries than with the few clients at the tables. A bald man sagged on his wall bench, sipping coffee from a thick china mug. A middle-aged woman with blue-caked eyelids hadn't taken off her coat with its fur collar, which she patted now and then as she devoured a large poutine.

The pea soup wasn't as thick as Maman's, but it warmed Rose. She was happy to be sitting with Leo in a diner where anyone who wanted could see them.

"Is Kenny still going up to your cabin in this snow?"

"All the time."

"He's one tough guy. You wouldn't catch me hiking into any woods with snow and bears all around."

Rose shook her head. "I've told you before. It's not that far north. There aren't any bears. And snow doesn't matter. The cabin's got a door and a wood stove." Leo had been far more exposed to the elements sleeping in his open-air tower.

For the fourth or fifth time he sprinkled more black pepper on his soup. "Kenny's the friend, isn't he? That day I met you when you were sitting by the canal. You said you thought you'd lost a friend. You didn't even want to talk to me, you were so upset."

She didn't look up from her bowl. "Everything's fine now."

"He seems like an easygoing guy. I can't figure out what happened to make you feel so bad."

"It was nothing he did." She crumbled a package of crackers into her soup, dunked the pieces with her spoon. She was too embarrassed to tell Leo what had happened that night in the cabin. Maybe one day she would, but not now, over soup in a diner.

The woman with the fur collar had finished her poutine in record time and lifted her hand to flag the waitress, her clasp purse already open to pay.

"He didn't make a pass at you." Leo scraped the last of his soup from the bowl.

"What do you mean?"

"I don't think he's interested in girls."

"How do you know?"

Leo shrugged.

Rose considered what she knew of Kenny. How happy he always sounded about seeing Jerome. And did Jerome ... like Kenny, too? There was a new thought.

Leo had finished his soup and sat back, clasping his hands behind his head. From where she sat, she could see the large clock over the cash. She would have to leave for the hospital soon. She wanted to talk to Leo about Yushi but felt nervous about how he would respond and what that would mean for them. She watched his face. "Yushi's thinking of moving out."

He pulled his hands from behind his head and set his elbows on the table. "What happens to you?"

She couldn't bring herself to say all the options Maddy had rattled off.

"Can you live there alone?"

"It's too big. I can't afford it." And she didn't want to live alone.

He stared before him, thinking. Then crept his hand across the table to touch hers. "You can move out, too."

Did he mean move to somewhere smaller? Or that they could move in together? She heard the phone ringing and the man at the cash calling orders. Two men with baseball caps over shaved, grizzled heads joked with the waitress.

Leo's fingertips stroked the back of her hand. "I can't ..."

Sadness sifted through her as she felt him back away from what she'd hoped — all the while she'd known he didn't want to live closed up in a box of walls. Still, she'd hoped.

"I can't," he began again, "live up in the city where you do. But what if you moved down here to St-Henri or the Pointe?"

The waitress suddenly loomed at their table. *"Vous avez finis?"* She snatched their bowls, not waiting for an answer. *"Café?"*

Leo shook his head so she would leave.

Rose needed to be sure she understood. "You mean, rent a place by myself or get a place together?"

"Well ..." Leo looked at her. "How about we try *together*?" He said the word carefully, as if trying out the sound. "But somewhere small, okay? Nothing fancy. I can pay half the rent, but I can't afford much."

Rose's heart beat with such excitement she could feel it in her neck.

He grasped her fingers more tightly. "I'll be with you, but I don't want anyone to find me. Will you sign the lease?"

She nodded.

Leo's face was still sober. "And you know, when the weather's nice again, I might want to go sleep —" He lifted his chin in the direction of the canal.

Rose remembered the lovely stir of cool wind in the summer, so high up with the city below.

Leo cupped his hand over hers. "You can come, too."

FARA

"Hey, Fara." Valerie wheeled a chair out of Fara's path as she walked to her desk. Zeery stroked her arm as she passed. "You look pale." Claudette's voice squeaked even higher with concern.

"I'm okay," Fara assured them.

"Was it strep?"

Fara shook her head. She'd only had a sore throat and flu, but she'd told the doctor about the shock of the break-in and he'd given her a week off work.

Everyone was solicitous, but her desk was the usual tornado wreckage of paper and the phone was ringing. With a grimace she answered. "Twelve surgery." An unidentified person wanted to borrow an IV pump. "Who's calling?" she asked. Lending equipment was an exclusively you-scratch-my-back arrangement. Departments that never lent anything didn't get anything. Not on her watch.

Nahi tapped his finger on the counter as he walked passed. "You tell me if you need help today."

The people at work only knew she'd been sick. She hadn't even told Zeery about the break-in. She would have had to explain about Ben, the suicide in the house, maybe even her own family suicide. It would all sound crazy.

She and Frédéric had decided not to report Ben to the police. She couldn't help it, she felt for him — another casualty of a dysfunctional family gone bust. She remembered how he'd leaped off the deck and bolted. He'd had a fright, too. She was pretty sure he wasn't going to come back. Frédéric wasn't as positive, but for lack of concrete proof that it was Ben, he finally agreed. Eric had already said that next spring he would replace their weathered plank fence with a proper one. It would be another practical and handsome Eric accomplishment, though Frédéric would have to spend a couple of days playing lackey.

The phone rang again. "Wait," she said when she heard Lynn's voice. She had to root through requisitions, manila folders, and consultations to find her agenda. "Okay, tell me now." She wrote *22B Wanderbeer 13:00 Dialysis* on today's date.

On the other side of the counter, a man said, *"Madame!"*

So early in the morning and already the greater public surged before her. "Yes?"

"I'm looking for a Greek."

"Does this Greek have a name?"

"A lady."

"I need a name." Fara had poked her finger into a rubber tip to begin the triage of paper on her desk.

"A Greek," he insisted. "A lady."

She didn't begrudge the Greek lady a visit, but if he didn't know her name, should he even be visiting her? She wasn't letting him wander down the hallway into rooms to look at patients in their beds. "Can you tell me what street she lives on? Or how old she is?"

"Old," he barked.

People should stay home if it was so hard for them to be civil.

Fara answered the phone. "Okay." She scratched Guang's name on her notepad to remind herself to tell Brie there was a sick call for nights.

"Madame!" The man clenched an impatient fist on the counter.

"Listen." Fara made a fist with her voice. "I can't help you if you don't know this lady's name, her age, or her address."

"A Greek," he insisted.

A Radiology porter dangled an arm across the counter to show her a slip of paper. In her test book she jotted *40A Johnston CT chest*. The porter had overheard the man badgering her. He spoke to him in Greek and told Fara, "He's looking for a Greek lady."

Fara smirked. "We've been through this. He doesn't know her name."

"Come on. How many Greek patients you got?"

"We don't identify patients by ethnicity. We use their names. Why is *he* visiting someone whose name he doesn't know?"

"She's the wife of a guy he plays cards with."

"You know he can't just go looking in rooms."

The porter pushed away from the counter and motioned with his head for the man to follow him back to the elevator.

Fara didn't trust the porter but didn't have the time to watch him. The intercom was buzzing. Claudette needed someone to bring her a Toomey syringe in an isolation room. Fara twisted off her chair. It was easier to get it herself than find an orderly or a nurse who wasn't busy. In the hallway she walked past a huddle of surgical residents standing outside a patient's room discussing her liver mets. If the patient or anyone in the room — or in the hallway — didn't already know she had cancer, they knew it now. Choice of treatment, prognosis, chance of recovery. In a hospital, privacy was a concept thinner than the curtains between the beds.

Back in the nursing station Fara saw that the Radiology porter had stepped behind the counter and was scanning the names on the patient list. "What are you doing?" she demanded.

He waved his slip of paper. "I forgot the room number you told me."

"The room number is stamped on your slip — the way it always is."

"Yeah, yeah, yeah." He walked away.

Fara knew he'd taken note of the rooms with Greek names. She wanted to follow him — or maybe just report him to his supervisor for still hanging around when he was supposed to be transporting patients to CT — but she had to find Brie to tell her there was a sick call, her phone was ringing, and a new patient, looking wary and lost, stood before her desk with a package from Admitting.

A week away from work and nothing had changed. Same old, same old. Maybe she and Frédéric should start a pastry business. Or something.

Anouk grabbed the remote for the TV and turned up the volume. She sat with her knees tucked up against Ben's legs. They were watching a comedy show that he didn't find all that funny, but she sniggered and looked at him with a bright face, so he pretended to laugh.

The man on TV brayed, "Kid says, But Mommy, why do *you* always wet the bed?"

Yeah, Ben nodded at Anouk. Good joke. Though what was the joke in laughing at what a kid couldn't understand? He sometimes thought that was his problem. He could remember too well what it was like being a kid.

He'd been damn lucky about what had happened at the house — that the new people hadn't called the police. The hippie lady had probably figured out it was him, but the more time went by, the more he felt safe. The police weren't interested in stories that were already a week old. This was the Pointe, too. Nobody came around doing DNA testing. He'd already ditched the key to the back gate.

"Don't you want to go to one of these shows?" Anouk leaned against him. "We could get tickets. It would be fun."

"Maybe." He wondered how much they would cost.

He shifted on the sofa, which he had to admit was comfortable, if monstrous in their small apartment. He'd been shocked when he'd walked in last week and seen the sofa with its overstuffed cushions crammed against the wall. He'd even taken a step back to check the number on the door. Surprise! Anouk cried. Isn't it perfect?

She still hadn't told him how much it cost. As she said, they were married now. Married people should have a proper sofa. Next, if he expected her to keep the place clean, she wanted a vacuum cleaner.

He liked that she was so serious about doing the married part right. He could always do a few overtime shifts to pay for the extras.

Dusk was grey with flakes drifting down lazily. Before Fara even saw the rink that had been flooded in the park, she heard the thwack of hockey sticks, the skitter and crack of pucks against boards. She had her scarf wound up to her cheeks, her cloche hat pulled low, but the kids on skates gyrated and wheeled with their jackets open. The scrape of their blades sliced the cold air.

She strode past the rink, under the railway overpass, around the corner. Up ahead, against the sky, the *R* that was missing from the Five Roses sign last week — FIVE OSES — had been replaced. The powers-that-be shone on the Pointe again. She smirked, not sure if she meant whoever had fixed the sign or the sign itself.

By the parked taxis on Wellington, two hookers in tight boots and leather jackets paced and circled. A taxi driver got a call, knocked hard on his window, and the closest one flung her cigarette to the ground and stepped in. He eased out from the curb and drove off. *Taxis did delivery service? Huh.*

The kitchen chair outside the *dépanneur* had disappeared. The man who usually sat there had gotten himself a second-hand parka several sizes too large for his bony frame. The red toque on his head wobbled like a garnish as he patrolled the sidewalk, the tilt of his spine slanting the enormous bell of his parka.

In front of Fara's house, a woman in a coat stretched over her broad behind rummaged in the back of a car. She tugged out a box and two bags she struggled to carry all at once. Fara recognized Maddy and called, "Wait! I'll help you."

"Thanks." Maddy's cheeks were red, her curls bristling out from under her hat, which was knocked askew. She handed Fara the bags and shoved the car door closed with her hip.

"You bought a car."

"Leased it. That's what my brother said to do. Mr. Business Head." She propped her box on the steps as she dug in her coat pocket for her keys. "Come see what we did in the kitchen."

For the last few weeks there had been trucks and vans parked outside Maddy's house. *Construction M&M, Bérubé Électrique, Global Sinks.*

Fara followed Maddy through what had been the living room but was now a large space lined with steel counters and shelves. In the kitchen the wood cupboards had been ripped out to make way for a large white refrigerator with double doors, a six-burner gas stove, counters topped with more steel shelves. Plastic binders ranged along the counter like a card trick.

Maddy spread her arms. "We've got fifteen restaurants committed and another three who want a look-see. They're sampling a couple of cakes to start, but you just wait. Quality desserts made with butter, free-range eggs, Dutch chocolate, and local fruit? This is going to take off."

"But how did you —" Fara stopped. The question was indiscreet.

"How did I what?" Maddy grinned. "Get the idea? I'm a genius."

"This must have cost a lot."

"My brother said to get a line of credit. Would you believe it? I bought this house for twenty thousand and it's now evaluated at *three hundred*." Maddy ogled the room in disbelief. "It's still the same house. It makes no sense to me — but I don't care. I can spend a hundred thousand and still come out ahead." She poured filtered water from a jug into the kettle. "Staying for tea?"

Fara draped her coat over the back of a stool pushed up near the counter. "Are you going to bake too — or just your friend?"

"Only if she wants me to make Polish poppyseed roll, which I doubt. She's the whiz with the cakes. I'm the cheerleader."

"You make a good cheerleader. You've got pom-poms in your voice."

Maddy held up a box of Earl Grey. "This okay?"

Fara nodded.

Maddy dropped two bags into a teapot and set mugs on the counter. "I needed a change. It's been years I've been working at the market. Sometimes I thought I'd die there. One day I'd be bagging a baguette and I'd keel over on the breads — those holy loaves we weren't supposed to touch with anything but gloves on."

She raked a hand through her hair. "This big old house, too. It needed a makeover. It was getting tired of me waiting for that crazy woman with the braid to come back."

Fara couldn't recall Maddy ever telling her about a crazy woman with a braid. "Is that one of the neighbours?"

"She was living in this house when I got here — in seventy-eight. Just after I had my baby."

Fara, who'd been tucking a tissue away, stopped with her fingers still in her pocket. "I didn't know you had a baby."

"Like you said with your sister, it's a complicated story. I don't usually tell people."

Fara started to form a question, but she saw how briskly Maddy grabbed milk from the refrigerator and opened the drawer for spoons. Better to wait and let Maddy speak at her own speed.

"No one knew where she came from, the woman with the braid. She just showed up one day." Maddy stopped and stared at the teapot. "I don't usually tell people," she repeated. "It's pretty awful." She paused. "She kidnapped my baby."

"How ...?"

"How? It was easy. We were stoned, asleep, drugged, wacko, you name it. And I was so stupid! I didn't even *get* that a stolen baby was more important than hiding a couple of bags of pot. That's how clueless I was. We didn't even call the police."

Fara remembered being a teenager — how all-knowing she thought she was, how naive in retrospect. Big with her own stupidity.

"Yeah ... I was only sixteen, and at first I thought it was for the best I didn't have a baby anymore. I had no idea what to do with her. My parents didn't help. They more or less told me to get lost, go find the father, whatever."

"The father didn't —"

"Forget the father. He didn't even know." She made a shoving-away gesture with her arm. "*I* didn't know until my teacher saw I had a big belly. Can you believe being so ignorant?"

She sighed and slouched on her stool. "It drives me crazy sometimes to think I've got a daughter somewhere in the world, and I don't have a clue what's become of her. She's twenty-seven, assuming she's still alive. She might have a baby by now. *I* could be a grandmother! She's my daughter and I don't know *anything* about her."

"That's ..." But Fara didn't even know what that was.

"At least with your sister," Maddy said, startling Fara with the sudden shift, "you've got some memories. Sure, she's gone. It's horrendous how you lost her. I don't doubt it for a minute. But she had a life before she did what she did. You had experiences, right? Things you can remember about her or that you did with her."

Fara gazed at her, not sure if she'd ever realized that.

"You can't believe," Maddy was saying, "how I wish ... oh, the silliest things! I wish I knew if my daughter has my hair or her father's. I don't remember much about him except that he had straight red hair. Maybe she does, too. Or maybe she's got his straight and my brown? Or my frizz and his red? Maybe she's got a big bum like I do and my mom did." She slapped her buttock. "For her sake, I sort of hope she doesn't or she'll never get jeans that fit."

Even if Maddy was turning it into a joke, Fara could hear how serious she was. "Maddy, I'm really sorry. I had no idea."

"Yeah, well. It's the past, right? Twenty-seven long years ago. The woman who took her obviously isn't bringing her back or telling her where she came from. All these years I stayed here because I figured it was the only way she'd ever find me again. I even bought the house." She slapped a hand on the counter. "Now I want to put it to good use. I'm starting this baking business with Yushi, who, as it happens, is the same age as my daughter. To me that feels right. Mind you ..." She lifted a finger at Fara. "I haven't told her any of this, and I'd appreciate if you don't. I'll tell her one day. First, let's see if we can make a go of this."

She pulled one of the plastic binders toward her and began flipping through recipes. "Listen to this — hazelnut torte with mocha buttercream. *Tarte à la crème fraîche* with redcurrant topping. Don't ask me where we'll get redcurrants, but Yushi wants them."

Johannisbeeren, Fara thought, surprised that she remembered the word. She hesitated then said, "My mother has redcurrant bushes."

"Do you think she'd give us some roots or cuttings? I could plant them out back."

"But you won't have enough currants to do anything for a couple of years."

"We intend to be around for a while. You wait and see. We're going to make a mark in the Montreal dessert scene. Look, we even have business cards." Maddy leaned across the counter for a lime-green box with an ivory top she opened. She handed Fara one of the smooth ivory cards embossed with a discreetly swirled font. *Rose en Amande.* "I wanted Marzipan Rose, but it doesn't work in French — *Rose en pâte d'amandes.* Too long and clumsy. So it's *Rose en Amande.* Almond Rose. And if people can't figure out what it means, maybe they'll be curious."

"I like the name. I think the whole idea is great and hope you ... break a leg?"

Maddy laughed. "For a pastry chef, it's probably crack an egg."

Over supper Fara told Frédéric about Maddy's new kitchen and showed him the business card for Almond Rose. She didn't tell him about Maddy's baby, though the story and what Maddy had said about the completeness of her loss affected her deeply. She felt dazed, as if she could still hear Maddy's voice.

While he did the dishes, she leaned against the window watching the Morse code of snowflakes against the beam of light from the high, hooded street lamp in the alley. The bare branches of Maddy's maple were like uplifted arms receiving the night and the snow.

"Do you want to go for a walk?" she asked.

"In the snow?"

"Just up to the canal and back."

The sidewalks hadn't been cleared yet and they tromped side by side, kicking through the white fluff. Snow had softened the edges of brick, stone, and asphalt. It was a hushed world.

"At work," Fara said, "they're asking me when we're going to have a housewarming party."

"Are we?"

"Maybe next summer, when people can spill into the backyard."

"Have you decided yet when to invite your parents?"

Her parents still hadn't seen the house. They didn't often come to Montreal, though they lived closer than Frédéric's two sisters, both of whom had visited, bearing housewarming gifts. One had even returned to bring their mother so she could give her blessing. Fara's parents had said they would wait until the house was finished. The rooms were all painted now, but there would always be work to do in an old house.

"They won't want to drive in the winter with the snow," Fara said.

"But they expect us to go see them at Christmas. It's the same trip for us as for them."

"They're older."

"Not *that* old." He didn't understand their indifference. Fara was used to it by now. Or rather, she had taught herself to expect no better. It was how they'd always been.

But Frédéric — dear Frédéric — was still willing to give them the benefit of the doubt. "How about you invite them? Your dad would like all the wood in the house."

Her father would see the slant of the door frames that had shifted with age. How Frédéric hadn't succeeded in sanding every last fleck of paint off the floors. That the kitchen counters should be replaced. The old cupboards too. That the cellar wasn't finished. Probably the only detail he would approve of would be the French doors. Her father should have had a son — or a son-in-law — like Eric.

She and Frédéric climbed the low hill off the road to walk along the canal. A broad swath of snow had settled between its stone and concrete walls. At the lock, water tumbled with a gushing force that kept a pool of black water open, where ducks swam or clustered on a rim of ice.

"Look at them," Fara said. "Inside their duvets."

She and Frédéric stopped to watch the ducks, one of whom squawked protest that they hadn't brought food. On the other side of the canal glowed the warm windows of the condos that used to be the old Redpath factory.

"You know who I wish could see the house?" Fara asked.

Frédéric turned to her.

"Claire."

He tucked a strand of hair under the brim of her hat, smoothed his fingers across her cheek.

She blinked, knowing she was about to start crying. "Today when I saw Maddy ..."

"Yes?"

"She said something about memories — how lucky I am to have memories of Claire. She made me realize I've let Claire's death ..." Her voice wavered and she took a breath. "She made me realize I've let Claire's death and the way she died totally eclipse her life."

Frédéric pulled her to him, but she lifted her head because she had more to say. "And that's wrong. It's so unfair to her. She died — she killed herself — okay! But she also lived for twenty years."

"Fara," Frédéric murmured.

She pressed her face into his chest and said it again to herself, because it was important. "She lived."

Fara sat on the bed with an envelope of photos. One by one she examined them, trying to place where and when they'd been taken.

Here was one of Claire at about three years old in a coat, hat, and boots in the snow by a city park bench, holding a beach ball. Fara could just vaguely recall the beach ball. Their parents wouldn't have known the striped balls were to be used at a beach in the summer.

Here Claire sat cross-legged on the living room floor of her apartment with Tiger sprawled across the cradle of her thighs. She was massaging his neck, her hand deep in his ruff. Tiger had stretched and flexed his claws. Fara had taken the picture and given Claire a copy. She'd never seen it in Claire's apartment, but when she'd emptied Claire's wallet after her death, she'd found the cut-out square of the cat, the edge of Claire's jeans, and her hand in the cat's fur.

Fara set the photo of Claire and her cat next to a collage frame with six openings. She wanted to choose five pictures of Claire at different ages.

From downstairs, even with the French doors closed, Fara could smell the banana bread she had cooling on a rack in the kitchen. Not everywhere in the house, but between the bedroom and the kitchen, scent travelled along a secret tunnel between the wires, planks, floors, and ceilings. In the morning, before the alarm went off, she woke to the smell of the coffee brewing on its preset timer.

Frédéric was working in the next room, assembling bookshelves. The whine of his new electric screwdriver cut across the yodel of opera he had playing on the radio. He didn't care for opera but must have been too focused on his new screwdriver to change the station.

There were a few baby pictures, but they weren't labelled. Fara couldn't guess which were of her and which of Claire. Both had had blond hair and blue eyes as babies. If she asked her parents, would they be able to say?

Here was a picture of Fara and Claire in matching wool dresses their mother had made. Fara shivered, recalling the itch of the fabric. Their mother hadn't lined it, and wearing the dress was torture. But each collar was adorned with a white crocheted flower. Fara set it next to the frame.

Also by the frame lay a photo of Xavier, the young man who'd killed himself. Fara thought Claire might like him as a boyfriend. Let the dead have a romance, why not? She'd chosen a picture where his eyes had a wry sort of warmth. She would have to cut away the young woman who was also in the photo, which would be easy since she wasn't touching him, only smiling coyly at the camera.

Fara wondered who had taken this picture of Claire in a midnight blue, strapless dress. Fara had never seen her wearing it because she hadn't gone to Claire's graduation. She was already living in Montreal and hadn't made the trip home. Had she even been asked? Graduations didn't use to be the extravagant affairs they were now. Still, it would have been Claire's last fancy occasion. Fara put the photo between the one of Xavier and the one of herself and Claire in the wool dresses.

Hanging the pictures felt like a way of showing Claire the house. And Fara, too, would see Claire every day and remember how she'd looked in life. How she'd been.

MADDY

Maddy scrubbed the bathroom sink, rinsed and swiped at the suds. The cleanser bubbles were harder to wash down the drain than the dirt. She peeled off her gloves, catching sight of herself in the mirror. Cheeks too bright, hair electrified. Muscled lines between her brows. Had she been scowling all her life? She poked her tongue at this harried version of herself.

When she'd finished cleaning, she would shower with the vanilla-scented mousse Gaylene had given her for Christmas last year. Wash and condition her hair. Wear her velvet harem pants and a thick turtleneck. A spritz of perfume, why not? Have a glass of wine and relax in the new upstairs living room. She'd paid the man who sat outside the *dépanneur* to come with a buddy to carry the sofa and armchair upstairs. His hips and spine weren't aligned, but his arms were firm as tree limbs. She'd seen him around the neighbourhood hoisting lumber and hauling sacks of cement. In the Pointe, he — not Leonard Cohen — was your man.

When she'd extended the kitchen into the front room, Yushi had suggested using the upstairs room with the balcony as a living room. Maybe next spring they could even replace the old wood balcony with treated pine and a wrought-iron railing. It was high time she stop thinking about this back corner of the house as the woman with the braid's room.

Maddy was committed — more committed than she'd ever been. All these years of working at the patisserie and staying in the house had suddenly revealed themselves as the long and necessary preparation for this venture.

And now everything was happening so quickly! Maddy sometimes had to plop onto a chair and remind herself that this whirl of change had all depended on *her* first step. Who was it who said you were free to make the first decision — like jumping out a window? But once you jumped, you couldn't stop yourself from falling.

Some of Yushi's bags and boxes already stood piled in the room that would be hers. Whatever could be transported by car would leave less to move later. Yushi said Rose had a friend with access to a van to move the furniture. He would help Rose move, and Yushi, too. Yushi was going to help Rose find a place. Her boyfriend would be moving in with her, but Yushi said he seemed as naive about practicalities as Rose was.

As Maddy carried the vacuum cleaner upstairs, she glimpsed Jim's tail flitting around a corner. It was the one beast he feared. She didn't even have to turn it on.

She hadn't quit her job at the patisserie yet. She didn't care what happened to the patisserie but didn't want to leave her old colleagues in a fix. Just now she was training Yushi's replacement. She would give notice the day before she left for her Christmas vacation. Her long record of employment at the patisserie gave her the advantage of being at the top of the seniority list — the only employee able to stay home during the pandemonium of holiday entertaining. She and Yushi would have their own pandemonium of last-minute planning.

When Yushi gave notice, Pettypoo snapped that Yushi needn't bother returning the next day. Moments later, everyone behind the counter could hear Zied bellowing from the kitchen. Was Madame crazy? It was too busy in this month before Christmas to work one person short! Pettypoo mounted the stairs, lips dry, face scarlet. Jaw wagging like a ventriloquist's puppet, she told Yushi that she would be expected to work her final two weeks. Yushi had stared at Pettypoo, not speaking, until the older woman backed away, fingers touching the gold crucifix at her neck. Behind Pettypoo's back Cécile gave Yushi a thumbs-up. Cécile had said she wanted to come to work for Maddy and Yushi when they were ready to start hiring.

Maddy scraped the head of the vacuum cleaner across her bedroom floor. If it weren't howling so loudly, she would start singing.

The drill of the doorbell echoed inside Yushi's apartment. Maddy stood on the landing, her breath puffing clouds. She'd carried up one of the empty recycling boxes that had been tumbled along the frozen sidewalk. On the side of the box was printed PROPERTY OF IRELAND. Who else but Yushi?

Rose opened the door with a questioning expression. "Yushi's in the shower," she said. She took the green box from Maddy and walked off down the hallway.

Maddy stepped in, unbuttoned her coat but kept it on, and headed into the front room. From the bathroom came the muffled drum of water.

Steps soundless, Rose returned and slid onto a chair at the table before a pad of graph paper. Squares were shaded to form a large *V*. She glanced up and saw that Maddy was looking. "It's an *oeil de perdrix*. It makes a ..." With her fingers she shaped a diamond in the air.

"You plan what you weave on paper first?"

Rose smiled, but as if to herself, not at Maddy. "I should. I don't always."

"Yushi doesn't always use a recipe, either."

"Yushi's good."

"The pillow you made Yushi looks pretty good, too."

Rose's smile faded. Didn't she like getting compliments? The conversation felt delicate — as if the wrong word might make her bolt.

She'd picked up a pencil and was using the tip to count squares. Her profile looked different with her hair pulled back into a short, stubby ponytail. Maddy was reminded of her mother, who'd always worn her hair in a bun. When she'd stood in the kitchen with her circles of dough and a bowl of cheese and potato filling, she'd had the same absorbed expression. The same high curve of her forehead. The silence, too. Her mother, immured in her Old World values.

Yushi always said Rose's taciturn manners stemmed from growing up alone in a cabin with her mother. What kind of a life must that have been for a child?

The shower had stopped, but Yushi still didn't appear. Maddy shrugged off her coat and sat on the sofa with a view into the hallway.

Into the silence Rose said, "Do you want some tea?"

Maddy understood that she was trying to be sociable, albeit in delay. "Thanks, but Yushi won't be long, I hope. We've got to move some boxes and there's stuff to arrange in the kitchen at my place."

"That's okay." The words sounded hollow. Maybe lonely? Yushi had told her she was Rose's first friend. Then along swooped Maddy, taking her away. Even if Rose had a boyfriend now, men were men. Women wanted women friends.

"You know," Maddy said, "you can always come visit Yushi at my house. I won't always be there. You can come see Yushi when I'm not home." Maybe Rose didn't understand that people could have several friends. "Yushi told me you're going to look for an apartment in St-Henri or the Pointe, so you'll be close."

Rose kept shading squares with her pencil. This must be one complicated weaving pattern.

From down the hallway a hair dryer roared. Yushi always looked as if she'd only just pulled on her jeans and raked gel through her hair. Who would have guessed that her careless appearance demanded such a lengthy toilette?

Again Maddy noticed Rose's quiet absorption in her task. The dangly yellow earrings she wore must be Yushi's influence. "Are you growing your hair?" she asked.

Rose tucked her chin close, as if embarrassed, then lifted it. "My boyfriend likes it."

"You'll be able to twist it up when it's longer."

"Or braid it. I used to have a braid like my mother did."

Maddy nodded, impressed. Those were the most words Rose had ever said to her at once.

Then Rose added, "She had a really long braid."

Maddy looked at her hard, nearly asked how long her braid was, and what else did her mother look like, but she told herself to stop. No more kidding herself about that woman. Wherever she was, she was gone. Rose's mother had been a woman living in a cabin in the woods somewhere up north. And she was dead now.

The bathroom door banged open and Yushi called, "Rose!"

Pencil still in hand, Rose walked down the hallway.

"There," Maddy heard.

More murmurs, then Yushi hollered, "I won't be long!"

"No problem!" Maddy called. But she felt restless now and stood. She paced to the hallway and back, trying to rid herself of the image of a long brown braid hanging down a woman's back as she eased a baby into a large bowl of warm water.

On the table lay the page of stepped angles and squares, which she couldn't interpret, but that Rose would use to create an intricate and beautiful length of cloth.

ROSE

Rose kept pushing the shuttle through an ever-tightening mouth of threads. Even as she knew it was time to stop, one hand sent the shuttle across and the other thumped the beater toward her. Time to stop, she thought. *Time to stop.* She finally jolted herself to a halt, stretched her foot to free the brake, and rolled the warp forward.

She was weaving cloth patterned with hexagons of brown, gold, and rust — autumn forest colours — for Kenny. He'd smiled shyly when she'd shown him, then said that if she sewed it up as a cushion he'd take it to the cabin, where they needed one for the sofa. She was pleased with how he'd adopted the cabin and was taking care of it, and only wondered later why she and Maman had never thought to plump out the old sofa with cushions.

She took advantage of having stopped to fill the kettle at the sink and plug it in, then considered the different jars of tea on the dresser. Ginger lemon, chamomile, peppermint, verbena. Leo thought it funny that she took the tea bags from their boxes and put them in jars — that she'd kept her cabin habits of protecting food from mice and weevils. She thought it funny that Leo believed insects and rodents respected city doors and walls.

He'd left early to go to the garage. Soon — except for work — they would always be together. She hugged her arms across her breasts and murmured, "Soon." They'd looked at a few places, but so far they were too expensive, or over a restaurant or a bar and too noisy.

As she waited for her tea to steep, she walked across the room to the window. The bike path was covered in snow, yet packed hard enough that Rose had seen the odd person trudging past, head lowered before the wind. More frequently she saw cross-country skiers gliding by. Swinging arms, scissored legs.

The canal was frozen and white except for the shadowed holes of paw prints angled from one bank to the other. Animals never crossed ice straight across. Even city dogs, who had never been in the wilds, kept that instinct. By the loading ramp, the sculptor's block of marble was gone. In October men had come with a lift to hoist the finished piece into the back of a truck. The marble had been swaddled in sheets of foam, wrapped in burlap, and tied with twine, yet the sculptor still hovered and shouted anxious instructions.

Curious, Rose had joined the others who had left their studios and ateliers to watch. Once the truck left, the sculptor invited them into his studio for tiny glasses of a clear liquor that smelled like candy but sliced a hot arrow down her throat. She'd seen the sculptor's name — Joachim — on the plaque beside his door, but she didn't know how to say it. His studio was far larger than hers. On a centre pedestal stood a hewn block of granite. He said that was his winter project.

He'd invited himself down the hallway to see what Rose was doing. Look at this! he'd cried. How do you have patience with all those blasted threads? There must be hundreds! And colour! Me, I address form — primary and pure. No distractions.

Annette, the painter, who had a studio upstairs, said colour *was* her medium. Colour and light.

Rose said nothing. She didn't trust language to explain what she felt about the design, juxtaposition, contrast, and blend of colour. How and why she yearned to make cloth.

She squeezed her teabag and dropped it in the garbage. With the mug next to her on the bench, she squinted at the length of cloth she'd already woven and decided to switch from rust to chocolate. She reached for her second shuttle, pulled the beater forward and back, and slid the shuttle across. The dance began again, the interlocking of colour and threads.

The landlord of the small building trudged up the stairs ahead of Rose, complaining about the climb. Four flights were too much for his old legs and heart. Too much, too much.

On the second floor landing he stopped to catch his breath. "You," he said to Yushi, peering at her in the dim light. "Are you going to live here, too?" Yushi said no, she had a place. She was helping Rose look. Neither mentioned that someone else would be living with Rose. It wasn't his business.

He glanced again at Yushi. "Where do you come from?"

"Ireland."

He frowned and launched himself up the next bout of stairs.

He unlocked a door and repeated what he'd said when Rose called to ask about the apartment. *"C'est petit."*

The apartment was a single room with a double window, a galley kitchen, and a bathroom off to the side. The refrigerator was spray-painted turquoise. Altogether the apartment was larger than her studio — and there was a refrigerator, a stove, and a bathroom. She could put Yushi's rosewood table, which Yushi insisted she borrow, against one wall, her bed and dresser against the other. Yushi peered into the kitchen cupboards and the closet, touched the radiators to see if they were warm, peered at the tiles around the small tub. The landlord watched but didn't speak.

Rose wished Leo could see the place, but he was working, and the landlord had said he had others interested in the apartment as well. Leo had told her to take it if it was good. They could afford the rent, and the address — in St-Henri, on the same subway line as the hospital — was perfect. At the window she looked down onto the back of a grocery store, where a beer truck was parked. A man was hefting cases onto metal rollers aimed into the store. Higher up, against the grey sky, she had a view onto the domed steeples of a church.

She remembered how she'd sat curled on the old sofa in the cabin after Maman's death, feeling alone and bereft. And here she was in Montreal — with Leo and Yushi and Kenny. Perhaps Maddy, too. The sculptor whose name she was going to learn how to say. Annette, the painter. That tall woman from the hospital who said she lived nearby. Other people who recognized her on her tube feeding rounds and had started to say hi and ask how she was. Who else might she meet in the years to come? Why stop at five friends?

Yushi joined her at the window. "Do you mind being so high up? You'll have to carry up groceries."

Four floors wasn't high. Leo's rope ladder was high. And stairs were a lot easier than a ladder.

She turned around and surveyed the room again. The table on that side, the bed on that side. A bed, a stove, a refrigerator, a bathroom. More comfort than she and Leo had known yet.

"I like it," she said.

"Are you talking to your friend or to me?" the landlord asked.

"To you." Rose looked at him. "To you."

ACKNOWLEDGEMENTS

Writing a novel is the long haul. Thank you to the friends who listened to me talk in circles around and through it — all of you. You know who you are. You were there in cafés, over pints of beer, tromping down city streets and along the river path, responding to letters and frantic emails.

Thank you to my colleagues on 4NW at the Jewish General Hospital in Montreal who aided and abetted my fictional re-creation of a unit coordinator's job; the long-ago Cow Café on John Street in Toronto, where I was actually paid (!!) to make cakes; Len Zorn and Glenn Zorn for demonstrating how to install French doors; Savitree Guness and her family for explaining the finer points of Trinidadian cuisine.

Thank you to the Conseil des arts et des lettres du Québec for their generous support of this project.

Thank you to a now defunct writers' group who read early drafts of early chapters: Danielle Devereaux, Lina Branter, Matthew Anderson, Kathleen Winter, Julie Paul.

Huge thanks to Anita Lahey for giving me insightful feedback on the complete draft. Her help was immense, necessary, and invaluable.

I am endlessly grateful to Shaun Bradley of Transatlantic Agency for her editorial input, ongoing belief in the book, generosity of spirit, courtesy, and good humour.

Thank you for the enthusiasm of the fine team at Dundurn Press, especially my editor, Shannon Whibbs, for her patience and expertise in shepherding *Five Roses* into the world.

As always, my love, appreciation, and thanks to Robert for everything else that makes it possible for me to write.